Joseph Carrabis

The Shaman

Northern Lights Publishing

Nashua, NH

ISBN 979-8-9878048-5-8

Library of Congress Control Number

Editing by Jennifer Day, Susan Carrabis
Cover and interior artwork by Sarah Bowden
        https://www.sarahbowdenart.com
Book design by Jennifer Day

The tale Gio tells in Chapter 104 - StoryKeeping originally appeared in The Write Festival's Fantastic Stories Anthology, Oct 2020, and again on Tall Tales TV, Oct 2022

Printed and bound in the United States of America
First printing September 2023

Published by Northern Lights Publishing
www.northernlightspublishing.com

Praise for The Shaman

"I love the depth and breadth of the mythology and different traditions."

"Settings are rich, emotions are flowing, imagery is on-point with 'wow' levels of amazing."

"*The Shaman* is Campbell's *The Hero's Journey* writ large in the modern world."

"The story is a primer for spirit work, thank you."

"Beautiful."

"It brought tears to my eyes. So profound."

"I felt emotional at the end and had to take a minute to pause and breathe."

"Although, as usual in a Carrabis story, some parts of this novel are uncomfortable, I enjoyed it very much. Gio needed to experience those things to learn and grow."

"This will be another healing book and perhaps a training manual for empaths and light workers."

"I had goosebumps on my arms and a smarting of tears in my eyes. Just amazing."

For Susan
(because everything should be)

And AJ
(who said I could)

To my Grandfather John
with whom all things were possible
I miss you, Buppa

To Grandmother Running Water
who said it's time

Thanks to
Jennifer Day, Susan, Sheila Oranch, David Nash, Elizabeth
Dougher, and Clarabelle Miray Fields
for reading and reading and reading until I got it correct.

Thanks to
Dr. Francesca Failla for help with translations

Thanks to all my Teachers.
If I didn't mention you it's because I respect your privacy, not
because I don't cherish the teachings you shared.

More than anything else
The Shaman
is dedicated to all who come after me
to help them find their way.

Walk softly,
Walk in Peace.

Also by Joseph Carrabis

Fiction
The Shaman
The Inheritors
Empty Sky
Tales Told 'Round Celestial Campfires
The Augmented Man

Non-Fiction
Reading Virtual Minds Volume I: Science and History
Reading Virtual Minds Volume II: Experience and Expectation
Reading Virtual Minds Volume III: Fair-Exchange and Social
Networks
That Th!nk You Do: 60 Ways to Be Healthy, Happy & Hold Off
Harm

Contents

Author's Note

The language used in this book may offend some readers. My goal is to use all the tools at an author's disposal and all the tools in my author's toolbag to create as exacting a sensory experience for the reader and to be as accurate to my creation as possible. Sometimes that means language which may offend some is used to create such exacting sensory images.

I've learned to accept my limitations and hope you'll do the same.

Characters, events, places, and things described, depicted, or referred to in this work are fictitious. Any similarity to actual persons, events, places, or things is purely coincidental.

The Shaman

The ability to perceive or think differently is more important than the knowledge gained. - *David Bohm*

Every great advance in science has issued from a new audacity of imagination. - *John Dewey*

Our perception of the world is a fantasy that coincides with reality. - *Chris Frith, Cognitive Psychologist*

The world is not what I thought, but different, and more! I have seen it with my own eyes! - *Mary Oliver, Upstream*

The most readily adaptable animal is the one with the largest repertoire of stored experience to call upon. - *Abby Smith Rumsey, When We Are No More*

There is no supernatural, there are simply things that are easily understood and/or controlled by almost everyone, and those things that are understood and/or controlled only by specialists. Those things need to be dealt with using different techniques, just as building a bridge needs to use different techniques and specialists than roasting a pig. People in these societies usually accept and believe in what we call magic, which refers to the technology they use to manipulate what we call the supernatural. - *Cara Richards*

Those who at the First Beginning
Were given the world,
the bushes,
the forest,
we meet them there. - *Zuni song*

Men's gods come and go as do their needs. But energies are forever and take what forms they will to best get their work done.

There are "logical values" beyond true and false. These values can be used to prove theorems in domains that ordinary logic cannot reach.

Humans hate what they fear and they fear what they do not understand. - *Linda Koerber, Eclipse Dancer*

...understanding is given only to those who make an active effort. Passive receptivity is not enough. - *Igor Stravinsky*

The walker and path are intrinsically linked. - *F.J. Varela*

...calls upon his auxiliary spirits, speaks in a "secret language" or the "language of animals," ... which constitutes a spectacle without equal in the world of everyday experience. The exhibition of magical feats (fire-handling and other "miracles") unveils another world, the fabulous world of gods and magicians, the world where everything seems possible, ... where one is able to disappear and reappear instantaneously, where the "laws of nature" are abolished and where a certain superhuman "freedom" is illustrated and rendered present in a stunning manner. - *Mircea Eliade, A History of Religious Ideas Volume 3: From Muhammed to the Age of Reforms*

What causes the first drop of rain to decide "I will become an ocean"?

When was the last time you saw something for the first time?

Childhood

Chapter 1

Incorrect Diagnosis

Yelling. There is a heat in the words. I'm suffocating.

Grandpa lifts me from my cradle, my only clothing a soiled diaper. "He is fine and he'll grow strong."

My mother reaches for me. "He's stupid, Pa. The doctor said he's stupid. Don't you understand?"

My father lights his cigar, drinks his wine. "We're in America now, Pa. A boy like that, we'll spend more time taking care of him than..."

Grandpa turns. I'm in his arms. I smell his clove aftershave, feel his rough beard against my ears, my cheeks, my head. He tucks my head into his shoulder. I'm crying.

"Shh, shh, shh, Gio. *Il nonno ti ha preso.* Buppa's got you."

My mother's hand is on my back.

Grandpa turns again. I feel Grandpa's strong heart against my chest. I hear my mother over his shoulder. "Pa, this isn't the old country. We're alone here. Who'll help us look after him?"

Grandpa lifts me off his chest, holds me in front of him. He's looking at me. Me. He changes. Becomes a thing of swirling winds and fire.

A thing of rising mountains and forming oceans. A thing of sounds and silences. A thing of cold and heat.

But always love. There is always love.

I feel him moving inside me. Every change, he moves inside me.

His two calloused palms are soothingly rough on my sides and back, his thumbs hooking under my arms and holding me in a gentle vise. "*Mi prenderò cura di lui.* I will take care of him."

My father blows smoke into the air, sips more wine. "Let him take him. We can't help you, Pa. I'm telling you that right now. We'll need all our money for ourselves. You can adopt him if you want, we won't stand in your way. *Procuratore* Calcazie'll draw up the papers. He'll be your son, all legal and proper."

My mother moans. "Pa, he'll be better off in a home for kids like him."

Grandpa puts me down, one hand stays on me, protecting me, making sure of me. I hear the flap of cloth, smell soap and water, talcum. He takes off my soiled diaper. Cool air hits my bottom and I pee a stream into the air, laughing.

"See, Pa? See?"

Grandpa cleans me, washes me, puts fresh clothes on me. Lifts me. He holds me against him with one hand, his other puts on his hat, reaches for his coat.

"Pa, you don't have a job here. All you have is your army pension and social security. That's not enough for you and Ma and a dumb little boy."

"He's not dumb and he's not stupid. I'll find work. The Old Work."

My father laughs. "You going to wave your hands and make him smart, Pa?"

Grandpa shrugs his coat over his shoulders, buttons me up inside, against him. "You okay, Gio?"

I smile. I am wanted. I am loved.

We walk out into the cold, cold night, his body a furnace warming me.

Chapter 2

Listen

My Buppa teaches me to listen.

People come to him. He sits me on his lap, puts a finger to my lips and whispers into my ear, "*Ascolta*." Listen.

Some people talk about their sick children. Some have trouble having babies. Farmers come when their horse goes lame or their cows won't milk. Sometimes women come because their husbands are... important?

I'm not sure that's the word.

But they all come to see Buppa.

Some men don't like their wives coming to Buppa. He talks to them softly, gives them something from his garden. They nod, shake his hand, walk away.

Sometimes he shimmers at them, his face like bright sunlight on a fast-moving stream. They run away.

"How come they run away, Buppa?"

"*Non ascoltano*." They don't listen.

He never touches anybody. Sometimes he claps his hands, sometimes he waves his hands as if writing in the air.

"How come you never touch them, Buppa?"

"*Questo è per te da fare. Quando sei pronto.*" That's for you to do. When you're ready.

Sometimes he closes his eyes and hums an old Sicilian tune.

———

We tend his roses in the garden behind the house. I point to the shed. "Do you want me to get the hose and sprinkler, Buppa?" Behind the shed, I hear the bees in the two hives Buppa keeps for honey.

He shakes his head and holds me close. "Close your eyes. What do you smell?"

The earth, black and rich and moist, not wet, not watered. Naturally moist, earth good for growing in.

The aroma of the flowers. Roses. Hyacinth. Jonquils. Morning Glories. Bleeding Hearts.

The smell of the May sun on the grass, on the vines, on the brick walkway through the backyard.

Our sweat, pungent yet soothing, the scent of strong arms and backs and legs doing good work, growing work, nurturing work, working with the earth, not against it.

Buppa's arms tighten around me.

He senses further than I do. I'm still learning.

"What is it, Buppa?"

He points to his nose and inhales slowly.

I inhale slowly, watching to learn what else I must do.

A cloud of thick perfume and expensive makeup.

"*Ascolta.*"

The sound of footsteps in the house. Voices. Grandma and someone else. A stranger. A woman. The sound of a long swishing skirt. The tinkle of fine jewelry bobbing on wrists, around a neck.

Grandma leads her to us. She speaks educated English. She isn't from our neighborhood. Nobody we know would know her.

Her husband is much older and Buppa has been recommended. She glances at me and her face reddens. She switches to Italian.

Buppa holds his hand up. He understands.

He takes his tobacco pouch and rolling papers from a pocket and fashions a cigarette. He lights it and gives it to her to smoke. It goes out when she inhales. He lights it again and tells her to smoke. Again it goes out.

A third time. It stays lit. The woman swells with the smoke. She coughs and looks around, holding the cigarette away from her.

Buppa takes it and crushes the burning end between his fingers.

"Take this to your husband. Give it to him to smoke before he goes to bed tonight. He'll work for you three times."

The woman laughed. "That's it? That's all there is? Do you think I'm some hill woman from the old country? Is this what you do for people who pay with chickens and bottles of wine?"

She reaches into her purse and pulls out a stack of bills. She waves them at Buppa and knocks the cigarette out of his hand. "We're in America now. I've got real money to pay."

Buppa stares at the cigarette, smoldering in the garden. "Three times," he repeats. "You'll grow fat from the third."

She stomps the cigarette, crushing it under the toe of her high heel, and spits on the ground.

"The child will be broken inside you."

She slaps Grandpa's face and leaves.

Grandpa buries the cigarette, weeping as if burying a child.

"What's wrong, Buppa?"

Chapter 3

Truth Like Wine

Buppa kneels on the ground and pats the freshly turned earth where he buried the cigarette, then looks up into the few cirrus clouds forming horsetails high in the blue sky. "People will come to you, asking you questions. Be careful what you tell them."

"You said to always tell the truth."

"To us. To me. To others..."

He lets it hang and I'm unsure. "Do you want me to lie to them?"

"No, Gio. Never that. Truth is like wine: a few sips and you smile and nod. Too much and you get a headache and your dinner goes *plah* on the floor." He makes a funny face and I laugh, then gently turns me to face him. "You must tell the truth, Gio, but listen to them. Pay attention when you answer. They will let you know when they've had enough truth, then you stop."

"How will they let me know?"

"A look. A sigh. Sometimes they'll nod and turn away." He acts each statement, showing me what to look for, what to see. "They'll fidget. Watch if they start rubbing their hands, tapping their fingers. Or their face will go cold, hollow, where before it was warm and full. Or their face will go like this." He makes different expressions. "And listen to their breaths."

"There are many ways to tell. You don't need to know them all right now. There's time to learn. But each different way means something different bothers them, makes them stop listening, makes them want you to stop answering."

He sits on the ground and motions me onto his lap. He hugs me, resting my head under his chin.

"Few people want all the truth, Gio. Most people want enough to believe they're right, they're doing the right thing, they're taking care of their family, they're being a good person. Tell them more than they want and they'll hate you."

"But you don't hate me, Buppa, and I tell you the truth."

"I'm not afraid of the truth and I know when your truth is not my truth."

"We have different truths?"

He points to a rose. "That flower's truth is it's a rose." He points to a morning glory. "That flower's truth is it's a morning glory. These are different truths. Both share a truth that they're flowers. Both share a truth that they grow in the earth." He points to the trees edging the garden. "They share that truth with the willow, oak, and elm. Go far enough and you find one truth that's true for everything, every person, every car, every plant, everything."

My eyes grow wide. "What truth is that, Buppa?"

He kisses my head and hands me my toy spade. "I don't know. I haven't learned it yet."

Chapter 4

First Lesson

Each day Grandpa and I practice. Some days I want to play and he turns practicing into a game.

"Gio, we're going to play Hide-and-Seek."

A new game! How exciting! "Okay, Buppa."

"I'm going to hide and you come find me. Okay?"

Oh, yes. Very much yes.

He takes me to my room and lays me on my bed. "Close your eyes. No peeking."

I scrunch my face and bury it in my pillow so I can't see. "You can count to ten? Count to ten, then you come find me."

Lower-Center-Relax-Breathe. The first lesson. Him, not me. I can feel it, feel him leave the room without him going anywhere. I'm still learning.

I count to ten. "Here I come, ready or not."

I keep my eyes closed. I never leave my bed.

The air swirls around me. Grandpa's helping me so I can learn.

"Lower-Center-Relax-Breathe, Gio. The first lesson."

He floats around me, touches me. I smell him near then far. I follow.

"Lower-Center-Relax-Breathe. You do it often enough, you practice every day, it gets easier and easier."

I race through the sky. "Yes, Buppa." I'm too excited. I move too fast, too far. I trip over a rainbow and am covered in cupcake sprinkles of multicolored mist.

His hand comes under me, helps me, keeps me up.

"Simple, Gio. Slow and easy. Learn slow, the lesson stays. Learn fast, you forget. Lower-Center-Relax-Breathe." He stays just out of reach, calling me further, guiding me deeper, each step, each move, each finding a part of Lower-Center-Relax-Breathe.

"You want to learn, Gio?."

"Yes!" I want to learn. To make Buppa happy.

"Good. Enough for today. Want to see how we do this? What it's for?"

"Yes, please, Buppa."

He smiles. His hands envelop me and guide me down.

We are back in his garden.

How did we get here?

Buppa smiles. Inside I hear, "You'll learn, Gio. In time, you'll learn."

His hands raise a rose blossom to his nose. He closes his eyes. I feel him go through the rose, checking for disease, for problems, things to mend. "Say hello to Rose, Gio. Lower-Center-Relax-Breathe until you can say hello."

I Lower-Center-Relax-Breathe. It makes it easy to follow Grandpa into the rose.

In a swirling mist, a great tree-like thing reaches its petals down for me.

"Are you Rose?"

A sound like sibilant thunder in my heart. "Yy-e-sss." Its leaves lift me to its flower, lying atop a thick stalk, a crown against the sky. Its voice again. Kind, giving, distant thunder carried on faraway winds. "Ta-a-ke f-f-rom-m m-m-e-e."

Bee is there. "Hehlloh, Gioh."

Bee wears glasses, same as me, to show me we're the same no matter how different we look. "Hello, Bee."

"Dihd Rohse brihng youh hehre?"

"Yes."

Bee shuffles aside, its legs and back weaved heavy with pollen like a woodsman's sweater even though it's summer. "Cohme. Tahke. Ehnjohy. Rehmehmbehr toh gihve sohmehthihng bahck. Youh knohw *Theh GihvehAhwahy*?"

Grandpa is teaching me The GiveAway.

"Buppa's teaching me."

"Mahy Ih shohw youh hohw Ih dho iht?"

"Yes, please."

I am with Bee, borrowing without knowing it. The world is a prism before me. Rose is still Rose and now it is Bee's Rose. I understand before Rose was my Rose.

We fly from flower to flower, rose to rose, bloom to bloom, through Grandpa's garden. Morning Glories to Tulips to Daffodils to Columbine to tomatoes to zucchini to peppers red, green, and yellow and back. Bee's sweater grows heavy and he sheds some grains of wool here, some there, each to their own, before coming back.

"Seeh? *Theh GihvehAhwahy*."

I have much to learn.

"Goh bahck nohw. Youhr Buhppah's waihtihng."

I return. Grandpa laughs. "You've been talking with Bee."

He brushes pollen from my face, my hair, my hands, golden with the stuff, catching on the breeze, flowing from me into the sky, a river of life.

Chapter 5

The Wild, The Shadows

Grandpa teaches me about Shadows. We walk through a forest and greet everyone we meet. "Hello, Tree! Hello, Ash! Hello, Ant! Hello, Spider!"

"Do you know who these are, Gio?"

"These are my friends."

Grandpa smiles. "Yes, they are your friends. They are *Shadows*, too."

"Shadows?"

"Yes. Everything here is a shadow of what really is."

"The tree is not a tree?"

"The tree," he points, "Is not *Tree*."

"It's a maple."

He laughs. "That maple tree is not *Maple*."

I hear the emphasis in his words.

"In all things, there is one which is the first of that thing. Everything else is a shadow of that first."

I watch a snail inching up a birch. "Where is Snail, then?"

"A place of such brilliance it casts its shadow so every other snail exists."

"But where, Grandpa?"

"*Home.*"

A simple word. I hear the emphasis. Not where Grandma sits spinning yarns, weaving, making me clothes. Some place *other*.

I put my hand by the snail. Its antennae tickle me. It waves them at me to see who I am. "Hel-lo, Gi-o."

"It knows who I am, Grandpa!"

"This is *The Wild*, Gio. Everything is known here. When you want to know something, go to The Wild. If there is an answer, you'll find it here."

A raven comes. It flaps by the snail, snatching it in its beak, flying away.

I cry.

"That is the way of The Wild, Gio."

"That snail was my friend."

"Is raven your friend?"

I sniffle. "Yes."

"And the birch tree?"

"Yes."

"But sometimes we cut down a tree for firewood. We load up the truck and take it home."

I am confused and answer slowly. "Yes."

"That is also The Wild, Gio. And all things in balance. If we take one thing, we give something back."

"The GiveAway, Grandpa?"

He nods. "Yes and no. Something very like and not."

I consider. "What happens when there are no more snails, Grandpa?"

He kneels and turns me to face him, his hands on my arms, holding me gently. "When there are no more snails, Gio, *Snail* is gone. When the last birch tree dies or is taken, *Birch* is gone. Do you understand?"

I nod. I don't understand and want to. It is important to Grandpa I understand. I can tell.

"Being the last...is a lonely thing."

I feel him, inside, looking, questing.

"I'm here with you, Buppa."

He frizzles my hair. "Yes."

"Are we the last, Buppa?"

"No, not yet. But there's not many of us left. Each time one of us passes, more of *The Knowledge* goes away, is lost." We stop walking. He kneels and looks into my eyes. "We must make sure nothing is the last. Sometimes The Wild takes the last and that's the way it should be. But we must never cause the last to be taken."

I understand. The Wild must be protected, saved.

"How do I do that, Grandpa?"

He stands and takes my hand. We walk back to his pickup. "That's enough for now, Gio. Today is a start. Others will teach you..."

He lets it hang. I feel something hiding. I feel it in his chest as he walks, as he talks, as he laughs, as he cries.

I play a game. "Our truck is a shadow of Truck?"

He laughs. "Yes."

"And Grandma is a shadow of Grandma?"

Big smiles. "Yes."

I stop.

"What is it, Gio?"

I look up at him. "Then you're a shadow of Grandpa?"

He nods. His eyes sparkle. There are universes behind them, un-explored and waiting. His mouth opens and something else answers, shaking the forest. "Yes, Gio. Now do you understand?"

I nod. "Yes." Now I understand.

My Grandpa comes back. "And soon I will go Home, Gio."

Chapter 6

The Childhood Door

Buppa stops, turns, lets me see him in another place. Somewhere beyond the moon, under the sea, through his garden, into the earth.

A big wooden door, made from trees and branches all woven together, leaves grow out of limbs making eaves and lintels. There's a little window but it's too high for me to see through. A light flickers through the glass. A candle.

"What's that, Buppa?"

"It's a door, a very special door. But only for you, Gio, not for anybody else."

"It's my door?"

"Yes, but only if you want to learn more. If you want to learn more you have to go in."

The door has no handle. I step closer, onto a mat of tightly woven hay and flax.

The mat opens eyes. It lifts and spins like it's caught in a whirlwind. It pushes me back, grows four legs, a spiky tail and a giant head. The woven flax and hay become golden fur. It stops spinning and lands on its feet, larger than me, larger than Buppa, larger than the door.

It looks down at me. "Are you afraid, Gio?"

"Yes."

"Good answer, truthful answer. Do you want to go in?"

"Yes."

"Why?"

I don't know what's expected. "To learn more?"

The creature smiles. It has many, many teeth, like needles. It drools. Its drool splashes and steams like acid on ground that isn't there. "Are you asking me or telling me?"

I want my Buppa. He's not here. He's always with me. Where's my Buppa?

The creature shakes its head and its golden fur ruffles. "Let's start again."

"Yes, please."

"Why do you want to go in?"

"To please Buppa."

"Good answer, truthful answer. I am the Guardian of The Childhood Door. Your Childhood Door. To enter this door, you must get past me. To get past me, you must tell the truth."

"Buppa says truth is like wine."

"Your Buppa is wise."

"How do I get past you?"

"You ask. But not now, not yet, not for a while."

"Oh."

"But now, for now, for this time, you can knock."

"On the door?"

"Yes and no. Knock on the door so you'll know where it is, so you'll always be able to find it when you need to, to tell the truth. That's the lesson. For now. For here. For this time."

I knock on the door. I feel a thump-thump-thump inside my body. "Oh!"

The Guardian laughs. "Do it again, Gio. Do you know where the door leads?"

I knock. Thump-thump-thump.

"It's me! I'm the door! The door is me!"

"Very good, Gio. The door is inside you. This is your First Door, the Childhood Door."

"But if the door is inside me and you guard the door…"

"Yes?"

"Are you my guardian, too?"

The creature laughs like rain on young leaves. "Very good, Gio! Very good!" My Guardian jumps into the air, spins, becomes a woven flax and hay mat again. "Now your Buppa's waiting. He has much to teach. You have much to learn. Someday you'll come back. I'll be waiting. Remember I'm here. It'll make it easier to find me."

I turn around and Buppa's there. He lifts me over his head so I ride piggyback. "What did you learn, Gio?"

"It's a big door, Buppa."

"Yes. It is the largest and safest door. For most people it leads to other doors."

"My door does all that?"

"Oh, no, Gio. That door is only for you. Only you can open that door. It will open easy for you. All you have to do is knock."

"The Guardian said to ask."

Buppa chuckles. "Maybe to knock on a door is to ask a question. Maybe?"

Buppa changes into a horse. "Hold tight, Gio. We have to get home and have dinner ready for Grandma."

I clutch his mane in little, tiny hands.

I wonder about my door, my Guardian. "There are other doors, Buppa?"

"There are always more Doors, Gio. You go through one to find the next one."

Chapter 7

Hide-and-Seek

"Where am I, Gio? Come find me!"

He starts with easy things, asks me questions to make me explore. "Am I in the garden?"

"I don't know, Buppa."

"Can you feel me in the garden?"

The garden is tough. He puts so much of his energy into his roses, his vegetables, his Brothers the Bees.

"You've been in the garden, Buppa. I can tell you've been there."

I feel a kiss in the air around my head. "Oh, come on, Gio. You and I worked in the garden yesterday. Am I there now?"

The air tickles my feet. I laugh, realizing. "No! But you're some place we walk to."

"Oh, you're so smart, Gio. Where am I now that is someplace we walk? Feel where I am. I left a trail. You can follow."

"Like Hansel and Gretel, Buppa!"

"Yes, like Hansel and Gretel but I won't put you in my oven when you find me."

I start crying.

"What is it, Gio? What's wrong?"

"What if I can't find you, Buppa? What if I get lost?"

Still playing the game, his words fill my head. "Gio, you will always find me. All you need do is want to find me. What did I tell you about getting lost?"

"Just take a step. If you're truly lost, any step you take is in the right direction."

I feel him smile. "Ah, you're so smart, my little Gio. Now, what's the first thing I taught you?"

"Lower-Center-Relax-Breathe."

"Exactly. Right now you're scared. You're afraid. That's okay, you can be. Just know that you are. What are your four bodies, Gio?"

I point to remember their directions. "Emotional, Physical, Spiritual, Mental." I know the words, not necessarily what they mean yet.

But Buppa teaches me.

"See how smart you are, Gio? You remember everything Buppa shows you. Now you have four directions. Soon you'll have many more."

"How many directions do you have, Buppa?"

The universe folds and expands in ways too numerous to count.

I laugh.

"Fear is your Emotional Body talking to you, pulling you off balance. So is joy, sorrow, happiness, sadness, ... Each are wonderful and too much, like anything else, can be dangerous."

I feel him warm me with each emotion he speaks.

"When any one emotion becomes too much, talk to your emotional body, ask it to come back to the center. Make it a game. Ask if it can find you there. Know what's happening and you control what's happening, it doesn't control you. Your fear makes you think crazy. Your emotions control your mind. Ask that body to come back to the others, tell it they want to play. Make them work together. You are stronger that way."

He waits, a warm cloud surrounds me, relaxes me, makes it easy for me.

"You like when I help you, Gio?"

"Yes, very much. Thank you, Buppa."

"Remember the feeling of me helping you. Remember my voice, the smell of my breath, my sweat, how my beard tickles your cheek when I kiss you. Remember these things and my help is always with you. Understand, Gio?"

"I think so, yes."

"So now, what do you do?"

"Lower-Center-Relax-Breathe." I feel myself swarming, hear buzzing, feel wings touch my face. "Not the garden! The hives behind the shed!"

"Which one?"

"The one with Mrs. Minerva, the new queen."

"Which one has Mrs. Minerva?"

I guess. "The one without Leonora. She abused her bees, wouldn't give them the honey they worked hard for, kept it all for herself."

Grandpa laughs. "You remember her? She forgot how to be a bee, let alone be a queen. We must always remember how to be who we are, Gio."

"I'm Buppa's and Grandma's!"

Hugs and kisses fill the air around me.

"Leonora's long gone now, Gio. Look again. No cheating."

Grandpa doesn't let me cheat. I have to be specific.

One hive sits on a green frame, the other blue. "The Green Hive."

"Oh, I make it too easy for you, Gio. I need to get another hive." Inside my head, Grandpa's voice. "I'm so proud of you. Good work, Gio, good work! Come back now, come back and we'll play again."

And so I learn to use my bodies to do what they can naturally do, and how to combine them to do what they do best together.

"Where am I now, Gio?"

I feel warm water surrounding me, see fish, bright corals, taste salt, hear whales and dolphins and things slithering deep in the sea. "You're in the ocean."

"Tell me more."

"It's warm. Not like here, at the beach. I can see through it."

"Tell me more."

Orange and white and black striped fish. Long, thin blue fish with long snouts. Big fish with wide, flat heads. Little, tiny silver fish moving like clouds in the ocean. Fish like giant saucers flapping wings in the water. Rainbows of coral too delicate to touch. Silver bottom sand. Plants waving in the currents like trees in the wind. Gray, green, and orange crabs walking carefully. Red and blue starfish prying open brightly colored shells.

"Tell me more."

The taste of the water, the smell of it. Its color. How far I could see through it.

Then childhood panic. "I'm under water, Buppa! I can't breathe!"

"Do you see a fish?"

"Yes, Buppa."

"Can the fish breathe in the water?"

"Yes, Buppa."

"Borrow from the fish."

I start choking, coughing.

All of him surrounds me, lifts me, returns me to my room, and takes me on to his lap. "Here, Gio. Come back to me, here. Come back to Buppa."

I come back, open my eyes, afraid, cling to him, cry.

He rocks me. "We'll go see John. We'll bring him some of Mrs. Minerva's honey. Maybe he'll make us some sweetcakes. Would you like that?"

John is one of Buppa's friends from a place called Africa. He's one of our friends. He makes sweetcakes with Mrs. Minerva's honey. He is also a master of *borrowing*, a way of learning. From anything.

Chapter 8

Friends

Buppa has many friends. They all know Lower-Center-Relax-Breathe and they all know something different. Buppa teaches me that. "We all do some things the same, we all do some things different." Sometimes when we play Buppa stops, shakes his head. "We need to see John. John knows about this." or "We should go visit Running Water. She knows how to do this." or "That's something Chan does better than me. Let's ask him to show you how it's done."

"You can do this, Grandpa. I've seen you do it."

"But I don't do it best. We need to have someone better than me show you how it's done."

"You do everything best, Buppa."

He smiles. "Thank you, Gio, and I do one thing best, maybe two things pretty good. The rest I can do if I have to but it's not what I do best. Everybody has one thing they're best at, sometimes two. But it's good to know what you can't do. Then you get to ask friends to help."

Buppa doesn't know it all. "Not knowing is a great gift, Gio. If you know you don't know, you can decide to learn. If you know you know, you've already decided not to learn. Never be afraid and never be ashamed if you don't know something. When you admit you don't know, that's when you learn."

We travel. Grandpa takes me to meet his friends. They talk together in voices I cannot hear, look at me, look back at Grandpa. They nod. Sometimes they shake hands, sometimes they hug.

They ask me what Grandpa teaches me, have me show them. Grandpa wants me to learn.

One friend, Daskele, smiles, pops into two separate Daskele who are the same Daskele, one on either side of me, helping me. "Training wheels."

Grandpa nods. "Thank you."

I learn of many doors. Some always start at the same door and then enter other doors beyond the first. Some people go through their Childhood Door only when they need to. They find other doors to different places they need to go. Some people can control their doors so that one becomes many and many become one.

I learn you never let someone enter your door and you never follow someone through their door, even if they ask.

Sometimes it happens by accident. Someone has to go find them. Beautiful Painted Arrow shows me. "Like Grandpa and me playing Hide-and-Seek?"

"Wonderful, Gio. Wonderful."

Daskele Lower-Center-Relax-Breathes and enters his door. Two of him come out the other side. He does it so quickly it's hard to follow. He takes me with him. I look at myself and laugh. I look funny. Not like in a mirror washing my face or when Grandma combs my hair. We look up at two Daskeles. "Which is real?"

"Ask 'what can we really do?', not 'which is real?' The latter assumes if one dies, so does the other. The former assumes infinite possibilities. When there are two of you, three of you, four, five, six of you, what can you do one of you could not?"

I clap my hands. "I can eat more of Mr. Zelli's ice cream!"

Grandpa and the Daskeles laugh.

Running Water Lower-Center-Relax-Breathes and a river stands where she stood, flowing water except it doesn't splash. I reach in. The water chuckles. "That tickles."

WildCat Lower-Center-Relax-Breathes and a huge brown bear rears up.

Chan Lower-Center-Relax-Breathes and shows me The Lion Dance.

I make mistakes.

They help me. "It might work better this way."

Or they ask me questions to guide me. "What happens if you do it that way?"

Never "Do it this way" or "Do it that way."

Always I must find my way, my path, and always they're happy to have me share their path for a while.

Like Buppa. Patient. Warm. Each meeting ends with an embrace, a hug, they rub themselves against me, animals leaving their mark. Beautiful Painted Arrow purrs like a cougar. "So others will know who you've been with, what you've studied."

On the rides home Grandpa always gets a load of peaches to sell from the back of his truck and he always gives me a great big one. The fuzz tickles when I eat and he wipes the juice from my chin, holds his handkerchief under my mouth so I don't stain my shirt. "Everything, everything, everything is your teacher, Gio. You decide what the lesson is."

"Is Bee my teacher, Buppa?"

"Yes, Gio. Yes."

"Is Spider?"

"Yes."

"Uncle John?"

"And Mary, too, yes."

"Running Water?"

"Oh, yes."

It becomes a game. "Toothpaste?" "Garlic?" "Anchovies?" "The gas station man?" and always a smile, a laugh, a "Yes," and always, "You decide what the lesson is."

"Yes, Grandpa."

"Never stop learning, Gio. Never stop learning. There are teachers everywhere. No one knows it all."

Chapter 9

Sensing

Grandpa sells peaches from the back of his truck. He sits me in the bed and lets me open crates. When no one comes by we play games.

"*Ascolta il gattina, Gio. Riesci a sentirlo camminare?*" Listen to the kitty, Gio. Can you hear it walking?

A favorite game Grandpa plays with me. I close my eyes, pay attention to my ears. I clap my hands. "Yes, Buppa! I can hear it walking."

"*Dove sta camminando, Gio?*" Where is it walking?

I listen, my eyes shut tight. I cock my head, right ear up, left ear up, right ear up. "On Mrs. Gianelli's fence. The one on the Caputo's side."

Grandpa smiles and kisses my head.

"Now look, Gio. Where is Grandma?"

It is hard not to hear. I cover my ears with my hands, open my eyes wide. "She's talking with Piantedosi the baker, Buppa. She says -"

"No listening. What's she doing?"

"She's getting bread for dinner."

"Anything else?"

Grandma looks in the dessert cases. She points to ricciarelli, struffoli, cannoli.

Grandpa licks his lips and pats his belly. "Yumm."

"How does Grandma know which ones to buy?

"She uses her hands. To taste."

I look up at him.

He picks up a big peach, red and yellow, from the top of an open crate.

"Is this peach sweet?"

I reach for it.

"Don't touch with your hands yet, Gio. Send your hands. Make sure it's safe."

"Safe?"

He turns the peach so I can see the other side. It's molded. The mold makes you sick if you eat it.

Grandpa teaches me to know when something will make you go *plah*. Grandma calls them poisons. You find them in food turned bad, sometimes mushrooms, often when milk is sour.

"Smell from here. Don't go there. Not yet."

"Okay, Buppa."

"Walk with me in the forest. Tell me what we can eat."

We never leave my room. I hear the forest floor, leaves and pine needles, long grasses bend over as we walk, always gentle so they rise back up. "Thhhank youhhh, Giohhh."

"You're welcome."

The evergreens greet me with the heavy scent of pine. The oaks roll some acorns in our path. A maple sends a little helicopter seed spiralling down beside me.

Grandpa puts his hand on my shoulder. "Do you see that, Gio?"

On a birch tree, at face level and clinging. A huge creature, cousin to Spider, bigger than any spider I've ever seen, and not familiar to me. Eight legs, not a spider, and blind.

"Walk slowly, Gio. It is telling us something. This is its land."

Each step brings us closer. The wind brings scents of fox and deer. Crows fly overhead. Raven lands on an elm branch and squawks at Grandpa. "Be careful. Gio doesn't know."

Grandpa nods. "Thank you. I'm teaching him now."

Crows caw at us. Raven hops from branch to branch, always over us, always a little ahead, making sure I'm safe.

The creature on the birch grows smaller as we approach. Smaller and smaller.

Raven squawks and flaps its wings. "Careful, Gio."

We stand beside the birch. The creature is so small. I reach for it and Grandpa pulls my hand back.

"Safe passage for me and mine, Tick?"

I hear a voice of "S"s. "Yesss. Sssafe passsage."

"This is Tick's land, Gio. Always ask before you go. And if Tick says 'No,' then stay away."

"Yes, Buppa."

"Remember the smells, the sounds, the feels. Remember what you see, if it's safe. Remember the tastes."

"Yes, Buppa."

He rubs my head. "Let's get home before Grandma knows we're gone."

I open my eyes. I'm on my bed. Grandpa is sitting next to me, looking at me, smiling.

Chapter 10

Cat

"Ascolta il gattina, Gio. Riesci a sentirlo camminare?" Listen to the kitty, Gio. Can you hear it walking?

I close my eyes, pay attention to my ears. "Yes, Buppa! I hear it walking."

"Dove sta camminando? Puoi camminarci sopra, Gio?" Where is it walking? Can you walk with it, Gio?

I listen, my eyes shut tight. I cock my head, right ear up, left ear up, right ear up. My body flows into the cat. My feet and hands twitch as the cat hurries along.

"It's crossing the street, Grandpa."

Grandpa, hovering above me, sees what I do not. I feel him descend, not in time.

My eyes open wide.

I run with Mrs. Gianelli's cat, rushing across the street and not fast enough.

A car runs over it, crushes it, kills it.

I still share with the cat. I roll, jumble, as the little cat's body rolls under the car, is crushed under the tires.

We scream together.

Cat comes. It takes Mrs. Gianelli's cat Home.

My first experience of death. Sudden. Violent. The part of me that listens, that walks, lifted in Cat's jaws at it gathers its Shadow Home.

It takes Grandpa two days to find me, to bring me back. He lays beside me on my bed the entire time, never leaving, until I return, safe but terrified, shaking, as if waking from a fever, chilled, afraid.

Grandpa lifts me in his arms, cradles me against him, calls to Grandma. "He's back, Sadie. He's safe."

Grandma comes in, wipes my face, my brow, gets fresh clothes from my bureau.

"I'm sorry, Gio. So sorry." Grandpa is crying.

I wrap my arms around his neck and kiss him. "It's okay, Buppa. I forgive you."

He hands me to Grandma and walks out. I hear him in the living room, Lowering-Centering-Relaxing-Breathing.

Sobbing.

Deep, belly-aching sobs.

"Is Grandpa okay?"

Grandma hugs me. "Yes. He needs time to forgive himself, Gio."

Chapter 11

Borrowing

John stands on his porch waving as we drive up in Grandpa's truck. He is tall and his arms are long and when he waves I wonder if he can gather clouds.

Uncle John laughs.

"Did John know we were coming?"

"Go give *Uncle* John these jars of honey." Grandpa makes sure I show respect.

Uncle John has an accent so he talks in my head. "A fish scared you, Gio?"

I hand him the honey. "I don't know how to borrow."

Sometimes Grandpa's friends ask "May I share how I do it?" to help me learn how they do something Grandpa does, something he is teaching me. They let me piggyback down their path. Sometimes we have to travel far and they become a ladder and I climb up their rungs and the ladder flies and you learn how to be a ladder and fly.

I piggyback and climb their rungs so I can borrow from them to learn how to do things, to understand my way, my path would be different from theirs and different is okay, it is the outcome that matters.

Uncle John loves sweetcakes made with Mrs. Minerva's honey. "Come inside and help me make sweetcakes. We'll put poppy seeds on them. You like that? And your Grandpa and Mary can make some good strong coffee to go with them. And while we're making sweetcakes, you can show me how you borrow and I can learn from you. You like that?"

Mary is John's wife. She's not as tall as John, only as tall a Buppa and John's chin rests on her head when they hug.

I wonder if Uncle John's head rests on Buppa's head when they hug. He laughs and holds his long arms out to Buppa and they hug.

Uncle John smiles. Buppa's eyes go wide and he nods at me. I laugh because Uncle John and Buppa always know what goes on inside.

She smiles at us as we enter. She speaks no English and no Italian, so when I'm there she teaches me their language, Lozi. John taught me how to say "I am John N'bmwe from Namibia" in Lozi, Igbo, Xhosa, and lots of other languages. John and Mary have a favorite phrase when things go wrong: the sweetcakes overcook or the coffee spills. "Oh, Yootsue T'a'Anjuu!" Mary's goats get in the garden and she whisks them out with her broom. "Oh, Yootsue T'a'Anjuu." John bangs a knuckle fixing their car. "Oh, Yootsue T'a'Anjuu!"

I drop a flower Mary gives me to hold and pick it up. "Oh, Yootsue T'a'Anjuu!"

Everybody laughs. Mary and John laugh so hard they have to hold each other up.

John claps my back. "Do you know what you say?"

"I don't know. I just like the sound."

"'Oh, Yootsue T'a'Anjuu' is 'Oh, Jesus Christ.' in our language."

I put my hand over my mouth and Grandpa laughs.

John pats my head and helps me put the flower back in its pot. "That's okay, Gio. We have different gods. I'll tell you about them sometime."

Between them John and Mary know fifty languages, all from Africa. "That's normal. You need all those languages to work and trade. We helped people make films in Africa because we could talk to everybody and be understood."

But their English sounds funny. And their Italian makes Grandpa laugh.

Today Grandpa and Mary play penny-a-point cribbage while John and I make honey and poppy seed sweetcakes and he teaches me how to borrow.

"Learn to borrow and you can borrow from anything. You always borrow with permission. You always ask. You only do it for a little while. You never borrow it all because that leaves them with nothing."

He pats a sweekcake into the best shape for cakeness and sweetness. "You be careful, Gio. Some people borrow without telling you. You feel them like an itch on the skin."

"People like us?"

"Oh, people like us, it's easy to tell. It's the ones not like us, the ones who want to get close but -"

I pat a sweetcake and he helps me shape it for cakeness and sweetness. " - never open their door?"

Grandpa laughs.

Mary pours some rich, black coffee into mugs. Her voice is a song in my chest. "You're such a smart one, Gio."

John pats my head and leaves me with a flour crown. "You sure you're not your Grandpa passing? I don't know, you know so much."

I pat the sweetcake the way he shows me. "It's me! Gio! I don't know how to pass yet."

He inspects my cake, gets close to it. "That's a good cake, whoever you are. I think I'll have to eat it now." He reaches for the cake.

Mary slaps his hand away. A melody in my heart. "Let the boy learn."

"Oh, Yootsue T'a'Anjuu, woman."

Everybody laughs.

"Those who never get to their door, they borrow by dressing the way you do, talking the way you do, telling people they know you when they don't. They study for a day, run away, and write books about everything they've learned."

"I'm going to make a sweetcake just for you, John."

Mary sits across the table and sings. "Do I get one, Gio?"

A little figure dances in the air over her shoulder. It holds a finger over its lips. I smile and look away, gather ingredients for Mary's sweetcake. "Yes, Ma'am."

"Be careful of them, Gio. They are the real dangers, those who know nothing and claim to know a lot."

"Yes, Uncle John."

He sits next to Grandpa. He presses Grandpa's chest then reaches out and presses mine. "I make sure you're not your Grandpa having fun with me." He licks his fingers. "Hmm...you don't taste like a sweetcake, either. Okay. I guess you're Gio."

"Oh, Yootsue T'a'Anjuu. It's me. Gio."

Everybody laughs.

John leans towards me, his coffee mug steaming in his hands. "Now, teach me how to borrow."

Chapter 12

The Immensity of Now

Buppa and I stand on the porch. He holds me, his strong, tanned arms making a seat for me to sit on. A man comes to us. He and Buppa talk quickly, quietly. Buppa shakes his head, no.

The man reaches out, pulls his hand back before touching Buppa. Holds his hands out, palms up. His voice strains. I feel it high in his chest, caught right below his throat, wanting to escape, afraid.

Buppa tells him to go away, come back later. He shakes his head as the man goes down the steps, out the gate, to his car, drives away.

He takes me inside. "What did he want, Buppa?"

"To cause pain."

"Will you do what he wants, Buppa?"

"I will do what he asked, not what he wants."

"You going to hurt someone?"

"Someone will be hurt, yes."

"You told me not to hurt people, Buppa."

"I won't hurt them. One person will wound himself. Another will be wounded but grow from their wound." He pauses, smiles, kisses me. "But more importantly, Gio, you will learn."

I'm excited. I love Buppa teaching me. I love his friends teaching me. "What will I learn, Buppa?"

"Come. Let's watch TV."

We watch *Tutor Turtle*. Tutor Turtle has a friend, Mr. Wizard. Every episode, Tutor comes to Mr. Wizard with something he read in a book. He reads about racecar driving, being a knight, captaining a boat, exploring the heart of Africa, being an astronaut; always something exciting and different.

Each time Mr. Wizard warns Tutor Turtle maybe his wish isn't the best idea, but Tutor begs and pleads and Mr. Wizard says okay and casts a spell and Tutor opens his eyes and is whatever he wanted to be this time around.

Tutor has fun and an adventure, but always something happens. He crashes the car or gets chased by a dragon or sinks the ship or faces a lion or flies into the sun. Right before Tutor Turtle is about to meet his end, he cries out, "Help me, Mr. Wizard! Help!"

Kindly old Mr. Wizard has been watching Tutor all along through his Crystal Ball. He goes *tsk tsk tsk*, lifts his wand, waves it over the image in the Crystal Ball. He says, "Drizzle, drazzle, druzzle, drome. Time for this one to come home," and there's a *poof!* and Tutor is sitting on the floor in front of Mr. Wizard.

Mr. Wizard helps Tutor up and cleans him off and listens to Tutor's say what a fool he's been.

Buppa loves *Tutor Turtle*. He always laughs when Tutor Turtle says "Help me, Mr. Wizard! Help!"

The man comes back. Buppa meets him on the porch. He holds me as before, making a seat of his arms so our faces are inches away from each other, so we see the same things.

The man holds money out to Buppa.

"*Non è quello che abbiamo concordato.*" That's not what we agreed to.

The man snorts. "That's the price I'm going to pay."

"*Partire. Non venire mai più da me.*" Go. Never come to me again.

Buppa turns with me in his arms,

"You didn't take his money, Buppa."

"It wasn't what we agreed to."

I remember my father yelling "Something is better than nothing" the last time my parents visited.

My Buppa knows what I think. He kisses me. "That's not true, Gio. We always do what we agree to."

"Even when other people don't?"

"Even when other people don't."

"Why?"

"Because we honor ourselves, what we do. Any agreement is really an agreement with yourself. You respect yourself when you do what you say you'll do."

"But then they're not respecting you when they don't do what they said."

"Doesn't matter. They're not respecting themselves." He tickles my ribs. "Remember what I said about thieves?"

I tuck that side and chuckle. "Yes. 'If I am a thief, you must steal'. So he stole from you?"

"He stole from himself. He doesn't know it. No one can steal from you unless you let them."

"You let him steal from you?"

He winks at me.

I clap my hands. "You knew he would do this! That's why you didn't want to do it when he asked."

He kisses me. "You're so smart, Gio."

"But you still did what he asked?"

"I asked The Universe what I should do. It answered, 'Do exactly what he asks.'"

"What did he ask you to do, Buppa?"

"He asked me...he asked me to change his son."

"Change his son?"

"He worries his son won't be what he wants his son to be. He asked me to change his son into what he wants his son to be."

"And you did?"

"I did because The Universe never wastes anything. I did because changing his son into the son he wants his son to be will rob him of the son he wants but teach his son respect and honor, for himself and others, something his father will never have and therefore cannot teach him. One day his son will be taken from him and he will mourn." He pauses. "And remember."

He rubs my hair. "You will help his son, and you will remember. But not for years yet."

He smiles. He smiles like he smiles at Tutor Turtle. But he doesn't laugh. "This would happen even if I did nothing."

"Then why did you do it?"

He laughs. "Every moment has many, many, many things happening in it. What we do in the *Now* changes everything that follows it."

"The *Now*?"

He takes my hand. "Let me show you."

He shimmers. Like sunlight on ripples in a pond. He gathers me into him and we go up.

Up, up, up.

"Look down, Gio. What do you see?"

"That's our house! That's our garden! And the beehives behind the shed."

"Good. Now we go higher. Now what do you see?"

"Is that the street where we live? That's Mrs. Gianelli's house." I start pointing. "And the Caputos, and the Gagliardis, and..."

He laughs. "Good, Gio. So good. Now we go higher."

Each time he asks what I see.

"That's the town where we live." "Is that America?"

Sometimes he helps me. "That's our world, Gio. A planet. The Earth."

Then he says, "What do you know about me, Gio. What's different about me?"

I sense. I smell. I taste, touch, and feel. "You're bigger!

He tickles me. "How about you?"

"I'm bigger, too!"

"Yes. Someday you'll meet Don Alejandro and he'll teach you how to do this."

"You won't teach me?"

"I'm still learning it myself. Now what else besides bigger?"

I look. I listen. I sense. I expand the way Buppa teaches me. "We're -" I search for the word " - thin?"

"Seems like thin, doesn't it?"

"Yes, Buppa. What are we doing?"

"Look down, what do you see?"

"The Earth. It's passing us. It's going around the sun."

He continues. We spread, grow bigger, grow *thinner* because there is no other word in any other language.

Our joints pop like stars exploding. Our bones crack like galaxies colliding.

And still we grow. Among the stars, beyond them. Bigger, bigger, bigger until we stop and everything stops with us. Nothing moves.

In all the universe, there is silence. A silence that can only be understood once everything stops.

"What do you see, Gio?"

I'm not sure. "I see...everything?"

"Yes. Everything at this moment. Like a picture, like a flashbulb. It seems like everything stops when the picture is taken but everybody keeps moving. The camera takes the picture so fast it seems nobody moves. To get here, where we are, we are moving so fast we are not moving at all, we are so big everything exists inside us. We become this moment in time."

He helps me open, experience, become.

"Remember this, Gio. Our purpose is to be here, now. Not to serve some imaginary creation. The Universe is Creation enough, and no one explores all of it."

"The Universe is big, Buppa."

I hear him inside. "The Immensity of Now."

Chapter 13

Go Wide

Grandpa and I walk down the street side-by-side. I feel Grandpa shift. He guides me from one side of him to the other, always holding my hand. I look up at him. "Buppa?"

He touches a finger to his lips then touches it to my forehead. I hear his voice inside. "Let's learn something new: how to talk two ways at the same time. Would you like to learn how to do that?"

Buppa always makes learning fun. "Yes, Buppa! Yes!"

Buppa speaks quietly inside me and taps his chest. You hear me here. I nod.

He clears his throat and makes a sing-song like when my friends and I play games. "AND YOU he-ear ME HE-ere."

I laugh.

Inside. Go wide, Gio. Go wide like Sidney and Anouak teach you.

～

"Let's go see Sidney today." Sidney is one of Grandpa's friends. He's from a place called "Bahama." Bahama is lots of islands strung like pearls on the neck of Yemoja. That's what Sidney says.

We take a boat to the island where Sidney lives. Buppa signs on as part of the crew for no pay if he can take me with him. The captain knows Buppa. "I'm sure we have an extra bunk for such a little one, Giovanni." Buppa and the captain shake hands.

The captain is Apolonus. "I'm from Greece, Gio. Do you know where that is?"

I point over the ocean and everybody laughs.

"You're right, Gio!"

Apolonus knows Daskele. All of Grandpa's friends know each other.

Buppa puts on heavy gloves and a helmet. "Time for me to work, Gio."

"What are you going to do, Buppa?"

Apolonus picks me up and we follow Buppa. "Do you know your Grandpa talks to Fire?"

"You do, Buppa?"

Apolonus laughs. "Your Buppa talks with everybody."

"Can you show me, Buppa?"

We stop on the deck beside sheets of metal and a big tank with a hole in its side.

"Fire is one of the oldest of the Old Ones, Gio. It has many children. We ask for its help to fix things."

Buppa picks up a funny, thin nozzle like we use in the garden except this one has two hoses going to it. The other end of the hoses go to two tall, thin tanks. Buppa opens the faucets on each. The funny, thin nozzle also has faucets and he adjusts these.

He snaps his fingers and a flame sprouts from the nozzle.

Buppa whispers to the flame. He points to the big tank with the hole and the sheets of metal standing beside it. The flame grows a little face and arms and hands. It looks where Grandpa is pointing and listens as he talks.

It nods and reaches for the big tank. Grandpa pulls his helmet down and goes to work.

Apolonus turns us away from Buppa's working. We head back to the bridge. "Your Grandpa will teach you how to talk with Fire, Gio. Your Buppa talks with everybody."

In port, Apolonus finds us a car. "Forty-eight hours, Giovanni, then we have to go."

"That's enough."

We drive to the ends of the earth and then walk a small path through the trees and grasses. There's a warm breeze and it rustles the palms overhead. We walk on crinkling casuarina leaves and I sneeze at the scents of pink hibiscus and yellow allamanda.

A deep voice booms through the trees. "Sweet, Gio. We call the breeze sweet, not warm."

Buppa smiles.

"Is that Sidney, Buppa?"

"He saw us coming."

The path ends at a little white sand beach. On the far side a hammock made of vines and leaves is strung between two palms. The tallest, blackest man I've ever seen climbs out of the hammock. He waves at us.

"Go say hello, Gio."

I run over the sand. The man sits on the sand and is still taller than me. "We going to play games, Gio. You teach me yours, I'll teach you mine. That be fun?"

I nod, excited.

"Your Buppa said I saw you coming. How could I do that, you think?"

I look around. The sun rose on the part of the island where Apolonus harbored the ship, now it sets.

I scratch my head. "You guessed?"

Sidney laughs. His laughter makes me shake like thousands of fingers tickling me and I laugh, too.

"Guessing is good. Going wide is better."

"Going wide?"

He points to the ocean. "You see Tico's boat? He's fishing two islands over. He's coming back now with dinner."

I shake my head. "Who's Tico?"

He touches foreheads with me. "Look at everything, not just one thing."

I fly across the ocean. It grows larger and larger yet changes somehow else, somehow other.

I feel the waves. "This is like Chan!"

"You know Chan? He's my brother, too. Like your Buppa is."

I feel the salt in the air as it rushes past me. My chest expands. My shoulders broaden. I see a dot.

Sidney goes wider and so do I. The dot on the ocean grows longer, sprouts a sail.

Sidney goes wider and so do I. The dot becomes a little boat. A man sits in it, beside him a net full of fish. He looks up, waves.

"Say hello to Tico, Gio."

"Hello, Tico!"

Tico stands up, points to the fish, pats his belly, nods.

Sidney pulls me up against him, my back to his chest. He gently rests his forehead on the back of mine and uses his hands to hold my head so as he turns his, I turn mine. We look away from Tico, across the ocean, north.

"Now, Gio. We join with no hands."

He slowly pulls his hands away and I still feel them there. Not hands, more like flowers, leaves.

"Easy, easy. Slow, slow. We ask Ataba to help us."

"Who's Ataba?"

"You'll know her when she comes."

Cool hands caress my head, play with my hair. The hands are large and graceful, soothing, made of water. I feel them joining Sidney's head to mine, a hat perfectly fitting both so we move as one.

"Ataba?"

A voice like air over ocean waters. "Hhelloh Geeoh." The ocean laughs.

"Good work, Gio. Now we go see a friend, Anouak."

"Where's he?"

Sidney whispers inside like Buppa does. "Ask Ataba to help us find him, Gio."

"Ataba, will you help us find Mr. Anouak, please?"

The ocean swells, waves rise, a woman smiles from beneath the water and carries us on her breath north north north.

Ataba opens the ocean to the horizon and beyond. Sidney and I spread ourselves, grow, cover the distance riding a chariot of wind.

"See those, Gio? Those are icebergs. Like ice cubes in a drink, but now in the ocean."

Wider, wider, wider until we see another dot in a frozen world.

"Is that your friend Anouak?"

"Can you ask him, Gio? Ask him who he is. Like we did with Tico."

We get closer. The dot becomes a man in a different kind of boat. He also has fish but no net. He looks up, waves, points to his fish, pats his belly, smiles.

Suddenly Sidney is gone and Anouak holds me. "Hello, Gio. Are you learning how to go wide?"

"Yes, Mr. Anouak."

He laughs. "There is no 'Mr.' in my language."

"What is your language?"

He speaks. Flowing sounds like the ocean around him, then back inside my head. "Sidney and I go wide the same but different. It is a form of Sees-Far."

"Seize fire?"

He laughs. "Not quite." He enunciates in my head. "Sees...Far...A way of knowing what is not around you. Being aware of what's happening. You start with here and go wider and wider until you know what's happening there." He holds up a fish. "You bring this to Sidney when we're done. He never had a fish like this."

I feel Sidney getting close. "Yes, sir."

Anouak and I touch foreheads. "Now you know what I know, but don't know it yet. When you need it, it'll be there. Then you come back and see me. We'll go from there."

I feel myself pulling away.

"Don't forget Sidney's fish. Tell him to bring me a coconut the next time he comes."

I sleep all the time going back on Apolonus' boat, practicing the things Sidney and Anouak taught me.

— ~ —

I go wide as we walk.

Buppa's voice is gentle inside me. "Go wide wide wide until you see it all."

I'm not sure what "all" I'm supposed to see but I do what Buppa says.

The people. They glow.

"Everybody's glowing, Buppa!"

"Very good, Gio. Tell me more."

Outside, I hear him speak. "Maybe we should go to Mr. Zelli's. Get a ice cream?"

I go wider and wider. It takes work. But it's fun.

The glow separates. A single white becomes four colors and not everybody's colors are the same.

"It's their bodies, Buppa! The glow is their four-bodies!"

"Oh, you're too smart for me, Gio. The colors tell you something. Someday you'll meet Don Alejandro and he'll teach you what to do. Him and others."

This is exciting!

"Tell me more, Gio. Tell me more."

I feel Buppa moving me. We taste each person's colors. "This person does this," and I tell Buppa what the person does. "This person does this," and I explain what that person does.

Grandpa speaks out loud and people smile hearing his words. "What kind of ice cream you like today, Gio?"

Coming down the street, towards us, a woman. Buppa slows me down. He helps me be careful.

"That woman has only one body, Buppa!"

I don't know how that can be. She is a pretty woman with a nice smile and long golden hair. She wears sunglasses but I look past them into her gray-green eyes.

A tide pulls on me, stronger than any Chan teaches me about.

Buppa is beside me, holding me back.

"Careful, Gio. Go slow."

She is a tall woman, almost as tall as Buppa. And she walks so smoothly, like she's not touching the sidewalk with her feet. She doesn't look at us, she doesn't look at anything, as if the rest of the world isn't there, her smile never changes, she never blinks. Her motions are smooth, practiced.

"How can she have only one body, Buppa?"

She passes us. Buppa guides me over to the side, away from the people walking along, back from the traffic.

"Look at her now, Gio."

The woman is hollow. She has no back, no sides, only a front, only a smile, nothing within. Look at her from behind and you see a mirror of what you saw in front but walking away from you.

"Now come back, Gio. Look with your eyes."

She walks on. She looks normal. No one would ever notice anything different about her.

"That is an Ellewoman, Gio."

I switch from eyes to wide and back. Woman, then hollow like the front of a porcelain doll, and then a woman again.

"All smiles on the outside, nothing on the inside. They mean us no harm but they can do us no good. It is their nature to take, to receive, and never give back."

I nod, remembering the feel of her, her scent, her taste.

"Expect nothing from them. Avoid them. Let them be."

We walk again. Buppa picks me up so I ride his shoulders. "I'm going to have pistachio. What you gonna get?"

Chapter 14

Steps

Matsuo and Furyada spoon soup into white bowls with flower pictures on them. "What shall we do today, Gio?"

"Can I show you steps?"

Matsuo and Furyada stare at each other then back at me. "Steps?"

Buppa chuckles. "Show them, Gio."

I walk to their back porch and look out over their garden. It's different from ours and called a *karesansui* with rocks and sand and little trees and a pond.

I take their hands and walk down to the steps until we're level with the karesansui. "This is where we are now, okay?"

They nod, their eyes watching me intently.

I go up one step.

"Should we follow, Gio?"

"Not yet. I have to see that I'm here so I can show you how to do steps."

They watch me intently.

"Oh, Yootsue T'a'Anjuu. I did it wrong."

Matsuo and Furyada hide their smiles. Matsuo whispers something to Buppa but all I can make out is "John N'bm'we."

"You know Uncle John?"

Matsuo laughs and holds his belly.

Furyada squats so our faces are even. "Good for you you know you made a mistake, Gio. Never *wrong*, just a *mistake*. Start again."

I stand by the garden with them and take one of their hands in each of mine. "See that we are here."

Matsuo nods. "Good so far, Gio. What's next?"

Furyada nods, too. "You can do this, Gio. Slow and easy, like everything else."

I balance my bodies the way Buppa taught me. I take them one step up. "Now see that we are here."

My eyes are closed and I hear the smiles in their voices. "Go on, Gio." "Yes, go on."

"And see that we are also there by the karesansui."

We turn from the first step and look back. Matsuo and Furyada are looking at me, smiling. I see myself by their garden. My eyes are closed and my face is scrunched with effort.

I feel Matsuo's other hand on my shoulder. "Easy, easy, Gio. Relax-Lower-Center-Breathe. Take your bodies with you. Go slow."

Furyada whispers into my ears by the garden and I hear it here. "Can you do this again? And take us with you?"

I take them with me one more step up, we turn, look back. The three of us are beside the garden, looking up. My face is relaxed. Buppa is using a special rake to create waves in the sand. One step up the three of us have their backs to us, staring into the karesansui.

"And again?"

Third step.

I feel Furyada and Matsuo beside me. "One more step, Gio. Can you do one more step?"

I feel a *Pop!* and we're up another step. Their energies are tickling me and I squeal covering my sides with my arms. "You helped me!"

Furyada, Matsuo and I are back by the garden, laughing.

Furyada goes up the steps. "I will make tea."

Matsuo kneels in front of me. "You did very good, Gio. Do you know there are lots of names for what you call steps? Our people call it *hareigia*."

"Hareigia."

"Excellent. You'll be speaking our language soon. Better than me!"

"What else is it called?"

"Oh, there are more words than I know of. Pretty much it comes down to awareness."

"Awareness?"

Furyada pours us tea. "Do you see that we're all here by the garden? Think of this as one level."

The tea is hot and delicious.

"You go up one step, you're on another level, right?"

I nod. There are sesame candies on a plate. Furyada is pointing at the steps back into the house and Matsuo slides me a candy.

"He thinks I don't see that, Gio. How do you think I see that?"

I look where he's pointing. "You're on the steps looking back!"

Furyada gives me a candy. "You're too smart for us, Gio."

Matsuo sips his tea. "Now go up one more step. How many levels is that?"

I count out loud. "The ground is one. The first step is two, the next step is three."

Buppa looks at the sesame candies on the plate. "If I go up a step, can I get one?"

Everybody laughs. Matsuo hands him the plate. "Every time you go up a step, you go up one level of awareness. From that level, you can look back at all the previous levels."

Furyada takes a candy. "Sometimes you have a problem and you can't figure it out, go up a level. Few problems can be solved at the level in which they exist."

Matsuo nods. "A smart man said that."

Furyada pours me more tea. "Remember, Gio. Levels of Awareness. Like steps."

Matsuo sips his tea. "Or shells. Layers. Remember, the further in, the further out."

"Thank you!"

"Let's go see what your Buppa did with our garden."

Chapter 15

Passing

Uncle John walks with me to the edge of his field where his beans grow broadleaf in the shadow of trees. I know most trees. Sometimes a new one grows overnight and Uncle John and Buppa take me through the seedling through its roots into the soil to feel the cool earth.

"There's someone wants to meet you, Gio. You like that? It's okay if we say hello?"

"I like that."

A tall, tall man walks out of the woods edging Uncle John's field. He moves quietly, his footsteps like whispers, and steps carefully, as if his rich brown sandals sense what's beneath them, making sure nothing is harmed, nothing is crushed. He wears garden-green silk stockings and his violet trousers flare with each step, and it seems he walks with the earth, not on it.

Uncle John and I sweat from our walk in the warm sun but the heat doesn't bother the tall, tall man. His shirt ripples like vanillaed cream in the slight breeze, and the black lines on his violet jacket frill like feathers when his jacket ruffles. His broad, banded white and yellow hat hides his face but his elegant beard, trimmed so closely to his chin, has gold and white highlights in it, depending on how it catches the sun. His bowtie is gold and lavender, rimmed with black.

"Say hello, Gio."

I offer my hand.

The man bends slowly, gracefully. A cloud of earth smells, growing smells, surrounds me. Buppa's garden, Mrs. Minerva's hives, John and Mary's fields, Chan's medicines, Beautiful Painted Arrow's flatbreads, chamomile, rosa rugosa, rose of sharon, clematis. Insects buzz around him, under his hat. Some crawl up his silk stockings, pants, and jacket. A spider builds a web between his chin and bow tie.

We shake. His hand is soft and reminds me of lamb's ear leaves. I look down. My hand is wrapped in a flower petal.

His other hand lifts off his hat. His face is a sunflower, his eyes bright yellow stella d'oro, his beard corn hairs flowing with pollen.

The wind tickles my ears. "Hhhelloh Geeeooh."

A new friend! "Hello!"

He stands up, pulls away, moves over the earth, carried by the wind, back to the trees. He leans against one, a mid-size oak. His legs merge into a single stalk, his shirt and jacket become petals and blooms, flowers burst from his hands, his hat scatters pollen to the sun.

The mid-size oak is embraced by a climbing clematis.

Something about the oak.

"Buppa?"

The oak pulls up its roots, lowers its limbs, grows smaller, its bark becomes Buppa's work clothes. The climbing clematis moves to another tree.

"Oh, you're too smart for me, Gio."

Uncle John stands behind me. "How did you like that, Gio? Your Grandpa played a trick and you found him out. How did you know the oak was Grandpa, Gio?"

I shrug. "It felt like Buppa."

Buppa picks me up, gives me a kiss, puts me back down. The three of us walk back to John's house, me in the middle.

"It's okay to see me as a tree, Gio?"

"It's okay. I know it's you."

Uncle John jabs his thumb into his chest. "How about me, Gio? You like me like a tree?"

"You can't be a tree, Uncle John."

Uncle John and Buppa look at each other.

"How come I can't be a tree, Gio?"

"I don't know."

"What can I be?"

"I don't know its name. It looks like this." I shape my hands like claws and scrunch my face and growl. "Grrr."

"You mean like this?"

John melts, shifts, his hair grows long, his clothes fade away, golden hair covers his body, his beard grows long, his hair goes unfrizzy and haloes his head. His face stretches out, his mustache becomes long cat whiskers, his eyes close and reopen as cat's eyes. His arms grow long and thick, his hands become paws, his fingernails claws that grip the earth as he walks. His nose grows large and pink. He sniffs me, hot breath enveloping me. "Grrr."

"Uncle John! You're a -"

Buppa strokes Uncle John's tawny hide.

"A lion, Gio. Uncle John is a lion."

"But Buppa, Uncle John doesn't look like any of the lions in my cartoons." Buppa and I watch cartoons on Saturday mornings. Sometimes I have to work the antennae, sometimes he does.

The lion roars with laughter.

"Uncle John is a real lion, Gio."

"You're a real lion, Uncle John!"

More lion laughter.

A moment later Uncle John is back. "You like that? I can be a lion for a little while. WildCat, that's his gift. Someday maybe he'll teach you."

"WildCat is a lion?"

Buppa laughs. "Usually a bear. But whatever he chooses, he doesn't have to change back. We *pass*. You saw me, you knew it was me. When you saw John, you knew it was John. How did you know?"

Silly question. "Because you're Buppa and he's Uncle John."

"Tell me more."

I don't have words. I make them up. "You have Buppaness. Uncle John has UncleJohnness. You are Buppa no matter what you look like. Uncle John is Uncle John no matter what he looks like."

John points to a short, strong man in a heavy shirt and pants working in the field. The man's gray hair and beard and thick black sideburns are so heavy I can barely see his face. Only the white streak of hair in the middle of his head let me know he's looking at us. "What about him?"

"He's a badger!"

The man stands up, waves, his face melts to a badger's face, his eyes sparkle. His voice is a hoarse grunt. "Ghello, Ghio!" He goes back to work, his face covered in heavy beard again.

At the other end of the field, at the far tree line, tall men and women come out of the woods and head to where Clematis grows.

Uncle John waves. "This is Giovanni's boy, Gio. Say hello, Gio."

They walk slowly towards us, towards me.

I give them my hand. Their hands are rough. Even the women's.

"Do you recognize us, Gio?"

Their faces shimmer. Grow bark. Their arms become branches, their fingers limbs, their hair leaves.

"You're trees."

Another shimmer. The people are back. The forest laughs. "Yes, we are trees. You have four bodies, so do we. Our physical-bodies grow but can't move. Not well. That is our way. This is how we explore. Will you remember us?"

"Always." I know Treeness now.

The men and women continue into Clematis' woods. With each step, a tree takes root, grows, sprouts, leaves, flourishes, seeks the sun, drinks deep waters, lets birds nest in its hair, insects burrow.

Buppa lifts me to his shoulders. He and John take long strides back. "What we do, what Clematis and the trees do, what Badger does, we do for a little while. You still know it's us, who we are."

"Why pass, then?

Uncle John watches the cars drive past his fields. "Not everyone can see, not everyone can tell. Sometimes we have to be and not let others see us being."

"Isn't that a lie, then?"

Buppa nods, watches the cars. "Where do you hide a leaf?"

I know this. Buppa taught me. "In a forest!"

"Where do you hide a grain of sand?"

"On a beach!"

"If someone only looks at the outside, refuses to see what we truly are, are we lying to them?"

Buppa reads me books that have stories about this. Some people on Grandma's TV shows do this. "It's like when we dress up!"

Uncle John runs his hands through the corn stalks as we walk. "Oh, you're such a smart boy, Gio. What else can you tell me about dress up?"

I reach up and feel the cornstalks leave his fingers. He leaves answers for me in the grasses. "But not like the Emperor who got new clothes?"

"Because?"

Uncle John lifts his hands from the corn stalks. "Come on, Gio. You can figure this one out."

Buppa lifts his hand to his face like he's drinking from a bottle.

"Truth! The Emperor lied to himself about not having new clothes. We can't lie to ourselves when we dress up." I correct myself. "Pass."

Uncle John's hands come back down to the corn, to the grasses. His knowledge whispers into me. "Oh, you're too smart for me, Mr. Gio. There's nothing I can teach you now."

"You'll always be able to teach me, Uncle John."

Grandpa chuckles. "Remember, Gio. When you can't tell and it can change, that's not passing."

Uncle John nods. "That's what Wildcat does. Maybe someday he'll teach you. You like that? He so becomes what he is that his other is gone, no more. You can't tell because it's as if his other never existed."

"You'll always exist, right, Uncle John?"

"Oh, I've got a way to go yet."

"And you, too, right, Buppa?"

"I'll always be in your heart, Gio."

Chapter 16

Slow

Grandpa teaches me to be aware of who I meet before I meet them. *"Guardali prima che ti guardino, Gio."* Watch them before they watch you, Gio.

It is like Steps, another *Levels of Awareness* training. I feel someone's vibration across a room, across a field, across a beach, on the other side of the street, on a bus, with Grandma in the market, it doesn't matter. They don't notice me but I know them, where we'll meet them and when.

Grandpa says what we do is old, old beyond measure, old beyond ancient. He calls it *Il Sapere*, The Knowing. *"Il Sapere sceglie il suo, Gio. Ha scelto te."* The Knowing chooses its own, Gio. It's chosen you.

"How do I know I'm chosen?"

"In all things, you have to ask to learn."

I want to learn. To make Grandpa happy. To make Grandma smile.

He lights two candles. One Grandma made, the other she bought. We sip espresso on the back porch and watch the candles burn, listen to the whispering of their flames as afternoon turns into night.

"What does Candle teach us, Gio?"

I study the two candles. I want to make Grandpa proud. "The bought one burns faster?"

"Are you asking me or telling me?"

"The bought one burns faster."

"What do we learn from the candles then?"

"Grandma's candle burns slower. It'll last longer."

He nods, smiles behind his espresso.

"That's what you've observed. Good boy. What do you learn?"

I rest my chin on my fist, my left leg crossed over my right, making myself look like Grandpa when he practices.

When he's learned something he raises his head, points his finger. "Ah ha!"

Grandma always chuckles. "What did you figure out?"

I raise my head, point my finger. "Ah ha!"

Grandpa hides behind his espresso. "What did you figure out, Gio?"

"Go slow, the lesson lasts."

Grandpa puts down his cup and pulls me towards him. His eyes grow wet. "That's it, Gio. That's everything. *Lento.* Slow."

He hugs me. His tears wet my face. "*Questo è il tuo diritto di nascita.*" This is your birthright. "Go slow, Gio. Learn well. Learn slow and it'll never control you."

"Does it control you, Grandpa?"

"Sometimes I fall."

Chapter 17

Little Lost Girl

Buppa stands me in front of him, on the sand facing the ocean. Chan adjusts my feet so they point forward and are as wide apart as my shoulders.

"You ever ride a horse, Gio?"

"At the *Festa de Sant Antony* I did."

"You remember how the horse felt under you?"

I nod.

"Feel like that now. Make believe you're on the horse."

"Giddy yap."

Chan smiles. "My people call this a horse stance because it's like you ride a horse. Make sense?"

Chan always asks if he makes sense. I have to show him I understand before he continues.

"Now put your hands out like this."

The shadow of Buppa's arms comes over me. I look above and behind me. He's doing the same thing I'm doing.

"What are you doing, Buppa?"

"I've got to learn, too, Gio. Chan does this much better than me."

Chan adjusts my arms, levels my hands, straightens my fingers, taps my belly.

"What do we do first?"

"Lower-Center-Relax-Breathe."

"Make sense?"

I Lower-Center-Relax-Breathe.

"Feel the ocean, feel its power, hear the waves coming in? They sing songs of distant lands."

My body rocks gently, back and forth.

"Let the ocean move you. Be its water. Learn where it's been. Feel where it's going. Taste its bottom. See what moves there in the deep, deep dark."

I rock with ocean, striking the land, feel its movements in my bones.

"This is *Waves*, Gio. We do this to learn the power of Ocean, this form of water, so we can draw on its power when we need to. Make sense?"

Buppa's head rises, his eyes open.

Chan's head rises, too. He follows Buppa's gaze. "You're needed, Giovanni."

"Finish the boy's lesson."

"We can practice more later. Nobody gets it the first time."

I stop rocking but keep standing, my arms outstretched, my fingers sensing the ocean. A shallow forms in front of me.

Chan claps his hands. "Gio! You make a liar out of Chan!"

〜

Officers Morelli and Clarkson talk with Grandma on the porch. Their police car is at the curb outside our gate.

They walk to us as we get out of Buppa's truck, their hats held in the hands in front of them.

Officers Morelli and Clarkson are friends. They walk through our neighborhood often. Sometimes Officer Clarkson wears shiny black boots and rides a motorcycle. Sometimes Officer Morelli comes by in a police car and I get to ride around the neighborhood in front with him. Sometimes he sits me on his lap while he drives and I get to hold onto the steering wheel. "Oh, we're in hot pursuit, Gio. Gonna get them crooks, Gio." He drives funny so we go all over the street.

Officer Clarkson sits me on his motorcycle and puts his helmet on my head. It covers my eyes and I can't see. He gets on behind me and goes "VROOM! VROOM! PUT-a-Put-a-put-a-put VROOM! VROOM! PUT-a-Put-a-put-a-put." We put on the siren and Grandma comes out of the house, a kitchen towel over her ears. "Shut that damn thing off. You'll deafen the boy."

Officer Clarkson turns off the siren. "Sorry, Mrs. Fortune. Just giving the boy some fun."

He looks at me and his face goes *Whoops!*

Grandpa and I laugh.

Grandma goes back in and comes out with a cookie tin. "You ask that Cheryl girl to marry you yet?"

"Doing it tonight."

"Gio, bring these to him."

I hand him the tin and he starts to open it.

Grandma snaps the towel. "No, no you don't. Those are for your girl to give you when she says 'Yes.'"

Officer Clarkson perks up. "She's going to say yes?"

Grandma looks at me. "What do you think, Gio? His girl gonna say yes?"

I shrug. I don't know how to see through time yet. Buppa says time is a place like any other. You can get there if you know which direction to travel.

Grandma laughs. "You bring those cookies, Charlie. In case."

Officer Morelli looks at Officer Clarkson. "I'm going to speak Italian, Charlie. No offense. So I'll be understood better."

Officer Clarkson nods. "Go ahead."

"*Abbiamo bisogno di te, Maestro Fortuna.*" We need you, Master Fortune.

I tug on Grandma's apron. "*Maestro* Fortuna?"

She lifts me into her arms and holds me close so we can whisper better. 'People call Buppa "Master" when their need is great."

Buppa nods. "They request the Old Ways and are afraid."

"*Una bambina è persa.*" A little girl's lost.

Buppa nods. "*Il ragazzo viene con me questa volta.*" The boy comes with me this time.

Officer Morelli shakes his head. He turns to Officer Charlie. "He wants to bring Gio with him."

Officer Charlie looks at me and then at Buppa. "I don't know, Mr. Fortuna. We suspect…This could be…"

"So he can learn. For later." Buppa pats my head. "Go help Grandma clean you up, put on fresh clothes. I got to wash, too. All this sand."

Buppa sends me the sounds of the ocean, of the waves, the feel of the water, our feet in the cool blue-green water, little crabs scurrying into the water, bubbles where clams sleep under the waves.

I feel the ocean move me. Remember Chan's lesson. Hear Buppa inside. "Good, Gio. Remember."

We get in the police car. "Can I ride in front?"

Buppa nods. "For now. You'll have to help me later, Gio. Do you want to help me?"

I get to help Buppa! "Always!"

Officer Clarkson lifts me over the back of the seat and puts me on his lap. "No sirens this time, Gio. Don't want your grandma mad at me."

I pout. He tickles me until I laugh.

Officer Morelli starts their car. He looks back to Buppa. "Where do we start?"

"Where did she live?"

Officers Morelli and Clarkson pull in the driveway of a big house. The driveway's as big as our street and has its own streetlights but they look like lanterns. Other police cars are there. A man and a woman stand on the house's front steps. In front of them on lower steps are police and men with cameras taking pictures. Officer Clarkson weaves his way though the crowd, Buppa behind him, me in Buppa's arms.

"Mr. Johnson, Mrs. Johnson, this is Giovanni Fortuna. He's come to help us."

Mr. Johnson stares down at Buppa and me. He turns to another man standing behind him. "Sandniggers."

Buppa laughs. Mr. Johnson turns back, his face red. Buppa smiles. "A lot of people make that mistake, Mr. Johnson, but I'm Sicilian, often known as the Black Italians. Our geographical location and many seaports brought a variety of people to our shores. No doubt I have some Sudanese or sub-Saharan blood in my veins, perhaps even Congolese or deeper in the Dark Continent."

Buppa speaks good English?

I didn't know Buppa spoke good English.

I'll ask him to teach me.

Mr. Johnson goes back up the stairs, into the house. Mrs. Johnson comes forward, offers her hand. Buppa has me shake it.

Pain...Pain...Pain...

I stop, pull back, hold Buppa tightly.

I hear him inside. He comforts me. "Good, Gio. Be brave. Learn. Do what Chan taught us. What you feel, it's like waves, right? Pain, nothing. Pain, nothing. Pain, nothing. You made the waves stop and form a shallow, remember? Do that now, Gio. Do that now."

Buppa keeps me close. He looks at Officer Morelli and nods at Mrs. Johnson.

"*La bambina è in casa.*" The child's in the house.

Officer Morelli walks up the steps. "We need to go inside, Mrs. Johnson."

Mrs. Johnson falls backing up the stairs. The people behind her catch her, don't let Officer Morelli through.

Buppa stares at her. He cocks his head. I feel him listen.

"Where is the little girl, Gio? Find the little girl."

Lower-Center-Relax-Breathe. I go in the house, past Mrs. Johnson, past the men standing behind her, through the door, up the stairs, down the hall, into the rooms, into the baths, down the stairs, ...

"Wide, Gio. Do as Daskele taught you."

I am two. One goes down the stairs, into the rooms, into the kitchen, through the house.

Two become three. One goes into the basement. We talk to each other, helping, guiding, looking. "What's in that closet." "Do they have a pantry?" "Where do those stairs go?" Three become four. "What's in the attic?

A presence. I reach for Buppa. "I found her, Buppa. I found her."

Four become three become two become one.

"Careful, Gio. Don't look. Not yet."

There's a big, old refrigerator in the attic.

Buppa surrounds me. I smell him. I feel and hear him. I taste him. Wanting me to learn, wanting to keep me safe.

"It's like Mrs. Gianelli's cat, Gio. Do you understand? Do you remember?"

I hear one of the people behind Mrs. Johnson. "You'll need a search warrant to enter these premises, Officer."

Mrs. Johnson. Not pain. Fear. Waves of Fear.

Fear...Fear...Fear...

I look at her. Fear ripples her skin, words on paper: Don't let them look in the icebox.

A little girl. Crumpled. Folded. Cold, dried blood. Her eyes are missing.

"SHE'S SEEN ME!"

Her teeth are missing.

"SHE'LL TELL PEOPLE!"

Her legs broken, shattered, the bones poking up through her dress.

I pull back, tuck my head into Buppa's neck, clutch him tightly.

"Help her, Gio. Be brave. I'm here. I'll help you if you need."

I gather her energy. There isn't much left. I let her borrow from me. Give her strength. Something floats above us.

An Old One?

Not an Old One. Close. Different. Waves on an ocean made solid yet flowing.

It takes her from me, thanks me.

I am back in Grandpa's arms.

Mrs. Johnson's skin ripples.

Buppa holds me close. He uses beautiful words again. "In the attic, in an old Frigidaire. Look in there."

He rocks me in his arms and looks at Mrs. Johnson. Buppa's face shimmers, changes. His eyes grow dark, different, like Mrs. Gianelli's cat's eyes, like Uncle John's when he's a lion.

Mrs. Johnson's face turns white. I smell her sweat, hear her heart. Her chest stops moving.

Buppa's face is back. "You knew all along, didn't you."

He carries me back to the police car. We sit quietly. I'm in his lap and he stares out the window, away from the house, away from the Johnsons, away from the police and camera people, away from me.

"Buppa?"

"Yes, Gio?"

"Are you angry at Mrs. Johnson?"

"Yes, Gio."

"How come, Buppa?"

He turns to me, his face shimmers, a cat's face. He lets me play with his whiskers. "Because I still have much to learn."

Chapter 18

Expensive

"What do you charge?"

The man at the gate doesn't know Buppa. People who know Buppa never ask what he charges.

People bring us things. "We just slaughtered one of our pigs, Giovanni. May I offer you some porkchops? Sausages? Bacon?" "We just slaughtered one of our cows, Giovanni. How about some fresh steaks or ribs? You need some hamburg? Sadie need anything for the sauce?" "Giovanni, I had good luck hunting today" or "Caught more fish than my family needs, Giovanni" or "Could you use some corn?" or "I brought you a basket of apples. Maybe Sadie can make a pie?"

Cartons of cigarettes, wine, sambuca. Brand new clothes. A bureau. A chair. Things. "If you can't use it, maybe you know someone who can?"

"The Universe knows, Gio. We want for nothing because we don't want more than we need."

"Yes, Buppa."

Buppa looks at the man outside our gate. "I'm very expensive."

The man speaks English and wears a nice suit, like the men at the bank who help Grandma. He looks down and smiles, strong white teeth against dark skin. He takes a billfold out of his jacket. "What's 'very expensive' mean?"

"What's it mean to you?"

The man chuckles. "No, come on. How much?"

"You haven't told me what you want me to do."

"Look, I'm only here because my wife -"

"Then your wife should be talking to me, not you."

The man stops. His billfold is still in his hands. "I don't have time for -"

"*Come mai non mi parli in calabrese?*" How come you don't speak Calabrian to me?

The man's ruddy features ashen.

Buppa moves, changes. I see part of him go out to the man, sniff him, a dog picking up a scent.

"*Hai lavorato duramente per perdere il tuo accento.*" You worked hard to lose your accent.

Buppa switches to English. He sounds like the man at the gate. "You went to...Harvard? Yes. Harvard. Studied hard. Good for you. Got your degree? Yes, got your degree."

The man steps back, his arms hang limp by his sides.

"And now you're a...*consigliere?*" Buppa holds his belly and laughs. "No, you're a lawyer, but you like the sound of *consigliere* better? Ha! *Alcuni dei vecchi modi ti stanno bene?* Some of the old ways suit you?"

"I -"

Buppa stares at the man. "Yes. You." Buppa shakes his head. "You could never afford me."

The man drops his billfold, turns, steps, turns back, picks it up, walks quickly down the street to a car, drives away.

"Are you expensive, Buppa?"

"Yes, very, and no, not at all."

I look down, purse my lips, furrow my brow.

He kisses my head, runs a hand over my brow, smoothing it. *The Knowing* leaves his hand, enters me.

"People not willing to change will pay any price to stay who they are. They want the world changed to suit them. That's expensive. But someone willing to change? I'm not expensive at all. They're already on their way."

He looks down at me, smiles. "Remember, Gio. All we do is help people realize what they want changed, what they're willing to change. That's all. Nothing more."

Chapter 19

An Instance of Time

"You remember when we talked about *Now*, Gio?"

I tell Buppa of the great things we shared in an instance of time.

"Good, Gio. Remember, not a *moment* of time, only one *instance* of time."

"Yes, Buppa."

"Now..." He looks at me out of the corner of his eye and smiles. "I show you the *Real*."

"The *Real*, Buppa?"

Buppa takes my hand in his. His palm tickles like lamb's ears on my feet. "Do you feel my hand?"

I chuckle. Buppa's having fun with me. "Of course, Buppa."

He increases his grip so I am held firmly, strongly, but not painfully. Tenderly. Knowingly. "This here, Gio. This is what is real now, yes?"

He teaches me an important lesson. I can tell. I nod, stop chuckling. "Yes, Buppa?"

The air around Buppa darkens, quickens. Little lightnings flash around him, become him. The lightnings surround me. "What is *real, now?*"

I am different. I feel the air. Little pieces of it. Like each piece finds a place in me, on me. For a moment I think I'm air. Then electric. I tingle. Buppa's dark sky surrounds me. I see different color balls, some with rings around them, a really bright one not far away. But also I feel fishes swimming in the sea, in lakes, rivers. Birds on branches, in flight. Strange animals loving the cold, swimming in icy waters, walking on different colored earths, breathing different airs.

"Gio?"

I have no words. "Oh, Buppa." It is so beautiful I cry. No words in any language he teaches me make the sound I feel inside. "Oh, Buppa. It is...it is..."

"It is what is *Real, Now*, Gio."

"Oh, Buppa."

We stay in the *real now*. "When you become aware of everything, you are *Now*. Everything else is imagined, everything else is remembered. Sometimes people are troubled. One body is greatly stronger than the others, puts demands on the others, controls the others. Which body do you think that is?"

Dark wisps of starlight tap my chin like Buppa's fingers when he's thinking. "You said imagined and remembered. The mental body?"

"Tell me more."

I...remember! "All bodies can imagine and remember, some do it better than the others."

"Yes. How can you tell which is which?"

"If I'm asking, I'm imagining. If I'm telling, I'm remembering."

"Oh, you're so smart, Gio. You already know more than me."

Buppa pouts and I laugh, then he smiles. "What else can you teach me?"

Buppa wants me to teach him. He makes teaching him fun. I can make mistakes and he teaches me how to teach.

"So some people, the troubled ones, they don't know what is imagined and what is remembered." I make sure I say it, don't ask it.

"Go on."

"But to know what is *Real*, what is you and not-you, you must be able to tell what is you and not-you." The darkness glistens into snow-covered sunlight. "So these people, they can't tell what is them and not-them."

"Therefore...?"

"They don't know what is *real*, what is *now*."

"Oh, you're too smart for me, Mr. Gio Fortuna. People are going to come to study with you, you know so much."

He tickles me and I laugh.

"Can we stay here, Buppa? Can we stay here forever?"

We are back on our porch and he is holding my hand. "No, not yet. But you can go there when you need."

"I can, Buppa?"

"Yes. Start with *Here*."

"*Here*, Buppa? We're here."

"Exactly. We are *Here*, *Now*, and it is *Real*. Remember these three things, Gio. They always are together, and together they make an *Instance of Time*."

I nod. I can feel the learning enter me. I close my eyes to help it find a place inside, not outside, not at what I'm looking at. "I will work to make every instance a good one." I open my eyes.

Buppa's crying.

"You okay, Buppa? Did I do something wrong?"

He shakes his head, holds me close, tears leap from his face and he rubs them into my hair. "No, Gio. You've just given me an incredible gift, perhaps the most amazing gift."

I want Buppa to be happy. I pull back and look him in the eye like he does with me when he wants to make sure I understand. "And I did it right *here*, *now*, and it's *real*."

Buppa's head lifts and he laughs.

Chapter 20

Funny Little Hats

Buppa puts a funny little hat on my head. He takes one of Grandma's bobby pins and puts it in so the little hat doesn't move. He has a funny little hat, too. He puts it on and takes another of Grandma's bobby pins so it doesn't move, either. He crosses his arms over his chest and puts one foot behind the other like a statue.

"*Stai come me.*" Stand like me.

I do.

"*Sadie, vieni a vedere i tuoi bei uomini.*" Sadie, come see your handsome men.

Grandma comes out and laughs. She laughs, laughs, laughs. She covers her mouth with the dishtowel in her hands. "Have fun."

"Where we going, Buppa?"

"To see a friend."

"Are we going to learn something new?"

"I am. You're so smart, though. I don't know."

"Oh, Buppa." I lean against him and he wraps his arm around me. I feel it when he shifts. Every time he shifts, I smell his clove aftershave and hear his whiskers bristle against his collar. He drives us through Boston to some place far away.

We get out in front of a row of houses all linked together. Not like where we live where there's a house then another house and then another house. Here it's like one long house made up of house-house-house-house-house-house-house. Each house has its own small yard and each yard has its own small garden. Each yard is separated from the yards on either side by a black iron fence. A walkway leads to a few steps to a door.

"That fence is no good, Buppa. Rabbits could get through easy."

A deep laugh makes me turn. "It is for the orphan and the widow."

"Gio, say hello to Rebbe Ben Lev."

"Hello, Rebbe Ben Lev."

"Hello, Gio."

Rebbe Ben Lev combs his hair so it looks like a pigtail on one side.

He laughs. "A pigtail? Really? I'll have to remember that."

His apron is made of string. It has knots and is full of holes. I wonder how he can wipe his hands when he cooks with an apron like that.

He laughs again and leans over me so his head is close to mine. "Want to know a secret?"

"Yes, please."

He looks back and forth to make sure no one else is around and whispers into my ear. "It's not for cooking."

"You listen the way Buppa does!"

Buppa and Rebbe Ben Lev laugh.

His laughter turns to chuckles. "What can I do for this smart young man today?"

"Buppa says we're going to learn from you today."

Rebbe Ben Lev looks surprised. He scratches his head and I see he's also wearing a funny little hat. "He did?"

"I like to learn."

"So do I. Let's see what we can learn together."

He goes up the steps and opens the door. I follow. I'm about to walk in and Buppa holds me back. He shows me a pretty little gold toy with all sorts of colors on it on the side of the doorway. "See this, Gio?"

"Yes, Buppa."

"Every time you see that or something like it, you kiss it. Like this." He kisses his fingers then touches the gold toy with the fingers he kissed.

Rebbe Ben Lev nods at Buppa.

"What is it, Buppa?"

"It is respect."

We go inside. Rebbe Ben Lev has us sit with him at a big table with all sorts of books on it. He sings in a language I've never heard before.

I lean towards Buppa. "That's beautiful, Buppa. What is it?"

"Shh."

Rebbe Ben Lev smiles when he finishes. "Can you read, Gio?"

"Buppa and Grandma are teaching me."

He opens a book. "What do you think this says?"

I've never seen writing like that before. "It's magical writing. Magical words."

Rebbe Ben Lev's eyebrows go up. He nods at Buppa.

"Do you know what it says?"

I run my hands over the magical writing. "It says Love."

Rebbe Ben Lev stares at me. He goes into another room and comes back with a small wooden box. The box has magical writing on it. He opens it and pulls out a badly knotted string.

"Do you want me to help you take out the knots, Rebbe Ben Lev?"

His eyes go wide. "I would love you to help me take out the knots."

My lessons begin.

Chapter 21

Sunday Mornings with Sambuca

Grandpa sits on the backporch watching his garden, listening to Mrs. Minverva and her children, sipping an espresso with a bottle of Sambuca by his side.

His espresso has more Sambuca than espresso, mine has espresso with a drop of Sambuca. And a sliver of lemon rind. To make it sweet. Delicious.

Still I cough.

Grandpa laughs.

"How come Grandma goes to church and we don't?"

He laughs. "She likes to play both sides."

"There are sides?"

He smiles. "No, not sides, only different understandings. People take sides. People without *The Knowing*. They create sides, differences. Reasons to say Me and Not-Me, but because they fear, not because they love."

"Have you ever been afraid, Grandpa?"

"Oh, yes. Many times."

"What do you do when you're afraid?"

"I decide to love, to respect, instead."

I sip my espresso. "I don't understand, Grandpa."

"May I tell you about one of my teachers?"

I love Grandpa's stories about his teachers. "Oh, yes. Please."

"Once I left home, I traveled to study. There are teachers everywhere."

I quote from memory. "Everything, everything, everything is your teacher, you decide what the lesson is."

He chuckles and ruffles my hair. "Yes. Good you remembered that. One of my teachers taught me any time we identify as some one thing we separate ourselves from everything that's not that thing. He thought that was an act of violence."

I frown. He smiles. "Remember the man who called us sandniggers?"

I nod, sip my espresso, touch my tongue to the floating lemon rind.

"He said that because he believes he's different from us. People believe they're different when they're afraid and they're afraid because they don't know who they are. Not knowing who they are, they decide others are different."

"Chan is different."

"Chan looks different, but how different is he?"

"He's a Lion when he does the Lion Dance. You can tell. We saw him at the Chinese New Year. I'm not a Lion."

"He'll teach you when the time is right."

"Running Water is a stream. I'm not a stream."

"She'll teach you when the time is right."

I smile over my espresso cup.

He lifts his cup so it hides all his face except for his eyes and he squints at me. "Ye-e-es?"

"I'm not a Buppa! Ha!"

"Not yet. Your children will teach you when the time is right. Ha!"

"But that means I'm not special."

He pulls me onto his lap and gives me a long hug. "You're special because you don't know how special you are."

"I'm your boy. That's why I'm special."

"Stay that way, Gio. Forever."

"I will, Buppa."

Chapter 22

Healing

A woman comes on a hot August night. Grandpa and I sit on the front porch watching traffic and sipping steaming hot espressos. A boy in blue shorts, white shirt, blue three button jacket, knotted blue bowtie and topped with a blue hat rides her hip. Her dark, mid-calf skirts seem heavy in this heat.

Her walk and clothing tell me she's not from our neighborhood or any other I know. Her long, thick, black hair hangs loosely about her shoulders, not done up, braided in a thick ponytail or held back with pins the Sicilian way, and she wears thick, rich makeup during the day, not for a special occasion. A strap over her shoulder supports a large, beaded purse which hangs like the udder on John and Mary's cow.

Grandpa smiles and nods as she walks past. She stops at our gate and opens it without asking, as if it's her own.

On the porch her steps are so light the floor doesn't creak and I can tell from the sound she wears expensive shoes.

Grandpa stands.

She talks in whispers and holds the boy out to Grandpa.

The boy is my age.

The woman puts him down. She pushes him at Grandpa.

Grandpa shakes his head and steers the boy back to the woman.

I come over and ask if the boy wants to play with me in the garden.

He pulls back into the woman's skirts.

Lower-Center-Relax-Breathe.

Grandpa puts his hand on my shoulder, a warning. I look up at him. He stares at me wide-eyed and shakes his head, no, pursing his lips.

Too late.

Pain. Raw pain. An animal caught in a trap gnawing its own leg to get free.

I cry, my body, my bones, my joints on fire.

The boy.

Such pain. How can he stand?

Grandpa yells - it is the only time I hear him raise his voice in alarm - and pulls me back. His four-bodies come together, between me and the boy, falling like thunder. A shield. He only does this to protect Grandma and me from things we can't see.

I snap back, released.

Grandpa moves me around him, holds me behind him, shrouding me, making sure I can't touch the boy, can't sense the boy.

The woman speaks hurriedly, quietly. She pushes the boy to him.

Grandpa kneels down. He is face to face with the boy. "How much will you pay me to heal you?"

The woman shrugs off her purse. She pulls a roll of bills out and hands it to Grandpa.

He stands, pushes her hand away, only touching the back of her hand, not her fingers or the money in them.

He kneels in front of the boy again.

"How much will *you* pay?"

The boy looks up to the woman.

"Momma?" His English is almost Sicilian.

She curses Grandpa in Italian and English.

Grandpa rubs his hands together and passes them over his mouth, pinching his lips.

The woman *stops*. Everything about her stops. She doesn't talk, she doesn't move. I can't hear her breathe.

Her eyes open wide. A tear slides down her cheek. It makes a little river in her makeup.

Grandpa's eyes never leave the little boy. "*Quanto, Davino? Quanto pagherai?*" How much, Davino? How much will you pay?

The boy reaches into a pocket and pulls out a licorice drop, sticky with lint, as if licked and savored then saved for the next rejoiceful lick, and hands it to Grandpa.

Grandpa doesn't touch it.

He looks down his nose at it and puckers his lips as if tasting it.

"Is that a licorice drop?"

"Y-Yes."

"Is it any good?"

"Yes. I got it yesterday from Crescengi's."

Grandpa sniffs the licorice drop in the little boy's hand. "Smells good. Is that an expensive licorice drop?"

"It's from the two-penny bin."

Grandpa nods and his brow goes up.

He keeps me by his side, one arm around me holding my arms at my sides so I can't touch the boy.

"Are you sure? That's a good licorice drop. You will give it to me if I help you?"

The boy looks around to his mother. She doesn't speak or move. She doesn't acknowledge him. He reaches for her skirt and Grandpa pulls his hand back.

"Are you sure, Davino. Not your mother, you."

The boy hesitates then nods, yes.

"One more time. Are you sure you want me to do this?"

The boy looked at the licorice drop in his hand. He hands it to Grandpa.

Grandpa takes it and licks it once to clean the lint off.

He spits into his palm and rolls the licorice drop there until it is shiny, then gives it back to the boy. "You take this."

"I don't want it."

"Maybe your Momma does?"

He hesitates then takes the drop from Grandpa's big hand.

"Will you save that for yourself or let your Momma have it?"

The boy turns around and holds it out to his mother.

She still doesn't move.

"If I pick you up, maybe you can put it between her lips. Can I do that? Pick you up?"

The boy holds his hands out for Grandpa to lift him.

I see the boy's legs. They are spindly, deformed.

Grandpa hums. He rubs his hands, covered with spit and black from the coloring of the licorice drop, up and down the boy's legs.

Grandpa winces several times as he massages them.

He cries out when he pats the boy's hips and thighs.

He does this for some time, rocking the boy and rubbing his legs and singing old songs, something hovers above him, something made of sound.

All the while he walks back and forth on the porch.

He stops on the far end, puts the boy down.

The boy runs to his mother, stops midway, looks down at his legs, looks back at Grandpa, continues to his mother.

"Good strong legs now, Davino?"

"Good strong legs. Thank you."

He lifts the boy to his mother. "Give your mother the licorice drop."

The boy pops the licorice drop into her mouth.

She breathes, she shakes, she cries.

She takes her son from Grandpa and kisses the boy as if he'd been lost to her for years.

Then she looks at Grandpa.

She looks around the porch. She lowers her boy and Grandpa doesn't hold me away anymore.

The woman lifts the hem of her skirt slowly, slightly. She says something in a husky, frightened whisper.

Grandpa laughs, deep and full from the belly.

He smiles and sticks out his tongue.

She screams, clutches her son to her and runs away.

I tug on Grandpa's sleeve. "Why did she run away, Buppa?"

He smiles and sticks out his tongue. The licorice drop is crooked in its hollow.

Chapter 23

The Orchard

"Where are we going, Buppa?"

"To see an old friend. To learn."

We pull into a farm that's nothing but orchards. "Who lives here, Buppa?"

A woman comes out of the trees. Her skirt is long and covered with flowers and vines. The wind swells it, lifting slightly. She walks barefoot, her feet moving like an ice skater's on a pond. Each step leaves a brushstroke of fresh green in its wake. She comes across the grass and cobblestone runoffs to the dirt driveway where we park. Her long black hair flows out of a scarf tied around her head and her blouse surrounds her like heavy rain clouds.

She walks up to Buppa and gives him a big hug. "Who you bring me today, huh?"

Buppa gently pushes me in her direction. She squats and tucks her skirt under her. "Is okay I hug you?"

She smells like apples and peaches and pears and watermelon and corn and...something else, something good, something delicious.

"Yes, please."

She pulls me into her. Her blouse swells around me, her skirt sweeps the dirt and wraps itself around me. She reminds me of pictures Buppa shows me of women statues, statues he knew as a boy back in Italy. She is soft and cushy and warm and safe. The flowers on her dress come alive and send their tendrils around me, tickling me. My hair becomes leaves, my legs root into the ground. My face becomes a star gazer lily and the wind catches my laughter.

Her arms gently push me back. "You gotta name?"

"I'm Gio!"

She looks up at Buppa and smiles. "I knew a Gio long time ago, far away."

Buppa smiles back. "Somebody else's turn now."

The woman stands, her blouse and skirt pulling back with her. "Gio, you hungry? You like eat fruit?"

"Yes, Ma'am."

She bends over a kisses my head. "Such a good little boy you got here." Her kiss smells like sunshine.

She offers me her hand. We cross the driveway and I look back. Buppa's not following us. I stop. "Buppa?"

"It's okay, Gio. You go with G. You'll be alright."

"G?"

"Okay I lift you up? Carry you?"

"How come Buppa's not coming with us?"

She kneels on the grass. "Because today is your turn. Is okay today is your turn?"

"Buppa said we came here to learn."

"Is a good thing, to learn?"

I think about Buppa's teachings. I Lower-Center-Relax-Breathe. "Yes." I open my arms, lift them, she gathers me in her blouse, her skirt billows and we move on the wind through the orchard, past apple trees, pear trees, wild watermelon vines, grapes climbing tree trunks, peach trees, and onto trees I don't know. "How come your name is 'G'?"

"Oh, it's a name, not my name. Everybody gives me different names because everybody needs something different. You want to see me different?"

"Yes, please."

She puts me down amongst the trees. She lifts her hands above her head and starts spinning like a dancer. Her blouse and dress blossom, her hair falls from her scarf and sweeps over her shoulders, chest and back. It's full of stars.

She spins and spins and spins and a woman stands on her toes in front of me even though G is still spinning. The woman has lots of arms and is covered in bright stones that reflect the starlight in her hair. Her face reminds me of Chan's but not quite.

G keeps spinning. A big, naked woman sits on a throne in front of me. G spins. A thin woman with a crocodile's head smiles down at me. G spins. A mountain talks to me with G's voice. G spins. I'm surrounded in cool river water. It reaches up and wets my lips. I open my mouth and a few drops fall in. The water is sweet. G spins. A woman in heavy clothes rides a big cat in front of me. G spins. A woman like in Buppa's statues says "Hello."

A moment later the spinning stops and the G I know stands before me. "But which one are you?"

Her hair climbs up under her scarf, her blouse settles back around her, her dress falls to the ground. "Yes, I am." She lifts me in her arms and we walk through orchards.

Her walking slows. We enter a ravine. There's a pool in the center. G's arms become harder, thicker. Her hair turns into leaves. The flowers and vines on her skirt race ahead, along the ground, into the soil. Her legs stop, her skirt turns to bark, her arms become limbs. I'm sitting in a tree.

A limb grows heavy. A beautiful light green thing grows in front of me at the limb's tip and falls into my hands. "A fig!"

The tree has G's voice. "You like figs?"

Buppa and Grandma give me figs for dessert. "Yes, Ma'am. Very much. Thank you."

"You know where figs come from, Gio?"

"From a tree?"

G's limbs reach up and lift me to the ground. "From this tree."

G is twisted and gnarled. Her trunk isn't straight and her limbs aren't even. "You don't look like other trees."

G shakes her leaves and becomes an apple tree. "You like this better?" Another shake. A pear tree. Another shake, another, then another. Each time "You like better?"

I wrap my arms around the trunk. "It doesn't matter what you look like, G. You're all beautiful, just different."

G is back. She has a big funnel shaped basket. All sorts of fruits and vegetables fall out of it.

"And I will always feed you if you take care of me, Gio. Always."

Chapter 24

Knowing

People come to Buppa asking to study.

He tells Grandma this one will not continue, that one will not learn. He pats my head as Grandma teaches me to stuff artichokes.

"How come, Buppa?"

"It is *The Knowing*, Gio, *Il Sapere*. It's a friend like everything else. But it is a friend that looks both ways."

I remember going to the library, him showing me a picture of a statue with two faces. "Like Janice?"

Grandma smiles. "Jan*us.*"

"Like Janus?"

"You can only go as far out as you're willing to go in, Gio"

"Yes." I have no idea what he means. I repeat something Chan said, my voice sounds like an old Chinaman's. "They get to their first door and stop."

Grandma and Grandpa laugh.

Grandpa lifts me so I stand on a kitchen chair, easier for me to pound open the artichoke leaves. "*Il Sapere*, the Universe, has special plans for you, Gio. You're one of its Chosen. Not everyone learns like you do."

Unfamiliar words but I know their meaning: I am loved.

"There will be great things in your life. Make yourself ready."

Chapter 25

Grandpa Smokes Cigarettes

We sit in the park. Bluejays squawk, cardinals tweet, chickadees chirp, and pigeons coo. They land a little ways away from us and hop closer, keeping their eyes on us, ready for flight.

"Did you bring the old bread?"

I rattle a bag I carried since we left our house.

"They want us to feed them."

"Do you want me to take out the bread, Buppa?"

"Not yet." Grandpa lights a cigarette.

"Grandma says that's bad for you."

"Grandma smokes, too."

I touch my chest. "It hurts here when you smoke, Buppa. Grandma, too."

"Maybe I can borrow from you. Grandma, too. Because smoking won't bother you."

"How do you know that, Buppa?"

"Because you have a gift I don't have. You can heal."

He borrows from me as he draws on his cigarette.

I cough. My chest aches and then the aching stops.

He borrows from me again as he inhales.

My chest doesn't ache.

"See? You heal. Remember that. That's something you can give to others. Healing. That's something I can't give."

"Buppa?"

"Even to myself."

Chapter 26

Mr. Giambatta's Car

Mr. Giambatta's car stops outside our gate. Everybody knows Mr. Giambatta's car but nobody ever sees Mr. Giambatta. People say his name quietly, like a prayer in a church, a loud whisper, "Mr. Giambatta," like they don't want anyone to hear. Some parents use his name to make their children behave. Toma broke a window playing ball and his mother came out of her house. "Better hope Mr. Giambatta doesn't live there."

Buppa plays a game with Chan. He plays it with Lee and Yao and Matsuo and Salomão and Uncle John and Brother Jonnie Rae. Everybody's game is the same and a little bit different. Every game starts slow and goes faster and faster until they move so fast no one can follow, their arms and legs a blur, their bodies here and there then here again.

Sometimes Buppa plays the game with me. He picks a twig up from the ground. "Practice so I don't touch you."

He plays the game with Chan and Lee and the others with their hands or knives or swords or other things I don't recognize. "What are those?"

I learn each is a tool where all my friends came from. They teach me how to use their tools.

"Do you like learning to use tools, Gio?"

"Yes, Buppa."

"Someday you will learn how to use a tool to make a tool."

"I'd like that, Buppa."

I work hard to learn the games. It's fun.

Buppa picks up a twig, lights the end with a match, blows out the flame and breathes on it so it glows, hot and red. "Practice so I don't burn you."

He makes me move faster and faster. Sometimes he gets close but the hot tip never reaches me. Chan and Matsuo and Uncle John and Salomão and the others ask if they can play their games with me. "Find your center, Gio." "Protect your center, Gio." "Learn your center, Gio."

I laugh. We have fun. These are good games.

"But you don't play these games with others, Gio. Not yet, anyway."

"How come, Buppa?"

Buppa thinks about it. "Because other people don't know how to fall."

A big man in a dark suit gets out of Mr. Giambatta's car. He has a broad brimmed hat and pulls it down, hiding his eyes. He looks up and down the street before opening our gate and walking to our porch.

"*Il signor Giambatta vuole che tu mi insegni come combattere.*" Mr. Giambatta wants you to teach me that fighting you do.

Buppa shakes his head. "No."

The man leans towards Buppa. "Do you want Mr. Giambatta to ask you personally?"

Buppa laughs. "If he wants. The answer will still be no."

The man turns and looks back at Mr. Giambatta's car.

The car doors open. Two other big men get out. One holds the door open and an old man gets out. He nods to the man on our porch

The man with the broad brimmed hat turns back to us. He pulls a gun out of his jacket pocket. Buppa plays his game. Now the gun's in Buppa's hand. Buppa holds it up. The bullets fall out, bounce, and roll down the stairs.

Buppa holds the gun flat in his palm. He offers it to the man.

The man steps back, down the stairs, almost falling as bullets roll under his shoes.

The men at the car reach into their pockets.

Buppa shimmers. "*Nessuno è danneggiato qui.*" None are harmed here.

The men fall back against the car, huddle against each other, their hands cover their faces.

The old man and Buppa stare at each other. He looks at the men huddled around his car, at the man now hurrying back to our gate, then back at Buppa. He holds his hands up, moves like he's washing them, then shakes his head and holds his hands palm out towards Buppa.

Buppa nods. They drive off.

"Did you play the game with them, Buppa?"

Buppa walks down our steps, collects the bullets, puts them in his pocket. "Remember I said be careful, some people don't know how to fall? People who don't know how to fall hurt themselves. I helped them learn how to fall."

"But you didn't hurt them, did you, Buppa?"

Buppa picks me up, holds me close. His face is cool to touch. His clove aftershave surrounds me like a warm silk. "You don't have to touch people to hurt them, Gio. Mr. Giambatta and his friends, they learn differently than we do." He stares where Mr. Giambatta's car was. "So yes, I played the game, yes, but not to hurt them, only to help them learn."

I think about what Buppa, Chan, Yao, Matsuo, Uncle John, Brother Jonnie Rae, and the others tell me when we play. I stare where the car was. "Did they learn how to fall, Buppa?"

"Oh, you're such a smart boy. You know so much there's nothing left for me to teach you."

"Do we know how to fall, Buppa?"

"We're learning."

Chapter 27

Mr. Zelli's Ice Cream

Grandma, Buppa and I walk to Mr. Zelli's ice cream shop, up two streets on the corner. Buppa likes the ice cream there. It's special, called *gelato*. Mr. Zelli has ice cream for his *L'Inglese* and *gelato* for us. Buppa says it's the best.

Buppa makes it a game. "What flavor is it, Gio?"

I answer quickly. That's too easy.

"Which of Mr. Zelli's helpers made this? Was it Antonio? Maybe Francesca? Or Anne? Who was it?"

I have to travel back through the flavor to feel the hands on the machine then go up the arms to feel the face. "Anne made this one."

"Go ask Mr. Zelli. What does he say?"

Mr. Zelli watches Buppa and me play. I say "Anne?" and he looks at Buppa then back at me.

"You asking me or telling me, Gio?"

"Anne."

He laughs and nods.

He asks what's my favorite flavor and sometimes I say "Paolo" or "Cozmo" because I feel the maker in the flavor.

———

I am older. Grandpa can't walk as far and I'm too big to sit on his lap.

We sit in Mr. Zelli's and still play our game. Now I must say who made the *gelato* before Mr. Zelli serves it, before he scoops it.

"Paolo."

Mr. Zelli shakes his head, no.

I stare at him. I swarm around the *gelato* still in the freezer chest, before he raises the lid. My face shimmers.

Grandpa puts his hand on mine. "Gio."

Mr. Zelli scoops the *gelato*. "I'm sorry, Gio. I lied. You're right. I didn't mean to upset you."

Grandma takes my other hand in hers, stares into my palm. "Mr. Zelli is our friend, Gio. He makes a joke." She stares at Mr. Zelli. "Not a good joke to play on a little boy, but a joke."

"I'm sorry, Gio. Forgive me?"

"Yes."

Grandpa taps my hand.

"Yes, Mr. Zelli. I forgive you."

"Thank you, Gio."

Grandpa licks his *gelato*. "Forgiveness is a gift, Gio. Give it freely. Accept it humbly."

"Yes, Buppa."

I haven't called Grandpa "Buppa" in a long time. He looks at me, shakes his head. "It's okay, Gio. I'll be alright."

———

Mr. Zelli makes frappes for us. "You only get frappes in New England. You know that, Gio?"

"Yes, Sir."

"And you know where you get the best frappes?"

"From you, Mr. Zelli!"

He makes mine extra thick.

He lifts his scoop and looks at Grandpa. "Which *gelato* today?"

Grandpa looks into his palms. "A frappe for me today, Angelo."

Grandma reaches out to him. He smiles, nods, repeats. "Like the first time we came to this country, Sadie. You remember?"

Grandma nods.

"Pistachio for me. Chocolate for my lady."

Mr. Zelli brings our frappes, sets them down, wipes the moisture from his hands then cradles Grandpa's hands in his.

"Never to worry, you know that, right?"

Grandpa nods, smiles. "Thank you."

"Is everything okay, Buppa?"

He takes a big gulp and pulls the cup away slowly with a big "Oh-oh" look on his face.

Grandma laughs.

"Look at me, Gio. I have a pistachio mustachio."

Chapter 28

The Safe Place

Grandpa creaks my bedroom door open. His clove aftershave tickles my nose before his whiskers tickle my ear. "Today's a special day, Gio."

I roll over and smile.

He sits down beside me, smoothing my blanket. "Today we go to a safe place. A special one. Today we go to your safe place."

I've never been. I've never heard him say anything about a safe place.

"My safe place?"

"*Sì. Il tuo posto sicuro. Il posto sicuro.*" Yes. Your safe place. The Safe Place.

"How will we get there, Grandpa?"

"You remember piggyback?"

I love piggyback.

"Let's go!"

I climb on Grandpa and am lost in a swirling wind.

"Yay!"

Grandpa laughs. The sky clears. We're on the path walking uphill. An old woman sits on an apple cart. "Hello, Grandmother."

"*Ciao, Giovanni!*"

"This is my boy, Gio. He needs to know there's a safe place. For him."

She smiles at me. One eye is swollen closed, the other weeps a milky fluid. "*Ti piacciono i biscotti?*" You like cookies?

"Yes, Ma'am."

"Here. Eat." She hands me anise biscotti.

"Yumm!"

She nods at Grandpa. He nods back.

"Let's go, Gio."

We go uphill and enter a town. Old buildings on either side of a dirt road, like on TV, shows Grandpa likes, like *Have Gun, Will Travel* and *The Rifleman*."

Something rolls down the street towards us. Towards me. It stops and falls flat on the ground. A mouth opens and closes. A single eye gazes up at me. A body with legs all around, nothing else. "Hello, Gio."

"Hello!"

"You're not afraid?"

"No."

"Good. This is your safe place, Gio. Do you know what a safe place is?"

"Umm...a place that's safe?"

The eye winks and the mouth laughs. "Close enough."

The legs kick it up and it rolls away.

Music comes from one of the buildings. Grandpa points the way. "Come on, Gio. More people for you to meet today."

Inside are six tall, thin, men with one leg each. They have no head. Their face is at the top of their tube-like bodies. They sing and it reminds me of the organ at Grandma's church. They chorus "HELlo, GIo!" Then each individually sings "How are you?" "How are you?" "How are you?" "How are you?" "How are you?" "How are you?" and then back as a chorus "HOW are YOU, GIo?"

I sing back the best I can. "I am FI-ine. THANK you. HOW are YO-ou?"

They laugh and their voices feel like fingers tickling my sides.

A woman with skin darker than Uncle John's and Aunt Mary's drags herself across the floor. She has no legs and no mouth. She stops beside me and I hear her in my heart. "Hello, Gio!"

"Hello!"

"You don't find us horrible?"

"No, Ma'am."

"Good, good."

Grandpa sits on the floor beside the woman. "What do you feel, Gio, being here?"

I look at Grandpa. What a strange question but it has an obvious answer. I feel what I feel with Grandpa and Grandma surround me without touching me. "I am loved."

Grandpa hugs me. "That's right, Gio. Exactly so. Here, you are always loved. Always remember that. Here you are safe because you are always loved. No one will come here to hurt you. No one can get here who wants to hurt you. This is your Safe Place."

I push away. Grandpa's crying. "What's wrong, Buppa?"

I don't call him Buppa often anymore. Only when I think he needs to know I love him.

"Nothing, Gio. But you must remember this place. You are always safe here because -"

The men with voices like organ pipes chorus so loud the building shakes. "We will not allow any harm to enter here."

The black woman drags herself away. "We will not allow any harm to enter here."

The thing with a mouth and eye wheels down the dirt street. "We will not allow any harm to enter here."

The buildings grow mouths, heads without bodies float down the street, legs without feet tromp by, all create a sound like warm water washing me. "We will not allow any harm to enter here."

"Remember this place. Should you need it."

"Yes, Buppa."

And we're home. I'm in bed. Buppa shakes some dirt off his pants. He brushes a tear from his eye.

Chapter 29

Council of All Beings

Voices dance over me like ants making a nest. I shake with the deep bellow of Whale's song and Elephant's answering trumpet. I am tickled with the chirping of Cricket the size of a bus. A spider wraps me in her web, places me on her back. Her chelicerae grate "Ha-angg-on-n" and she balloons up into the sky.

"Where are we going, Grandmother?"

Her chelicerae grate again. "Coun-n-c-cil-l-o-of-f-A-a-ll-Be-ei-ingg-s-s. Yy-you-ur-r-Ggrannd-d-ffa-a-ath-ther-r-i-s-s-wai-ai-ait-t-inn-g-g."

We descend through clouds, through fog, through mist, through water, through waves, through oceans into the earth, through boiling rock and land on an island deep in the sky.

"Buppa!"

He lifts me in his arms. "Are you ready, Gio? Are you ready to meet your friends?"

The island grows and grows and more and more arrive. Uncle John and Running Water and Apara and Chan and Joe Swota and Erdös and Yao and Matsuo and Timbe and Rose and Bee and Spider and Moose and Hummingbird and Hawk and I recognize them even when they don't look like how I've seen them before.

"You're passing!"

"Do you see me who I am, Gio? Do you see me who I am?" It's a game to them, too!

My friends teach me to play their games and ask me to teach them mine.

Then a voice I've not heard before. A voice of fire, like a mountain. A throat clears and it sounds like trees falling in a forest. The Universe spins before me. "Hello, Gio."

"Hello."

A wall of sky offers me its hand. It's filled with stars and planets and galaxies. It breathes on them and they swirl in its voice.

"Who are you?"

"Your friend."

Whale offers me its fluke. "As am I."

Wolf offers me its paw. "As am I."

Moon pours itself down on me. "As am I."

A hand forms underneath me and Earth lifts me up. "As am I"

Each in turn, offering, asking, *balance*.

The fire mountain, the wall of sky, the spinning eternity, my friend who holds stars and planets and galaxies in its hand, clears its throat again. "We are honored to have you among us. Welcome."

Grandpa comes up behind me. He rests his hands on my shoulders. "This is my son. My grandson. Keep him in your care."

The wall of sky forms a face and looks at Grandpa. "Always, we will be with him. But as with you, so with he. He must choose which path to follow."

Grandpa nods. I feel his hands resting on me, holding me, hoping for me.

"Now, Giovanni, rest."

I hear Grandpa's heart. I feel his hands. They shake a little. "I have many more things to teach him. I have no time."

Apara places her hands on me. "I will teach him."

Uncle John comes forward. "I will teach him."

Running Water, Daskele, WildCat, Chan, all of Grandpa's friends, each in turn, come forward. "I will teach him."

Spider, Wolf, Moon, Orion, Dog, Moose, Nebula, Mountain Lion, Hummingbird, so many others, come forward. I am brushed by web, by paw, by light, by star fire. I feel the weight of antlers, the cold of space. I smell the breath of mountains and oceans and skies and earth.

Each in turn. "I will teach him."

Others come forward, others I don't know. Friends of future times. "I will teach him."

Grandpa turns me to face him. He's crying.

"What's wrong, Buppa?"

"Nothing, Gio. I know you'll be safe. You'll learn. I have one more thing to teach you, then I must go."

"Go where, Buppa?"

We are back home. He looks at his palms. He goes into the kitchen, to Grandma making coffee. He looks at his palms again, confirming. "About a week, Sadie. I have about a week."

He teaches me a song.

Chapter 30

DeathSong

"You promised."

"Gio."

"You said you'd never leave me."

"Gio."

"I won't do it."

"Gio."

I turn my back. I won't face him. I won't I won't I won't.

I feel his arms encircle me, hear his voice inside me. "Do you feel me, Gio?"

I don't answer.

"Gio."

"No, I don't feel you."

He withdraws. The energy that cradled me, rescued me, taught me, pulls back.

I spin, reach out, fall into his arms. "No, Buppa. No. Don't go, Buppa. Don't die. I need you. I don't want to go home."

He holds me against him. I feel his heart, not strong. His arms are weak. Still he holds me. I hear his breath, smell his clove aftershave. He rubs his beard stubble against my forehead, he sings an old song. I see that thing made of sound. It hovers, sees me watching, flutters in the light, fades away.

Inside I hear. "Am I with you now, Gio?"

"Yes, Buppa. Yes."

He taps my chest. "As long as you keep me here, I'll never leave you. Remember, this is what is real. Do you understand, Gio?"

I sob. "This instance..." Another sob. My stomach aches with my tears. "...of time."

"I've done all I can here, Gio. I've learned all I can learn. Is it right for me to stay?"

"Yes."

He chuckles. His chest rattles. "Gio."

"No."

〰

Grandpa's death shocks no one. Every morning he stares into his still calloused, once powerful hands. He holds Grandma and holds me. "Six more days." "Five more days." "Four more days."

Each day, quiet, patient. "Come sing with me. Start with your hands, here." He places my hands on his chest, over his heart. It misses a beat. Then strong. Then another. Then strong.

I learn his song, his rhythm, his path. To guide him. To help him. To find his last door. To shape the universe he travels to.

In seven days.

"Will I know everyone's DeathSong?"

"Yes."

"I don't want to know everyone's DeathSong."

"Remember, Gio, always look for the good."

I don't want to. "I will."

"Promise?"

"Yes."

⌣

Today he says nothing. Grandma lifts me in her arms and takes me to Mrs. Gianelli's.

Grandma holds me close. I feel her heart, hear her breaths. She kisses me. "Yes, Gio. Yes."

She whispers to Mrs. Gianelli who takes me from Grandma and cradles my head against her chest. Grandma rushes out. Mrs. Gianelli speaks Italian to Mr. Gianelli, but their dialect, not Sicilian. I know some words, not all.

Mr. Gianelli runs into their kitchen, picks up their phone, calls the police.

Mrs. Gianelli asks if I'd like some *latte e bustaciotti*, milk and cookies. Mr. Gianelli goes to our other neighbors. People gather. Some go in our house.

A siren.

An ambulance comes to our home. Mrs. Gianelli looks out the window. I slide off the kitchen chair and out the back, through Grandpa's garden. His roses, his morning glories, his lillies, all his flowers, his peppers, tomatoes, squash, none face the sun.

They look to our house.

The bees are gathered on the outside of their hives. They're not buzzing, their wings unmoving. The hives are silent.

I go inside. Men are rushing around Grandpa. They put him on a rolling bed.

He lifts his head, smiles, touches his palms to mine.

My hands burn. Itch.

A final gift, my legacy, the marks I bear.

He breathes and the house shakes. It's already mourning.

Inside me, Grandpa's voice. "Sing my song, Gio. Open the door for me."

I breathe with him, our breaths make a bridge for him to cross.

The ambulance people want to hurry. Grandpa makes them stop.

He takes my hands and places them on his chest, over his heart. My two small hands in his. I feel him there.

Inside, his voice. "Never raise your hands in anger, Gio. Never hurt or harm others with what you've learned."

"Yes, Buppa."

"Now, Gio. Sing for me now."

I sing his song. Doors open in the sky.

My spirit-body moves from me. His waits. Something sails above us, like waves on the ocean clothed in gray.

"Who is that, Buppa?"

"Another friend. Take me to it. It will help me the rest of the way."

"I want to go with you, Buppa."

"No, Gio. Not yet. Not for a long while. But I'll be waiting. Don't worry. And I'll have peaches for you when you get there."

I help him. Grandpa's friend spreads huge wings that shed gray waters, a weathered sail fluttering on the horizon.

Grandpa smiles. It takes Grandpa's hand from me.

The ocean's robes turn from gray to white at Grandpa's touch. They flow over him leaving the creature's wings free, catching the wind, lifting.

Grandpa is gone.

I wave goodbye.

Not all lessons are joyful.

Adolescence

Chapter 31

Alone

Mourners form a quiet line three city blocks long. Officers Morelli, Clarkson, and half a dozen others come and direct traffic. People bring food. Cheryl, Officer Clarkson's wife and heavy with their second, kisses my forehead and holds my hand.

Grandma and Grandpa pass within a week of each other.

I sit in the house alone. I go outside and tend the garden, talk with the bees. They are lonely, too. The garden knows. Our best friends are gone.

The grasses, the flowers, the trees, the birds, all comfort me. The tomatoes, the peppers, the squash, all tell me they will feed me.

Mrs. Gianelli calls my parents. They come and go through Grandma and Grandpa's things.

My father finds Grandpa's vendor's license. "Here." He holds it out to me. "You want this? You sold peaches with him, right?"

He pays some men I don't know to load Grandpa's truck with furniture while my mother and father drive off.

Mrs. Gianelli does the *malocchio*.

I tug on her sleeve. "No, Mrs. Gianelli. Grandpa said never use what he taught us to hurt people."

She stares down at me and her eyes water. "Oh, Gio. You've learned so much. But not to worry. I can't do the *malocchio*. Not like you." She leans over and kisses me. "And you're right. You do what your Grandpa said. What was it he said? Always look for the good? That's you, Gio. Always look for the good."

I sit out in the garden and talk to the bees.

My parents come back. I hear my father going through the house, down the hallway, past the rooms, through the kitchen, through the vestibule. The back door slams.

I feel his heat as he approaches. He grabs my arm, spins me around. "Are you too stupid to get in the car? We were halfway home before we realized you weren't in the backseat. Christ."

He sets fire to the hives. The bees flee. Alice, Mrs. Minerva's granddaughter and the new queen, screams as her wings burn away.

My mother pours bleach on the flowers and the garden.

My father stands in front of me, stares down at me. "Get in the car."

"No."

His hand slams across my face and my head snaps with the impact. "Don't ever talk back to me, Gio. Ever. I'm not your grandfather and I don't put up with his bullshit. Understand?"

The pearls from Grandma's jewelry box encircle my mother's neck. I reach up to feel the ocean in them, something Grandma let me do, and my mother slaps my hand away, her hand quickly returning to adjust them, fondle them.

"You'll start school this Fall. You'll be behind but you'll start anyway. Maybe you can learn to read and write."

"I can read and write. Grandpa and Grandma taught me."

"Oh, yeah?" My father takes a pencil and little notebook from his pocket, writes something. "Read this."

"I can't read handwriting, only words in books."

He laughs. The smell of his cheap tobacco and wine covers me like flies over the dead.

My mother shakes her head, pushes me towards the door. "I told you he was stupid."

Chapter 32

Talking with Thunder

Mrs. Woodbury turns the classroom lights on. The afternoon is dark and heavy with black clouds swarming as far as we can see. A crack of thunder rocks the school. Some students laugh, others cluster against the far wall's blackboard. The recess bell rings. I stand by the door.

"Where are you going, Gio?"

"It's recess time."

"We're not going outside today."

"I want to go see my friend."

"No one's going outside for recess today. Can't you hear the thunder?"

"My Grandpa told me Thunder is my friend. That's who I want to go see."

"Yes, Gio, we all know the wonderful stories your grandfather told you."

I walk into the school's hallway.

Mrs. Woodbury hurries after me. "Gio, we're not going outside."

Lightning opens the sky, the flash so bright it leaves shadows on the ground, in our classroom. I remember Grandpa telling me about Shadows and watch these fade.

Thunder rolls across the sky like a bulldozer, flattening trees and street signs, pushing them down, leaving them little strength to stand again, but they do.

I remember Grandpa's teaching: All things return.

"Yes. They don't understand."

Thunder rumbles an answer. I nod.

Hank comes up behind me, pushes me. "Don't be stupid. You can't talk to thunder."

Mrs. Woodbury says nothing.

"I can teach you to talk to Thunder, Hank."

He pushes me again. Other kids join in.

Mrs. Woodbury says nothing.

Thunder bangs against the window beside where Hank stands, shakes it, just the one window, trying to get in. Wind races up the street, lashing trees, snapping leaves from limbs as if cracking a whip.

Everybody jumps back.

I gaze into the clouds. "You frighten them, Brother, Sister."

Thunder rolls away.

Jimmy watches the storm, his eyes wide. He nudges me. "Can you do that again? Make the storm come close and go away?"

I Lower-Center-Relax-Breathe.

Fierce lightning rips the sky. A huge bolt halfway to the ground. It splits in two, legs reach to the earth. Above, arms lash out, gathering clouds. A head, a mouth, flashing eyes.

Lights go out in the school, on the playground, in the houses, on the street.

A hand reaches down from the sky and slaps the top of the school. It shakes. Pictures fall. Children scream. Teachers scream. Mr. Samuelson, the principal, stands in the doorway. "Everybody okay here?"

Children hide under their desks.

Thunder pounds the windows.

"Get everybody into the basement. Who has a radio? Did somebody drop a bomb? I've never seen weather like this."

Children run into the hallway, follow Mr. Samuelson to the next classroom, Mrs. Woodbury is a hen gathering chicks.

"You mean like that, Jimmy?"

Mrs. Woodbury spins me away from the windows, pushes me after the rushing children. Her lipstick and makeup show like a clown's mask against her white face.

"Shut up, Gio!"

Chapter 33

The Bird

I watch it fall from its nest from my bedroom window. Each day for a week I stand guard as its mother flies off in search of food. It keeps its head down each day, I think resting, waiting, until she returns and then it raises its head, chirps, squeaks, bobs, demanding attention, seeking her gullet, her open beak, the nourishment she provides.

Today it wobbles in the nest, hops to the edge, its flight feathers not formed, and plummets over the side.

I rush outside. I don't dare touch it, spread my scent on it, its mother would not like that.

I take a sheet of paper with me, slide it gently under its squawking little body, blowing on it to move it onto the paper, towards its center, to cradle it in my palm, get it back up into its nest.

But there are no low limbs for me to climb. Its mother chose this tree well. I wrap the white ball of fluff in my pocket, go back into the garage. Father keeps ladders on the wall, too high for me to reach, too heavy for me to hold.

I go to the shed. Locked.

Back into the house. Mother keeps a folding step ladder beside the refrigerator. Sometimes she needs something from a top cupboard or cabinet shelf.

I pull it out, drag it. It is bigger than I am.

Outside, up against the tree, not high enough, even if I leap.

A knock on a window. I hear it slide up. "What do you think you're doing?"

"This bird fell from its nest, Dad. Help me put it back."

"Get back in this house, now."

"It's just a little bird, Dad. Help me get it back into its nest. Please."

I hear its mother twitching twigs in her nest, seeking her chick.

"I said get back in this house, now."

"Please, Dad. Just this once. I won't bother you ever again. Just help me just this once. Please."

But I go too far. I realize too late.

The front door opens. His workshirt and chinos crisply crackling as he strides up to me, his hand out. "Give me the bird."

"No."

He backhands my face. My head spins. The world darkens. I stumble.

"Give me the bird."

I bring my face forward, blink, clear my eyes. "You'll hurt it. I know you will. You won't help it. You don't care."

His hand comes back, spins me in the other direction. My head aches. My ears ring. I taste blood on my lips. A trickle leaves my nose and stains my shirt.

His eyes go to the lump in my shirt pocket before I can move.

He lifts the chick out, places it on the ground, brings his full weight down on its tender neck, fluffy body, as it chirps, asking food from a giant who offers only pain. His hand grabs the back of my neck, lifts me, throws me forward. "Get in the house, I said."

The bird chirps from her nest, flies down, pecks through the crushed chick's remains. I glance back. "I'm sorry. I'm sorry."

"Shut up. Get in the house. Now."

Chapter 34

Money

My father's fists come down to emphasize specific words. "ARE. YOU. THAT. GOD. DAMN. STU. PID?"

I can't feel my face anymore. My arms hang limp by my sides. "Do you THINK ANY of that GOD DAMN STUFF is REAL?"

I have been in my parents' house two years. Every day Grandpa's teachings are beaten out of me.

"He MADE it ALL UP!"

One of my teeth hangs loose from my jaw.

"You GOD damn STUpid LITtle SON of a BITCH!"

He backs away, dancing around me, backing me until I feel our living room walls surround me, a boxer driving his opponent into a corner of the ring, choosing his targets because he knows his opponent is going down, he knows he can end the fight but taking his time, savoring the destruction of his foe. "You think what he did was real?"

I slump against the wall. He uppercuts my belly, my chest, my face. The force of his blows keeps me standing. "Then GET ME some

MONey. He never taught you how to do that, did he? GOD. DAMN. MON. EY."

His hands go down. He rubs them, one in the palm of the other, deciding. I slump to the floor. His kicks take over where his fists have stopped. "MONey. WOO WOO me some MONey."

My mother stands behind him, hands across her chest, and shakes her head. "I told you he was stupid."

One final kick and the living room goes away. "Stupid little shit."

I am in the dark. I smell clove aftershave. I remember his lessons. "Everything that happens happens because it must, Gio. Learn from this."

Buppa never lied.

What am I to learn from this?

I hear Buppa's voice in the dark. "To heal."

Chapter 35

Saucy

Wayne stands on his porch, arms crossed over his tiny chest, feet spread apart, looking tough. "My mother says you can't play with us anymore."

"How come?"

"You cheat. She saw you."

I look up to a second story window in Wayne's house. His mother stares back down. I stroke the back of his dog, Saucy. "What did I do?"

"She doesn't want you to play with us anymore."

Saucy licks my hand.

"Then I'll play with Saucy."

Wayne big brother, Kurt, comes out of the house. "Go home, Gio. We don't want you here."

Kurt hits people smaller than him. Saucy hears his voice and hides behind me.

"What did I do?"

"You cheat at Hide-and-Seek. My mom saw you."

"What did I do?"

Mrs. Morley bangs on the window. I look up. She points at me and snaps her hand away.

Kurt laughs. "Go away."

"How did I cheat?"

Kurt runs at me.

Saucy comes around me, snarls, sinks her teeth into his leg. He screams.

Wayne screams at Saucy.

Mrs. Morley comes out of her house carrying a frying pan. She hits Saucy on the head. Saucy yelps but doesn't let go, sinks her teeth in deeper.

Mrs. Morley hits Saucy again. I hear Saucy's skull crack. She falls over, her tongue, the tongue that licked my face, hangs out. I watch Saucy rise up and go into a field of flowers. I follow her, make sure she's safe, well, until I hear Mrs. Morley yelling towards the open door of their house.

"John! We have to take Kurt to the hospital."

Kurt cries. "No, momma, no."

She looks at me, quickly raises the frying pan and lowers it slowly.

"You did this, Gio. You turned our dog on Kurt. Get away from here, from my house. Never come back. I don't want you near Wayne or Johnny or any of us ever again. Do you hear?"

I sit on the ground, stroking Saucy's fur, feeling the life flow away, the body grow cold. "What did I do?"

She raises the frying pan again.

I remember Grandma. The *malocchio*. The way she did it, the words she said, the song she sang. She told me not to do it, ever, it was a bad thing.

I asked Grandpa and he shook his head. "We can not know the good unless we know the bad. Promise me you'll always work to let the good win."

"How will I know when I'm doing bad?"

"You will know."

I make the sign Grandma made. I make the sounds. Mrs. Morley steps back, drops the pan on the ground, clutches her head, clutches her chest, gasps for breath, falls to the ground, twitches.

Mr. Morley comes out of their house, sees Mrs. Morley twitching on the grass. "Gretchen? Gretchen?"

Grandma said not to do it. Grandpa said let the good win.

I don't care.

I watch the last of Saucy pass over, her peace more important than anything else in the world to me.

I cry, another friend lost.

I leave.

Chapter 36

25¢

I stand in front of the bookrack at Rexall's Drug Store in the Champagne Plaza. My hand is in my pocket and clutches a quarter I stole from the change my father keeps on his bureau.

My mother brings me here every week. We come on Fridays, the day her medicine runs out. She makes me sit on a chair by the door. Today I follow her and see her in the backroom with the druggist. They smoke funny cigarettes that don't smell like Grandpa's cigarettes.

"You shouldn't smoke cigarettes, Mom. They'll make you sick, like Grandpa."

The druggist laughs.

My mother slaps my face and shoves me back out into the store.

I hold my cheek and feel tears run down my hand as I walk away. The druggist and my mother talk as I walk away. "Hey, Rose. He's just a kid." "Shut up and mind your own business."

I stop at the bookrack on my way to the chair at the front of the store. One book catches my eye; Zenna Henderson's *The People: No Different Flesh*.

The People? No Different Flesh? That sounds like something my Grandpa would say.

I take it off the rack, open it, read some pages here and there. My chest tightens. I want to cry.

The people in this book do some of the things Buppa and his friends do.

Some of the things Buppa taught me to do.

Some of the things I do.

I Lower-Center-Relax-Breathe

These people. They hide. So no one will know. I remember one of Buppa's lessons, "If they learn what you can do they will hunt you down, and if they find you, they will kill you." A memory of old, old days.

Lower-Center-Relax-Breathe.

It was not a lie. There are others. Hiding.

I promise myself. I will find them.

I take the book and hurry to the checkout.

The woman there smiles at me. Her eyes twinkle. Her face changes to a fox's. The fox-woman winks, takes my money, hands me the book, and has a woman's face again.

My mother comes up behind me. "What are you doing, Gio? Where did you get that?" She takes my arm and shakes me until I can't think, can't Lower-Center-Relax-Breathe.

I scream at her. "I bought it."

My mother slaps my face. "Where did you get money to buy a book? You stole it, didn't you. And this woman caught you. You're a thief, an evil, evil thief."

The woman's face shimmers. Can my mother see it? She grabs my mother's hand and lifts it from me. My mother stops moving.

The woman turns my mother's hand palm up. Her eyes open wide and she shakes without moving. Her palm opens.

The woman drops the quarter in it.

"No, ma'am. Gio -" The woman smiles at me. "That's your name? Gio?"

I nod.

"Gio didn't steal this book. It's a gift." She drops the quarter - my quarter. My stolen quarter - into my mother's palm. "And here's a quarter, the price of the book. If you're concerned, give me the quarter." Her eyes become fox eyes and her nose a fox nose. Her fox-eyes close slightly and her fox-nostrils flare. "But Gio keeps the book."

My mother doesn't move. She doesn't breathe.

The woman lets go of her hand. My mother shakes her head, stares at the woman, closes her hand around the quarter, hustles me out and into our car.

"Doesn't matter. You don't know how to read, anyway."

Chapter 37

The Gunshot

I hear my name screeched across the wind. I can't breathe. Fluid fills my lungs. My neck wobbles. My head falls to the downy feathers on my breast. My eyes close. My mother flaps her great wings, her eyes scanning scanning scanning and unable to see where the bite that kills comes from. She takes to the air, calls to her kind.

There, far away, a human raises a rifle and takes a sister's life. We are gathered together by an Old One and go on to the Place of No Shadows, the only comfort our mother has at her loss.

I lay in bed shivering, rise up, hurry on clothes, fumble putting on sneakers, silently close our back door before my parents wake, the sun just cresting the horizon, its arms pulling it into a blue sky.

My name comes from the west. Stars still show on that horizon, twinkling sugar descending on southern New Hampshire mountaintops.

I run through fields, through trees, through woods, along a path worn low to the ground but shielded with vines from knee high up.

Whatever travels here is small, travels nightly to the river, to food, to feed, to teach its young, the great circle of life, Grandpa taught me, the Earth called me. G, I remember her words to me.

My name is screeched again, something bites my chest, my head sags to another feathered breast.

A honk, a goose, a mother, her children in danger, wounded, hurt, dying, by a man's hand.

I borrow, I see through her eyes. Not a man, a boy. I know him. David Savin, he has a gun, a rifle, an airgun, a BB gun.

She watches him from across a small glade, her wings full of sunlight.

He takes aim. I hear the *pthew* of the rifle, a moment later I feel another gosling's breast shatter.

She tucks, dives. He raises his rifle towards her.

I scream, place myself over the remaining goslings. "Don't shoot. You're killing them."

She veers, not knowing if I'm a new threat to her remaining chicks, her attention diverted.

David laughs. "I know. That's why I'm shooting them."

"Stop it. How would you like it if someone came by and shot you? While your mother and sister watched? How would you like it?"

He hesitates, turns, slings the rifle over his shoulder, great white hunter, he, walks away.

The goose returns to her nest, her wings wide, honks, threatens.

"It's okay, mother. I won't harm your chicks." I slide away, my jeans and shirt wet from morning dew, my sneakers squeaking water as if water is breath.

She gathers her remaining children, hurries them into the water, swims up, away, deeper into the straights, to the middle, to where her children might be safe.

I watch them go then stare at her nest. The chicks she left are bloody, feathery balls, their eyes dull, their beaks open, their feet cold, their gooseness gathered to a safer place.

The sun is higher in the sky. I wept and slept. I stand.

A chuckle. A *pthew*. A sting. A small hole in the thigh of my jeans. My blood trickles, makes a small ring.

David Savin laughs.

Chapter 38

Martin Can't Play Bach

Seventh Grade Music Appreciation Class. We meet every other week. Mr. Schroeder helps us understand what music gives us culturally, historically, psychologically, ...

Students talk through class. This week's *Laugh-In* routines become litanies. "Heah cum de Judge, Heah cum de Judge"

Mr. Schroeder has patience. He comes up with entertaining, educational ways to help us appreciate music.

Nobody listens.

Martin practices piano daily. The piano in his house is next to the family's dinner table, where the dining room flows into the living room. Go from one to the other and the piano is there, waiting. Everything stops in Martin's house when he practices piano.

He reminds me every day that his family and my family are different. He emphasizes that we are less. He doesn't say we are less, he says we're Catholic and he's not, we're Italian and he's not, his dad owns his business and my dad doesn't.

I borrow, realize he's not even sure how we are less, it's what he's heard, what others said, been told his people are different from mine and that is enough.

He shows me a violin his parents bought him. "It's over two-hundred years old."

"Gee. It's too bad they couldn't afford to buy you a new one."

His mother comes out of their kitchen, stares at me, shakes her head, snaps a dishtowel over her shoulder, goes back into their kitchen, Martin shakes his head the same way his mother does. "You're so stupid. I pity you."

I look.

"Pity doesn't walk with you, Martin. Hate does. And Fear. They're right there, behind you. They look like this." I borrow from Hate. My face shimmers. Martin screams.

His mother comes out of the kitchen. "You'll have to go home now, Gio. Andrew has to practice."

Practice? "My Grandpa taught me how to practice! Can we practice together?"

She shakes her head, her hand on my back, guiding me towards the door. "No, Gio. It's time for you to go home." She pushes me outside. The door closes.

I look through the door window and borrow from Hate and Fear. My face shimmers. I see their reflection. A ghoulish thing, fearful, boastful, shameful. I smile at Martin. He screams again. His mother pulls a curtain across the window in the door. I hear her hurry him away.

～

Martin is Mr. Schroeder's favorite. He sits at the piano as class begins. Mr. Schroeder steps back, lets him play.

The students gather. They quiet.

Martin plays for most of the class. He plays Beethoven, Haydn, Mozart, everything a good piano student learns to play.

I look around the classroom. The little figure, the one who dances, isn't there.

I play piano. We have one in our basement. I play when no one's around, when no one is listening. I play Bach because of the precision, the clarity, the elegance of it. The little dancer and I become friends. It wheels and spins and flies to my rhythms. Even my mistakes cause it joy.

Bach reminds me of Grandpa, his teachings. I bathe myself in sound when playing Bach. It is, to me, rapturous. I play Bach and I can do things Grandpa taught me.

"What is your name, Little One?"

It puts a finger to its lips. It's not time for me to know.

I and the others listen to Martin play. He plays as written. No interpretation. No "Martin" in his playing, only the notes on the page, none out of place, not a skipped beat.

I feel a feather on my shoulder, hear the little dancer jingle bells, sound its flute, crash its waves. "What is missing?"

I listen. "There's no music. It's only sounds."

The Little Dancer spins. I hear Simon&Garfunkel's *My Little Town*

...and then there's a rainbow

but all of the colors are black.

It's not that the colors aren't there,

it's just imagination they lack...

"Good, Gio. Good. Hear the whole orchestra, not just the piano, not just the flute, clarinet, or guitar. Hear everything."

"But who are you?"

Its finger goes to its lips. The bell rings. It's gone. Students gather their things, move on to the next class.

Martin gets up from the piano.

"Geez, Martin, all those lessons and no Bach?"

Martin looks at me, shakes his head, snorts. "Nobody plays Bach."

I stand at the keyboard, play Bach's Two-Part Invention #8, an easy piece. "I do."

Martin slows and stops, not looking at me, looking straight ahead.

"You study with Mr. Belisle, right? How come he doesn't teach you Bach?"

Martin's face crimsons.

I remember Grandpa's lessons, listen.

"Oh, you've never learned any Bach."

Martin faces flushes from crimson to white. His hands shake, his shoulders sag. His books slip from his hands, fall back to his desk.

I watch Hate and Fear come and rest beside him.

SpiritTalk. Something Grandpa taught me. "How come Martin doesn't play Bach?"

They show me, they share. They reveal. I understand. "Oh, okay. Mr. Belisle doesn't think you can play Bach. He hasn't taught you any Bach because he doesn't think you're ready for it."

Hate and Fear merge. Martin shakes, his eyes redden. Hate and Fear birth a new energy, Shame. Martin's face changes, almost shimmers. "Shut up! Shut up! Shut up!"

I remember one of Grandpa's rules; do not go where you're not invited.

Uninvited, I understand. Sharing what I understand, I cause pain.

Do not go where you're not invited.

The look on Martin's face, Hate and Fear becoming Shame, the pain in his voice, the pain I put there.

Our mistakes are our greatest teachers.

Chapter 39

Cory

I feel other people's pain. I don't know why.

I forget things Grandpa taught me or remember them when I shouldn't.

Cory always knocks my books out of my hand when we're walking between classes or takes pencils out of my pocket or trips me going up the stairs.

He reaches for my pencils but this time I catch his hand. I *Go Wide*. I don't mean to. I don't remember how to.

I don't remember how to stop.

I go into him, share his memories, feel him, his life.

He stops being someone who steals my pencils and knocks over my books and becomes a boy. Human. Me.

"Your mother doesn't like you. She tells you you're the reason your father left. She doesn't say that to your brother, just you. Every day."

His face reddens. Mucous trickles from his left nostril. He licks his lips.

"That's why you never bring a lunch. That's why you always come with a quarter. To buy a coke and a Twinkie. That's not a lunch."

Water fills his eyes. "Let go of me."

"Don't hate yourself because others hate you, Cory. That's not right."

"Let go of me."

Galaxies swirl around him. My heart merges with his and follows it down, down, down through the air under the soil into rock, under mountains, tasting minerals, coursing through lava until we stop at the center of his earth. I see the fires there, the twisted, broken creatures stoking the flames with his family, his mother, his absent father, feel the heat of his rage at not being loved.

"It's not you you hate, it's what's happening to you."

We are between classes. The tardy bell rings.

He jerks his arm back but my grip is strong.

"Let go of me."

I drop his hand.

He hurries off.

He hated his life and directed his hatred at me, somehow sensing I cared and understood.

Not all teachers are obvious.

Chapter 40

Tommy

"Stupido bastardo, vattene."

My father only speaks Italian when he doesn't want people to know what he's saying. When he's around mother and me he speaks in English. When he speaks Italian he whispers loud enough for people to know he said something, not what he said.

Tommy stands at the foot of our driveway flexing his biceps. "I'm strong enough."

I help my father fix our cars. Change the oil, tune-ups, new shocks. I wipe sweat from the mid-August sun. I switch a 9/16" socket wrench from right to left hand and extend my right. Tommy likes to shake hands. "Hi, Tommy."

"Hello, Gio. You're Gio, I'm Tommy."

I look around, don't see his mother or father. "Do your folks know where you are, Tommy?"

"My mother said I could come and see my friend Gio if I don't get in the way. I have to look both ways when I cross the street. I'm strong enough." He flexes his biceps again then holds his hand out to my father whose head is under the hood, his hands stained by the engine. "Hello, Mr. Giangregorio. I'm Tommy."

My father switches to English. "Time to go home, Tommy."

"I'm strong enough. I can help you fix your car."

I look for Tommy's parents, don't find them. "Tommy, let's get you home. I'll be back in a minute, dad."

"We have to look both ways before crossing the street, Gio."

My father never looks up from under the hood. *"Stupido bastardo, vattene."*

One block down, two houses over, I knock on Tommy's door. His mother opens it, her brows knit, her face tight. "You alright, Gio? Is everything okay? Tommy wasn't bothering you, was he?"

Tommy shakes my hand. "You have a very nice father, Gio."

"Thanks, Tommy. Everything's fine, ma'am. Just wanted to make sure Tommy got home okay."

She looks at me, into my eyes, and nods. "Thank you, Gio. I understand."

Tommy goes inside. She closes the door. I hear Tommy singing. His mother joins in. A little figure dances, puts a finger to its lips when I'm about to ask its name. A moment later I'm back holding an oil filter wrench while my father jacks up the car.

"Stupido bastardo."

You wouldn't call him a stupid little bastard to his face, would you. You wouldn't say that around his parents, would you.

You think speaking Italian makes you smarter than them, better than them. But you only speak Italian when you don't want people to understand.

Because you won't say things to their face that you'd say behind their back.

Because you're a coward. A stupid, ignorant coward.

My father rolls his creeper further under the car. "Hand me the wrench then get the oil filter ready."

I don't practice any more. I am beaten if I practice. My father shouts as he strikes me with his belt. "You'reInGodDamnAmericaNow." I am beaten if they even think I practice.

I hand my father the wrench and dab my finger in the bucket of used motor oil, spread the drop at the end of my finger around the gasket of the oil filter to form a better seal, hand it to him, listen to Tommy and his mother sing. His father's voice joins in.

They laugh as they sing. The little figure dances over them. I want to ask its name but the pain of being caught, being seen, being discovered.

Grandpa's "If they learn what you can do they will hunt you down, and if they find you, they'll kill you," a memory of old, old days.

I listen to Tommy's family singing and my father cursing underneath our car.

You don't understand why his parents don't put him away. You wanted to put me away.

His parents don't put him away because he's loved.

I hate Tommy.

I hate the fact that his parents love him.

And then I remember Cory.

No.

There are some fires that should not burn.

Chapter 41

Unexpected Journey

The old woman with one eye swollen shut and the other weeping milky fluid offers me a biscotti. "How did I get here?"

She holds the biscotti out to me. I take it. "Thank you." Almond-pistachio. "This is delicious. I haven't had one of these since -"

She nods, says nothing, points up the hill.

I look downhill. There's a town in the distance, not mine. "How did I get here?"

A man with four legs, no arms, just two legs where his legs should be and two more where his arms should be, crab walks up the hill, stops before he passes me. "You got here without meaning to, Gio. But that's okay. Part of you remembered."

I feel my face. The swelling isn't there. The swelling from Father hitting me. Punching me. Because I backed his pickup out of the garage to get the mower to do the lawn.

"Did I give you permission to drive my truck?"

"I had to get the lawnmower out of the garage."

"Did I give you permission to drive my truck?"

"Didn't you tell me to do the lawn?" I turn to wave at the lawn. When I turn back his fists come at me, one, two, three, four times.

"Where's my father?"

"Not here."

"Can he get here?"

I hear the organ voiced men in chorus up the hill. "NOT here, NO-o, GI-o."

The old cookie woman offers me another biscotti. "*Qui sei al sicuro, sempre.*"

I remember. "Yes. I'm safe here. Always."

The man with no arms wraps two legs around my shoulders, hugs me.

I hug him back. He lets go. "Come on, Gio. Everybody's waiting. Wants to say hi. It's been a while since they've seen you."

"How...how come..."

"Because real monsters are only hideous on the inside."

Chapter 42

Spider's Eyes

I take Mr. Fliescher's psychology class because the exercises intrigue me. One of us looks into a classroom strewn with obstacles once then closes our eyes. A blindfold is administered. Mr. Fliescher and the other students stay back against one of the walls and only intervene if the participant is about to trip over a chair or bump into something.

They blindfold me.

I remember John N'bm'we's teaching.

I navigate the room effortlessly. I say hello to specific students as I near them.

Mr. Fliescher pulls off my blindfold when the exercise is over. He puts the blindfold over his own eyes, takes it off, turns it around, put it back on, takes it off.

"How did you do that?"

I point to a corner of the ceiling. "See the spider up there? I asked if I could borrow her eyes and she agreed. I used her eyes to find my way around."

"No, seriously. How did you do that?"

I remember Grandpa's teaching; Tell them the truth, they'll never believe you. "How do you explain how I did it?"

He unfolds and refolds the blindfold, puts it on, takes it off, shakes his head. "That's the best case of spatial memory I've ever seen. You could make money with that."

"No." I laugh. "I can't."

Chapter 43

Mrs. Johnson's Dress

Mrs. Johnson teaches Film Studies. She wears long sleeve blouses, shirts, even on the hottest days. Sometimes when she writes on the board her sleeve slips down a bit.

There are bruises, yellow, blue, black, brown, there.

Today the entire class goes to The State Theater on Elm Street for a special matinee showing of *The Heart is a Lonely Hunter* starring Alan Arkin and introducing Sandra Locke. A similar class from West Side High attends the showing. They are loud, raucous. They laugh and make jokes about what happens on the screen.

I am Mrs. Johnson's favorite. I don't know why. Perhaps because I can thread the class's projector. We watched *An Occurrence at Owl Creek Bridge* because it fit into the class time slots. Everything else is scenes from different movies and Mrs. Johnson explains the emotions we should be feeling when people touch or smile or eye each other on the screen.

Point-of-View is everything. She reminds us of the Burt Lancaster-Deborah Kerr romance in *From Here to Eternity*. "You have to get into the character's head. See how the director reveals their lives through small, intimate moments only the camera can see?"

I watch Mrs. Johnson's small, intimate moments watching *The Heart is a Lonely Hunter*. I sit with her in the back of the theater, hear her sighs, feel her throat tighten at scenes in the movie, at Mr. Singer's loss, at Mick losing her virginity, at realizing she'll never realize her dreams because her father can no longer work.

My arm is on the armrest between us. Her hand comes over and gently like a butterfly tasting a flower rests on mine.

It is hotter than the sun in the theater.

I hold up my drink in my other hand and turn to face her. "Would you like some of my Coke, Mrs. Johnson?"

She takes her eyes off Arkin and Locke and Keach and Rodriguez and Tyson and returns my stare. Her eyes flash down to her hand covering mine.

She pulls it away. Her face radiates heat in the darkened theater, only reflections from the screen showing her thoughts.

She feigns a smile and her eyes return to the screen. "No, thank you, Gio. Thank you, no."

The movie ends. It is an hour to the close of school and we're given the rest of the day off. The West Side High teacher walks up to Mrs. Johnson, apologizes for his class, for having brought them, they were his responsibility, and he failed because of them, thirty-five times, once for each student.

Mrs. Johnson smiles, nods, says not to worry, it's not his fault. He stumbles, almost kneeling in front of her in the emptying theater's dim lighting, a knight falling before his Queen.

I catch him by the arm, lift him up. He stares at me. "Thank you." He hurries away.

"Would you help me bring these things back to the school, Gio? I know it's late. You're not working anywhere after school, are you?"

"I have time, Mrs. Johnson."

We walk back, a notebook in each hand. "Did you like the movie, Gio?"

"Yes, very much. I didn't know other people could feel such pain."

"Pain, Gio?"

"Yes. When Mr. Singer's conducting the music after it's stopped because he can't hear it's stopped, the look on Mick's face. She knows something he doesn't, something he'll never know, never experience or share, never understand. Or when Mr. Singer learns his friend Spiros died, realizing he's lost the only thing that had meaning in his entire world, that made life worth living."

We pass Grace Church. A circular sprinkler waters the lawn in sweeping arcs that spill onto the sidewalk. Mrs. Johnson bumps into me avoiding it. My arm goes around her waist to steady her.

"You okay, Mrs. Johnson?"

She takes a deep breath, pulls away. "Yes, Gio. Thank you." She watches the ground, where she steps, then quietly, "Do you feel other people's pain, Gio?" It is not her teacher's voice. It is a question among confidants, friends.

"All the time. It's how I am."

"What's it like, Gio?"

I laugh. I have not shared such things since Grandpa died. "Like a beautiful song played too loud."

I feel liberated, free. I test her willingness to listen and nod towards the church. "Father Werner says I'd make a great martyr but my glasses are too thick."

She shifts books so they're all in one arm. Her free hand reaches for my shoulder, rests there. "That's not true, Gio."

I laugh. "What, that I'd make a great martyr or that my glasses are too thick?"

The halls are deserted by the time we get back to the high school. Mr. Brown, the principal, is playing Elton John over the school's PA system. He announces each tune like a DJ on an all night clear channel radio station, something he does to mark the end of the day. We enter Mrs. Johnsons' classroom. The late afternoon sun is casting long shadows and the classroom is painted in shades of dusk.

I hold the books, the notebooks, the cards. She takes them, one by one as I stand behind her and hand them to her, over her shoulder, and puts them snugly in the cabinet in the back of the room. I stand close. I've run out of things to hand her. She looks over her shoulder up at me, sees me gazing down the front of her dress, my eyes filled with the curve of her breasts.

We hear Mr. Brown over the PA system. "And now, Elton John singing 'Teacher, I need you'." A moment later

Oh teacher I need you

like a little child...

She takes one of my hands and guides it to her. Over the PA

You got something in you

to drive a schoolboy wild...

She guides my other hand around her hips, helps me lift her dress, rests my hand on the dampness there, leads me to the table we put the projector on.

You give me ed...u...cation...

She holds me close, helps me find my way, whispers, "Go slow, Gio. Go slow."

in the lovesick blues...

Her arms circle me, she clutches me and arches her back, groans.

Mrs. Johnson's small, intimate moments.

～

A week later Mrs. Johnson is gone. Mr. Henry is teaching Film Studies and we watch war movies and westerns. John Wayne and Randolph Scott, great American heroes.

I ask what happened to Mrs. Johnson. Guidance counselors and administration look at me but don't answer.

I miss being held close, knowing someone cares. I remember Grandpa holding, loving. Not the same, but show an animal a little kindness and it's your friend for life.

Chapter 44

Bill Lutter's Cats

Bill Lutter kills cats. Any he can find. He catches them and breaks their legs so they can't get away then puts firecrackers on their bellies and watches them explode.

He terrifies me.

More than any bully, more than any angry teacher, more than my parents in their rages, he terrifies me.

Grandpa said, "Everything, everything, everything is your teacher, Gio. You decide what the lesson is."

What is Bill Lutter's lesson to me? You could be me, Gio. Why aren't you? It's vengeance, Gio. Vengeance for being helpless, for being smaller and weaker than everyone else.

I know. I understand. Bill Lutter feels my rage but lets it out differently.

In the quiet of my bedroom, my parents out, I take out my vengeance on my pillows, mimicking wrestling moves I see on TV: Chief Jay Strongbow, Argentina Apollo, and Ivan Putski warring weekly with The Iron Sheik, Ivan Koloff, and Superstar Billy Graham, always the clear line between black and white, good and evil, the simple definitions Grandpa gave me long ago.

Like discovering something's truth, go far enough and you get to the one yes/no question that must be answered for all the other questions to be asked. Answer that one and all the confusions go away.

"One step at a time, Gio. One step at a time."

Grandpa never saw shades of gray, his world was black or white and always full of color.

My parents see only shades of gray and insist I do, too.

Bill Lutter watches me as I watch him catch a cat. I feel the bruises on his back, his sides, where his father beats him. He gets between his father and his little brother until he can't stand any more, standing as his older brother did before him. I hear his mother scream, "Not the face, George. People will ask questions if you hit the face."

She sacrifices her sons for a big house and a nice paycheck, her comfort a greater need than her children's safety.

This is not the way of The Wild. Animals will sacrifice themselves to protect their young, keep their bloodlines active. Grandpa and I walk in the forest. He stops me, pulls me back, points. Turkeys rise from the ground, puff themselves up, spread their wings, form a feathered wall, challenge a black bear getting too close to their nests.

"Would you do that for me, Buppa?"

A tear slides down his cheek. "Yes, Gio. Yes."

I grab Bill Lutter's shoulder, spin him around so he's facing me. Too thin, too lean, flaxen hair, aquiline nose and a smooth, hairless face. His green eyes flash at me. I grab his wrist, his arm holding the cat.

"Let me go."

"Put the cat down, Bill."

"No, it's not your cat."

"Put the cat down, Bill."

I work on farms in the summer, mills during the school year. Grandpa is correct, I'm tall and strong.

Bill punches me with his free hand.

"Put the cat down, Bill. Do you think killing cats is going to stop your dad's beating you?"

He punches me again.

I catch his fist, spread his arms. The cat drops and runs away.

A short man, thick black hair and eyes, oriental features and wearing green overalls, a janitor's uniform, his name stenciled in red on a white patch above the chest pocket and too far away for me to read, stops and watches us.

Bill yells at him. "What you looking at, Gook? My brother's in 'Nam fucking your mother."

The man continues to observe, makes no motions.

"Please stop hurting cats, Bill."

"What are you going to do about it?"

What am I going to do about it. I remember Mrs. Gianelli's cat run over by the car, still hear its screams, still feel its life gathered by Cat and carried away.

I share this with Bill.

He screams.

He wrenches his arms, struggles, can't break free, kicks my legs, knees my groin.

I let him feel it all but won't let him get lost, won't let Cat take him away. I could do nothing, then.

I let go of Bill's arms. He falls, convulsing, feeling his bones breaking, his insides twisting, and no way to escape.

The janitor man is gone. How long did this take?

But Bill will not bother cats again.

I hear Grandpa. "Everything, everything, everything is your teacher. You decide what the lesson is."

We learn from everything or we learn nothing.

Bill Lutter teaches to protect the weak.

Like Bill himself.

Chapter 45

The Liberation of Lady

Samantha pulls me into an empty classroom. She looks around, not moving until the sounds of people coming and going to class quiets. She hands me a note written on folded notebook paper. There's some stains on the paper when I unfold it. I'm not sure what they are. I read "Show us your tits or we'll tell Mom and Dad."

I stare at the note. The smell of the stains becomes obvious to me. I want to wash my hands.

"Did you?"

She crosses her arms over her chest. "No."

"What do you want me to do?"

"Tell my brothers to stop it."

"I can tell them. But it won't matter. If they're going to tell, they're going to tell."

Samantha collapses into a chair behind the door. She kicks it closed. Her face reddens, her eyes water.

"Maybe they won't say anything."

She snorts, shakes her head, looks out the windows. She rubs a bump on her nose. She calls it her ski jump and hates her nose. "I'm going to get it fixed, you know. Someday I'll have enough money and get it fixed."

"You really think people care about a little bump on your nose?"

"It makes me ugly. I'm tired of being ugly."

"I don't think you're ugly."

"You don't think anybody's ugly."

Samantha and I do not have a good relationship. She seeks me out when she needs comfort, arms around her, a warm body beside her.

But I am not kind to her, either. Grandpa would not be happy, but much of Grandpa is forgotten.

Or misused.

I use Samantha as much as I am used by her.

———

Samantha invites me to meet her parents. I stand in the kitchen doorway. Their dog, Lady, a loving mutt six years old, wags its tail as it leans into my legs, waiting to be scratched.

Samantha walks over to her mother washing dishes, a tall woman, thin, her shoulders slumped, her body hanging over the dirty water as if an albatross pulls her down. She sees Samantha, not me, and half smiles. "Never marry a man who's stupider than you are. You'll live to regret it."

"Gio's here, mother."

Her mother turns to face me. She pulls a towel from her shoulder, wipes her hands and hides her face as it reddens. She breathes, slow and deep, keeping her face hidden too long, before wiping her forehead and opening a bobby pin with her teeth to fix a stray lock of hair to her head. Her nostrils flare and her eyes fix on me.

"You want to date my daughter?"

A huge green serpent, its scales glistening, its tongue flicking out, sensing me, wraps itself around her. Like her, it keeps its eyes on me.

"Yes, ma'am. Unless you'd rather I not."

It is Fall and I still carry my summer tan from working fields on a distant farm. My arms show a sinewy strength from long days of such work. Her eyes and the snake's flow up me, floor to head, stopping indiscriminately. When she does, her mouth opens for a moment and she pants, one, two, three quick breaths, then her eyes continue their inspection. The snake's eyes stop when she does, its eyes fixed where hers are, its tongue snaps out, samples me, its mouth opens, it shows me its fangs. Poison drips in small, lethal drops falling to the floor and smoking like acid.

"What do you want of me, Snake?"

"To wrap myself around you, to exhaust you, to drain you and leave you spent, to show my daughter what to do with the likes of you."

"What have I done to you, Snake, that you want to do such to me?"

"So my daughter will not make the same mistakes I have."

"But they would be her mistakes to make."

"Crippling, killing, destroying of the soul and dreams. I will end you before I allow it."

"Tell me not to date your daughter, Snake, and we'll have done with it."

Samantha's mother shakes her head, pulls back a bit. "I'm sorry. Did you say something?"

"Yes, I'd like to date your daughter unless you'd rather I not."

She shakes her head again. The stray lock of hair comes undone and sweeps across her forehead. She turns back to her dishes. "You'll have to ask her father. He's in the barn with the boys."

Samantha takes a clean towel and dries dishes. Lady follows me, nipping my hand, wanting attention.

The barn is dark, needs work. It is not a working barn, not anymore. A rough voice comes from the stalls. Lady falls back, stays outside. Young male voices chuckle. Hay flies over the wall into the next stall. I step closer.

"It doesn't matter what your mother puts on when she goes to bed. Whatever she puts on always ends up around her armpits." The rough voice laughs. The young voices chuckle.

There's a heavy iron ring latching a storm door in the center of the barn's floor. Across from the stalls are two bales. "This used to be a milking barn. Or they had two milkers here."

A broad shouldered man's head comes up over the side of the stall. "Who're you? What are you doing here?"

"Gio. I'd like to date your daughter."

"She's only fifteen."

I nod towards the bales. "Was this a working barn once?"

The man comes out from the stall, pitchfork held in both hands, in front of him, its tines towards me. He's followed by his twin, younger, thick muscled but thinner, standing shoulder height to their father, the rough man. Next comes another, chest height to him, then another, coming to his belly, and a last, standing pocket height to the rough man.

He walks towards me. "You know farm work?" A howling dog circles him, snarling and nipping at anything it nears, running in circles, biting its flanks, flea ridden and peeing on anything it can.

His sons put distance between themselves and him as he nears me. "Some."

He hands the pitchfork to shoulder height boy and grabs my hands. "Show me your hands."

Days of baling hay, milking, tending animals, shucking corn, picking beans, harvesting tomato and squash leave my hands calloused and thick.

Shoulder height boy, the muscular one, snickers. "She's got a funny nose, doesn't she?"

The man doesn't let go of my hands. He holds them, squeezes. I look at his son. "Haven't noticed."

I reverse the man's grip, something Chan taught me. He lets go, pulls his hands back, rubs them together.

The circling dog pulls back, hides behind him. Lady walks up behind me, small steps, unsure. She taps my leg with her nose. I reach down and scratch between her ears. "So is it okay if I take Samantha out?"

The rough man runs his hands up his forearms, the tendons not used to the motion Chan taught me.

"Yeah, sure. Go ahead."

The oldest boy snickers. "She's got a funny nose."

~

I read the note she handed me again before gingerly folding it and putting it in my pocket.

"I'll come over tonight, talk with them. But it won't do any good."

I enter their house and stop. There's no scent of Lady. "Where's Lady?"

The muscular one points over his shoulder. "Dad chained her in the barn. She kept barking during a football game he was watching and wouldn't shut up. Then she peed on the floor and that was it. He put her out there to punish her. His team was losing, anyway."

"It's Thursday. The last game was Monday night. How long she been out there?"

"Since Monday night. We can only go to her once a day to bring her food and water."

I run to the barn. A heavy chain goes from Lady's collar to the iron ring in the center of the floor. She whimpers when she sees me. Her tail gives a tentative wag.

I sit down next to her. She lays beside me, puts her head in my lap. Her eyes are rheumy. Her waterbowl is empty. There's mold on her food.

I hear the man with the circling dog come to the barn door. He stands silhouetted in the doors, staring into the dark, seeking. "Get out of here."

"Why are you doing this to Lady?"

He comes towards me, fists clenched.

I stand up. Smile.

He stops, looks around. The pitchfork rests against the wall with rakes, shovels, axes.

"Not used to someone actually standing up to you, are you. Don't know what to do when it's not a dumb animal or your kids or your wife, do you."

He backs out, shouts towards the house. "Call the police. Someone broke into our barn." The muscular son and chest-height come out, stand behind their father.

I sit back down, pet Lady. "And not a mark on anyone? Not on me, not on you? Just a sick, starving dog chained in a barn? Your barn? That'll go over big, don't you think?"

He moves quickly, picks up a sledgehammer. "I said get out."

"Did your boys tell you about the note they gave Samantha? 'Show us your tits or we'll tell Mom and Dad.'?"

"That's disgusting."

I reach in my pocket, pull out the note, folded to fit in with my pictures. "I have it here, if you want to see."

The two boys recede into the darkness.

"Who taught them to do something like that? Any family where the brothers blackmail their sister with statements like that, to do those kinds of things. There's got to be a problem there, don't you think? They didn't learn that in books or at the movies. Maybe on the streets?"

He clenches his fists. The whimpering dog circling him, stops, rears. The man sneers, the dog snarls.

I stare past the man, look at the dog.

I am tired of cowards in men's clothing.

But I've learned that cowards are easy to deal with. Feed them their fear. They'll grow fat and fall to the ground, unable to move, their bellicosity turned inward at their own failings.

"Tell me, dog, what do you fear?"

The dog vomits up a long ago meal, wallows in it, laps up what doesn't stick to its fur.

I show the dog what it doesn't want to see, the Snake wrapping itself around me, licking me, writhing under me. The Snake becomes the rough man's wife, held in equally rough hands that move tenderly, lovingly.

The Snake-wife circles the dog, hisses, shows its fangs. "In less than a year's time. Before he graduates high school. Cuckold and giving me something you never could."

The man's hands clench, open like talons, but there's nothing for him to grab.

I smile at him.

The snake-wife constricts around the dog. It screams with the rough man's voice. The dog becomes the man, his wife becomes fully the snake and she crushes the life out of it. "And safe. He'll never brag or boast about my conquest."

I laugh, remove Lady's collar. The chain clatters to the floor. She runs past the man into the night.

My ears follow Lady, running through the woods, free. I know a family not far away. I've never met the father, a Harvard professor of some kind. It's a place I go when I need to be safe. I show Lady the way.

Chapter 46

Dating

Rox's fork pushes the chicken lo mein across her plate. "Samantha said you told her a year ago we'd be dating now." The China Dragon is not good Chinese food. I remember Chan, Yao, and others cooking for Grandpa and me after we practiced, the scent of garlic, fennel, anise cleansing me as much as Grandpa's washing me before we ate.

"Yes. I remember."

"Did we even know each other then?"

"It was the end of the day. Your locker was across the hall from Samantha's. She knew you from homeroom. She introduced us."

"Did we talk?"

"I said hello, you said hi."

"And from that you knew we'd be dating in a year?"

From the energies you carried. From the spirits around you. From your smell. Your fear of home. Of wishing the bus would go slower or pass by your stop, not let you know, of walking slower and slower as you neared your door, of the heaviness of your books as you walked up your steps, of not wanting people to find out about your mother and father.

The drinking until they pass out on the couch. Your mother flirting to enrage your father. Your father's raging because he believes he's failed. And you not knowing what else to do. Wanting safety, wanting escape. Wanting comfort. "Yes."

"But how? How could you know?"

I shrug. "Likes attract?"

Chapter 47

A Silly Game of Cards

Mrs. Langlois' journalism class. She sits on the edge of her desk, fans herself with pages of homework. All the high school's windows are open. No papers ruffle on desks, no flags wave hanging from their wall mounts. Soft green painted walls sweat on this hot Spring day. Clothes stick. Female teachers blot off makeup before it runs. Sweat gathers in bras like runners finishing a marathon. Male teachers roll up their sleeves, some revealing WWII, Korean, and Viet Nam War tattoos, all loosen their ties, discard their sportscoats. Deodorants fail.

Students slump in their chairs. Mrs. Langlois looks around the classroom at half-lidded eyes. "Let's play a game."

A few students shuffle. One or two perk up for a moment.

She pulls a pack of Zener cards - wavy lines, circles, squares, stars, and crosses. Cards used in ESP tests - from her desk, stands in front of us, holds one up so only she can see it, and asks us to tell her what it is.

"I don't want to play."

"That's fine, Gio. Do your homework, read a book, just keep yourself occupied."

Everyone else plays and laughs. Dennis Beauchamp does well, better than chance. Mrs. Langlois congratulates him.

I start calling out cards as she holds them up. Some cards before she sees them. One or two before she holds them up.

I forget Grandpa's warnings.

But this is no game. Not like Grandpa's games. Her mind is so open. Sometimes I ask the cards what they are simply to alleviate my boredom. I forget Grandpa's other rules: Don't go where you're not invited. Do not do what you're not asked to do.

Mrs. Langlois holds up a card.

I call it.

"No, Gio. That's not what it is."

I come out of my seat, point my finger at her. "You're lying."

The only reason people lie to me is to hurt me, make fun of me, make a fool of me.

Not Mrs. Langlois.

She is testing me.

Mrs. Langlois quickly turned the card, showed everyone in the class.

"He got it right," she exclaimed, keeping her eyes on me, moving behind her desk for protection.

The class remained silent. No rustling of papers. No fluttering of flags.

"He got it right."

Chapter 48

Saturday Night Sex

Samantha puts an ice cube in her mouth and moves it to her cheek with her tongue. The ice cube melts so she drools a little. "Let me know how this feels."

She goes down on me, hands and mouth working in unison, prolonging me until I'm involuntarily thrusting into her mouth.

She feels me climaxing and brings the ice cube forward, touching it to the tip of my penis as I ejaculate.

"Arrgh."

"Good, huh?"

We no longer date. In school, Samantha doesn't acknowledge me, ignores me, makes fun of me. But every Friday, before the final bell, she hands me a note telling me where she'll be babysitting and what time to come by.

I calm my breathing. "Where did you learn that?"

"Tina told me about it."

"Don't tell me you've slept with Tina."

"Tina's been sleeping around since seventh grade."

"That I know and it's not what I asked."

"What do you care who I sleep with?"

I squirm back into my pants. They've been down by my knees the entire time I've been on the floor.

Samantha still has a ski jump nose but it doesn't matter. Boys don't care about it. Scott tells me the guys line up outside her house the nights her parents go away. "She's a good time girl, Gio. If somebody has a problem, she puts a paper bag over her head. The eyes and mouth are cut out. She calls herself The Unknown Hooker. She fucks, Gio. You think anybody cares what she looks like?"

She fucks. So do I. Her mother and half a dozen other of my friends' mothers. Martin's, Gary's, Michael's. Some teachers. Some of the women in the mill where I work after school. Cashiers where my mother shops. Sometimes a few women in the church basement between services. I take clingwrap from the church kitchen, wrap it around myself so they'll feel safe. I teach Ms. Warburton one of the things Samantha taught me.

"Do you think my glasses are too thick?"

She shakes her head, her mouth too busy to answer.

They all give me gifts when we're done.

Mrs. Koloutis is the first. She offers me a twenty dollar bill.

I remember a *Dobie Gillis* episode: Mrs. Osborne holds a coin in her palm and offers it as a bribe to Maynard G. Krebs. "How about a shiny new dime?"

Maynard looks at the dime in her palm then back at her. "I'd rather have a dirty old quarter."

The price of indiscretion is high.

Their pocketbooks open.

I can make more money in a single night than I can in a year on the farm, at the mill, in the warehouses where I work because I, more than their husbands, more than anyone else they ever knew, can "Go slow, Gio. Go slow."

Finally some things Grandpa taught me have a purpose beyond getting hit at home or laughed at in school.

Samantha practices on me.

I practice on Samantha. I shift my motions to draw out her sighs, her screams, the digging of her nails into my back, across my chest.

It's a fair-exchange.

Chapter 49

Hooksett Sand&Gravel Company

"You knew they were coming." Gary stares at me under the quarter moon, his size bulked by his father's hunting jacket and wool-lined jeans.

~

I stopped, cocked an ear to sounds no one else could hear, *listened*, Grandpa's *Ascolta*.

"Get everybody together, Gary. We have to leave. Now."

"Why?"

I shrug. "Never mind."

Blue lights bounce off the far side of a sand mound, rhythmic detonations of unseen, quiet cannon. A man's voice amplified through a bullhorn rolls through the mountains and valleys of crushed stone, dives into quarries and echoes back ten-fold, causes ripples in mounds of sand.

I don't know why I'm here.

People know I knew all Mrs. Langlois' cards. "What else can you do, Gio?"

"Nothing."

"No, come on. What else can you do?"

I look down, hide the fact that I'm looking at their girlfriends' bellies. "Nothing."

Except I start their cars when they can't. "You flooded the engine. Give me a minute." I raise the hood, ask Car if it's okay, tell them when something needs looking at. "Your carburetor's gummed up. Have it cleaned." "Your head gasket's weak and going to blow. Get it into the shop before you go anywhere." "Your master cylinder's leaking. Get a new one before your brakes give out." "Your number three cylinder is fouled. A can of engine cleaner will fix it."

"You can tell that just by looking at it?"

"I help my dad fix our cars."

And I know when gangs from rival schools are waiting outside arenas, between the school and Holman Stadium.

And what they've brought with them.

"You saved our asses, Gio. But how did you know?"

The Wind tells me. Or I see through Old Ones' eyes. Or The Moon looks down and tells me what she sees. Or I feel their energy, their malevolence, on the street. They walked this way and left their residue like a trail for a good hunter to follow.

Instead I shrug, look away, want to ask, How come you did not? How come nobody else can do these things?

~

There are close to a hundred of us scattered in the valleys between the sand and gravel mountains. Blankets are spread on several mounds. People hurry back into their clothes.

Several police cars wind through the valleys, stay on solid ground, don't run their tires in cloying sand.

Gary buries a sixpack in the sand as footsteps approach. "How did you know?"

Chapter 50

The Protest

Veterans Memorial Park on a wet September night. Different people take the stage and tell us what's happening in Viet Nam. None of them are soldiers. Busses line Elm Street two city blocks in either direction. People have come far and wide to learn about the atrocities. None of them are soldiers, either.

I learn today that at 18, I am 21. A friend in Montreal tells me to come north for five years and when I return, I'll be ten years younger.

Debbie Drake and Joan Noosum wear flag bandannas and green on white peace signs painted on their cheeks. They walk through the crowd shouting "Yeah, Yeah," and punching the air with their right fists. Sometimes a black man takes the stage and tells us how his people won't hurt their people until his people are free enough to make up their own minds who to hurt.

Debbie and Joan punch the air. "Right On, Brother! Right On!"

At the back of the tents, where the park's grass meets the sidewalk, between the protesters and the food vendors and hawkers and peddlers selling out of the back of their station wagons, men with crutches stand on one leg. Some are in wheelchairs. I talk with them. I offer my hand. One reluctantly offers me a prosthetic claw, watches me as I take it and shake it, returning only as much energy as he delivers to me.

One man, still whole, watches me. I feel him move around me, run his tongue over me, smell me.

In the middle of talking with one armed and no legged men, he walks up to me. "You don't want to go over there."

"Excuse me?"

"They won't know how you can do it but they'll figure out what you can do."

"What are you talking about?"

"Someone will catch on. They'll make you a Hunter-Seeker. You'll go in front, to warn the others, to protect them."

"What the fuck are you talking about?"

"Or they'll make you a Down. You won't see combat. Not up close. But they'll make you use your Voodoo-Eye to tell them what you see."

"What the fuck are you talking about? What Voodoo eye?"

He pulls me out from the others, into the rain, now heavy, the rat-a-tat-a-tatting on car and bus roofs and spray from passing cars and splashing in gutter puddles raising a mist in the last of the summer's heat. "Listen. The least you'll get off with is becoming a Sympathizer."

"Sympathizer?"

"They'll make you listen in on people's thoughts the way a radio operator listens in on radio transmissions. They'll make you do that until you wake up one day and realize you've been raping people, mentally raping them."

Somebody yells from back under the tents. "Anybody seen Bruce? Bruce Rudd? Ruddy? Where are you, Ruddy?"

"You'll wake up and realize you've violated the most private part of them, and they never even knew. Then there are two options. You either become a Down -"

The voice is louder. "Ruddy?"

Another voice joins in "Colonel Rudd? Bruce? Time to come home, Bruce."

" - a sociopath, essentially -- or a Mystic. Downs are controllable due to their own depravity. Mystics aren't controllable, but if you go Mystic, they won't let you leave."

The voices are close, demanding. "Anybody seen this man? Colonel Rudd?"

"They won't let you leave." He pushes me away from him, turns to a peddler selling red, white, and blue Peace flags, all sizes. He picks up the largest he can find, wraps it around himself. "Ooh, ain't I pretty! Ooh, ain't I pretty!" He dances a coochy-coo using the flag as a stripper uses her fans.

Two men come up in military uniforms, the first I've seen here. One lifts a walkie-talkie from his belt. "Found him. On Elm, in front. We'll get him across the street. Yeah."

An ambulance travels south, pulls a U-ey, parks on the far side of the park, across from us. Two men emerge. The four gather him. "Come on, Ruddy. Let's go home."

One reaches into a pocket and pulls out a syringe. "I'm gonna Lormey him."

"Do it."

"Ooh, I'm so pretty. I'm so pretty. Ooh..."

I feel the man pull away from me, the sense of him lost like tears in the rain.

"Hey, you owe me twenty bucks for the flag."

One of the men runs across the street to the peddlar, hands him a bill, whispers something. The peddlar nods, looks at the bill.

Across the street one of the men closes the ambulance doors. "Anybody know how he got out?"

The side of the ambulance reads "Manchester Veteran's Affairs Medical Center Hospital."

The peddlar holds the bill under his wagon's dome light. "A fuckin' Benjamin. Can you believe it? A fuckin' Benjamin for a flag I paid two-twenty for by the case. Oh, man, this is my day."

Back under the tent, Debbie and Joan punch their fists in the air.

Chapter 51

Father Werner

"You want to become a priest?"

Samantha's accused me of attacking her, grabbing her breasts. She tells Father Huntress, people at church, word spreads. I arrive early to put on my cassock, prepare to sing in the choir.

"It's what I'm thinking now."

It's true, I did, but only because we got rough and I didn't remember the signal, the safe word.

~

She meets me at the door and wears only a cat mask. "Let's do some bondage."

"Okay."

"I brought these straps." She shows me black leather belts. Lets me hold them.

"Where'd you get these?"

"Tina."

"Tina's teaching you a lot of stuff?"

"Tina says the way to man's heart is through your mouth."

"My mouth?"

"Doubt it."

She calls stop and I don't. "Like giving it away? I'm only for practice until you get it right?"

"Stop."

"Let's see what happens when I pull this strap up here."

"You're hurting me."

"That's the idea, isn't it?"

Wrists to ankles, ass in the air, breasts flattened on the hardwood floor. I penetrate too hard, too fast, not caring. She screams. I ball up her bra and stuff it in her mouth, go back to more work from behind, a breast in each hand so I can steer her while I ride.

I never looked at Samantha before. Now I do without knowing why.

A mule, beaten, whipped, wanting to suffer because that's all it knows, finding comfort in the lash.

My bodies center. I'd forgotten how to do this. Inside a whisper. "This is not right."

I pull out mid-stroke, dress, unbind her, drive away.

〜

John, a choir tenor, pulls me aside, tells me what's going on.

"You're kidding."

"Is it true?"

"After everything we did, her complaint is that I grabbed her breasts?"

"She says she has bruises to prove it."

"Have you seen them?"

He blushes.

I laugh.

Father Werner finds me in the kitchen between services. "Is the priesthood really what you want?"

How come he doesn't ask? Or accuse? Or stare? Or whisper to others? "Because I'll write you a recommendation, if that's really what you want."

I nod. "Seems like the safest bet for me right now, don't you think?"

His eyes flutter for a moment, resting on my face. He nods back. "Yeah, I think so."

"Pity my glasses are too thick, huh?"

Chapter 52

Cramps

Denise wrings her hands. She sits across the aisle from me in the back of study hall and whispers out the side of her mouth. "Can you tell?"

I gaze down her thin, just starting to ripen teenage body, through her clothes, through her skin, into her abdomen, into her womb. "You're not."

"You're sure?"

I sigh, frustrated with the role I've been given. Because I can "read minds" I must be able to do anything. Girls follow me seeking absolution from the Pope. Girls from other schools are introduced to me. In *Caesar's Pizza* on Elm. In *Sabo's Subs* at the corner of Bridge and Union. On the bus. They call me at all hours.

My mother wants to know what's going on.

"Did you get somebody in trouble?"

I laugh. She slaps my face. "I asked you a question."

I laugh again. "I got them all in trouble, Ma. And I stole Dad's Excalibers to do it. What do you think of that?"

Her hand goes to her chest. She backs away, turns and hurries off.

Diane flattens her blouse. "Maybe you didn't get a good look. Can you look again? Is that how you do it?"

———

An ache in my testicles, penis, and low in my gut, below and behind my navel. Not continuously. One or two days out of every week. Sometimes a dull ache, sometimes I can't get out of bed.

I masturbate. Everything's working perfectly. No blood in urine, stool, semen.

Grandpa's lessons; keep questioning everything. The obvious answer is obvious because that's what you know how to answer. Know more and other answers are obvious. Know enough and the questions are more important than the answers.

I observe myself, a *Level of Awareness* exercise. "Use one of your bodies to observe the others at work, Gio. Then let the other bodies follow the first. You'll be over there watching yourself over here."

Lower-Center-Relax-Breathe.

The pain depends where I am, who I'm near.

Places where women gather, where most men don't go or aren't welcome - convents, nunneries, women-run diet clinics - the pains come regularly, monthly. Places where women are with men - offices, grocery stores, drygoods shops, school - the pains come and go depending who I'm near.

Madeline, thick bodied and round breasted since junior high, sits across from me and winces.

I match heartbeats, body rhythms against my will

The pain is intense. My abdomen contracts for her, with her.

A beautiful melody played too loud.

I stop her pain so I can breathe.

I reach out to her, touch her cheek. She slaps my hand away and shrieks, "Don't touch me, Freak."

Mr. McGarry pulls me from my desk, not looking at me, looking at Madeline's chest. "You okay, Ms. Tehopolis?"

She nods blankly, not aware of him or his question. Her hands fall into her lap. She looks down, then up. "Yes. I'm okay, Mr. McGarry."

He pushes me ahead of him. "Wait for me in the Principal's office, Gio."

I look back at Madeline. "Pain's gone?"

She stares as Mr. McGarry hustles me out of the room.

It takes a while. I either avoid girls in the most pain or touch them "by accident." I knock a book to the floor and touch their hand handing it back.

Word does get around, though. A student teacher sees me absently staring at her stomach. I'm not paying attention where my gaze falls. She turns and runs down the hall, hiding in the teachers' lounge until Mr. Dean escorts her from the building.

I do it for myself, not them.

My body isn't designed for the problems they experience. The pain wanders around inside me until it finds something similar enough to land in.

I stop their pain to get rid of my cramps.

It is the first hint of what is to come.

———

Michael bumps into me as often as possible. I did something to Denise, he doesn't know what, but her friends know she's late, I touch her, and she runs to the girls' room purse in hand.

I relax her, take away her anxiety, help her body do what it wanted to do for days, nothing more.

Michael doesn't know this. All he knows is I touched his girl, whom he thought pregnant, and she's thankful.

What he knows is I did something for his girl he couldn't. I made her smile and asked nothing in return.

Michael is known for his violence. Lauren gets word to me through Vicky through Rox through Diane through Denise to Debbie to me. I've touched each, eased their pain, their anxiety.

The boys have plans for Gio. Tell him to stay home tonight. This weekend. Forever.

The boys and I gather at Gary's house to drink beers. His parents are out 'till late. Everybody comes over.

I bring a *Lowenbrau* six pack. I share freely.

Michael arrives and Gary guides him to a chair across the room from me.

I don't know all of what I can do. I do know I can't always control what I can do.

And I know the creature inside me is tired of people's stupidity, people's games.

But people never learned how to listen. They can't hear "Leave me alone."

Gary invites everybody except Michael and me to watch a movie on his parents' new color TV in the living room.

I sip my beer, lift it in salute as he closes the door when they leave.

Michael sits in his chair, breathing. He cracks his knuckles. Shifts forward to get up.

I turn my head slowly, like a gun turret, focus on him.

Didn't my Grandpa say he always had more to learn?

Maybe I do, too.

"Sit down, Michael."

He falls back into the chair.

"Don't move. Don't speak. Don't open your mouth to cry for help." I separate my rage and place it by the closed door, a gatekeeper, a threshold guardian.

"You and I are going to have a talk."

He struggles inside his own skin. His muscles tense, twitch, flick but his body doesn't obey.

"I don't give a fuck about Denise. But that shouldn't concern you. What should concern you is that I don't give a fuck about you."

I sip my beer.

"You planned to hurt me? To bloody me? To leave me in an alley somewhere for the police to find?"

I sip my beer, hold the bottle up to the light. There's not much left. Another mouthful.

"You don't know what hurt is, Michael."

Sip. Hold up the bottle. Still some left.

"But you're about to find out."

I finish my beer. I walk over to him. He's weeping, fighting to shake his head, no, no, no.

I touch him.

All the pain gathered for the past few years of high school, all the anxiety, all the fear, all the prayers, all the long rides to NYC abortion clinics, all the weeping, all the beatings from parents from all the girls from all the boyfriends waiting behind the door passes from me into him, into his head, his heart, his lungs, his gut, seeking seeking seeking as it did with me for months until it found a home.

I blink and give it all to him.

I step back. He vomits, soils himself, puddles himself into the chair, convulses to the floor, unable to escape, unable to hide, his intestines roiling, fighting to change from male to female so the pain can find a home, rest. He cries. A dry, hollow sound because breathing isn't easy. The pain crushes his lungs, cracks his joints like a deepsea diver's getting the bends.

Gary pounds on the door. "Mike? Mike? Don't kill him, for Christ's sake, Mike. We said we wouldn't kill him."

They said they wouldn't kill me.

I chuckle.

I laugh.

I double over, my laughter like spit drools down my chin, wets my shirt, forms a tiny mucoidal puddle on the floor, mixes with tears because I can't catch my breath because I laugh so hard.

I stand, wipe my eyes, shake myself, dry my chin on a sleeve, and look at Michael make puddles of his own on the floor.

I shake myself once more. My breathing slows. This isn't right.

I pull my anger back. The door bursts open. Gary and the others fill the room. They see me, standing, empty bottle in my hand, Michael on the floor, his mouth bleeding where he bites his lips and tongue, his body in a broth of his own wastes, curled into a ball they can't pull apart.

I hand Gary the bottle. "Nice party. Thanks for inviting me. See you around."

Driving home I hear Grandpa, inside, his voice. "Never raise your hands in anger, Gio. Never hurt or harm others with what I teach you."

"They aren't worth my time, Grandpa. Fuck 'em."

It is six months to graduation. I score 1550 on my SATs. I quit school. I leave town.

Chapter 53

Orientation

I feel a vibration during freshman orientation. I scan the students, the dorm parents, the advisors, finally drawn to the stage, to a girl, Helga, talking. She's on the orientation committee. The vibration is from her.

It frightens me. It is like the cramps but worse, much worse, and is localized: my hands, my right arm, my left leg.

She mesmerizes me.

The pain shifts. I hear her. She'll never have children. She won't even try.

Lower-Center-Relax-Breathe.

There are close to a thousand new students in my class not counting transfers.

Lower-Center-Relax-Breathe.

The main orientation is over. We mingle. I move to the side of the auditorium, away from the crowd, away from the groups. Helga's pain continues in me.

Guardali prima che ti guardino, Gio. Look at them before they look at you, Gio.

I feel her vibration, where she is in the crowd, mingling.

Guardali prima che ti guardino, Gio.

Someone offers me a plastic cup of fruit punch. "Yeah, sure. Thanks."

"There's some cookies and cake over there. Help yourself."

"Thanks."

Helga walks with a limp. The pain in my left leg.

Someone taps my arm. "Come on, Gio. Gio, right? Let's meet some people."

My right hand's fingers go numb. I can't hold the cup.

Someone hands me a cookie. I fumble it with my left hand, can't get my fingers around it. I stare at my hands, now strangely feminine and deformed. Short thumbs, two broad fingers each, palms too narrow to place things in.

Helga stands in front of me. A thalidomide child.

She is beautiful.

She reaches for a cookie. Her body rocks as she moves. I am too close, too mesmerized to back away. She brushes my arm. Her eyes brighten, her pain goes away.

She stares up at me. Her brow knits. She looks into my eyes. I wince as her pain finds a new home.

She shakes her head, pulls back, we no longer touch, her eyes fall back into shadow, her pain returns. "Excuse me."

I turn and walk away.

Chapter 54

The Ellewomen

There's a note in my mailbox. Come to the billing office. Settle your account.

An old scent, a taste, a feel, warns me away.

My bowels churn approaching the billing office, a low, gray, squat building, it reminds me of a crab scurrying on the shore of a grass lined sea, its claws snipping here, snipping there, doing enough damage to wound but never enough to incapacitate, always following, preferring the taste of living flesh over the taste of decay.

Lower-Center-Relax-Breathe.

I felt this before, but when?

The nausea stays. My spiritual body is drawn within, through the gray walls. I sit on a bench, close my eyes, center to keep it with me.

A classmate stops in the middle of doing an errand. "Everything okay, Gio?"

"Just need a moment."

My classmate looks from me to the billing office. "Yeah, these people suck you dry."

Yes. Suck you dry. Leave you empty.

I enter the office, walk up to the window, show my ID to the tall woman on the other side of the glass.

She smiles, her eyes not focusing on me or my ID. I'm not sure she's heard my words.

She says nothing, walks to a filing cabinet, walks as if her feet don't touch the floor, smooth, practiced. Her back is to me as she shuffles through folders seeking my name.

I hear Grandpa. Go Wide.

The woman has no back. She is hollow like a porcelain doll.

An Ellewoman.

The scent overwhelms me. The taste gags me. I want to run away, hide. There are only women here, on the other side of the counter, the delineation of payer and payee. Some have their backs to me.

All are Ellewomen.

What a perfect place to hide, beings who take and never give back.

All the women facing me focus their eyes on me. Those with their backs to me turn and join, a group of gargoyles staring down, watching the crowds.

None speak, all have cold, pleasant smiles, now turned to me.

"Leave us, One Who Sees."

I lift the note received in my student mailbox.

"Be free of us, One Who Sees."

The note smokes in my hand, catches fire, but the fire is cold and drawing, not hot, not warm, not soothing.

"Go from us, One Who Sees."

I nod, back out of the office, out of the building, trip backing down some stairs.

Smoke rises over the low, squat, gray building, but no fire alarm sounds. The crab waves its claws, caught in a hot broth, unable to escape. I hear its screams as cold, boiling water stills its heart.

My classmate is on his way back from his errand. "How'd it go in there?"

Chapter 55

Talking to God

"You talk to God." A dorm mate stands in my doorway. "When we're in prayer groups and everybody's praying, I watch you."

"So not everybody's praying."

He hears an accusation, not an observation.

I laugh, turn back to my studies. "Not everybody prays when they're supposed to."

"Except you. You become quiet. It's like you're gone, you're not in the room with us anymore. We expect you to disappear, grow wings or something."

"We?"

"And in the cafeteria, when we say grace..."

I shrug, my back to him.

"What's it like? To talk to God?"

He asks about Lower-Center-Relax-Breathe without knowing its name.

No one asked me this before. They ask winning horses at the track, winning lottery numbers, can you make someone love me, am I pregnant?

I hear Grandpa. "What do you do?"

"Let me show you." I Lower-Center-Relax-Breathe. I never paid attention to myself doing it, only experienced it.

I cast off a Level of Awareness and pay attention, *Ascolta!*, listen as if I am my Grandfather doing something someone needs done.

My voice changes, lowers, resonates. I'd never noticed how much tension I carried in my body.

Tension. Fear. Anxiety I would not be heard.

My dorm mate grows increasingly tense as I relax.

All around me things still. I forgot that Nature pays attention, that Nature hears. My heart beats steadily, an internal drum echoing through my flesh into my room.

"What is that sound?"

I whisper, my voice like waves breaking on oceans faraway. "My heart."

"What are you doing?"

"Imagine a joy formidable, a joy so great you ache for its release. It constricts your throat like a noose and enlarges you like the first rains on the first seas. Imagine a love that guides, embraces, accepts without question, that is always there for comfort, for succor."

I touch my chest, feel my heart beating strongly, soundly, rhythmically. "Your body, this body, is your foundation, your anchor, a momentary home for what you really are. It is one part of you, not all of you. You leave it here so you can go elsewhere, be something else, or use it to travel until you learn other ways, or travel and take it with you if you need but that comes later, much later." I echo Grandpa's long ago teachings. "Be willing to learn. To know you don't know. No one knows it all. Everyone...everything...is your teacher."

A blast of wind. A door slams.

I fill myself. Back.

"That's what it's like to talk to God."

My dorm mate is gone.

Chapter 56

Lilies

Dr. Blake hires me from a pool of work-study students. "Be at my lab at three o'clock."

"What are we doing?"

"Message transmission."

Message transmission? Like when Grandpa and others and I talked without talking?

"I look forward to it."

I hurry to the building, up the stairs, anxious to be on time my first day, and stop.

My arms are bleeding. Deep cuts from long knives run the length of my body. My forearm and hand are severed from me.

And the screams, the terror. My vision clouds and I can't breathe. My bowels want to release and I hear, "Save us, Gio."

A request.

Messaging?

Does anybody else hear this?

No, they used my name. Whoever calls knows I and I alone can hear.

I hurry to Dr. Blake's lab.

He stands at the bench closest to the windows, another student beside him. A row of Peace Lilies, their broad, green leaves and pure white flowers trembling in no wind, line the top of the bench. Dr. Blake holds a single-edge razor between his fingers. His free hand gently holds a broad, green leaf. Several cut leaves, cut stems, cut stalks litter the floor between him and the student. There's an oscilloscope behind them. Next to it some kind of recording device like I've seen in TV shows with lie detectors, polygraphs. Its needles quiet as the pain goes away.

"Hello, Gio. Mark's helping me take notes. Could you gather the cut leaves and throw them in the trash, please?"

I gather the sliced tissue slowly, lovingly, comforting a friend in their last moments of life.

I remember walking in John N'bm'we's fields, meeting The Standing Ones and their kin, and watch the Peace Lilies wonder what they've done, what are they doing here?

"What are you doing here?"

Dr. Blake stops, his eyes move from the leaf he holds to me. "What did you say, Gio?"

He felt me talk to the lily because he wounds it in his hands but he doesn't know what he hears, what he feels.

"This is your research?"

He nods. Mark nods with him. "Yes. Messaging. Plants respond when another plant is cut. Nobody knows why. We're researching to see if messages are transmitted by electric fields."

"Yes. Also sound. And smell. And thought. And -"

Blake chuckles. Mark joins him. "An amusing theory, Gio, but there's no evidence to support it. We're collecting evidence."

I lift the recorder's printouts, scan them and point to different sections. "This is when you're thinking about cutting but don't know which plant you'll cut. This is when you've decided on a plant to cut. This is when you're approaching the plant. This is when you're about to cut. This is -"

"How do you know that, Gio? Where you standing in the door watching? I didn't see you. You should have come in."

"You'd show the same patterns, probably wilder ones, if somebody came at you with a razor and cut you, wouldn't you?"

Dr. Blake steps back from the lilies, from me. Mark follows.

"What are you talking about, Gio?"

"And if you saw this happening to someone else, someone you loved, cared about, how would you respond?"

Dr. Blake glances at the phone on the far wall. He holds the razor differently, defensively.

I shake my head, walk out.

I get to the bottom stairs, to the doors to outside, and double over as the lilies scream, their sounds, their language, the sound of vowels, all breath, made by the wind moving through leaves, their shaking in their pots, unable to escape.

What am I to do?

How come I can remember then not?

I must relearn, learn again, learn more.

But from who?

Who will teach me?

When nobody I know knows?

Chapter 57

The Master Musician

Jack plays music in his dorm room late into the night on a compact stereo his parents gave him as a high school graduation present. He plays Stevie Wonder's "Songs in the Key of Life" and Elton John's "Goodbye Yellow Brick Road" and The Beatles "Sgt Pepper's Lonely Hearts Club Band" and "Abbey Road" and America and Yes and several dozen others.

Not with every song but with several songs I see a wisp, a shimmer, a cloud strewn face above the turntable, atop the speakers, sometimes in the center of the room.

Sometimes a body forms. Twirling, dancing.

It comes with the music.

I see it when I listen to some Bach, some Beethoven, some Rachmaninoff. I see it sometimes in Music Appreciation class. Listening to African drums. To Taiko drums. Some Muslim calls to worship. I see it when some chazzans sing. Bagpipes. Indian flutes.

I remember seeing it when Grandpa sang his old Sicilian songs. The shimmer is familiar, like an old friend lost in time and rediscovered, a favorite childhood toy whose touch floods memory.

"Who is that, Buppa?"

"A friend."

This friend went away when Buppa died. Music wasn't allowed in my parents' house. It came sometimes when I played Bach.

This friend is in all music. Birdsong. Whalesong. Elephant calls. Buffalo running. Seal bellows. Trumpets, clarinets, violins, instruments I can't imagine.

Always there to those who listen. *Ascolta.*

Jack studies English. He likes Folklore and Fable. One book is cover out. C.S. Lewis' *The Lion, The Witch, and the Wardrobe*. A lion smiles down at me. Children are at his side.

Uncle John? They wrote a book about Uncle John?

"What's this book about?"

Jack glances up from his albums. "A magic place you get to by wishing and dreaming, and a powerful lion who children meet there who protects and teaches them. I think you'd like it. Kind of sounds like the stuff you talk about every once in a while, and -"

The rest of his words are lost. Another book slides forward, falls into my hand, the pages open. "The Pied Piper of Hamelin."

Stevie Wonder sings about going back to Saturn.

"What did you say, Gio?"

"Nothing. Love the music. I'll have to remember it."

"I got some more albums. Hang around."

Yes tells me it's my move cause it's time, it's time in time with my time.

I look at *The Pied Piper*. So familiar.

My bodies - it's been so long since I felt my bodies - throb. I hand Jack the book. "Got to get back and study."

"See you tomorrow."

I pass the dorms, head into the woods to a place I know. Quiet. I sit.

My bodies resonate. Chirp. Their interactions like insects rubbing their legs together, birds answering each others' calls, organs filling church halls, drums shaking the world.

The mist forms in front of me. It spins, it turns, it twirls and churns and I bathe in sounds I'd forgotten existed.

"Hello, Gio."

"You're my grandfather's friend."

"I knew your grandfather. I know you."

"I don't know your name."

It spins. The Pied Piper stands before me, flute raised to his lips.

It spins. A man in a kilt plays bagpipes loud enough to deafen me.

It spins. Bach sits at a clavier scribbling onto sheets of music.

It spins. Indians sit around a fire singing and beating drums.

It spins. A half human, half insect creature with an enormous penis plays flute and laughs at me.

It spins. Ancient soldiers sing a unified chant preparing for war.

It spins. A rabbit stands like a man, its long ears flap against the sides of its head as it dances, flute at its nose, the sound of insects buzzing.

It spins. Some men beat the side of a long canoe-like boat while others paddle through ocean water.

It spins. The earth rumbles.

It spins. Glaciers shatter.

It spins. The moon sings around the earth.

It spins. The sun quakes.

It spins. The universe comes into being.

It spins.

And spins.

And spins.

The mist clears. Sound solidified stands before me wearing a cloak of colors that shift with each sound the creature makes.

"I am Music, Gio. All music. You don't need an instrument to make me, only ears to hear me."

I reach out. It forms a hand that touches mine. My mind explodes with sounds. My body vibrates as if wanting to shake apart. My heart weeps and cries for joy. My spirit takes flight and Music goes with it.

"Listen."

I fall asleep in the dark, dark woods, bathed in warm sounds, protected, comforted, loved.

Chapter 58

The Other

Student government meets in a room off the Student Lounge under the cafeteria. A quaver as I approach. Several people sit around a large conference table in the room. I feel an...*other*?

I have not felt *other* since I was a child with my Grandfather. Now I do? Here? My parents tell me all my childhood experiences were my imagination, that Grandpa was a drunk storyteller and nothing more. Now every day brings back more memories, more experiences, greater realities long forgotten.

Have I finally found *other*?

I taste, I touch, I feel.

Otherness, not *other*. Something similar but foreign, alien, too different to be *other*.

I enter the meeting.

We discuss next semester's plans. One is not paying attention. He feigns attention. He is elsewhere. In the room.

His eyes go to the speaker, to his notes, to his watch, to his soda, to someone in the room. He focuses but not long enough to be noticed.

And he smiles.

He nods at the speaker, sips his soda, makes a note. He looks around the room absently until his eyes lock onto the next person in the room but not long enough to be noticed.

And he smiles.

Someone leans over and whispers something to him. He smiles and nods, then puts his finger to his lips, whispers, "Shh," and holds his hand out between them, palm out. The other person chuckles and leans away. He nods at something the speaker says, looks at a painting on the wall.

He prepares, his energy surges, a weightlifter readying for a heavy lift.

The next person is a woman I know, someone I talk to. I call her *mi pequeña animadora latina* because I don't speak Spanish and it makes her laugh. She's a friend who seeks me out because I listen without judging and help her find her way.

She is weak, vulnerable.

To him, prey.

I feel him surround her, look for ways in.

Part of her knows, understands, the animal part tenses, sensing a threat is near but her mind too schooled to see where.

I wonder at him, his intention.

A taste I know. Grandpa and his friends warned me.

He will hurt her. If he can. He wonders if he can. What it would take. If anyone would notice. How long would it take. To use her. Control her. Manipulate her.

And when tired, cast her away to deal with shameful thoughts he will make sure she has.

All part of his calculations.

But to hurt someone you must recognize them as someone, as individual, recognize their personhood.

He does not. He recognizes her vulnerability, something exploitable, something to be used, drained, discarded, what's left left to rot.

I close my eyes for a moment.

Lower-Center-Relax-Breathe.

Another student nudges me. "Don't fall asleep now, Gio. It's Q&A in a minute."

My eyes half open. I smile. My emotional body flows from me around my friend.

Comfort.

I breathe a moment for her. To relax her. She sighs. Her fear is gone. Not so him.

He stares at her openly, unable to get in. There is no entry. There is always entry.

What stops him? He pales, hastily makes a note, pours a glass of water, spills a bit, someone offers their napkin, helps him clear it up.

"Everything okay, Larry?"

He wipes without looking up. "Yeah, just...is it hot in here? I got a little dizzy. Can we open a window?"

The leader agrees. "Yeah, it is a little stuffy. Bill, Sherry, mind opening a few windows over there? Tyler, could you get one of the back ones, get a breeze going in here?"

He recovers quickly, his face flushes back to normal. "Thanks, Ed."

He makes a note. He shrugs. He'll investigate. He moves on. To me.

His eyes meet mine. I nod and smile. I mouth "You sure you're okay?" and all the while I wrap him in a vise. He can't get in, he can't get out, he can't move.

He sits and stares because that's all he can do. All I'll allow.

Did you think you were the only one who could do these things?

He wants to look away. He struggles to move and I don't let him.

This is what others feel when you enter them.

He reaches out to me. I don't let him enter. I do not listen. I hold him, still.

The vise does not tighten. He does not move. No body is active. Emotional, Physical, Spiritual, Mental; immobile.

I do not enter. I hammer, my words like mallets on his skull, on his face, already bruising, purpling, his teeth loosening in his jaw and no one notices a thing.

You use your talent to harm others but you've never been harmed. Not this way. Because...?

I forget he cannot answer.

Ask differently.

What do you remember?

His memories play before me. His fingers twitch. He knows he can't escape and he doesn't know what it is I am.

You do this because you can. Because you believe yourself better than others. It never occurred to you someday you'd find someone better than you?

His arms twitch, his chest pops as he works to break my hold.

You thought you were special, unique?

There is no one that unique.

I pull back, completely, in an instant's part of an instant.

He snaps forward, scattering his soda, his water, his notepad skims across the table, his pencil snaps in his fingers.

The people beside him back away.

Someone calls the college's resident nurse.

The next day he approaches me in the cafeteria, introduces himself to me. "I want to apologize for yesterday's meeting."

He surrounds me. I create a shell with my physical-body as the center. "Don't worry about it. Ed talked too long, anyway."

He squeezes gently. I yield to the pressure.

He nods, smiles. "You're Gio, right? What's your major again?"

He pushes from one side. I let myself fold.

His smile turns into a sneer.

"Theology. Theology and Physics."

"Right."

He prepares to invade. I call out to a friend, a dying star, a nova. It gives me permission to release its cataclysm in his mind, pour its heat over his body.

His face goes white, blank, the smile and sneer gone, his eyes open wide, unblinking.

Never do this again. To anyone. Ever.

I remember Grandpa, his friends. I hope.

I'm not the only one who'll be watching. But I am the least of those who will.

"Nice meeting you, Larry."

Chapter 59

Roseanne

People come to me and ask about God. They come at night, in private. They clutch their Crosses and Bibles to them as they ask about their relationship with God, with others, with themselves.

"You can ask yourself. I'm neither priest nor confessor."

They turn rigid, as if told to jump from a plane sans parachute, not knowing how to fall.

I wait for a friend in the early Winter sunlight of a girls' dorm lounge.

Roseanne comes and sits with me. She tucks her thick, blue-nylon covered legs under her and leans forward, arms resting on her black, red, and yellow plaid skirt, the white sleeves of her blouse billow out, hiding her stomach, her chest, and she adjusts her red on black blazer, pulls it down, pulls it into place. Her long brown hair leaves spiderweb shadows on her face. The sunlight catches on a gold pin holding her collar tightly around her neck and reflects a jagged sword wound on the far wall, cleaving a picture of Jesus in two, a biker's scar giving personality to the blue-eyed, blond-haired mage.

"What can you tell me about me?"

I look at her.

Her large brown eyes fix on me, challenge me.

Lower-Center-Relax-Breathe.

I look at the Spirits, the Energies around her.

SpiritTalking. It's been so long. I didn't know I still knew how to do this.

She's not challenging. She wants to be found out.

Four spirits surround Roseanne: Jesus upside down on a rightside up Cross, his legs spread on the arms of the Cross and his arms nailed down, over his head; A man in a blue suit walking in a circle, talking into it; A fire with a heart pulsing in the center of it; A mouse scurrying after a piece of cheese, eating it, vomiting it back out and starting the process all over again.

I look back at Roseanne. "Are you sure you want to know?"

"Yes."

"You're sure you want to know?"

"Yes. I told you, yes."

"I will ask you one more time, to be sure, to be positive: You want me to tell you what I can learn about you?"

One of Grandpa's rules: Ask three times. To align the bodies.

"Yes. Are you stupid? I said 'Yes'."

I look to her spirits. "What do you want Roseanne to know?"

It is a chorus. Many voices. A beautiful song played too loud.

There is so much to share. So much she must know.

"You are troubled."

Roseanne rises off her legs, sits back down, crosses and uncrosses them.

"No, I'm not."

"Okay, my mistake." I stand up, walk towards the door.

The spirits around her scream for me to return.

"What do you think is bothering me?"

I come back, sit down.

Her Spirits are anxious to be heard. Roseanne has not listened to them, talked with them since a child.

Lower-Center-Relax-Breathe.

Ascolta! I listen.

"Are you sure you want to do this, Roseanne?"

She stares at me. It is not a game anymore. She knows they are talking and I am listening. Whatever troubles her, whatever her secret is, it will be known.

Spirit Talking. Share what the person can't hear, doesn't want to hear, must hear to remain whole, sane.

"You already know what's troubling you. What you want is to be punished for it."

"I have no idea what you're talking about."

I stand a second time. "Okay, like I said before, my mistake."

She grabbed my arm. "Tell me."

"Tell you what?"

"Tell me what I want to be punished for."

"That's not my job."

"You don't know anything."

"You're right. I don't. You found me out. I'm a big faker! Bwa-ha-ha-ha."

And I am tired of bowing at the Temple of the Stupid and forget: Never cause hurt or harm.

I smile. "You're terrified someone will find out about the affair you had with that married guy. What's his name? Jim? John?" I listen. "Joshua? That's it, Joshua. He's married, 38 years old, two kids and a pregnant wife. He tells you where to meet him. The BlueBird Motel? That's right. You're supposed to meet him there riding home from what? School? Work? No, something that's both. Oh, you taught... what was it? Oh, Vacation Bible School. So you spend your mornings teaching kids about Jesus and His Church then your afternoons taking it in the mouth, up your ass, any way he wants to give it to you. You show up on your bike. He has a room ready, the same room each day. He helps get your bike into the room."

I look over her head, a little to the right. The upside down Jesus frees himself from the Cross, nods, walks away. The mouse stops vomiting cheese.

"Wait. What? You're afraid your pregnant?"

I focus onto her belly, beneath her clothes and into her womb. "You're not. Don't worry. Probably just anxiety making you late."

Roseanne stands, strikes me across the face, runs to her room. Her screams echo down the dorm hallways.

I listen to her dorm mates gather around her. "Don't worry, Roseanne. Only Jesus really knows your heart." "He's an agent of the devil, Gio is."

Their illogic sickens me. Obviously others beside Jesus can know her heart. Either me independently or me in league with the devil, but in either case, their premise is false.

I hear Grandpa's words, long forgotten.

Truth like wine.

~

Roseanne wakes in the middle of the night, her period puddles her bed. She cries, can't stop. The dorm mother rushes in. Roseanne confesses. Everything I said is true.

How could I know?

People avoid me. Whatever it is I do, I know their secrets. Sherrill masturbates in her room. Charles walks around with pictures in his shorts.

I remember something from Mrs. Langlois' journalism class: News is something that someone, somewhere, doesn't want published.

Their fear isn't someone discovering their secret, it's someone knowing their secret and not caring. I have no interest in their news. My lack of interest tells them they are unimportant.

Learning they are unimportant terrifies them more than anything I can do or ever could.

Chapter 60

Search

Jess looks up at me, her head on my lap. She swallows, smiles, and says, "Stephanie wants to know if you can find her two little brothers."

The backseat of my 1964 Mercury Comet is cold on my buttocks. It is a cold, clear, late Autumn night. The windows are steamed except for a clear patch on the windshield revealing the crescent moon, its horns up, The Maid, accepting, gathering, collecting, as it rises over the sea at Singing Beach. Its light catches my face full on as sweat trickles down my chest. The DJ queues up another song on the radio, the volume low. I don't pay attention, too busy raising myself off the cold seat to pull up my pants.

"She's already mentioned you to the police."

Maria Muldaur whispers over the radio.

Midnight at the Oasis
send your camel to bed
shadows painted on faces
traces of romance in our heads…

Jess straddles my hips.

"She told them you're psychic."

I push her back, look into her face.

"I know, you're not psychic. You said you're not psychic. But you always know when I'm having my period. You know when people are in trouble. You find things that are lost and you always know what people are thinking."

Come on 'till the evening ends
you don't have to answer
you know there's no need to speak
I'll be your bellydancer
and you'll be my sheep

She pulls up her jersey, pulls my face into her breasts.

You won't need no harem, honey,
when I'm by your side
you won't need no camel
when I take you for a ride…

I lean back in the seat. She lowers my pants.

The moon beams through the windshield. My grandfather taught me to walk them, to gather them in my hands to make lampshades. I learned anti-gravity, FTL, time-travel, and teleportation from those who traveled with me. Its light always warmed me.

Now its light is cold.

~

I offer no peace, no comfort, only what I've learned. The two boys are lost, their guardian dead.

"How do you know this?"

"No idea."

"Are you making it up?"

"Don't think so, no."

"Can you prove anything you say?"

"Go look where I said."

The boys' parents want to pay me to help

I shake my head. "That's not how I do things. Sorry."

The police want me to help, ask me to be their consultant.

"Sorry, no. That's not how it works."

One knows me, knew my grandfather.

"You knew my grandfather?"

"We could use your help. Didn't he help the police? Didn't you?"

"Let me think on it."

An ancient enemy, an Old One my grandfather and his friends warned me of, one I've seen but never recognized, sits beside me.

"Hello, Gio."

"Go away."

"I've followed you all your life."

"You've hidden yourself from me all my life."

"I've taken the form of this one, then that one. But only for a while. To do my work. Borrowing? No, Passing. That's what you call it? Passing?"

"Leave me alone."

"Join me. No one will ever know and in time even you will forget."

I close my eyes, fight to remember.

Lower-Center-Relax-Breathe.

I *push*.

It screams, flees down the hall, up a wall, through a window.

A deputy hurries back to me. "What was that sound?"

"An ancient enemy."

"Huh?"

"Ignorance."

Chapter 61

Mi pequeña animadora latina

"Why won't you sleep with me?"

Laurie sits on my bed, her legs crossed at the ankles and tucked under her, her long tartan skirt hiding more than is necessary. Long black hair flows down her shoulders, her chest and arms. Her white blouse highlights her olive-skinned hands and full face in the light of my desk lamp. A small cameo, a gift from her mother, Laurie the first in her family to go to college, and they are so proud, holds her blouse's collar tight at her neck as ruffles frill out at the buttons.

"Why won't you sleep with me?"

Her dark eyes watch me, her full lips quiver.

"Are we just going to sleep or will you want more?"

"You sleep with everybody."

"No, I don't. I won't sleep with you."

The door to my dorm room starts to close, a design flaw in the building and the hanging of this door. If the door closes and she is in my room, the god-fearing administration will cause trouble for her, her dorm mates will ostracize her, the good, Christian boys on campus will make fun of her and assume she's an easy feast.

I focus on the door. "Stop."

The door stops.

I ask my Grandmother Spirit to weave a binding on the door, to ask it to stay open. Her eight eyes glisten, she nods as much as Spider can, and the door swings wide to let the hall light in.

Laurie's deep, dark, bright eyes fix on me. "Please why won't you sleep with me?"

The fawn lying down at her feet looks up at me. A tear leaves one eye. It wants to become a doe but doesn't know how to grow.

"Do you want me to hold you while you sleep? While you fall asleep? I'm happy to do that."

"You know what I want."

Her people are from a place different from mine but stories are told, not of me or mine, but of her people similar, not in her family but in families known, back in the hills, back in time, back in place.

"Laurie. My little latina cheerleader. *Mi pequeña animadora latina.* Did I say that right?"

She laughs. "I want you."

"What you want is to be loved. To know you're loved."

"Is that so wrong?"

"Is it so right to ask another to give it to you when you know they can't?"

"How do you know you can't?"

"Do you remember orientation? Your whole family came to help set up your room and see you off. I rode my bike past your father and brother struggling with a chest and stopped to help. And -"

"My grandmother couldn't take her eyes off you. She told me she felt one like you back home. She called you *un protector, un hombre mágico.*"

"But I'm not your protector and I'm not your magic man."

"I love you."

"I know."

"You're the only one here who listens."

"I'm the only one who listens now."

The fawn stands. A pool forms at its feet. It lowers its head, drinks, eyes alert, always on mine, quick away and back again, ears moving as if listening to the wind. Laurie stands up, comes to me, sits in my lap without asking, I offer without denying, and hold her while tears wet the front of her blouse, little drops tamping down the frills.

And then a kiss, on her eyes.

Fawn, grow. Your deer eyes will see another who will love you in ways I never can.

"Will I meet someone like you?"

"Better than me."

She laughs. "Better than you?"

"Yes. Shall I tell you about him?"

I follow her path and tell her what will come. She thinks it's a game. She laughs when I explain how they'll meet, how they'll grow, how they'll wed, their children, how their children will grow.

Then I stiffen.

"What's wrong?"

"That's all. No more stories to tell."

She pushes herself back from me. She kisses the tears on my face. "What is it?"

"Your life will be so wonderful, *mi pequeña animadora latina*. So wonderful. I'm jealous."

I push her from my lap. She stands and gazes down on me.

"I have studying to do, *mi pequeña animadora latina*."

A kiss and she leaves my room. I ask Grandmother to release her binding, to ask Door to close. The latch sounds and I burst into tears.

In her path, in twenty-five years, on a warm September morning, *mi pequeña animadora latina* and the man who will mean more to her than anything else, the man who will make her forget we ever talked, will be working and laughing side by side, look up, and see an airplane fly into their office.

Chapter 62

The Exorcism

I sit in a cushy, blue chair in the student lounge underneath the cafeteria. Outside, in the dark of early night, is a small parking lot followed by trees followed by a pond. There's movement I can't make out and I blink, not realizing my eyes become cat's eyes and all the nocturnal suburban woodland activity is revealed to me. I smile, sense whiskers forming, and blink my eyes back before Cat invites me to prowl.

Norm, Teri, and Lynne stand around me, their hands on my head, shoulders, and back, praying to Jesus to save my soul because Professor Strunk, Dean of the two-person Psych department, said anybody who engages in prophetic utterances is in league with the Devil.

Nothing is said about accuracy. Accuracy is irrelevant. If you prophesy - not even reveal the future, just reveal the truth - you're in league with the Devil.

Correction, _The Devil_.

Correct emphasis is important. There are so many.

What would he say if he saw my eyes a moment ago?

The lounge lights dim. The signal it's nine o'clock, head back to your dorms unless you scheduled a study room. Most of those lights are out, their doors locked from the inside, the small rooms perfect for trysts, the stench of sex tickling sensitive noses.

One student, I don't know his name, always schedules the study room at the end of the hall, away from the stairs, far from the smells of the overhead cafeteria. He can't afford a dorm room and sleeps there. He showers in the gym and shaves in the men's room next to the stairs leading outside.

I slide meal tickets under his study room door when no one's around, when I'm sure he's asleep, leaving my dorm despite watchful eyes, Lamont Cranston without the cape, hat, or scarf.

A night watchman comes through the lounge, stops to listen to Norm, Teri, and Lynne pray, their hands gentle on me, and keeps walking.

Do I do what they need me to do? What they expect of me? Do they really believe what they do has meaning?

It has meaning to them, isn't that enough?

You give them eyes but they cannot see.

Shall I let them see?

I give to them from me.

The room fills with human size rabbits, Harveys in all shapes and sizes, dragons, whales, squid sporting mortarboards, their tassels pending graduation, cougars, bears, spiders the size of elephants, candlesticks in monk robes sprout legs and nod as they walk past.

Norm, Teri, and Lynne pray louder, their hands clench me. They shiver and stink of fear.

I remember. Don't hurt or harm.

I rock back, out of their grips, the lounge empties, my chair falls backward, I somersault and rise on my feet.

"Thanks. All better now."

Chapter 63

Different Universes

Professor Ball stands at the blackboard in Quantum Mechanics class, his hand scribbling equations too fast for us to follow.

Eileen beams up at him. "You really know this stuff."

"Hey, I'm a wiz at this."

The class laughs.

He lifts an eraser.

I raise my hand.

He erases a set of equations.

"Excuse me, Professor Ball. I'm not through copying your equations."

He smiles at Eileen and his face sours as he raises his gaze to me. "You should write things down faster. You'll never keep up the way you do things."

The students stiffen.

"I seek to understand."

He shakes his head, turns back to the board, raises the eraser.

"Not yet, please."

He turns back towards the class, towards the students, towards us, towards me. He glances down at Eileen then back at me. His nostrils flare. "You just don't get it. You didn't get it last year and you don't get it this year. Why don't you do the rest of us a favor and just quit the class."

It is an order, a statement, not a question.

The class becomes quiet.

The stiffness in limbs, in chests, in breaths, becomes palpable. Eyes go wide but peer down. Note-taking stops.

Professor Ball turns back to his board.

"If you truly were the wiz you claim, you could explain this to me in a way I would understand. Your real anger, your real frustration and rage, is because you can't answer my questions. Your inability to reframe your knowledge in a way I can grasp, to only teach what you were taught, to answer my questions about the basis of your statements, tells you you're not the wiz you claim to be. If you were the wiz you claim, you could say this so any could understand. That's why you rage at me. Face me and you face the imposter you know you are."

He stares at me. His face reddens. His chest tightens. His hand whitens holding the eraser. The chalk in his other hand cracks as his fingers clench the cool, yellow-green stick.

"You're locked in a tower of your own ignorance, and like Rapunzel, you can't get down."

The students become mannequins sitting at desks, pens and pencils in hands, eyes fixed on notebooks, a display window's idea of a class paying attention.

Professor Ball breathes.

"It is this disparity hitting you square in the face that kills you. You can do the physics but you can't understand how the physics is done. I understand how it is done, but not the way you do it." The mannequins rotate, face me. "Your physics eludes me. Let me show you mine."

I hold my hand out, palm up, touch my middle finger and thumb, pull them apart. A bubble forms. Inside is a universe, perfectly formed.

All students' eyes are wide on me, on the bubble, on the universe within. I hold it up and offer it to Professor Ball. "You're trying to understand how the universe formed, but your own beliefs stop you from understanding the universe's true nature. You can't accept the possibility that what you call The Big Bang might have been someone snapping their fingers to bring this universe into existence."

The classroom, the desks, the blackboard, the students, Professor Ball, the pens, pencils, chairs, desks, the building, the trees outside all begin to quaver.

"Oops. Sorry. My bad. I haven't learned to prevent leakage."

I collapse the bubble. The quavering stops.

The room remains silent.

I gather my things, head for the door. "But I agree, you are correct, it is time for me to go. Close to, almost." I turn before I walk out, walk away, preparing to leave this form of education forever.

Then my second bad. I can't resist. I smile at the class first then directly at Professor Ball. "But do remember, if you ever start taking things too seriously or think you're so much, we are all talking monkeys on an organic spaceship flying through this universe."

One of the students, not Eileen, comes up to me in the library. "What did you do in there?"

I consider. Does anybody really want to know? "Ever read Julian of Norwich? *Revelations of Divine Love*?"

The student pulls back slightly, shakes her head, long brown hair ruffles and blue eyes fix on me.

"And he showed me more, a little thing, the size of a hazelnut, on the palm of my hand, round like a ball. I looked at it thoughtfully and wondered, 'What is this?' And his answer came, 'It is all that is made.'"

She keeps her eyes on me, continues to shake her head and shrugs.

"Hold out your hand."

She moves in slow motion but not slowly, only normal speed slowed through quavering quantum space.

I become the creature in Julian's vision and put a universe the size of a walnut in her palm.

She looks down at it. "What is this?"

"Everything ever made."

She closes her hand around it. Her eyes meet mine without fear and I replace the creature in her eyes. "What does it mean?" she asks.

"The universe is much larger than what you see, what Professor Ball can understand, what science comprehends. Keep questioning. The people asking questions are the wise ones, not the ones claiming they know the answers."

Chapter 64

The Fair

Some fellow students ask if I'll drive them to the Topsfield Fair. I invite Laurie because she rarely leaves campus and tell her we're going as friends, nothing more. She agrees and hopes for more.

Six of us pack into my two-door Comet. We haven't left the parking lot and my fellow students grumble about who'll sit next to whom on the way back, should we stop and rearrange seating on the way out, who'll sit next to whom if we go to Pewter Pot for coffee after the fair.

I pull over less than a hundred feet from campus, turn around, drive back.

"What are you doing, Gio?"

"Making sure Laurie and I can enjoy the fair."

My car thus emptied, Laurie still snuggles against me in the front seat. "You don't take crap from people, do you." It's a statement.

I don't respond.

"There's a lot of talk about you on campus."

I drive. My hands stay on the wheel, don't move towards hers, turn on my headlights as night covers the land.

"I worry about you."

I look at her. A tear slides down *mi pequeña animadora latina*'s cheek.

"Thank you, and you don't have to."

"I don't like what they say."

"I probably wouldn't either. That's why I don't pay attention."

She leans into me, pulls back, shuffles over to the passenger side, folds her hands in her lap. The vinyl upholstery crackles slightly due to the Autumn evening's air.

"You don't have to do that, Laurie."

She brightens. I feel a small sun has gone nova in the car beside me. "You mean that?"

"I mean tonight, and only for tonight, let's be on a date. To the fair. Nothing more."

She takes off her colorful Central American knitted hat, a gift from her grandmother, pushes up against me, and rests her head on my shoulder. Her thick, black hair covers my jacket chest and arms like soft clouds preparing to rain. "Will you kiss me?"

I don't answer, smile, we turn into the fairgrounds, park the car. "Do have something special you'd like to do or see?"

She weaves an arm through mine, pulls herself close beside me. "How about some greasy fair food?"

"You know what that stuff does to your insides?"

"You know how good it tastes?"

She opts for barbecued chicken on a stick, I get a hot Italian sub with everything on it. It's not hot and its heritage is doubtful. "How's the chicken?"

She smiles with a ring of barbecue sauce circling her lips. "Disgusting. Want some?"

We share a coke as we walk the grounds.

"How come the animals come right up to you?"

"How come they don't with anybody else?"

We go towards the rides. She pulls me towards the FunHouse. "They don't have things like that in my country. We honor the dead."

"Wise move."

"Let's go."

"I'll hold the coke."

A witch takes our tickets and cackles. "Buckle up, dearies."

I nod. The cart catches and we slither forward.

"You ever been on one of these, Gio?"

I shake my head as she grips my arm tighter. "No. I honor those who've moved on, too."

We're in the dark. Lights flash. Someone screams. A bloodied man lunges at us with a knife in hand.

Laura screams.

Frankenstein comes through a door above up, he reaches, his hands barely miss us.

Laura clutches me.

We move through a spider web, its gossamer strands gently flailing us. Things with eight eyes hiss on both sides.

Laura tucks her face into my chest.

Vampires. Werewolves. Ghouls. Zombies. Axe murderers. Knives and hacksaws and rifles.

And the witch smiles as the ride ends.

I disentangle Laura. "You okay?"

She's shaking. I give her my jacket.

"Won't you be cold?"

I shake my head.

"You never screamed. You never jumped. I had my head buried in your chest and your heart kept going sure and steady. Didn't any of that bother you?"

"No, I know it's not real."

I see a sign for a FreakShow and head towards it.

Laura slows. "I've had enough for one night."

"You wait here. I'm curious."

She doesn't let go. "No, I'll come, too. I'll keep my eyes closed, if that's okay."

The barker sees Laura already shaking. "Hey, it's none of my business, but there's some pretty severe stuff in here."

"I'm curious."

"He's curious."

He opens the door for us. "Suit yourselves. You got five minutes to see ten freaks. Thirty seconds per. Most people don't last the five." He smirks. "Most people don't last one."

"Cover your eyes, Laura. Pull your hat down over them."

I hold her close. Guide her among the cages.

Cages.

The Snake Man.

The Headless Wonder.

The Inside Out Woman.

The Occulting Twins. One child has another, smaller child growing out of his side. It is the smaller child who speaks, controls the movements of the other.

Captain One-Eye.

The Girl with Two Mouths.

No Face.

The Six Breasted Woman.

The Backwards Boy.

Mr. Two Dicks.

Some of them mock Laura's fear.

I don't react.

They yell, scream, curse. Rattle their cages.

Cages.

I walk slowly. Observing each. Wondering if any of them know the weeping-eyed grandmother who gives me *biscotti* as I climb the path to a village where these people would be considered whole.

Back in the car, I turn the heater on. "Want to get a coffee?"

"Nothing from you, Gio. I could hear them. I peeked at one or two. They were hideous. Monsters. And not a thing from you."

"I've seen...different."

She pushes away from me, shakes her head, a fresh tear slides down her face. "Because you see those kinds of things every day, right? The FunHouse didn't bother you, the...people in cages didn't bother you. Because you see those kinds of things all the time, don't you?"

Chapter 65

The Miracle

An afternoon at the mall. The crowd comforts me. No one knows me, no one fears, no one hates.

No one cares.

There is solace in anonymity, invisibility, oblivion.

I window shop, buy a pistachio ice cream, wonder if I have a mustache. A record store's having a sale. I hesitate. An album of hymns, gospel, a christian rock group, Phil Keaggy perhaps, would please my college brothers and sisters.

But the Master Musician might also dwell within its walls, something I do not want.

I pray silently. A clear sign. Something to let me know Buppa was a fool. I guess better than most, that's all there is. Or to let me know there is no one god but many, and not gods per se, simply those who are different, but different in ways that are wondrous, glorious, captivating, breathtaking.

And loving.

Always with Buppa's teaching there was love.

Not so any other teachings I remember. They came with the hand, the fist, the whip, the threat.

All others taught their fears, not their hopes.

I want a clear sign. I do not wish to decide. I wish to be told. To have it all explained. So clearly, so cleanly, I can not argue, can not debate, to have it all presented so sweetly and plainly there is no counterpoint anyone can offer. Something to let me know there's been a meaning, a purpose, for everything I've experienced in my life, that I'm not just some fool who's been made sport of.

I will go with Christ.

There are more of them than there are of me. It will be safer. One of the crowd, I'll be unknown, anonymous, invisible, and if it ends in oblivion?

I won't be around to care.

So be it.

I purchase an album of Gregorian Chants and hope The Master Musician isn't within the album's jacket when I get home. I have no stereo, no player, but it doesn't matter. I bought the album, the decision is made.

Back in the parking lot, I open the door to my car, pull back the seat, prepare to toss the album in back, only bring it out when I need a defense, a buttress, a counter to my brothers and sisters who only see me as sin.

There's a package on the floor behind the driver's seat.

I didn't put it there.

No one else has keys to my car.

And I am not one to forget.

I lift the package, feel a box, lift it out.

The Chronicles of Narnia!

The seven book set. Pristine. Never touched, never opened. No price tag anywhere to be found.

How?

I lean against my car, weak. I asked for a sign, to be told, to be guided, to have the decision made.

No one else had keys to my car.

I sit, shaking. Tears fall from my eyes to the box set.

I drive back to my dorm, lock my car, have to hold the railings going up the stairs to my dorm, to my room, the box set held tightly against me by my right arm, my left hand out, a blind man realizing he can finally see.

I pass Jack, show him my gift, my redemption, my salvation.

"I asked for a sign, Jack. I asked for God to let me know what was right and what was wrong, and He put these books in my car."

Jack smiles. "I'm happy for you."

"You don't know who did this, do you? This isn't somebody goofing on me. Tell me this isn't somebody goofing on me."

He takes the box set, opens it, rearranges the books. "This is the order they should be read." He hands me the opened set. "I'm happy for you."

I go to my room, sit, and stare at the package in my hands.

For the first time since Buppa I believe I am loved.

Chapter 66

Helga

Helga, beautiful, thalidomidic Helga who becomes graceful when she's around me, whose pains cease in my presence, finds me in the library, alone, the table where I sit stacked with Old and New Testament, Apochrypha, Gnostics in their original languages. I search for stories similar to Grandpa's teachings. Most are lost in the myths of the world. The *Malleus Maleficarum*, Baring-Gould's *The Book of Were-Wolves*, and similar books are water in the desert.

"I hated you when I first saw you on Orientation night."

"Thanks, I guess."

"I don't know why."

"Just lucky, I guess."

"People are frightened of you."

"They hide it well."

She sits, pushes the books aside, takes my current volume from me, closes it, takes my healthy hands in her three-fingered ones.

My hands always ache in her presence. She has no left leg, only a stump and prosthetic, and her womb, ovaries, and uterus are misshapen.

My left leg attempts to shrivel away. My guts twist and churn. It is a price I gladly pay when she is near.

"God has a special plan for you, Gio. You're one of his Chosen."

I shake my head, hearing another time, another voice. Grandpa's *Sapere*.

"You should expect great things to happen in your life."

"They already have, Helga. I met you."

Her eyes water.

"You have to leave campus, Gio. Tonight. Now."

I cock my head, furrow my brow. I remember Lauren to Vicky through Rox through Diane through Denise to Debbie to me.

Lower-Center-Relax-Breathe.

The campus Spirits talk.

Ascolta. Listen.

I raise her deformed hands to my lips, kiss them.

My Spirits talk.

Ascolta. I listen.

It is not my misshapen hands or missing leg or contorted ovaries or uterus or womb.

It is for Helga, so deformed she doesn't believe she'll ever be loved, my body aches.

Chapter 67

Not Yet

My car is gone, a motorcycle more convenient to my travels. I ride it on mountain roads, some remembered from drives with Grandpa.

Where are all his friends?

My friends?

And those I thought would befriend me? I bought their music, read their books, joined their churches.

No.

Still I am cast out because they are vigilant, watchful, for their *other*. Sometimes I forget and *do*. Sometimes I share.

And when I do I am quickly branded *OTHER!* If not *other*, then sick, strange, a monster. Even when they want what I can do, they're terrified when I do it.

All these years and nothing's changed. Still, I wonder: Am I a freak? A sport? Some genetic oversight? A stray gamma-ray struck me as a fertilized egg in my mother's womb during mitosis?

The one who seemed most like me revealed as a sadistic prick bastard. I told him there were others. Were there?

Are there?

Where?

How come in all this time I find no one who can do for me what I can do for others? Just one, anyone, who can *Ascolta*, listen to me, to what's going on inside without my having to state it.

My bike roars up a steep mountain road, one unfamiliar to me, one with no guard rails, as if someone paved the topmost ridge of the earth where it touches the sky. Look left, a fifty foot drop, look right, ninety feet or more.

Who made this road up here?

I could go over the edge. I could turn my wheel just ever so much, punch the throttle, relax my hold on the handlebars, go over the side, over the edge, let go, off into infinity, flight.

I remember Grandpa teaching me to fly.

Or it was a dream. All a dream. A fantasy told to children, to a child, to this child, to stop the pain of memory, of parents that didn't care, that didn't want.

Sure. Why not.

I crank the throttle, steer straight where the road curves ahead.

And over the edge...

I don't go.

A wind rushes up the side of the mountain, tearing trees up from their roots, moving boulders, lifting streams coursing down its side, making a bridge, making a wall, catching my tires like a motorcycle daredevil cage in a circus sideshow, the handlebars taken from my grip, the throttle released from my hand, the bike comes to rest in the middle of my lonely road.

A whirlwind gathers in front of me, moving earth, mountain, stream, sky into a face centered in its swirling cloud.

A voice of fire, like a mountain. "No, not yet. You're needed. Elsewhere."

I get off my bike, let it fall to the ground.

I cry.

Chapter 68

The Wilderness

Jack sits in a chair in my dining room, an opened, well-worn box set of *The Chronicles of Narnia* in his hands. David Bowie screams *Five Years* from the countertop clock radio.

Jack passes the box set back and forth from one hand to the other and looks around my dining room like a basketball player deciding who'll receive his pass. "I put them in the backseat of your car."

I stare at him from the kitchen. "I came into your dorm room when I found them. I said it had to be some kind of miracle because the car had been locked and there were no signs of forced entry. They were in a bag on the floor and nobody would have seen them. I wouldn't have seen them if I didn't put some laundry back there."

"You had a habit of leaving your car keys on your dresser and your dorm room unlocked."

"With everything I've gone through since then? All because I found those books? I asked you if you knew anything about it. You just told me to read *The Lion, The Witch, and The Wardrobe* first."

He stares up at me.

"I asked you, Jack. You. I asked. Did you know who put them in my car."

"You asked if I knew how they got there."

"Big fucking difference, don't you think?"

He looks at the boxed set in his hands. "You said you were leaving. Said you had to go before you got lynched."

"You let me believe in a lie all this time, Jack. Do you know how long I thought I was insane, hearing voices, seeing things, convincing myself my grandfather got me in some kind of cult. I prayed every day for goddamn Jesus Christ to save me from what was going on around me, in my head."

He looks away, his eyes on neither the books nor me.

"And all because there was no way to explain those books being in my car except some kind of miracle."

"You wanted them."

"I didn't want to be lied to."

"I wanted them to be a gift."

"From who? Jesus Christ?"

"I didn't want to spoil the moment for you."

"So you perpetuated a lie for how long? You heard me tell people about this one undeniable miracle in my life and that's why I chose Jesus for how goddamn fucking long and you never pulled me aside and told me the truth?"

"You had such strong faith."

"I had such amazing stupidity. Jesus Christ, Jack. Jesus fucking Christ. I could have been doing something else."

"I didn't want you to be disappointed in Jesus."

I laugh so hard I gasp for breath. "Disappointed in Jesus? Fuck that. I've been disappointed in Jesus since the day I met people who told me they were Christians. And all this time I'm wondering 'what? One fucking miracle and I'm supposed to live on that for the rest of my life?' One fucking miracle and the rest of my life goes south but stupid fucking fool that I am, I hold on to that one fucking miracle because I'm an idiot, a moron? Is that what you wanted, Jack? Another schmuck for Jesus?"

"I didn't want you to lose respect for Jesus."

"Don't worry about Jesus, it's you I've lost respect for. I'm not disappointed in Jesus, I'm disappointed in you. I've wandered in a goddamn wilderness for all these years because of your lie?"

He stares up at me. His face tightens and his eyes fix on mine with a challenge. "I didn't lie, I omitted a truth."

I laugh. There's no other response available to me.

"You've been carrying this for how long? You've got to be sick inside, brother. Your stomach and your heart must be rotting if you could do this to another human being since I left school."

All the energies flood back into me. Voices I thought lost. Voices I thought were demons and devils.

Now I know they were.

But only because I believed others more than I believed myself.

Meister Eckhart's teaching: Fear the hand held out to you and you see a demon's talons, love the hand held out to you and you see an angel's wings.

Now I know the voices' names and the speakers' functions in my life: Guides, Guardians, Totems, Power Beings, ...

Once always with me and now unheard for so long.

Jack sits and weeps. His tears flee his face, slither down the sides of the boxed set, stain the carpet between his feet.

How do I repay him for what he's done.

Grandpa talks to me. "*Tratta gli altri come se fossero te.*" Treat others as if they were you.

I would want forgiveness therefore I must give it to others.

And now I am free. I know the truth and it has set me free.

It thunders. Rain beats against my apartment windows like storm waves on the ocean.

I go outside and let the Universe baptize me.

The sky clears and Jack follows.

I take my apartment keys from my pocket and toss them to him. "Rent's all paid up through the end of the month. It's yours."

Chapter 69

A Moment of Eternity

I park my bike at the curb, take off my helmet, leather gloves and jacket. Her house is how it's always been, facing the ocean, the last house on an old street, built before such a view was precious, built when its distance from the town center made the land cheap.

I visit every week I wander, regardless of distance or time, knowing there is a secret here, knowing today is my last visit.

I ring the doorbell.

"Come in."

She never locks her door. I warn her every time.

She sits in her wheelchair, shrugs.

I rustle the paper bag from SeaSide Confectioners. She perks up. Her face turns towards me, blind eyes searching. "What did you bring me?"

"What makes you think I brought you something?"

She laughs. "What's in the bag?"

"Hold out your hand."

Arthritic, fingers bent, unable to grasp, to hold. I take something from the bag making as much noise as possible and put it in her palm.

She lifts it to her nose, inhales rich molasses and brown sugar scents. "Seafoam. I love Seafoam." The crumbly brick of candy goes in her mouth.

I shake the bag. "Where do you want the rest?"

"Right here, in my hand."

"Your sugar…"

"To hell with my sugar. It's my sugar, I'll do what I want with it."

"You're my girl."

"Why do you keep coming by?"

"Habit?"

"You waiting for me to die? I'm not leaving you anything. My family saw to that."

"I'm not waiting for you to die."

"I'll die soon enough."

I know. I will miss her. She knows.

"Do you know why you started coming by?"

I'm ashamed. My face grows hot.

"It was because of Linda, wasn't it?"

"We were friends."

She laughs. "Haven't seen her in years."

"Me, neither."

"What became of her?"

"She transferred to another school. I think…I think I frightened her."

"Sleep with her?"

I cough.

"Doesn't matter. You were patient, I'll give you that. Doesn't tell me why you keep coming back, always bringing me something sweet."

"The stories you tell…fascinate me."

"Did you know I knew your grandfather?"

"What?"

"Long, long ago. I remember he carried a little boy around with him. Was that you?"

"You knew my Grandfather?"

"I couldn't get pregnant. He had me smoke a cigarette. I called him a fool. He said I'd miscarry. I did. Couldn't have children after that."

"I'm so sorry."

"Everything worked out, though. My husband died, left me rich. I married a man who had a family and needed my money. We had a good life. I would've liked to have children of my own, though."

"I don't know what to say."

"I thought you kept coming by for spite, one day you'd tell me who you were and tell me your grandfather cursed me."

"Not our way."

Her palm cradles a piece of Seafoam, her hand stops midway to her mouth. "You're like your grandfather?"

"In some ways. A little. I guess."

"I'm going to die soon."

The Seafoam goes in her mouth. I study her palm as she reaches for another.

Yes. She will. Soon.

"Know what I'd really like?"

"Kids of your own?"

She laughs. "My husband and I used to dance. I was quite the dancer. Did you know that? Every Saturday night, the Stardust Ballroom. We really cut the rug, as they used to say."

"I didn't know."

Her hand reaches out to me. Arthritic fingers work to hold mine. Seafoam crumbs filter through my fingers. "I'd love to dance with him again. Forever. Can you do that?"

I lean over, kiss her forehead.

A final gift. I shape a bag of oceans, of stars, fill it with a Moment of Eternity.

"Sure. I can do that."

Chapter 70

Hall of Mirrors

I recite the numbers in reverse order they were given to me.

Abrianna, the grad student testing me, is impressed. "You only hesitated a moment at the beginning, then you went right through them. What were you doing when you were hesitating?"

I had to find the spirit watching me read the numbers. Spirit memories are better than mine.

But I don't say that. Instead, "Organizing my thoughts."

I match words by category. First the words are given to me randomly, then the categories randomly. My guides are amused by the Two-Legs' tricks and tell me what words go with what categories.

Abrianna calls Dr. Parker over and shows him her notes on me. "He's amazing."

Dr. Parker's eyebrows lift slightly. "Impressive, surely. Do you know what hyperthymesia is?"

"No, but if you hum a few bars..."

Abrianna chuckles and bats her eyes at me. Dr. Parker smiles dismissively. "Have you always had a good memory?"

"I don't remember."

"Would you be willing to take part in a different kind of study?"

"What's the pay?"

"Two-hundred dollars for an eight hour session. All you have to do is relax while we monitor you. Nothing painful, nothing intrusive or invasive. Ever hear of a sensory-deprivation tank?"

***

Dr. Parker shares the lab with Dr. Caico in the basement of one of Duke University's old Trinity buildings. My skin goosepimples and the stone walls sweat from the cold. I stand outside a room with a legend over the door reading "Hall of Mirrors." The room is lit by the green backlight of computer screens. Students carry clipboards back and forth. A few wear lab coats and swagger, giving directions to the others. There's a strange tomato scent I can't place.

A picture window in one wall reveals the next room. The floor is an array of cables leading to a bizarre looking washing machine.

Abrianna spots me outside the door and comes to get me, light on her feet. She wraps an arm through mine and pulls me into the computer room.

"Gio's here, everybody."

There's an uneven chorus of "Hi, Gio"s. Some wave. A few heads come up from computer screens.

"Dr. Parker'll be here in a few. Hungry? Thirsty?" She points to a pizza box and an ice chest of sodas.

"Got any water?"

Swagger One comes over, checks my vitals. "Okay if we draw blood?"

"How much you going to take?"

Swagger One has Dr. Parker's smile.

Abrianna brings over a tray. "I'll do it, Gio. I'm a phlebotomist."

"I thought you were a Presbyterian."

***

Dr. Parker goes over my tank data with me. "You fell asleep?"

"If you say so."

"Your body went into hyper relaxation. Sleep beyond sleep. But your mind was extremely active. Were you hallucinating?"

"How would I know?"

"Any strange feelings or experiences?"

"No more than usual."

〜

Drs. Parker and Caico sit across from me in a study room. "Your reactions are fascinating, Gio."

"Thanks."

"Unfortunately, we can't use you in our studies."

"Did I pee in your tank or something?"

Dr. Parker smiles. Dr. Caico genuinely laughs. "No, your results are so far off the norm we can't use them. You'd skew the study, make it worthless. We're researching normal people. You're not."

"Not normal?"

Dr. Parker shakes his head. Dr. Caico reaches across and pats my hand. "It's not a bad thing, Gio. You're kind of like a world class athlete. Give you the ball and the rest of us might as well get off the court."

"How about we look for a bunch of world class athletes and form a team?"

Dr. Parker shakes his head. "We don't have the research funds for that."

I shrug, stand up. "Okay. Can I get a copy of my results? My folder?"

"I doubt you'd understand them."

I repeat conversations he and Dr. Caico have had, explaining the flaws in their reasoning. I mention a few of their lectures and offer suggestions on where the literature is obsolete. I explain how a few of their research paradigms will result in flawed papers.

"How do you know these things?"

My Guides laugh. I chuckle with them. "I studied you while you studied me."

Dr. Caico looks from me to Dr. Parker and back. "Jack, we've got to get him in our program. We have some openings, don't we?"

I take my folder from his limp hand. "No thanks. This will be enough. It's all I wanted, anyway."

"What do you want it for?"

I want it because my Spirit Guides told me to get involved in this study. They tell me I'll need it someday. "It'll be a good conversation piece. May save my hide someday."

Chapter 71

Atlantic City

"Hi. We haven't met. I'm Randy Westphal. I run this casino." He offers me his hand and subtly nods at the two men who escorted me to his office. They leave, close the door. His cerulean eyes quickly inventory me as he smiles. His suit fits without showing creases or folds as he moves, nor does it bunch when he reaches into his vest pocket. He pulls out an initialed gold case, pops it open. "Cigarette?" His thick black hair is as smooth as a helmet on his head. Two gray patches flare above his temples, back but not far, like some kind of sports league insignia.

I shake my head, no.

"Smart. Damn things'll kill you. Mind if I smoke?"

I shrug.

He closes the case without taking a cigarette, puts it back in his pocket. "Nah. Damn things'll probably kill me, too."

His office is plush, dark, with windows that look down on the entire gambling floor. He motions me to a well-cushioned chair on one side of a heavy, polished oak desk large enough to serve as a pool table. "Would you like a drink?"

"No, thanks."

"Okay. Good, good." He sits on the edge of his desk, next to me but at an angle, friendly but protected, his hands holding each other in his lap as if in prayer, and smiles as he talks.

I remember some of Grandpa's teachings. Watch the face, the hands. "*Ascolta.*"

"Let's get right down to it. How do you do it?"

"Do what?"

He cocks his head, lowers his eyelids. "What's your name, kid."

"What am I doing here?"

He purses his lips. Turns to a phone with enough buttons to dial Moscow, taps one. "Jimmy, can you put the Klondike feed on the big monitor, my office? Thanks."

He lifts an equally well buttoned remote from his desk and points it at a wall. The wall opens to reveal a bar with twelve equally sized television screens laid out 4x3.

A moment later a skycam's view of the top of my head, the table I played at, the dealer monitoring me, and my hands on the cards fills all twelve screens as a single, unified image. One. Big. Monitor.

"That you, kid with no name?"

Another of Grandpa's lessons; tell as much truth as people can handle but never lie. "Never seen my head from that angle."

Randy Westphal chuckles. "Kid - and I do wish you'd tell me your name - you're young - what, twenty-five? Twenty-eight? - and that's cool, but you're stupid, and that's not."

"I really don't know what you're talking about."

He points his remote at the big monitor of twelve screens. My hands move over the cards, back and forth, forth and back. I listen to the cards tell me how they want to be played.

I win.

The dealer opens a new deck, shuffles, lays out the cards.

My hands, back and forth, forth and back, I play, I win.

A new dealer, a new deck.

I win.

Another dealer. Another deck. The dealer holds a card. My hands move over the cards. They tell me one of their brothers is missing.

I shake my head. "I'd like another deck, please."

On the big monitor, the two men who escorted me to Randy Westphal's office stand on either side of me. "Would you come with us, please?"

I look back at Randy Westphal. "I win a few games and you pull me into your office?"

He shakes his head, picks up his phone, presses a button. "Jimmy, the last twelve tapes of the kid, one on each monitor. Thanks."

In most of the screens I'm wearing the same shirt.

"Twelve times in two months. No idea how many times you were here before we caught on. You got greedy and being greedy makes you stupid. Most sharps grow a beard or shave one off, grow out their hair or shave themselves bald. They at least change their clothes. You didn't think to take your winnings and buy new clothes?"

"Clothes were never a big thing for me."

He presses a button on the remote. The screens go dark. "You sure you don't want a drink?"

I shake my head.

He presses his remote. The wall closes.

"So, what happens now. Your men break my legs or something?"

"You been watching too many Godfather movies, kid - and you still didn't tell me your name. We don't do that anymore. Some might, we don't. But we will put your name - if you ever tell me what it is - and your picture in what's called a BlackBook, kind of like being black-balled. All the casinos have copies, we share information back and forth. We don't compete; there's enough Chasers and Fish - every day folk. People who don't know what they're doing - to go around. But we share information on people like you. People who we think cheat. Even if we don't know how you cheat. And you're never allowed near a table again. Anywhere. Ever."

"I can live with that."

"I knew two others who did something like you do."

"You knew others like me?"

"I've been in this game thirty years, kid. Since before you were born. I've seen everything." He watches me. "You know you just gave yourself away, right? You basically admitted you know you're doing something. Want to tell me what it is?"

"Who were the others?"

"One died in a nuthouse in upstate New York, the other committed suicide. Both say - said - the same thing. They said they couldn't stop the voices in their heads. You hear voices in your head, son?"

"Do you hear voices, Randy Westphal?"

He claps his hands and laughs. "Christ, you got balls, kid. Balls are good, but you're still stupid and that's another bad mix; balls and stupid. I hear voices when my bosses talk to me. Listen, there's two ways this can go. One, I offer you a job. You work for us, let us know when somebody like you is working the tables."

He pauses, waits for a response. I offer none.

"B, you go in our BlackBook and we let everybody know you can't go near a table. You come in with someone, they can't go near a table. You pass outside a palace, everybody in the palace is suspect. We don't do anything else. But we're the nice guys. Other guys might see the Book, they're not so nice."

"Is that a threat?"

"It's a warning. Advice. Call it what you want. Whatever you can do, they'll want you to do it for them or not at all."

"Kind of like your offer, isn't it? Work for you or go into your book?"

He shrugs.

"Can I have time to decide?"

"Sure. You done deciding yet?"

I laugh. "No way I can keep myself out of your book?"

He looks at me, raises his eyebrows, snorts, then looks back into his hands. "Look me in the eye and tell me you don't do anything, you're just a lucky sonofabitch, and promise me you won't be lucky here or any place else ever again. Can you do that, son?"

I look into his eyes. Grandpa's lessons are still strong in me. Even when I don't remember what they are.

"I thought so. Those other two couldn't lie, either. You can't lie and you got some kind of Woo-Woo only a few people know about. Is there a club for you guys? You all get together and share your secrets? Any women in your club?"

I look away.

"Let me ask you another question. What you do - and I don't care what it is - does it only work with cards? Can you do whatever it is with people?"

I stare up at him.

"I've been waiting for somebody like you to show up for the past two years. My wife's got cancer. We've tried everything. The doctors are giving up."

The old energies surge. The Universe flows into my hands. I stand up, almost against my will. "Take me to her."

Chapter 72

Be Well

I'm riding south on the interstate and a guy in a BMW cuts me off, pulls in front of me and brakes hard to take his exit. No directional, just get out of my way.

I go onto the shoulder then into a ditch, holding on, letting the bike slow on its own, hand off the throttle, downshifting, engine braking, steering clear of the green slime covered ditch water and rocks and fallen tree limbs.

I take a moment. Breathe. See his car at the bottom of the exit going right. I spin my tire getting back up to the ramp and follow him.

I'm honking my horn and flashing my light. He gives me the finger.

He pulls into a parking lot. I follow him. He drives around the lot a few times. I play pickle, my bike faster than his car, more maneuverable, I can weave back and forth and eventually he stops by the door to a building.

People stare.

I pull up beside him. He hits the locks on his doors. I shrug, fold my arms across my chest, lean back against the sissy bar, wait.

He looks around. He waves at people. Nobody moves to help him.

I laugh, pull up my visor. "Guess you've got quite the rep, fucker. You got a car phone? Maybe you should call 911?"

His eyes widen. He reaches into the backseat, pulls up a phonebag, holds up the phone, snickers.

I snap the phone antennae off his car, snicker back. "Yeah?"

The guy holds his hands in front of his face like he's praying. His eyes redden. A tear slides down his cheek, through fuzz that someday if he's lucky might turn into a beard.

This is not how Grandpa lived.

I focus on the guy in the car with the tear sliding down his face. "What?"

This is not what Grandpa wanted for you.

I grab the driver's door handle. "What did you say?"

This is not how Grandpa said you should live.

I put my visor down, back away. "Sorry, wrong car."

I trade my bike and leathers for hiking gear and cash. My backpack weighs heavy on my shoulders. It carries my world: some books, two days change of Spring/Fall clothes, two days change of Summer clothes. I wear them all in Winter. Two rolls of toilet paper. A notebook and pen. Soap. I stop where there is work and a college or university large enough that an extra face is a clerical error and not a concern.

Today there's a convocation in the gymnasium. A guest speaker. A great man. A Nobel Laureate in Chemistry although his field is Physics. Science always interests me - Grandpa said always keep learning - and I attend.

The gym dividers are tucked against walls, the telescoping bleachers collapsed to make room for rows upon rows upon rows of chairs. I sit in 16L3: Row 16, Left, 3rd seat. There are forty-eight rows, each has a left, right, and center, and each section has fifty seats.

The entire campus is here.

He talks about receiving his Nobel in Chemistry and how it was a mistake. "I told them, 'If you had a physicist working on this it would have been solved years ago.'"

Everyone laughs.

He segways from confusion in the Nobels to confusion in life. How we all must find our paths, must learn our way, must remember what our grandfathers taught us as children.

What our grandfathers taught us as children?

We must pay attention to the energies in our lives, where they lead us, what they can teach us, how they can guide us, give us meaning, make us whole.

Energies in our lives? Guiding us? Teaching us? Making us whole?

We must grow, expand, become.

I go wide.

A gentle strength guides me away.

He keeps talking, uninterrupted.

Lower-Center-Relax-Breathe.

Go wide.

A gentle hand, like my Grandfather's, concerned that I learn from my mistakes, cradles me, redirects me.

The student in 16L2 whispers, "You okay?"

"Uh? Yeah. Just really into what this guy's saying."

"Yeah, heavy stuff."

The address is over. We exit the gym and disperse through the parking lot. I smell the evergreens encircling the cars, their musk carried by the warm morning, lifted by the bright sunshine.

Something passes through me. I stumble, brace myself against a car.

There is a voice inside me. "Oh, there you are. Hello, Gio. They said I'd find you here."

Every experience I've had, a drowning man's life passing before him, each memory held up, inspected.

Experiences. Situations. My responses. Fascinate.

"Capture moonlight in your hands."

Something my Grandpa taught me.

"What did you learn?"

To hold wonder.

"Shape it."

I make a lampshade brighter than the light it covers. Grandma smiles and cuddles me. Grandpa kisses me as she holds me in her arms. "Good, Gio. Very good."

"What did you learn?

To fashion gifts of what I do.

"Walk up a moonbeam. Hitch a ride on sunlight."

I remember.

A way to visit some of Grandpa's friends. Some of my friends. I'd forgotten.

I feel a smile.

"Good. Learn."

The gentle hand pulls away.

"No! Wait!"

Students and professors, administrators, walk around me and stop, stare. "You okay, young man?"

A limo climbs the slight hill out of the parking lot. A hand waves as a face pulls back into rear seat's shade.

"Good to meet you, Gio. Be well."

Teachers

Chapter 73

Home

They said?

I am known?

The possibility terrifies me.

I am more familiar with the lies parents and schoolmates tell me than in the memories of Grandpa and his friends.

Three hundred miles later I knock on my parents' door in the early afternoon. My mother answers.

"Oh. Gio. I didn't expect you."

"No one expects the Spanish Inquisition."

She frowns, unaware of the reference. "Do you want to come in for a while. I could make coffee."

I am not welcome, not even as a guest.

We sit in the backroom sipping coffee. She eyes my pack. It leans against the banister that stopped me from falling downstairs. "Is that all you have?"

"I don't need much."

"The college called. They said you quit." Her upper lip curls and her face transforms to a dog's snarling. "Like you did in high school."

"Point of view error."

She shakes the idea away, not wanting to consider.

"Do you know how much money that cost, sending you there?"

"Is Dad coming home tonight? I want to know if he can get me a job in the meat packing plant."

"The usual time, five-thirty, six o'clock. He won't get you a job. You're too much of a risk. He'll pull strings for you and you'll disappoint him. You always do."

"I have a high art."

"Can you make sense for once in your life?" The dog's face is gone, replaced by a viper, coiling upon itself, not coming near me.

"Why do I frighten you so?"

"You don't know what you're talking about."

Lower-Center-Relax-Breathe.

"You hate me...no, that's not it. Close, but not quite"

My eyes close, my nostrils flare. I track the scent like a wolf tracking a hare.

"Not me."

The smell is wrenching, hideous, the smell of offal left in the August sun.

"Grandpa. You hated Grandpa?"

"Stop it."

"No, but closer. What did Grandpa ever do to you?"

She raises her voice. "Stop it."

Mine remains calm. "What did Grandpa - "

I hear Grandpa's voice in her head, a memory. "You'll never *Know*, Daughter. That's okay. Not everyone can."

I focus on the energies around her. I remember one of Daskele's teachings: "Know the energies in a person's life and you know them better than they know themselves."

"You hate me to hurt Grandpa? Because he wouldn't teach you?"

She bangs her cup down on the end table. "Shut up."

"Wow, Ma. That explains a lot. All those times you schemed ways to put something over on dad. Trying to show your dead father how clever you were? That you deserved to learn? To be taught?"

She stands and screams at me. "Shut Up!"

I remember Grandpa talking with his friends while I ate sweetcakes and sipped milk flavored with coffee. "*The Knowing* chooses its own."

"You are lucky it chose your boy, Giovanni."

"Yes."

I stand, lift my pack. "It had nothing to do with Grandpa, Ma. It had everything to do with you. But what originally turned your heart black?"

A spirit hovers over her. So strong. Undeniable. My head cocks left, my ears upturned, a dog hearing its master's voice. My father, standing in his work clothes, forcing her to bend over in front of him. His head bursts and is replaced by a donkey's, its ears standing straight and focused on her, braying so loud and sounding like laughter. My mother whimpers as he forces himself in.

I laugh, shake my head and laugh.

She sits tightly, not relaxed, at an angle to me, like the Queen of England in an interview caught off guard, unprepared for some question, the dignity of her office questioned, revealed as tainted by someone who should know nothing.

"What? What are you laughing at?"

"Is Dad still talking about all the sex I got when I was in high school?"

The viper collapses, crushed under the weight of a bloating donkey, now fully a donkey, crushing her as it falls upon her, exhausted.

"Is he still jealous? What, you didn't think I could hear him talking, telling you how great it must be to be free and fucking whatever caught my eye?"

The garage door motor whirs to life.

"I'll ask Pa if he can get me a job. If not, I'll be off."

The queen is gone. All that remains are robes, bloodied and torn, covered in filth and excrement. She keeps her face turned from me and there is no power in her voice.

"Go away. Get out. You're not staying here even if he does get you a job."

She faces me, a glint in her eye, the hint of a smile on her face.

"I told the nurse when she brought you to me she had the wrong child. I was right."

I laugh. The hint of her smile flees at the sound, her eyes dull.

"Remember what I said before, Ma? 'I have a high art'? It's from Archliochus, a Greek poet."

"So?"

"I have a high art: I wound with great cruelty those who wound me."

Chapter 74

Phobos

A pink, far-sighted rhinoceros wearing black-and-white polka dot boxers and readers stands on the other side of my bedroom.

How did it get in?

I can't hear the clock tick. I look up and see the second-hand stopped, frozen in time. It is dark, the windows open, the screens untouched. Moonlight stops halfway between sky and earth. Some stars *twink*, others *kle*. None do both. The sky has stopped. There is no wind.

The pink, far-sighted rhinoceros stands in front the sliding doors to my His-n-Hers closets, the Hers with no Her to fill it. His front legs are behind him, massive legs turned into massive arms clasping hooves turned into hands.

It brings its hands forward. It's holding a pointer like those used by Mrs. Woodbury when I didn't keep quiet.

It whacks the foot of my bed and bellows with a voice like cannon-fire. "Do I have your attention?"

I nod vigorously.

I hear an old-style movie projector clicking as film winds through it. A black-and-white movie appears on my closet door as if it's a movie screen.

"This is your life." Whack on the screen.

Another projector starts up. A different film. A color Super-8. On Hers closet doors.

"This is what your life could be." Whack.

He backs up until he's beside my closet doors and looks over his readers at me. The movie continues flickering along.

"This is your life." Whack.

He walks over to Hers closet doors. "This is what your life could be." Whack.

Back and forth. Every painful episode of my life on my closet doors, a colorized Jimmy Stewart's *It's a Wonderful Life* going into the future on Hers.

Back and forth and back and forth and whack and whack and whack and whack and finally a deafening *WHACK!* on the foot of my bed.

Isn't anybody else in the apartment building hearing this?

Cannon-fire from the far side of the bedroom. "Because this is your life, not theirs!"

The movies end, the reels of film flap flap flap as the projector keep them spinning.

"What am I supposed to do?"

"Decide!"

The rhinoceros is gone.

Except for the tip of the pointer, writing in the night over my bed.

"Phobos. Call Now. 1-800-U-DECIDE. Operators are standing by."

The clock ticks, the moon shines, a breeze moves the curtains, stars twinkle.

I look back. The pointer and writing are gone.

Chapter 75

Knock, knock, knock

A big wooden door, made from trees and branches all woven together, leaves grow out of limbs making eaves and lintels. I can see through a little window. The flickering light is a candle. On the other side of the door, sitting at a table, the flickering candle casting large shadows in the empty room, I sit reading a book. The book lies flat beside a tray of Granny Smith apples, strawberries, bananas, and (I squint to be sure) peaches. Another tray has some asiago and a breadboard sports a steaming loaf of *pugliese* bread, a slice cut off. The me in the room has a wine glass in his hand. I take a sip, look up, see myself looking in, smile and lift the glass in salute.

I haven't had a meal like that since Grandpa and Grandma passed. So simple, so delicious.

I step forward, onto the mat of tightly woven hay and flax lying in front of the door.

It lifts, spins, knocks me back, away from the door. It grows four legs, a spiky tail, a giant head, golden fur.

"Hello, Gio."

"I'd forgotten about you."

My stomach growls as the scents of the bread, the cheese, the wine, the peaches, and other fruit filter out to me.

"You're hungry?"

"I didn't realize how much."

"Are you afraid?"

"Not anymore. Is my Buppa in there? I didn't see him."

"No, only you can go through this door."

"I already have. I'm in there."

"How many times?"

"What?"

The creature smiles, its many needle-like teeth show clearly. It drools and acid steam rises from a ground that isn't there.

"Do you want to go in?"

"May I please?"

"Do you remember how to knock?"

I open my heart. It knocks three times.

The Guardian stands aside. "Good answer."

Chapter 76

Grandmother Running Water

"Come in. We knew you were coming."

A tall, older woman, full-bodied but not fat, her face and hands darkened from fieldwork, sits behind a glass counter in a Native American craft shop. She hunches over something she works on, I'm not sure what, and it has her focus. A little bell over the door jingles as I walk in.

I look around. There's no one else in the store. "I'm sorry. Are you talking to me?"

She doesn't take her eyes from her work. "Yes, Gio. I'm talking to you."

"You know me?"

"You're John's boy."

"I think you have me confused with someone else. My father's name is Joseph."

I feel her smile but can't see her face. "Not him. John. Giovanni Fortuna. John's boy."

The craft store changes to a woodland setting. The woman sits in a cove, except now she is a stream of sparkling, flowing water hunched over something in front of her.

"Running Water!"

"You remember me!"

I rush forward. She looks up. It is her. I can tell by the water's sound. I put my hand in the water, wiggle my fingers. The water chuckles. I pull my hand back and the standing stream becomes my teacher, my friend, sitting over a glass counter in a Native American craft store.

"You said 'we' knew I was coming?"

"Look again."

The small store is filled with Spider, Wolf, Whale, Coyote, Hummingbird, Cougar, Mountain Lion, Mountain, Ocean, Moon, Stars... All my friends from childhood. "You're all here."

Spider's chalicere grate. "A-a-ll-w-aa-a-a-ys-s-s-be-en-n-w-w-wi-ith-th-y-yo-ou, wa-aa-ait-ti-i-nn-ng."

Grandmother Running Water comes out from behind the counter, opens her arms to me. I am a child again and she holds me while I cry.

I am so happy.

Chapter 77

Tae-Sek

Five-seven. Asian features. No English. Thick, rich black hair poking out from a green janitor's cap, the name of the company in red letters on a white background in front. He tips his cap to me and his hair rolls like a wave about to crash on his high forehead of a beach. Laugh lines like lightning bolts radiate from the corners of his eyes and mouth.

The night foreman introduces me. "Tae-Sek, this is the new guy. He's going to be working with you. Okay?"

Tae-Sek smiles and nods.

"Show him where the supplies are."

Smile and nod.

"Give him his own cart. He can work beside you until he figures things out. Alright?"

Smile and nod.

The foreman pulls me aside. "Look, nobody knows how much English this guy understands, so if you have any problems, just come see me, okay?"

"Yeah, sure."

Green overalls, "Tae-Sek" stenciled in red on a white background over a chest pocket with either a pen or mechanical pencil sticking out, I don't know which, he stands beside his janitor's cart.

I hold out my hand. "Hi, Tae-Sek. My name's Gio."

He nods, pulls a mop and bucket from his cart and holds them out to me.

I take them. He turns and pushes his cart.

I follow him to the killing room floor. Blood everywhere from eight hours of slaughtering cattle. Longer if it's a high production day, holidays coming up, higher demand. Workers line up barrels of offal for a forklift to transport to the loading dock leaving a stench like a battlefield without the explosions.

"Worked here long?"

I can't tell if he nods. He says nothing, just keeps walking.

I bring Jules Verne's *Twenty-Thousand Leagues Under the Sea* to read during breaks on my second night. Tae-Sek doesn't talk.

On my third night he watches me read.

"Do you read, Tae-Sek?"

He smiles and nods.

"Do you know Jules Verne where you come from?"

Smile, nod.

"Where do you come from?"

Smile, nod.

Break ends. We go back to work. I walk behind him.

I mimic what he does, the way he does it.

To learn.

I may not know who or what I am, but I'll be a damn good janitor if nothing else.

That'll make my parents proud.

Grandpa and Grandma wouldn't mind. Always do your best no matter what you do.

The next night he pulls an apple from a pocket inside his overalls. He twists it in two equal and clean halves in his hands. He holds half out to me.

"Thanks, Tae-Sek."

Third week of eight-hour nights. I walk beside him. I watch. I mimic his moves as best I can.

Sometimes he corrects me. He moves my hands to different positions on the mops. He shows me how to follow the natural gradient of the floors so water always collects in the same spot.

One night I pick up a mop and he shakes his head, no, and wags his finger at me.

"What is it, Tae-Sek? What am I doing wrong?"

He takes the mop from me and places my hand on his stomach.

I'm touching a rock.

He keeps my hand there and inhales. His breath moves through him like lava through a mountain. He motions me to keep my hand on his stomach, takes my mop in his hands, and starts on the floor.

He moves the mop in rhythm with his breathing. Exhale push, inhale pull, relax. Wax on, wax off. Focus.

"But don't concentrate."

I pull my hand away and stare.

He mops the floor.

"What did you say?"

A deep, sonorous voice with a hint of laughter. "Don't concentrate."

"You speak English?"

He stands and looks at me, the handle of the mop across his chest, in his hands, slightly resting on it. "*Aniyo, yeong-eoleul moshaeyo.*"

"Beg pardon?"

"Don't concentrate. You use only one body if you do that." His mouth never moves from its wry smile.

I looked around. "Okay, enough fun with the new guy. Who else is in here?"

Tae-Sek taps my chest with the mop handle. I hear a sonorous voice. "Blink."

Two great cats circle him. They shift from lion to panther to tiger to jaguar to tom to bob to lynx to cougar and a dozen other felines I've never seen and back, with each step a cat flows into the form of another, characteristics and behaviors shift from one to the other. Tae-Sek's head is bowed, his face hidden by the brim of his janitor's cap. His hands run along the cats' backs as they walk around him.

I open my mouth and he looks up, no longer a man, not even anything Asian, a muscular feline dwarfing the big cats around him, dwarfing me, his cat-eyed face, neither flat like a man's nor pointed like a cat's, and furred, as are his hands, both striped like a tiger's and spotted like a leopard's. His fangs are large but not like a sabertooth's. He sniffs the air in my direction and his eyes, black with red pupils, focus on me. A paw-hand places a pad-finger on my lips, silencing me.

"Blink."

I blink again.

Tae-Sek stands before me. A petite Asian man.

My legs buckle.

His hand swoops under my arm. He holds me up. I weigh two of him. One and half, easy.

He doesn't strain.

The deep sonorous voice, a man's voice speaking with the purr of a great cat, inside me. "Time to learn."

～

We are in a park, middle of the summer, a warm, sunny afternoon. I wear sweatpants, a t-shirt, socks and sneakers. He wears his green janitor overalls and cap.

He puts my hand on his chest. "*Nal mil-eo jwo.*" Push me.

He doesn't move.

"Push me."

I shove.

He stands, smiling, unmoving.

"Put your shoulders into it."

I look around. Someone seeing this might think I'm attempting to hurt him.

I put my shoulder against his chest, lean, brace my feet, groan, grunt.
Nothing.

I sweat, breathe heavy.

"Better, not good, and better."

I stand up.

"Here, like this."

He puts his hand on my chest. Lower-Center-Relax-Breathe. Something lifts me into the air. I fly back about fifteen feet.

"Now I show you this."

He kneels, bows to the earth, says something so softly I can't hear, a private prayer.

He places his palm on the earth. Lower-Center-Relax-Breathe. I feel the earth shake under my feet.

"To do that, you must ask."

Hence his prayer.

"Now again." He puts my hand on his chest. "Lower-Center-Relax-Breathe. Each time, your bodies unite, come together."

Ah. Emotional moments. Lost in thought. In prayer. Running and getting in the zone, you don't know how far you've run and could go on forever.

"Each is a body taking control, being first among others. Sometimes this must happen. But to do this -" His hand flashes forward faster than I can follow. His overall cuff snaps like a whip. " - you must have all bodies together."

I put my hand on his chest.

"Lower-Center-Relax-Breathe."

I do.

His eyes close. I feel hands on my different bodies, something not felt since Grandpa's gentle touch. He guides my bodies like building blocks. "This one a little more here. That one a little more there. More right. Down. Lower. Lower. This one, more here."

"Now!"

He falls back maybe five feet.

"Very good, Gio! Very good. You practice. Move things, yes. Also move through things. Move a little, be in things. Or separate a body to do a specific thing, something the other bodies can't do, even together."

A tear leaves his eye. "Also a defense when the time comes."

I look at him, unsure.

~

Tae-Sek hands me an apple. I cleave it in two with my hands and offer him half.

He smiles. "*Ige uli majimag bam-iya.*"

He rarely speaks English to me, wanting me to use all my bodies to understand his words, echoing one of Grandpa's lessons; People speak with more than words. Learn to listen to everything they say.

"This our last night together?"

He nods and looks at me with cat's-eyes. The transformation moves over his face and he stands over me, a cat-like being again, a shape he's shared only three times in our work together.

He looks down at me and purrs. "Time for you to meet another."

I nod. I know this. This is how it happens. To understand is to accept, to learn is to grow.

"Why did you - "

The paw-hand places a pad-finger on my lips. "You protected my cats."

Chapter 78

A'bli'g'moodj

I sit in the back of the lecture hall, a class on psychometry, the scientific measurement of mental capacities and processes and personality, what can be measured and what can't.

I'm in the lecture hall by accident. I stop at large colleges and universities because I can sleep in a chair or claim I forgot my meal ticket and no one cares. I slept in the back of this lecture hall and stayed for the class.

The professor stands beside an overhead projector, a map of the brain at the top of the screen, a picture of WWII pathologists removing a dead soldier's brain in the middle, a phrenology chart on the bottom. "We test for needle movement. We're not really measuring what someone does because people are too complex. We only measure what we know how to measure, not necessarily what needs to be measured. We search for what we already believe is there to be found."

He looks down, shakes his head.

"Real learning happens when the unexpected occurs, when the unprecedented presents itself, when our brain - in western and modern society - exhausts itself. Then we become sensitive to what's beyond what our heads tell us should be there.

"But not all of us. Few of us, really."

His eyes rove the class, resting on me.

He knows I don't belong.

"Few."

The campus clocktower tolls the end of class.

The professor laughs. "Saved by the bell."

I rearrange my pack as students shuffle out. The professor approaches, his eyes intent on me, my features. I turn to hide my face, hurry my packing, prepare my excuses.

An ocean wave washes over me, founders me. I come up for air.

The professor holds out his hand.

"Hello, Gio."

⌇

"We have many names and titles depending on many things. I am Roger, professor of psych and communication sciences at Harvard. I am Ch'i Lin and teach roots of western philosophy at the Beijing School of Economics. And sometimes I am A'bli'g'moodj."

We stand in the center of twelve men and women sitting in a store loft near the intersection of Routes 9 and 128 west of Boston. Windows on all four sides let the afternoon light in.

I am beside and slightly behind him. I glance at him, wondering. This is A'bli'g'moodj? The Frog Prince?

He nods towards me. "He is Mani He."

I've never heard that name before.

"I've asked him to help me teach today."

"You did?"

A nervous laugh from the circle.

He smiles. "I did. Someone draw the blinds, please."

Two men and two women rise, each takes a wall, the blinds are drawn. Mid-afternoon dark.

A'bli'g'moodj invites me to sit on the floor with him. There is a small incense burner on a pedestal between us. He lights a piece of charcoal, pulls a tobacco pouch from his pocket, sprinkles some on the glowing ember, breathes on it, a wisp of a flame spouts.

"Blow on the flame, Gio. Let it know you're a friend."

I lean forward.

He shakes his head. "The first lesson."

I nod, pull back. Lower-Center-Relax-Breathe. Eyes close. Lean forward. A long, controlled breath. It lasts minutes.

He says to those gathered. "The first lesson, and the power of Breath."

Murmurings.

What am I teaching? What are they learning from me? What am I learning from him?

"When we met, you sensed something. What did you sense, Gio?"

"The water? The ocean?"

He nods. "Very good. There are people who've read of the ocean, who can tell you lots about it, but who've never experienced it. A friend of mine, a river engineer from the mid-west, saw the ocean for the first time and thought, 'There's got to be one hell of a dam out there somewhere.'"

Laughter.

"But the point is, you cannot share what you have not experienced."

Something Grandpa said: Don't feed someone when you're hungry.

"You may provide information, but not knowledge. Enough knowledge, experience, you might gain wisdom."

I know the reference: T.S. Eliot.

"Some people say the opposite of wisdom is ignorance. Incorrect. The opposite of wisdom is folly."

The small flame flares briefly, swirling the air above it, sparks like microscopic fireflies flitter before me.

"Go back, Gio. Go back."

Direction is meaningless. A word. I understand the meaning, the knowledge.

I'm caught in the swirling firefly dust, pulled in from its edge. Winds gather me, lift me. I leave the room, leave the intersection, leave Massachusetts, the continent, carried by the winds. At the edge of the atmosphere radiation from the stars collects me and takes me higher, somewhere out in space.

The voice. I remember from childhood. "Lower-Center-Relax-Breathe, Gio. Remember The First Lesson."

Some other energy, gravity, takes the sun's place. I'm traveling faster than light. Swirling nebulae surround me, collect me. A spiral armed galaxy.

There is a pause.

I move towards it.

Faster, faster, diving into the galaxy as if into oceans, spinning spinning spinning...

But not me. Everything around me. I am held safe in some center.

I'm getting smaller and smaller and smaller.

Through whorls of gas, of stars, along currents of light, through the atmosphere, through the room, through the smoke, through the flame, into the charcoal, untouched by the heat, through to its center.

I see its separate molecules, its atoms, its electrons in clouds over a pulsing of particles and then into these.

And at its center, I stop. The wisp of a flame, swirling, but in the shape of a man.

"Who are you?"

I remember. The voice of fire, the sound of a mountain. The flaming man holds its hand out to me. It's filled with stars and planets and galaxies. It breathes on them and they swirl in its voice. "I am WhirlWind. I share all that I am with you."

"What are you?"

The flaming man explodes into hurricanes and tornadoes and storms on the sun and planets circling and nebulae and galaxies and the universe itself.

"I am all things that spin."

A'bli'g'moodj calls me. "When you're ready, come back, Gio. Come back."

I Lower-Center-Relax-Breathe, but in reverse, turning, changing, returning to the room where I started.

The people stare at me. Their faces show alarm.

A'bli'g'moodj rises from the floor beside me and takes a seat in the circle.

"Now, Gio. What can you teach us?"

Chapter 79

Jean Reveaux

New Orleans in the middle of summer. Heavy rain for about five minutes. The clouds release their burden and are dispersed by the sun. It boils Lake Pontchartrain, the Mississippi Delta, and the shrimping channels of the Gulf into a fog it gathers into his arms. Soon it can't bear the weight and again releases their waters back to them as heavy rain. The pattern repeats throughout the day.

The rainbows are glorious. Sit in any one spot along a brick, stone, or plaster exterior wall too long and little green lizards scurry over you. Some become familiar and wait for crumbs. They don't like saltines. Little balls of rye bread are a favorite.

I wonder if they use them to make fly sandwiches.

I sit on a wooden bench with a cement base. My pack rests beside me, leaning against the armrest. There's a park behind me, obscured by a small board of bus schedules, public events, meetings, and church invitations. Someone's tacked a few business cards there. One of the little green lizards climbs up the base and stops, watching me, from the far side of the seat. It's got one front leg lifted as if hesitant to put it down, as if it might make too much noise.

I have a package of melting raisinettes in my shirt pocket. I pull it out and shake a few onto the bench between us. "Raisinette?"

A deep voice comes around the notices. "Chester, you don't eat no Raisinettes. You know they gives you gas."

A small, wrinkled black man appears. He's dressed for this heat: woven leather huaraches with no socks, light khaki pedal pushers, and a sky blue cheesemaker's shirt open in front. The little green lizard turns and looks up at him. It taps its feet like the bench is too hot to stand on; left front-right rear, right front-left rear, left front-right rear.

"Ah, go ahead. You know I can't say no to you."

The little green lizard moves faster than I can follow and swallows the Raisinettes one by one, not chewing.

When there are none left, the lizard looks back at the little black man. It flicks its tongue out and wipes its left eye.

"You got any more Raisinettes?"

I hand him the box. He puts it in his shirt pocket and sits on the bench, on the far side of the lizard.

"Come on."

The little lizard crawls up his pants leg, his shirt, and into his pocket. It sounds like he's rummaging through the box of Raisinettes.

"Don't you shit in my pockets now, hear?"

The little man looks at my pack. "You got laundry?"

"Yeah."

A bus size version of Chester pulls up. The scales on the side of its body form stairs leading to an open air interior with seats. No one's onboard. The little old man climbs in, turns, holds his hand out to me.

"Come on. Chester and me, we know a place. Good learning there, too."

~

Jean Reveaux is a Vooduan "low-down" papa man. He nudges me. "I watch you long time, my man. You're a good waiter."

I nod.

"You practice. What your Grandfather taught you. Very good."

He knew my Grandfather?

He nods at my unspoken question. "You work at your lessons from Tae-Sek and A'bli'g'moodj much. That's good."

He knows Tae-Sek and A'bli'g'moodj?

He nods again. "You're a good listener, too. That's very good."

I shrug.

He smiles. Bright, strong, white teeth. His canines are longer than most people's. He catches me staring and shakes his head. "*Ascolta.*"

"*Tu parli Siciliano?*" I ask. You speak Sicilian?

He shakes his head, still smiling. "No, your Grandfather does."

I say it out loud. "You knew my Grandfather?"

He laughs and slaps his skinny thighs. His N'awlins patois is gone. "Everybody knew your Grandfather, Gio. He was strong. We all worried when he passed over."

"Worried about what?"

"Every time one of us passes over, a little more of *The Knowledge* is lost. He said he taught you all he knew."

"He did?"

"Do you remember your Grandfather's garden?"

Joyous memories race through me. "Yes. Very much."

He smiles and pats my thigh. Chester pops out of his pocket, rolling a Raisinette between little lizard lips. "You are his garden, Gio. He left all his knowledge as seeds in you for us to find and water."

I lean back, wondering about my life. About Mrs. Langlois, Mrs. Johnson, about college, Helga, my wanderings, Tae-Sek, A'bli'g'moodj.

How many more have there been, watching me, waiting?

"How'm I doing so far?"

His patois is back. He pulls his shirt pocket open wide and looks in. "Chester, did you piss in my pocket?"

The lizard bus stops in front of a laundromat. Jean taps my arm. "We get out here. Come on."

The laundromat is empty save for a mid-forties couple, a young boy and a young teenage girl. The man, boy, and girl are dressed for New Orleans summer. The woman is covered head to toe, only the skin of her face and hands exposed to the air. She carries a scent of sickness, one I'm unfamiliar with. Washing and drying machines, dented with white paint chips flaking off, are a few stairs down from street level. Lawn chairs in need of new webbing run the length of the center of the room. At the opposite end of the laundromat are a few more stairs leading up to a small room with sparkling, brilliantly white machines, their logos proudly intact on their fronts. No dents or dings I can see. There are padded chairs there. I see a table with magazines on it, and a water cooler at the far end. A sign hangs above the entrance to the small room: "Whites Only"

The man points at the small room. "Only sheets and underwear up there, Rose."

Jean hurries down the stairs towards them. "Oh, no, no, no," he said. "Only white folks can do their laundry up there. There's no colored folks allowed."

Afternoon light comes in the laundromat windows. Jean's ebony skin seems radiant, almost transparent. He walks up to Rose, closes one eye and stares at her with the other.

He inhales deeply, grabs her arm and pulls it to his face.

Rose pulls back. "Let go of me. Jim, stop him. Get him away from me."

The man, Jim, doesn't seem to notice.

Jean puts her arm down by her side. "I know what that is. I can fix it."

"Jim?"

Jim sorts clothes.

Jean pulls up the woman's sleeve revealing reddened, scaling, flaking flesh.

"This. I can fix this. Do you want me to fix this?"

Rose says nothing, frozen in the heat. Jim carries a basket of laundry out the door. The boy and girl follow.

Jean holds a finger up to Rose. "You do your laundry. I'll be right back."

I follow him outside. He takes Chester from his pocket. "Chester, you know that juice we made last week? Now we know why we made it. Go fetch me the bottle. Hurry back."

The lizard bus pulls up. Jean puts Chester on a seat. The bus runs away on stubby lizard legs, its lizard feet slapping the pavement as it hurries away.

"You got a watch?"

I hold up my wrists and shake my head, no.

"Doesn't matter. We stop time if we have to."

I hear a siren. Instead of the ee-EE-YOAR-EE-ee-ee-EE-YOAR-EE-ee it goes ee-e-or and fades. A police car crawls past us.

The lizard bus pulls up. Chester is on the seat nearest the door. A small green glass bottle with a white screw-on lid is next to him.

"Ah, you're so good, Chester. You're so good."

Jean picks up the bottle. Chester jumps to his hand, runs up his arm across his chest and into his pocket. "Remember, no shitting in my pocket."

Inside, Jean gives Rose the tiny bottle. "You take a drop of this and rub it in. Just a drop. You'll be fixed." He snaps his fingers. "No time flat."

Jim comes in. He looks from Rose to Jean to me and back. "Everything okay, Rose?"

Rose opens her pocketbook. "What do I owe you?"

Jean wags his finger and shakes his head. He says nothing. He walks out and taps my arm on the way. "Come on. Our bus is waiting."

I sit beside him. Chester pokes his head out and flicks his tongue at me.

"She didn't pay you?

"Not yet. I'm too expensive. She'll pay you in -" he rolls his eyes as if following a rainbow from one horizon to the other " - twenty years."

"What's in the bottle?"

"Your future."

Chapter 80

Grandmother Apara

A beautiful, blue-eyed, middle-aged woman meets me at the door of a small home overlooking a tidal pool on the Rhode Island coast. Her long, white hair flows down her shoulders and covers her tie-died blouse like a veil. She reaches for me and her hair mantles around her as if she moves through clouds. The palm of her hand rests against my chest, her dark-skinned fingers move slightly, sensing. Her touch is warm, not hot.

"You have a strong heart."

"Thank you."

She welcomes me into her home and guides me to a large room. No furniture, blue walls that match her eyes, a stone fireplace with two small, charred logs on its grill, and a bay window, a smaller window on each side stand as acolytes, each open to let air in. I can hear the ocean, the waves breaking in the distance, and closer, gulls.

We walk across a thick carpet that reminds me of sand paintings. She moves like a flame tendered by the wind. I'm not sure her bare feet touch the floor.

She sits cross-legged beside the fireplace and motions me to join her. She is blind.

"Four-Body Discernment is the ability to tell where a person is in relation to their Four-Bodies. It can be quite helpful in determining how to help people through different problems and situations in their lives. I use Four-Body Discernment because it is simple and elegant." She pauses, cocks her head, listening to something I can't hear. "Each technique, ceremony, ritual, aspect, at its center and done properly and well, is simple and elegant."

I nod, then look away. She can't see what I do.

She laughs, reaches over and pats my leg. "I may not see, but I can borrow."

I scan the room. Who is she borrowing from?

"From Wind."

My foolishness, my lack of understanding. "I didn't know that was possible."

"Now you do and you're that much closer to your path. Every mistake gets us closer to our path. So long as we recognize our mistakes we can learn from them. People who never make mistakes have no teachers."

"Thank you."

"May I?"

"Yes, please."

I feel her move within.

"You SpiritTalk. You SpiritTalked with -" I feel her sifting through my memories " - Roseanne, when you went to college, and others." I feel her inspect my experience with Larry. "Often these tools overlap. Use Four-Body Discernment with SpiritTalking and you know which Spirits talk for, to, and from which body."

"My work with Larry. I upset you."

"Four-Body Work - helping people find their Centered-Selves. This is not like being focused or centered. Those terms have quite different meanings for us - comes after Discernment. Your work with Larry -"

she waits for the best word, the correct word " - You fear that you could be him."

I pull back, pull myself in. My words come quickly. "My Grandfather taught me there is light and dark in all of us."

She lifts her hands from her lap, palms up. A cloud forms between them. "We can seek our own light only if we recognize our own dark, Gio."

Her statement. My fear. She asked a question, I didn't realize. She asked herself, not me. My fear made me answer.

"I -"

"Calm, Gio." She draws my fear from me, gathers it in her hands. The cloud grows, darkens. I hear miniature thunder. Her hair is lifted, lit by St. Elmo's fire.

Her eyes light, cat's eyes made of flame. She sees through me, finds the pain, the fear, pulls it slowly, gently, Androcles drawing the thorn from the lion's paw. "The real question, what did you learn from him?"

Lightning arcs through the room. A bolt sears my heart. I weep. The pain. The cloud hovers over me, releasing its rain on my cheeks, neck, and back. I pull my hair from my eyes and look up at the cloud, white again.

Grandmother Apara's face gazes down.

"I learned..."

The cloud is gone. Grandmother Apara sits across from me, her blind eyes fix on me. "You learned...?"

"I learned to be like him one must first be alone."

The room fills. Cougar, Moose, Coyote, Whale, Spider, Wolf, Hummingbird, Hawk, Mountain Lion, The Standing People, Ocean, Mountain, ...

Beyond these, others, smiling, waving, happy, joyous...

They surround me. I am their center.

I've been here before.

"A Council of All Beings."

WhirlWind forms. "You are never alone, Gio."

The Council fades, the mists part, the thunder quiets, the storm stills. I see Grandmother Apara sitting across from me.

"Is this how it is for everybody?"

"This is how it is for you."

She scooches next to me, pulls me into her, her hair flows around me, blanketing me, comforting me.

"I don't fear becoming dark."

She holds me close.

"I fear being alone."

"Yes."

Chapter 81

Saotome

Four of us face Saotome, one of us on each corner of the mat. Each of us smooth our *aikidōgi* prior to our attack. Saotome teaches us *taninzugake*, defense against multiple attackers. The woman left of me and the woman across the mat from me smile at Saotome and their brows furrow. They don't smile with their eyes, only their mouths. The man to my right smiles fully, nods at Saotome, lowers slightly like a wrestler, and waits.

I neither smile nor lower my stance. I watch Saotome genuinely smile at us. He smiles at the women and lowers his gaze to the mat after smiling at each, smiles broadly at the man. He turns to me, blinks, smiles, and inhales deeply.

I watch him.

They don't wait. Was his inhaling a signal?

They rush forward.

Saotome kneels beneath their outstretched arms.

His movement began before they did.

Didn't they see it?

The man and one woman collide. He grabs their ankles, rises, steps back, turns slowly, their legs entwine, they're pulled into each other, their *ukemi*, their fall, fails.

They crumple onto the mat, a black and white blob of flailing arms and legs inexplicably bound together.

The other woman avoids the falling mass, punches into Saotome's exposed gut.

His arm moves inside hers as he turns into her, guides it over his head where his other hand is waiting, captures her hand at an odd angle.

Saotome kneels, his hand holding hers continues in its arc. She flies over him, spins in two directions at once, lands awkwardly, doesn't fall correctly, rolls to the side, off the mat, doesn't protect her head, sits up stunned, holds her head and blinks her eyes.

I am halfway from my corner to Saotome, my right hand forward as if holding a *tanto*, a knife, and continue towards him.

He smiles and is in front of me faster than I can follow, takes my hand in a gentle grip. My hand opens against my will. He reaches into my open hand, takes it firmly in his, as if shaking hands.

He looks into my eyes and smiles. "Friendship."

～

"How come you didn't disarm me, Sensei?"

His English is heavily accented. My Japanese doesn't exist. "I stop attack."

I consider.

He smiles. "You learn better."

"You did disarm me."

He turns his head slightly, waits.

"You stopped my attack by offering me friendship."

His brows go high. "Friend. Best defend. Best attack. Always friend first." He nods.

I clap my hands.

"Come. Teach you -" His mouth works slightly. He frowns, his eyes look around searching. " - cutting."

"Cutting?"

"Don't know word. For now, cutting."

He sees me frown and shakes his head. "Not cutting?"

I explain Dr. Blake's wounding the lilies to him.

He pulls back, his eyes wide. His head shakes in disbelief. "Not cutting." He takes my hand. "I show you."

He lifts two *bokken*, wooden swords, from a wall rack and hands me one. "Follow." We go outside to a field beside his school. He takes one *bokken* in two hands, raises it in front of himself, slowly brings it down as he exhales, his move timed to his breath, his eyes closed.

He opens his eyes and smiles at me. "Cutting. You do."

I lift my *bokken*, do what he did, open my eyes and he shakes his head. "Do again. Learn better."

Fifty strokes. Fifty "Do again. Learn better."

He stands me behind him, moves my arms around him so I hold his wrists as he holds his *bokken*. "Now?"

"Now."

He *cuts*. I feel the earth rise up through him, move through his arms, out through the *bokken*, separating what is from what should be. I let go, step back, shaky.

"Cutting."

I nod. "Cutting."

———

I fail cutting some five-thousand times by my count. Earth circles the sun, galaxies spin, the universe sighs.

"Do again."

I lift my *bokken*. The earth rushes up through me, down my arms, into my *bokken*, its movement matching my breath.

Saotome pats my back. "Good cutting. Now show you more."

"More?"

He winks. "Follow."

We take our *bokken* and walk to the edge of the field, to a dead patch, to withered grass, flowerless shoots. He touches the tip of his *bokken* to the dried earth, cuts up.

A blade of grass comes out of the soil.

He moves slightly to his right and repeats.

Another blade of grass shows itself.

He continues. "You cut now."

I stand beside him. Move slowly, don't have his smoothness.

"Borrow."

I borrow. A blade of grass comes forth and whispers on the wind. "Hhellho, Gheeho."

Saotome steps back, watches, makes suggestions.

The sun sets. He hands me his *bokken*. "You go, go as friend, cut."

Chapter 82

Grandmother Paula

She sees me straining, rests her hand on my arm, sends her peace into me, relaxes me. "You're having difficulties with this. Any idea why?"

"My Grandfather did this so easily. I probably forgot something he did or taught me."

"I don't believe you."

Her Vision goes through me like a dispersion grid. I am me on one side and a rainbow of me on the other. She looks at the colors, rocks back, claps her hands, laughs.

"What's so funny?"

"You forgot your Grandpa didn't know what he was doing."

"Huh?"

"What's the First Lesson. Use the First Lesson to find the real challenge."

Lower-Center-Relax-Breathe.

A glowing wall growing and fading to the sound of a ticking clock but never getting closer, only larger. The Past. Something I read in a book. You can't outrun time. The Second Law. "This violates the laws of physics. We shouldn't be able to do this. It negates the Second Law."

"Important law, is it?"

"Foundational."

"Did physics work before this Second Law was known?"

"Of course."

"Do you think your Grandfather knew about this Second Law?"

"Doubtful. Not as such, anyway."

"So he could do what he could do because he didn't know he couldn't do it?"

I laugh.

"Are there laws of physics we don't know about yet?"

"Of course. Without question. New laws are being discovered all the time, old laws go away as our understanding grows."

"Good. Use those laws nobody knows about yet."

BOOM!

The Smithsonian's grasses have become upheld swords encased in Winter's ice and morning's light. A guard greets me as I enter the main doors. "Help you find something?"

I give Grandmother Paula's name.

He pulls a notepad from his pocket and draws me a map on a clean sheet of paper, puts an X on it. "You get there and wait. She'll find you."

A staircase later I stand at the railing of a beautiful diorama of Pre-Columbian living.

Squeaky wheels, water sloshing, and the scent of industrial cleaners come around the corner. A mop handle juts up from a bucket on wheels and both are followed by a white haired, petite, middle-aged, fair-skinned, bespectacled woman in janitor coveralls. She stops when she sees me.

"What do you think? You know anything about these people?"

"Not much. I came here to learn. Meeting my next teacher here."

"Your next teacher?"

"If she'll have me."

"She a hard one?"

"Never met her. Only heard stories."

"What've you heard?"

I shake my head. "Sorry, it'd be gossip. Nothing I know firsthand."

"Come on. Sharezees. Tell me the gossip."

I quote one of Grandpa's lessons. "I will tell you your story and as much of my story as you care to hear, but I will never tell you someone else's story nor will I ever tell your story to someone else."

"Wow. That's pretty severe, don't you think?"

"I don't know the woman personally. And besides, everything I've heard is other people's experiences of her."

"She good looking?"

"I've never met her."

"Never seen a picture? Nothing like that? How'll you know when you meet her it's her?"

"Maybe I should move along."

"You give up too easy."

"Okay, fine. How will I know her? By her smell."

"Doesn't wash, does she? And you want to study with a woman like that?"

"It's not a smell like that."

A cloud envelops me. A scent I've not detected since my time with the Grandmothers Apara. The janitor's coveralls are replaced by regalia. "Something like that?"

"Grandmother Paula?"

~

I knock on her office door. She checks her watch. "A year to the minute."

"As you said, Grandmother."

"What have you learned?"

"How to practice."

She shook her head. "No, no. That's what you've *studied*. I want to know what you've *learned*."

I laugh and quote one of her first lessons. "To learn anything you must learn everything."

She checks her watch. "We have one week. Then you go and learn again. But for two years this time."

"Can't I stay here with you? Longer?"

"You could and you'd only learn what I know. This is how the Universe does things. We are the Universe learning about itself." She taps her chest. "When this body dies we return with all the knowledge we've gained, everything we've learned, all the questions we've answered. Sometimes we move on, sometimes we come back to answer other questions."

"Sounds like reincarnation."

She shakes her head. "Sounds like how the Universe works. Reincarnation works bottom up. The Universe works top down. But the pyramid is inverted. It balances on its tip. People provide the foundation. Or not."

I nod.

"So what have you learned?"

"There's one practice I'm not getting. My Grandpa could do it. Any time he wanted. I can't do it at all."

She cocks her head, her brow furrows. "Show me."

Chapter 83

Brother Jorje

"I have no idea of what you need to know. All I know is what I need to say. The only way you can teach me what you need to know is if you ask me questions. Because I am the Teacher, I am the one being taught."

I take a moment. Brother Jorje is a Russian Orthodox monk by day, Buza player when he can, and has spent time with Daskele. He is shorter than me and almost twice as wide through the chest and arms.

He teaches me control.

I'm not good at it.

He laughs. "A Healer must heal themself before they can heal others, a Pathfinder must find their own path before they can help others find their paths. That's the way it is for all of us. Before we can go out, we must go in. We can only go as far out as we're willing to go in. Through these things we can help others learn how to do these things."

Brother Jorje is the epitome of Grandpa's "expensive." I read him *Sherlock Holmes* stories. Holmes tells Watson, when all the logical answers are exhausted whatever remains, no matter how illogical, must be *the* answer.

Brother Jorje laughs. "Did you hear? Holmes knows the first lesson: When you strip away all that isn't, all that's left is what is."

"That's the first lesson?"

"The first lesson for you here now with me: Discover what you're doing in your life automatically by becoming aware of what you do with intention."

I consider, nod.

"Or not."

"Huh?"

"Most of us are aware of those things we do consciously, intentionally, and which things we do nonconsciously, automatically, habits healthy and not. Gain control of consciousness and you learn where the boundaries between intention and habit lie."

"Ah. Or not."

"You're going to teach me how not to have control."

"I am?"

"I hope so. It's the only way I'll learn how to show you how to have control."

"You will?"

"Yes. To do what you do with intention. Act with intention and no one gets hurt unless you mean to hurt them."

"Grandpa told me never to harm or hurt anyone with what he...and others...taught me. Teach me."

"Your grandfather was a wise man."

"You knew my grandfather?"

Brother Jorje laughs. "My hair is gray but not that gray. Not yet. He was before my time. I'm sorry I never met him here."

"I sometimes remember him. It's like being with him again."

"Perhaps you are."

I look down, shrug. "Perhaps."

He lifts my chin and stares into my eyes. His eyes are tapestries of stars, constellations from cultures across the globe. I stare back. His face becomes a blue, snow-capped mountain, a stream flows down the mountain's face and becomes a clear rushing river. The river speaks to me. "Both-And, not Either-Or."

I nod.

Brother Jorje's face returns. "Now, show me how to begin."

Chapter 84

Ailo

"It's time for you to learn LifePath Work. Ailo is good at that. I'll tell him you're coming."

Ten days and four thousand miles later I am in Lapland, two hundred plus miles north of the Arctic Circle, naked in a hut made from downy birch and spruce branches and covered with bear hides. Brightly colored Sami clothing is neatly folded on sleds outside. My L.L. Bean arctic gear rests in a pile on the snow beside them.

I struggle to breathe because of the heat. A fire burns in the center, its flames so intense rocks placed on it crack. A circular hole at the top of the hut vents the smoke out, a door made of pitched pine planks lets air in. Men, women, and some children, all naked, sit around the fire showing no discomfort.

Ailo steps outside, comes in with a handful of snow, drops it on my head. It turns to water and cools me. "Breathe." His voice is high for a man his size and sounds like the Aurora crackling, a cold that burns.

"I'm trying."

The adults chuckle. Josef, who brought me the last two-hundred miles, laughs. "Yes, you are very trying."

"Reminds me of a Native American SweatLodge."

"It's traditional. It's the way we do things. Everyone starts here."

Ailo picks up his drum. He speaks and Josef translates. "This is how I do it. Remember to Lower-Center-Relax-Breathe."

Josef taps my arm. "Definitely breathe."

Everyone chuckles.

Ailo speaks again. Josef translates. "I'll start and carry you until you're able to follow."

I feel Ailo's presence under me, in me, lifting me.

"Piggyback!"

Ailo frowns at me and looks at Josef.

"My grandfather and his friends use to do this when I was a child, so I could learn from them."

The Aurora crackles inside me. "Yes. Your grandfather." Ailo smiles, strong teeth in an arctic tanned face.

Josef places some logs on the fire so they form a cradle and places a stone in the cradle's center. "We'll go slow. Let me know when we've gone too far or you need to rest."

Ailo drums. A few moments later he sings. Others join in. The heat lessens. I feel cool night air on my naked body and remember peeing when Grandpa took me home. Ailo stands over me. His body melts, flows to the ground, his arms become forelegs, his head sprouts antlers, his body grows fur whiter than the snow I traversed to get here.

A white bull reindeer. His Power Being. Not a normal reindeer. He stands as big as a bison. I remember a line from C.S. Lewis' *The Lion, The Witch, and the Wardrobe*, "He's not a tame lion."

The Aurora crackles in my chest. "Piggyback. Like your Grandfather taught you."

I climb carefully onto his back.

Each step is between shadows and light, bright and dark, each step a year back through my life.

"Where are we going?"

"To your decision."

Snows give way to forests to plains to cities to streets to the street I grew up on to a confrontation I had with Richie Forsler on an early Summer afternoon.

"Remember this?"

I nod, look away.

"You must see."

I clutch his fur, bury my face. This is not happening. I am not naked riding a white bull reindeer the size of a bison down the street where I grew up, the white bull reindeer is not taking me to Richie Forsler's house.

I feel the arctic cold but only for a moment. Ailo shakes his head as if tossing snow from his antlers. A hind hoof reaches up and scratches his side, almost dislodging me. Everything stops. Nothing moves. Richie is on his porch, a saltine cracker with peanut butter held in a hand fixed between table and mouth. His mother walks away, locked in mid-stride. I see their old black-and-white TV in their living room, a scene from *One Life to Live*, unchanging, the image still on my eyes in afterglow as I look away. No sounds. Silence.

"Do you wish to stop?"

I look at Richie. His house needs work. The porch where he eats has loose boards and can't support the weight of a full-grown man. His mother is sick. She has trouble walking and will return to teaching at the end of summer. His father, also a teacher, left in the middle of the school year, taken with his student-teacher, moved several states away after emptying out their accounts, leaving Richie, his five brothers and mother to find their own way.

"No. If I am to grow, to learn, I must go through this."

Ailo raises his muzzle and bellows, Auroras and Nightfall leaping from his mouth. "Good."

I sit up, shake my head. It is heavy. My shadow shows antlers growing.

Richie's mom comes out, wipes off Richie's face. "Ready to go to the park? You coming with us, Gio?"

I look at Richie's mom's car. The sides are rusted. The muffler needs patching. Three days out of five people watch him and his brothers push their car because the starter motor won't catch. The other two days one or more of them walks downtown, a gas can in their hand.

My mother and father have the finest cars. Father works hard, brings home his paycheck, wants his dinner on the table at 6:30 sharp, and knows what we're having each night because mother cooks to a schedule.

"Yes, Ma'am."

The Aurora comes down, gathers Summer, the street where I lived with my parents, Richie, his mom, their car, in its lights and takes them up into the arctic night. I sit by a fire but not in a hut. Ailo is across the fire from me, drum in hand. He has the head of the white bull reindeer but the body of a man. The reindeer raises its muzzle and chants.

"Continue?"

"Yes."

Paths form in the snow. Paths branch off from the paths. Other paths branch off from those. Some stop abruptly and redden. Others continue toward the ocean, to villages on the horizon, to a woman and child, to an academic institution, many paths.

Ailo points to one. The longest. It goes through the woods, emerges on the other side, dives under the sea, rises on an island, wraps around a volcano, climbs into the sky, to the stars, beyond.

WhirlWind is there, waiting.

"That's the path you chose. That's your LifePath."

"I don't recognize some of it."

"Most of it hasn't happened yet."

"Why that path?"

The bull reindeer bellows. "You chose compassion. You chose to risk. A small risk now, a great risk then. You did not know if Richie's mom's car would be safe. You chose love over fear. That choice shapes your life."

"I helped push their car back home."

"Richie's mom knew she didn't have enough gas to get there and back. She hoped you wouldn't come. But you did. And when it ran out of gas and she sat in the driver's seat, crying, you said, 'Don't worry, Mrs. Forsler, we can take care of this.' You went back to the playground and gathered boys to help you and Richie push it home. You made it a game: who could push the furthest without resting. You told them only special kids could push a car really far. They had to practice."

"I was reading *Tom Sawyer.*"

The paths spread from one like branches from a tree, branches to limbs to twigs to stems. They are uncountable. "What about the other paths?"

"Why salivate over food you're never going to eat?"

A man, older, his beard and hair gray, his eyes dull but his Vision sharp, walks towards me on the One Path. I stand as he approaches. He holds out his hand, roughened by work, smoothed by years. "Hello, Gio."

"Are you my teacher?"

He laughs gently and shakes his head. "No, I'm what you've learned."

I look at Ailo, confused.

The man still holds my hand. He clasps it in both his. "A lot's going to happen between now and me, Gio. Remember this: I wouldn't change a thing that's happened in our life, not one thing. But I never want to repeat it. Any of it."

He shakes my hand, nods at Ailo, and walks back up our Path, each step causing the Aurora to come down and fill his footprints with colors from the sky.

"That's me. Down that path. Later in life."

"You learn." The reindeer chuckles. "Sometimes it takes a while, and you learn."

"Thank you."

We're back in the hut. I open my eyes. Everyone smiles at me. The fire still burns. The rock has cracked.

Ailo says something. He nods to Josef. Josef hands me a drum. "Now it's your turn."

Ailo whispers. The Aurora crackles. The cold that burns. I hear in my heart. "You do me."

Chapter 85

Little Bear and Red Feather

"Do you know how to wash dishes?"

Little Bear teaches executives how to be better bosses. Executives pay ten thousand dollars a day for his trainings and his classes are always full.

I know him as Little Bear, a WarChief. He never speaks his white name to me.

"I would like to study with you."

"What's the name of your company?"

"I'm not with a company."

"Then why are you here?"

"I want to learn."

He is shorter than me, his face and hands are reddened from the sun. His face is smooth. No laugh lines. No frown lines. He doesn't blink and his eyes ask questions I don't know how to answer.

"I don't teach your kind."

I offer my hand. "Thank you for your time, then. Sorry to trouble you."

He takes my hand and a vice made of lightning crushes it. My arm goes numb. I'm alone in a canoe on the ocean. There's a spear in my hand. A small salmon swims beside me. The canoe has a mouth and eyes.

"Spear the fish."

I hesitate.

"Spear the fish."

"No."

"Why not?"

"I'm not hungry. There's no need."

"Your village needs the food. Spear the fish."

"Prove my village's need is greater than the fish's."

I'm back in the training facility. Little Bear lets go of my hand. "Do you know how to wash dishes?"

I rub my arm to get feeling back into it. "Yes, I know how to wash dishes."

He writes a note on a small pad and tears off the top sheet. "Meet me there at that time. We'll see if you know how to wash dishes."

～

I didn't know orphanages got this large. I know there are orphans. I know there are this many. I know there are more.

But I have no experience of it.

A statistic, a number, is not a child with suppurating wounds who's given up hope, is not a toddler sister protecting her two younger brothers because she knows the blow will come, not where, not when, only that it will, is not an abandoned brother and sister who climb over shelves looking for scraps of food, anything edible, and if it crawls, then edible it is.

Little Bear stares at me. "Leave now if you want to. Right now you don't know anything. You're still safe from this, from..." He hesitates, smiles. "*Knowing.*"

I shake my head. "No, let's get started."

His gaze narrows. I feel him evaluating me, seeking weaknesses. "You're sure?"

"Yes."

Unseen hands prod me, gouge me, push me, pull me.

"Last chance. Back out now if you have any doubts. Remember, you can't *unknow*."

I cock my head at him. I smile. I chuckle, then laugh. I place my hands on his shoulders and draw him close, hug him. "Thank you for asking me three times, Grandfather. I didn't realize what you were doing. Thank you for teaching me."

I let go. He nods.

I follow him down dark corridors to a huge kitchen.

I did not know there were this many dirty dishes, pots, pans, pitchers, knives, forks, glasses, cups, saucers, bowls, spoons, on the planet. They line counters, butcher blocks, prep tables, fill three sinks, are stacked on the checkerboard-styled linoleum floor.

"Roll your sleeves up, Gio. We've got a lot to teach each other."

~

We meet at his clan gathering. His daughter has just wed. Per tradition, she and her mate feed all in attendance. A small cabin off to the side serves as kitchen because it has a large, black cast iron wood-burning camp stove and a well water fed pump. A bright red feed pipe comes up from twelve-inch-wide floorboards worn smooth by many footsteps, the pump's green arm and the blue basin under the spout giving it a bizarre festive appearance.

I'm pumping water into a pot to put on the stove. Pots, pans, cups, spoons, and bowls are stacked on a huge table commanding the center of the cabin.

He leads a middle-aged man with graying temples, smoothly shaved, aquiline features, and weekend casual - designer jeans, polo shirt, Docksiders without socks - towards me.

"Gio, give him a towel and a sponge."

I reach up to a shelf over the pump.

The man pulls back, puts up his hands, palms out. "Wait a second. You didn't tell me there'd be so many." He reaches into his back pocket and pulls out a small address book. "Is there a phone around here? I can get a team here in an hour, maybe less, to do this place up right."

Little Bear turns the man around. "You can leave now."

"But..."

Little Bear shimmers. I wonder if the man can tell. He does step back. His brow furrows as he looks at Little Bear.

"Okay, okay."

He leaves.

Little Bear reaches up to the shelf and grabs and towel and sponge.

"He wanted to learn?"

"No, he wanted to spend money."

~

Every weekend for more than a year, "Meet me here at that time" or "Meet me there at that time."

Some weekends my hands want to fall off. Sometimes the detergent burns them. Sometimes my skin cracks. I bring gloves.

"No. Bare hands here."

"Alright."

Sometimes my stomach surges from the filth. Hercules had it easy at the stables compared to this. Sometimes my eyes burn from the steam rising from what I scrub clean.

Always there is learning. We spend a day washing and a night studying.

"Come, we have to talk to Tree." "Come, Wolf wants to teach you something." "Come, there are stars you've not seen before." "Come, Fire wants to talk to you."

Back at it the next day. Where do all these dishes come from?

And each time, sitting in the corner in a rocker, knitting, knitting, knitting, Little Bear's wife, Red Feather, listens. Sometimes she chuckles. Often she smiles.

Today Little Bear takes the towel from my hands before I start, stands between me and the sink. "Don't you ever wonder where all these dishes come from?"

"All the time."

"Guess."

"Somebody must be doing lots of cooking."

Red Feather laughs. Little Bear looks at her then back at me. "Good answer. You know I'm not any good at this, don't you?"

"Could've fooled me."

"Red Feather, she really knows this stuff. Lots better than I do."

I look at Red Feather. She meets my eye. I smile. She nods.

"She's the one who does all the cooking."

"Wow." I nod to her. "Who do you feed?"

She puts her knitting down. "The hungry."

"Okay."

"Are you hungry?"

"Umm...yeah, now that you mention it."

The piles of dishes are gone. The pots, pans, colanders, mixing bowls, everything is neatly stacked on counters and shelves. Steam rises from a pot of coffee on the stove.

"Good answer." Little Bear smiles. "Red Feather and I think it's time you learned how to cook."

Chapter 86

Han

Han, a tiny Bhuddist *Bhikkhu* in *Kāṣāya*, a monk in ceremonial robes, who can't remember when he was born yet remembers Halley's last passing clearly and says his country's had three names in his lifetime, stands in front of myself; Hiraku, from northern Japan on my far right; and a young, blonde, fair-skinned, blue-eyed woman standing between us.

He smiles at Hiraku and points to a young, leafy elm across a small green from us. "Go there."

Hiraku takes a step.

Han holds up his hand. "No."

He smiles at the young, blonde, fair-skinned, blue-eyed woman standing next to me. "Go there."

She smiles, bows, takes a step.

He holds up his hand. "No."

He smiles at me. "Go there."

I shake my head. "I don't know how."

He smiles and nods. "Yes."

We stand at the foot of a mountain. "Follow me." He starts at a pace difficult to maintain, zigging and zagging, sometimes down a slight grade, more often up a steep one. If he follows a path, I can't discern it. Once or twice he steps on loose gravel but never slips, never slides, never falters.

My eyes focus on foot placement, not on him, not on the path he follows.

I take a step.

"No."

I look up. He's some fifty feet up on the other side of a steep incline. I bring my booted foot back where it was.

"No...what?"

"No step there."

I look at the ground around me. "Why not."

"Bad step."

He lifts a stone in one hand it would take me two to lift and tosses it a footfall ahead of me.

The rock surface cracks and falls inward, a man-size hollow shows underneath. "Bad step."

I stare down into the man-size hollow, see the razor sharp rock edges, an iron maiden made of stone.

I catch a flutter of *Kāṣāya* and he stands beside me and smiles. "Tired?"

I nod, hand to my chest. "Thank you, and yes, tired."

He motions as if bringing a cup to his lips. "Drink?"

"Yes."

He moves his palm over the stones around us. His face is relaxed. He hums. A chipmunk races between his sandaled feet into a burrow. His hand reaches out and touches the ground.

Water burbles through the stones and grasses.

"Drink."

I cup my hand, let it fill with water, lift it to my lips.

He removes his *Saṃghāti*, the outer, top layer of his robes, and snaps it over our heads. It unfolds into a tent and anneals itself to the rock walls of the crevice we're in, covering us.

"Rest now."

———

My eyes open to see him standing above me, surrounded by sunlight. The air smells mountain clean, none of the sourness of urban and suburban air. I stretch to pump blood into my stone-numbed body.

He smiles. "Go now."

"Aren't you hungry?"

He looks at me.

I point to my mouth.

He shuffles me to the spot where he stood. "Watch." He Relaxes-Lowers-Centers-Breathes. "You do."

He watches, holds up a finger, manipulates my body slightly, moves my feet, shifts my hips, pulls one shoulder, pushes another. "*Gua Shai Bong*." He mimics Relax-Lower-Center-Breathe. "Do."

Something fills me. Hunger is gone, thirst is gone. Aches are gone. "Go now."

———

He turns and continues his ascent. Half a mile up I signal for a rest.

He shakes his head. He points to the ground he stands on then to the patch I stand on. "*Dū!*" Look!

I shake my head.

He's beside me in an instant. He points to the ground he stands on then to where I'm standing. "*Dū.*" Look.

I shake my head a second time.

He slaps the side of my head and a rock slide rolls down my face. He points again. "*Dū.*" Look.

"You mean *Go Wide*?"

He takes my hand, closes his eyes. My Grandfather's voice mixes with his. "Yes, Gio. *Go Wide.*"

The mountain is latticed with lines of all colors, some as fine as spider silk, others as broad as house beams.

Han holds up his arm, points to the veins in his wrist. "*Dū?*" See? I nod.

He points to the path he walked. I see a strong red line. He points to the path I chose. No lines.

Han's irises become horizontal slits, his pupils take on the bright orange color of a spider silk thin line. "*Deinsāy nī**." Walk this line. He points at his eyes then to a line the same color and width.

I follow the line for ten feet, making sure each footfall touches the spider silk.

My feet stop aching.

His irises widen until his eyes are vertical bars of blue pupil. "*Deinsāy nī**." Walk this line.

It feels like the earth moves me over it rather than I move over the earth.

"*Txn nī* dū tidtām.*" Now, watch. Follow.

There is no effort. No hunger. No thirst. I am not tired. Breaths come easy.

He points to the lines. "*Dū.*" Look.

He steps on a line and the earth rises to meet him, lift him, make his moves easy and light.

"*Hěn txn nī*?*" See now?

I laugh.

He laughs with me and nods. "*Hěn txn nī*.*" See now.

He steps quickly, neatly, gingerly, Fred Astaire and Gene Kelly and Gregory Hines and Savion Glover and Michael Jordan together in a tiny Thai body, and in one move he stands beside me. He touches me softly, takes my head in his hands and tilts it until my focus is on his sandaled feet.

He stands on a red line, like a plumb line but not straight.

I feel him laugh.

I remember an old landscaping adage. "There are no straight lines in Nature."

He laughs and the mountain joins him. He shakes his head and rocks roll downhill.

~

My steps are not as graceful.
No, not correct.
My steps are not as loving.
I shake my head.
"*Pid tā. Dū dī kĥn.*" Close eyes. See better.

~

I follow the lines - *Look* - easily now.

Each night we rest on a conjunction of lines, each morning we stand a moment on a blue line and are refreshed. Water follows orange and gray lines. Yellow and indigo meet where edible things grow.

We near the top of the mountain. There is no effort in the climb.

Except today I see a color I've never seen before.

Han steps in its direction and stands in the air.

He offers me his hand.

I smile, shake my head, wave his hand aside, take a step, and fall six feet down the slope of the mountain.

Han tucks his robes, jumps, lands beside me, helps me to my feet, brushes me off.

"*Khrng tx p thĥı* dī kừā nī*.*" Do better next time.

~

The lines. I thought they were ley lines. Bound to the earth. I put my limitations on the Universe.

The earth has lines over its surface, into its depths, and extending out into space. Sometimes our journey around the sun passes us through strange energies instruments can't understand.

Times of great rejoicing. Times of great sorrow. Times of war. Times of peace.

Each time depending on a line and whether we align with it.

Some lines move as things move, the Old Ones laying down new paths for us to travel.

Some bind the earth to other worlds not yet known. Others who follow them visit us often. Others, others like ourselves, technology bound, can't follow the folds, the meeting of lines, and they travel slowly or not at all.

All things are tied together. Pathfinders know the lines, follow them, find things for themselves and others.

Challenges are avoided and successes come easily when you follow the lines. Something comes easy? Your bodies align with that line. Something's difficult? Han's *Gua Shai Bong*, a *Feng Shui* for the body, aligning it with the energies of a place, a time, a need, a wish, a deed, change a challenge into a blessing.

It takes time to allow the lines to be, to sing their story, to listen to the strings of the Universe and walk their vibrations, the ultimate highwire act.

To follow the Universe's heartlines.

~

Han offers me his hand. I nod and walk amongst the stars.

____

Chapter 87

Huong Jo and Tonno

A man two-thirds my size, his skin brown and smooth, his eyes bright and on me, takes my hand, turns it harshly, forces my wrist up. His eyes rove the lines of my palm, the tips of my fingers, the size and shape of my knuckles and wrist.

He holds my hand out to his partner, Tonno, and my body contorts to ease the pain caused by the power of his movement, my wrist and elbow and shoulder twisting as if held in the grip of a master aikidoist or *gyakute* teacher.

Tonno stares into my palm, my hand, and looks up at Huong Jo, paying no attention to me, to the pain I'm in.

He shakes his head, no.

Huong Jo nods, agrees. "*Tidak, belum.*" No. Not yet.

～

A year passes. I deboard the ship, shake the captain's hand. "I may be back before you leave. Will you need me to help crew?"

347

He laughs. "You won't be back. Not on this trip." His grip strengthens, I feel something surge up my arm, into my chest. He winks at me. "Maybe next time, maybe not."

I stare into his eyes. He turns me to face the dock. Huong Jo and Tonno stand there, wave.

The captain gives me a gentle shove. "How is it written? Not all who wander are lost?"

Huong Jo takes my hand, offers it to Tonno, my body relaxes, moves with theirs, there is no pain in my joints. Tonno smiles. "*Hō. Samaya bhayō.*" Yes. It's time.

Huong Jo is a Dukun, a traditional Indonesian sorcerer, Tonno is Dzankris, a traditional Nepalese shaman. One will teach me the ways of the forest, the other the ways of mountain.

I lift my pack to my shoulder. They shake their heads. I drop my pack on the dock. They walk. I follow.

〜

Huong Jo scoops soil into his palm, lifts it to his nose, inhales deeply, eyes closed. Shadows rise from the small piece of earth, dance. His eyes open, he watches, smiles.

He exhales. The shadows fade back into the soil. He takes my hand, holds it palm up. He pours the black earth soil into it and tension races up my wrist and elbow and into my shoulder.

"*Katakan padaku di mana itu.*" Tell me where it's been.

Lower-Center-Relax-Breathe.

A spirit's face forms in the soil, in my palm. It stares at me, bares fangs, growls.

"*Kamu takut.*" You are afraid.

I stare back at the spirit rising from my palm. "Teach me to not be afraid."

The demon's nostrils flare. Its eyes widen. Its face reddens. The soil turns to lava in my hand.

I hold it with searing flesh. "Teach me to be brave."

My hand cools. The lava quivers like a pool of fresh rain. The demon's face changes.

Tonno shakes his head. *"Hō'ina, tapā'īṁ parivartana garnuhōs."* No, you change.

The creature rises fully from my hand, stands before me. The lava I held empty from my hand becomes its surface, its skin. It cools and becomes flesh.

It is me. I smile.

Huong Jo comes beside us. *"Pelajari tentang hutan, pelajari bagaimana Anda hidup. Pelajari gunung, pelajari siapa Anda."* Learn of forests, learn how you live. Learn of mountains, learn who you are.

It takes me the better part of a year to learn how to live.

Huong Jo takes my hand, turns it to see my palm, smiles, nods.

I stare into his eyes. *"Terima kasih telah memberi saya permulaan."* Thank you for giving me a start.

He laughs. "Your language is improving."

I glare at him. He speaks English? I should have known.

He turns me to face Tonno. Tonno takes my hand. There is no pain. *"Mērō pālō."* My turn.

⌇

My lungs ache. I am cold. Ice crystals form in the air when I exhale. My legs are taffy and bend in impossible directions. The earth rumbles and sends shock waves up my spine.

Tonno turns to me. His eyes glitter like specks on stone caught in glaciers. *"Tapā'īnlē hānakā pāṭhaharū birsanubha'ēkō cha."* You have forgotten Han's lessons.

The only word I recognize is "Han." Recognition brings his teachings back to me.

Lower-Center-Relax-Breathe.

So many teachers.

I am a fool to believe I can learn from all.

The mountain shakes, knocks me off my feet.

Tonno stands on one side of me, Huong Jo on the other. Neither offer me their hand, neither help me up.

They are unaffected by the cold, the shifting earth, the rarified air, the steady pace.

I get my legs under me, stand.

Lower-Center-Relax-Breathe.

"Help me, Han."

Lines appear in the earth, up the mountain's side, reach into the sky, wrap around stars, sheave the rock I stand on, go into the earth, lead to the sun. Blue lines offer this, red this. Follow water lines when thirsty, follow growth lines when hungry.

But always take only what you need.

I remember.

Tonno and Huong Jo nod. Tonno continues up the mountain. "*Ajha rāmrō.*" Better.

I look down, turn around, gaze in all directions, and laugh. "We've been walking uphill for a year." My laughter shakes me until tears of joy wet my face.

We've been walking uphill for a year and never left the plain on which we started.

Tonno and Huong Jo cock their heads at me, lean towards me. My laughter doubles me over. They wait for me to stand. I hug them both. "Thank you for this. Mountain has taught me who I am."

Tonno leans even closer. *Ani timī kō hau*?" And who are you?

"An absolute beginner. Always."

They applaud. Tonno takes my hand, checks my palm. "You begin to understand."

He speaks English, too.

I laugh.

〜

I hug Huong Jo and Tonno on the dock. They weep. Huong Jo gives me a handful of earth, Tonno exhales and I smell high mountain air. I lift my pack from where I dropped it many lifetimes ago. The captain waves at me from the ship.

I drop my pack back down.

Huong Jo and Tonno applaud. I hug them each again and they are gone.

Chapter 88

Dharghie

"All our knowledge comes from *Tjukurrpa*, the Dreaming. Wisdom comes when we understand what we know." An old, short woman, her skin blending into the night, sits across a small pit from me. She stands, pulls a stick from the pit and uses it to draw a circle around us.

"This is now *Boro*. We'll work here." Her speech is the halting English typical of bilingual aborigines. Behind her is a bark hut. She unslings a dilly bag from around her shoulder, sliding the strap down her arm and placing it by her side. Far above I see The Southern Cross. Halfway up from the horizon I see my old friend, Sirius, shedding rainbows into the night. There are Taurus, Aquila, Scorpius.

The woman fills the pit with pine bark and broom bushes. She spits into it and it catches fire. "Find some stones, put them on the fire."

I look around me, see some stones, take one, toss it on the fire, see another, reach for it. It hisses and is as hot as fire itself. It sprouts legs and waddles away.

The old woman laughs. "Not that one. That's a haunted stone."

"How do you tell the difference?"

"You learn."

She is dot painted with red ocher and white gypsum. Sweet smelling white swansdown covers her arms and head and a short twig goes through her septum.

"You like yams?"

"Yes, please."

"Have to cook them first."

"May I help?"

She teaches me how to construct a good cooking fire with stones, leaves, grass, and earth.

"We need help." She makes a sound like a birdcall. Rain winds gather over our heads, release a fine mist onto the burning pit.

She reaches in and pulls out a bouquet of smoking leaves, tosses them into the air and they fall higher and higher until they become *Bunjil*, The Great Eagle.

She points, her finger following *Bunjil*'s flight into the stars. "He shares our fire with the ancestors."

"The Milky Way?"

"Smoke from the ancestors' fire to some, a river to others. Build a canoe so you can travel from here to your home and back when you need."

The moon is on the horizon and has a cat-like face. A long shadow comes off the horizon as something runs towards us.

The running shadow shortens as the cat-moon rises. Soon I see eyes reflecting the fire light. It becomes a form low to the ground. I make out something dog-like. White fangs appear as its muzzle opens, a spotted tongue lolls out.

Much closer now. It is a dingo. In three strides the dingo becomes a man, as dark skinned as she and wearing a shining rock necklace. It continues running towards us, slowing only as his features become obvious in the fire.

The man stops beside the woman, lowers himself to the ground, becomes half-man, half-dingo. She rubs behind his ears and smooths his pelt. "Hello, Desert Child."

The dingo-man licks her face. "Hello, Dharghie. What need do you have of me?"

She takes the shining stone necklace off him and tosses it to me.

"For me?"

"For now."

She nods in my direction. "See this one?"

He peers over the fire, bares his fangs. A low growl comes towards me.

"Shh. He grows like us under the skin."

Dingo-man is suddenly beside me, his movements faster than I could follow. He sniffs me. For a moment more dingo than man. He lifts his leg and pees on me.

"Hey."

Dingo-man laughs and sits back by Dharghie.

She laughs. "How do they say it in your country? You're his little puppy now?"

His piss dries on me. My skin is dark like the night.

She pats Dingo-man's back. "Bring him to me, Desert Child. Teach him to make a canoe, ride the Great River, sail the cosmic ocean, climb down the Dreaming Tree of Life."

He nods.

She inhales and the fire, the hut, the dingo-man, the earth, the universe are drawn into her, leaving me floating in the dark.

I wake up, throw the covers from me, turn on a light.

There's a dark patch on my chest.

I smell urine.

Eyes glow, rise up on the far side of the room. A paw turns into a hand.

It is held out to me.

"Come."

～

Dingo-man guides our canoe through the midnight skies. Beneath us the earth -

He shakes his head, points with his paddle. "Mother."

I nod. Beneath us Mother turns through half a day's light. We come to a tree -

"Dreaming Tree."

We come to Dreaming Tree anchored in the dark center of a field of stars.

Dingo-man shoves his paddle down into the cosmic ocean, the Great River, and anchors us there as well. He nods me towards Dreaming Tree.

"You want me to get out? Up here?"

He rocks the canoe and I tumble out its side, falling until I grasp leaves and limbs and bark. They slide through my hands, tearing flesh off my palms. I slow. I hold on. Catch my breath.

Far above me Dingo-man grunts, lifts his paddle, sails on.

I descend.

~

I stand inside her circle.

"Are you hungry? Eat."

Yams smoke in her fire pit.

"Thank you."

She mixes red and black tints in stone bowls. "We live from epoch to epoch."

A river forms in front of me, chest height, reaching from horizon to horizon. It sings to me, sounds of nature, voices talking, animal movements, stars colliding, Totyerguil throws his boomerang and it becomes the Corona Borealis, its song the story of his battle with the great snake before it kills him.

My eyes close. I focus on the sound surrounding me in the waters.

"You hear that?"

"Yes, I do."

"It is a songline."

"I hear it. And feel it. A vibration from the earth. What another teacher calls *leylines*."

"Yes. They crisscross the land, all land. It is how we communicate our stories and knowledge."

I step up into the river, bathe in the sounds.

"It is good you can hear such things."

———

I get a bag of yams and place it on my chest as I lie down.

There is a second paddle in the canoe. Dingo-man grunts and points to it with his.

I help guide us down the River of Dreams.

At the Tree Dingo-man paddles furiously, battling a current in a calm river.

The canoe thumps against an unseen shore.

Dingo-man steps out and beckons me to follow. We're inside the old woman's circle. He lifts a didgeridoo and clapsticks from the canoe.

The old woman points to her fire. "Are you hungry?"

"May I offer you some yams I brought?"

She looks up and smiles at me. "Good son. You're learning."

———

Dingo-man hands me a paddle. He sings to the stars while I guide the canoe.

———

She sits on the other side of the fire pit. A small, black, fan-tailed bird lands on her right and takes human form. It is followed by a red lizard on her left and a small, prickly lizard in front and a little to her side. It places yams on the fire and builds it for cooking.

She sees me watching them. "Ancestor spirits."

The small, prickly lizard human says something and I help with the fire.

The old woman stares at me. "You understood what Ancestor said?"

"It asked me to help build the fire."

The small, black, fan-tailed bird person laughs. "Go far enough back, we all spoke the same language. Now we use different words but we still talk about the same thing. Inside, we all speak the same language still." It looks at Dharghie and nods at me. "This one listens good."

The lizards grunt agreement.

Small, black, fan-tailed person leans in to her. He whispers loud enough for me to hear. "You didn't know that?"

—〜—

I understand Dingo-man's song, share it with him. He looks at me, smiles.

"Kinship binds the communities, not only to each other, but to the stars above, and the earth below and the plants, the animals, the very rocks and landscape."

"You speak?"

"You listen?" He turns completely into a dingo, nothing mannish at all. "But most important, it binds me to you, you to Mother, the Ancestors to us all."

I nod.

He raises a paw, rakes my chest, leaves his mark on me. "You can find your way now."

"No, wait - "

"Not my little puppy anymore."

He leaps out of the canoe. There are no paddles. I sing.

—〜—

The old woman is by a different fire pit. Still inside a circle drawn in the dirt, but no bark hut. Behind her a string hammock is strung between two Matchwood trees. "How did you get here?"

"I sang."

"You shouldn't be here."

"This is where my song brought me."

She blinks and her eyes are replaced by the fires she tends. "Take my fire from me."

"No."

She slaps me hard. My face stings and my jaw aches. "Take it."

"No."

She raises her hand again.

"What have I done that you treat me this way, Mother?"

"Ah, you're a man now? You wish me to treat you another way?" She lowers her arm. Her body transforms into a young, long-legged woman's. She dances around the fire, around me. She shakes her bottom at me, invites me in. Grabs my arms in a grip I never knew she had. "Will your clever stick do what is needed?"

I pull free, back away. "No."

Her arms still reach out to me. They're covered in feathers. "You want to learn my magic, then?" Her arms become wings, her nose and mouth replaced by a curved beak. She lays on the ground, opens herself to me. "Take me now?"

"I come to learn from you. Is this one of your lessons?"

She rises over me, now a man.

He has a blade in his hands.

I am naked.

His blade flashes in the firelight. He severs my penis and scrotum, catches them and throws them into the fire. "Bleed like a woman, if that's what you want."

My belly swells, my breasts fill.

I scream, breathe, push.

And give birth to a boy baby. Me.

I'm surrounded by Animals. Dreaming Ancestors. A Council of All Beings and all the beings are First Ones.

Australites fall from the sky and encircle me, giving me their power.

The man drops his knife and becomes the old woman again.

"You brought forth life."

The child grows and I'm absorbed into it.

"You traveled through the Realm of the Unborn? You carry Old Magic. Men must go through several ceremonies to understand women.

Men are barren and inferior. A few men, one or two, can become women, give birth. You became woman."

She rubs charcoal over my body and puts a smear of white paint on my nose.

"Our time is done. It is the Grandmothers' turn next."

I touch myself, curious to know if all pieces are back where they belong.

The old woman laughs.

Chapter 89

Grandmothers of the Three Women's Nations

A dark cloud surrounds me. I feel a cool mist, smell coastal waters, hear feet running along a seashore, children playing in the breaking waves, prairie buffalo grasses tickle my thighs, crickets chirp around me, grasshoppers hop and take wing around me, their wings buzzing as they pass, spiders build webs around my feet, the scent of a cooking fire comes to me, fat melting in an earthen pot, the songs of tribal ancestors color the air around me, clear lake waters lap my toes, the scent of aspen pine, mountain oak, birch, ash, and elm, a moose calls, an eagle high overhead answers, loons call my name, a bear and her cubs fish some thirty feet from me.

Ocean, Prairie, Mountain.

The cloud separates into three standing flames, resolving into women's forms, a mix of smoke and heat until the flames submerge into flesh and three women encircle me, old and not old, young and not young, dark skinned and light, voluptuous and lithe, evocative and shunning.

They are maiden, mother, crone but shifting, never staying one too long. There are three of them but there's only one of them.

Their faces.

They are not hidden but I cannot see them.

One approaches. "You carry your Grandmother Spirit on your male side and your Grandfather Spirit on your female side."

It recedes and another steps forward. "You carry strong women's medicine."

I know those voices. I've heard them before.

"Grandmother Apara? Grandmother Paula?"

The last shade approaches and the second recedes.

"But you've never given birth."

That voice I do not know, I do not recognize.

The three shades swirl around each other, around me, and the dark cloud returns. A hand, old but strong, forms in the darkness and takes mine, draws me in.

~

I stand in the center of a star field, a great circle divided into thirds converging under my feet, one third is a beach bounded by storming ocean, one a wind-swept prairie, one rises quickly into a mountain, its forest climbing up its sides like an earth tinted, flowing cloak.

The voices speak in unison and then separately, answering questions before I ask.

"The Intersections of Eternity."

"Studying the Rays of the Moon." "Learning the Ways of the Lake." "Discovering the Meanings of the Horns."

The one whose face is hidden solidifies before me. "Only two other men have been allowed to learn these things in our lifetimes."

The one with Grandmother Paula's voice solidifies. "Men birth ideas. Some ideas become seeds and take root in others. But men cannot birth other men, cannot birth women, cannot have children."

The one with Grandmother Apara's voice takes shape. "Without knowing how to bring life, they take it."

"Learn how to bring forth life." "Teach it to others." "Teach men not to fear the woman waiting inside them."

Their voices unite into a wave as high as the heavens crashing onto the land, a tornado of fire as wide as the earth scorching the plains, an upheaval creating chains of mountains. "Before it is too late."

The water recedes into a dry ocean bed. "Before it is too late."

The tornado churns the land until nothing can grow. "Before it is too late."

The mountains collapse and fall into dust. "Before it is too late."

I sit in the center. "Teach me. Before it is too late."

Chapter 90

Anouak

"How is my Brother Sidney?"

"I haven't seen him in a while."

Anouak guts and cleans cod on the shore. Gulls wait impatiently, take flight when he throws something he can't use - not often - and fight over it. Ringed seals gather and watch.

He points with his knife. "He's right there."

I turn and look. "Where?"

"Didn't he teach you to go wide?"

I do. Sidney waves from his hammock. One dark leg hangs over its side and rests on the sand. It gently rocks him back and forth.

"Did you give him the fish I caught?"

"Yes."

"You've traveled a long way. How did you know I'd still be here?"

"I didn't. I hoped."

He throws me a piece of cod. "Eat that quick before these thieves take it from you."

A gull pecks my heavy mitten as I snatch the cod from it.

"What made you hope?"

"Something told me you'd help me learn how to listen. I'm afraid I've forgotten how to listen."

He speaks with my Grandfather's voice. "*Ascolta.*"

I stare at him. He tosses a cod head to a seal. "You didn't hope. You heard."

"I heard?"

"Listen."

~

The Aurora Borealis are dancing in the distance.

Anouak shakes his head. "Listen when they talk."

I strain.

"Singing?"

"Who?"

Some of the Aurora seem to break off, separate. Forms shape. Beings as tall as the aurora itself. They cover the distance in two strides and collapse to tall human size as they do, NBA basketball players made of dancing red and green and violet and yellow light.

More break off, stride to us, appear as tall human forms, without diminishing the aurora itself.

We are surrounded. They sit on the ground with us.

I look around. "Should I add more wood to the fire?"

One of the creatures opens its mouth. A sound comes out. The song of suns. The fire grows without fuel.

I lean towards Anouak. "Are they hungry? Should I cut up some fish?"

Another opens its mouth. A sound of oceans, of the deep. Fish leap out of the water, near the shore.

"What are they saying? What is their song?"

"Learn their language."

"How?"

He laughs. "What is the First Law of Semiotics?"

I stare, my eyes widen, I cock my head. "You know semiotics?"

"No, I know you know it and I know your language."

"Yes, your English impresses me."

He shakes his head. "You hear. You don't listen. I don't know English. I know your language."

"My language?"

He reaches over and taps my chest. "Isn't that how your Grandfather did it?"

"Did anybody not know my Grandfather?"

The Aurora laugh. I recognize it as laughter. It is the sound of electrified snow falling: staticky and whispery and soft and coming down from the sky.

I laugh. "Yes. Everybody knew my Grandfather."

One of the Aurora taps my chest and I hear them inside, church organs and whale song and avalanches and waves lapping beaches. "Learn your own language and you know the language of all things. Earth, ocean, fire, sky, and all things within them. Learn to hear yourself first, you learn how to hear others. Talk to others, others listen. They listen. Listen, they talk to you."

One by one they rise from our fire, step back, rejoin the infinite.

Anouak watches me closely. "They are from a distant time, when all things spoke the same language. The cod, the gull, the seal, the caribou, the whale, the snow, the sea, the sky, the stars. All spoke together."

"A Council of All Beings."

"Learn to listen. Isn't that what your Grandfather taught you?"

"Yes. Listen. To all things."

He nods, gathers his things into his umiak. "And then?"

"I learn to listen more. Listen better."

He pushes off and waves as an Aurora walks over to him across the water. "Did you hear?"

I nod. Understanding.

"Listen well, listen better, and at some point you'll learn to ask."

Chapter 91

Brother Andrew

"Twenty-three."

Brother Andrew teaches me Levels of Awareness.

"And me?"

"Thirteen."

"I have level envy."

He laughs. It comes up from his belly and shakes the walls of his cell. He speaks colloquial American English once you get past his accent. "Is that useful to you?"

"Not really."

Months ago I felt a presence, a touch like the gentle hand which guided me back to my grandfather's ways forgotten for so many years, so gentle I questioned its existence and so overwhelming it couldn't be denied. Slowly it steered me, always allowing me options, always waiting to see which I'd take, never forcing me closer, always accepting my decisions.

"Yes, that was me."

"How long were you watching me?"

"Since your Grandfather passed."

"You knew my Grandfather?"

"One of my teachers."

"He never mentioned you."

"He never mentioned you."

"Then what made you watch me?"

"A gift to a friend."

He tells me things I've done in my life. Not sharing my memories, he recounts them as a first-person witness, as if standing beside me, silent yet watching.

"Levels of Awareness."

He studies mathematical physics as a hobby, a relaxation.

"To validate what we do?"

He laughs and shakes the walls of his cell. "To validate what it claims."

"Teach me."

"Start with the senses, the bodies. Each body has a preferred direction, the points on a compass. Each body dominates a sense. This is natural. Beyond these we each have our own directions. Some more, some less. We travel in those directions. Sometimes we share directions with another. Travel those directions together, a life partner. Travel those directions opposite each other, a challenge. Perhaps a teacher, perhaps a friend, but not someone you can tolerate long.

"Often paths intersect, come together, move apart. Rarely do they change. We can develop more, develop less, but one's South is almost always one's South. We say someone loses their direction; we mean they're not following their path any more.

"Sometimes we must help someone find their directions, relearn their path. Align them with the Universe."

He takes my hand and I see myself as a child in my parents' house. The child-me steps off one of Han's lines. One of his, but different.

Mine.

"You, for example, forgot your way. You found it again and things got both easier and more difficult. Easier because you relearned who you are. Difficult because to be who you are meant not being who others needed you to be."

I see myself as a young man not long ago. The not-long-ago me rejoins my line.

"That's part of LifePath Work and Levels of Awareness: finding someone who needs you to be you and is willing to let you be you even when it hurts them."

He releases my hand.

"That is Love."

Levels of Awareness isn't easy.

"Yes and no. Like the Steps Matsuo and Furyada taught you long ago."

"You knew Matsuo and Furyada?"

"My teachers, thanks to your Grandfather."

Lower-Center-Relax-Breathe.

"Good. *Go Wide.*"

I do.

"Excellent. Stay like that. Now *Go Up.*"

I splash back into myself like water in a basin. "Up?"

"Whatever that means to you, do it."

"That's all the instructions? 'Do it.'?"

"Lower-Center-Relax-Breathe and that's all the instruction you need. Lower-Center-Relax-Breathe and you figure it out."

Lower-Center-Relax-Breathe.

"*Go Wide.*"

I do.

"Good. Now Listen. Just Listen. Do nothing but Listen."

My body slows. My bodies gel.

"Lower..."

Yes.

"Center..."

I can do this.

"Relax..."

Easy to do.

"Breathe..."

Done this many times.

"*Go Up.*"

Somehow the air above me clears yet I feel myself slip through a barrier, a membrane, and it dissolves, goes away, a cataract I was never aware of. My head, above the barrier, goes wide, but not my head, my head on a new body, different bodies.

Brother Andrew chuckles beneath me. "The four bodies of one body."

"Like the Kabbalah?"

He laughs. "Can you *Go More*?"

I pull myself through. The membrane is gone. I stand on nothing and look down from the ceiling of the cell.

"What do you see?"

I tell him, share details I'd not noticed before, his monastic life suddenly larger than I could imagine.

My self suddenly larger than I could imagine.

"Matsuo and Furyada explained?"

"Enhanced."

He nods. "I'll accept that. Can you *Go Up* one more?"

Easy.

"Wonderful. Now *Go In*."

The puddle splashes in the basin again.

Brother Andrew chuckles. "You did good for your first time. I'm proud of you. You learn well."

"What do you do when you get to the point where a given level is natural to you, is constantly available, is where you naturally are?"

"Then I have the next level."

"You said I have thirteen directions?"

"That's all I can see from where I stand." He fades, becomes a monolith, its top haloed in stars.

"Will I ever need more?"

"If you do, they'll be there. Let's work with what we know we have."

I nod.

"And one thing, Gio."
"Yes?"
"Should you discover you have more than twenty-three, let me know. That way I can have level envy."
We laugh.

Chapter 92

Two Bears

He adjusts a pair of glasses, pushing them up his nose, blocking his view of me with his hand. He lowers his hand and his gaze is on the brook down a small field from his house. Drum frames season on carpenter's staging at the foot of his porch. Sunlight dazzles off the water and dances on the drums, giving the impression they wiggle when there is no wind. "I work with apprentices ten years minimum before allowing them to care for drums on their own."

I nod.

"Have you studied before?"

"With my Uncle John who made drums for people practicing *Oya*. He taught me some."

"John? *Oya* John? John N'bmwe?"

"He was my Uncle John."

He focuses on me. Looks at me over the top of his glasses. Stares me up and down. I feel him Lower-Center-Relax-Breathe. He slaps his thigh and laughs. "Sorry. I'm used to so many *wannabes* I didn't look. My mistake. What's your name again?"

"Gio."

"You're Grandfather John's Gio?"

"You knew my Grandfather?"

"You're the one who put his mark on SilverHawk's and EagleFeather's drums?"

"You'll teach me?"

"Tell me."

～～

SilverHawk looks from behind the counter as I enter her store. She's with a customer and nods at me with a "With you in a minute" smile.

There's a display of drums on one wall. The cash register *ka-ching*s and the customer leaves. SilverHawk is beside me before the door closes. "You looking for a drum?"

I pick up one, lift a beater, thrum a beat.

The store shakes. Displays rattle. People crouch slightly as if balancing on a rocking ship or feeling an earth tremor.

Everyone looks at the drum. SilverHawk's store is silent except for the release of held breath.

I return the drum to its stand. "Nice drum."

SilverHawk's gaze goes from the drum to me. "I've never heard a drum sound like that."

I browse and chat with SilverHawk's assistant, Three Crows.

Other people pick up the drum and beater and quickly put them back, fire to the touch. One woman gives it a whack, almost dropping it as a shockwave goes up her arms, into her chest, shaking her breasts, contracting her stomach.

But the drum doesn't sound. It thuds.

I walk back to the drum, lift it, take beater.

Drr-uuu-mmm!

SilverHawk gets a shopkeeper's glint in her eye. "So, you going to buy it?"

"No. Not quite yet."

Her shopkeeper's glint fades. "Oh."

~

"What did you do if you didn't buy it?"
"I asked if Drum wanted me to have that drum."
"You've met Drum?"
"I've been introduced."
"Tell me."

~

I stop for a frappe on the way home. I get pistachio and I always think *mustachio* when I taste pistachio. I hear John N'bm'we's voice, smell his gentle breath enveloping me, feel his tender hands tap my little chest.
"You tap this drum to find Drum."
"My chest?"
"Your heart."
I smile.
I remember, Uncle John. I remember, Aunt Mary.
I tap my chest. "I'll use this drum to find Drum.
Uncle John's voice surrounds me. "Your chest?"
"My heart."
Aunt Mary hides a smile.

~

Two Bears looks through the trees to the sky. "Getting late. Best go inside."
Deer hide, bear hide, cow hide, all stretched on frames in his living room, hallway, dining room. Beside each, a different tanning solution. I catch the scent of one and pull back sharply.
"Brain tan." He goes into the kitchen and comes back with two steaming mugs. "Tea. It'll make it better."
"Thanks."
"What you describe is what I teach."
"Just stuff I remember from Uncle John."

"Good stuff. 'What's the first instrument we hear?' 'Where and when do we hear it?' 'What's the only instrument we carry with us at all times?'"

"Uncle John said, 'Creator gave each one of us a drum, and proper drumming echoes the heartbeats we hear in our mother's womb.'"

"You know FourBody Work? How DrumWork is linked to it? And JourneyWork?"

"I'm here to learn."

Two Bears laughs into his steaming mug. "Good answer. You learn well."

"Uncle John said if someone is properly trained, they don't have to listen to drumming to journey."

He shakes his head and smiles. "He was one of the best of us."

"Do you all know each other? After a certain point of learning?"

"Don't you know a lot of us?"

"I have no idea."

"Aren't you one of us?"

"I'm not anything like those I study with. You included."

"That's why you're one of us."

"How many of you - us - are there, then?"

"Enough."

"Do you know everyone?"

He guffaws. "Hardly. But this is how I think of it: you like music, you learn to play an instrument. Maybe the clarinet or recorder. Maybe that's your instrument and you stick with it. You get better and better. The guy teaching you knows he can't teach you any more and sends you to the next guy. Then that guy can't teach you any more and he sends you on. Eventually people come to you and you tell them stories about the folks you've studied with and still study with."

A silhouette, a black tube with silver ornamentation a little over two feet long, spins in the air before him. It slows, stops, and a ghostly clarinet forms.

"One day comes and you realize there's only five or six people who play at your level. You can't get together all the time but you know who each other are. And when you do get together, my god the music you play."

Other silhouettes join the first.

"Or maybe clarinet isn't your instrument. You try piano and guitar and end up on, I don't know, flugelhorn or something. But it's the same thing. You get to that place and you don't all play the same instrument but you're all at that level. You can't all play the same instrument. The music couldn't happen. It's the different voices that make the music whole, make sure no one instrument dominates."

More silhouettes. An orchestra. His hands make slight, rhythmic motions like a conductor calling his musicians to pianissimo. The silhouettes merge and fade.

"Make sense?"

I remember what other teachers taught me. "Yes."

"Good. Did John show you how Drum demonstrates your life? Or how DrumWork has a place in LifePath Ceremonies?"

"I can't even imagine how you'd hear the power of Drum's beat."

"Then that's where we start. But finish telling me about Drum."

A doe stands over me in human form, reaches down and takes my hand. "Please get up."

"Where are we going?"

It turns away from me but still holds my hand and leads me like a child. We step from my bedroom to a mesa complete with scrub and hardpacked earth all around.

Singing and drumming come over a rise, and a flickering light glows up into the cold, night sky.

Doe turns to hurry me along and I see stars reflecting in its eyes.

Over the rise I see all the Animal Spirits circling a great fire. Drum floats in the center of the fire, constantly burning and being renewed. The Animal Spirits dance around the fire, dance around Drum, sing a DrumWaking Ceremony as Drum transforms itself into the drum in SilverHawk's shop.

"Why are the Animal Spirits here?"

Doe pulls me towards the dance. "You are BearHeart."

Drum calls me into the fire. It points into the desert night sky as my flesh sears and heals, my body constantly burning and being renewed with Drum's.

Drum dances in the center of the fire, the sky spins overhead. Drum draws me closer. The Animal Spirits' singing and dancing enters me, shakes me, moves me, transports me.

I am burned and healed so Drum's Spirit and mine can merge.

Drum comes into me, into my heart, and I move with its beating into a sea of stars.

~

Two Bears slings a drum across his back. "Come outside with me. Time to build a fire."

I gather some wood from a stack on his porch.

"I've never heard of a DrumWaking like that. Doesn't matter. Time to get started. We'll start with DrumWork and DrumKeeping, then the WakingDrum of my people and the Celtic DrumWaking because I learned it and should pass it on. Then there'll be CleansingDrum, SmudgingDrum, WelcomingDrum, BreathingDrum, and JourneyingDrum. Finally we'll get to HealingDrum, HeartDrum, Powersong, and TalkingDrum."

I set the fire.

He hands me the drum from SilverHawk's shop.

"How do you know this is the one?"

He holds it so the firelight gleams on it.

My handprints are there.

~

It is my last night around Two Bears' fire and I sit alone surrounded by drums from all cultures, all parts of the earth, and they sound as one when I strike them.

I lift the beater and the drums merge into Drum from the Animal Spirits' fire.

It falls into my hands and I hear my heart echoing off his skin, boom boom Boom Boom BOOM BOOM BOOM BOOM BOOM.

"Drum, are You my teacher?"

BOOM!

I fall through Drum into a world where only sound exists. "The Only Time I am Drum is When Someone Strikes me."

Chapter 93

Matthias Kaonohiokala

"Your fear gets in your way."

"Lava is hot."

Matthias Kaonohiokala steps calf deep into the lava. We walk here from where his helicopter lands a quarter mile away, the flattest, closest place to this lava flow. My boots are steaming. He is barefoot.

"Maybe it's because you're...whatever you said. I can't repeat it... Hawai'in?"

He shakes his head. "Child of Pele." He holds out an arm as thick as a good-sized tree trunk, offers me a hand as broad as a warrior's shield. "Come. Learn."

~

We meet in a mall on the big island. He takes his kids to a movie. His children look like children. He looks like an oak with its top leaves on fire.

"Do oaks grow in Hawaii?"

He cocks his head at me, frowns, and slowly shakes his head. "No."

He sees me working to not stare at his hair, so red it can't be natural. His eyes go up as if to see what I'm seeing. "Never seen a *kānaka ʻōiwi*?"

"Pretty sure I've never seen one. I'm not sure I could pronounce one."

He laughs and it resounds from a chest bigger than a flesh covered barrel. "I trace my ancestry to Nanaula."

"I trace mine to a small town in Sicily where my grandfather comes from."

"Maestro Fortuna. Yes. A good man."

"You knew my grandfather?"

"We all knew your grandfather."

His children climb up and down him as if he's a mountain, or they're hummingbirds flitting about a rhino. He's a head taller than me, evenly tanned, and built like a cross between a body builder and professional power lifter. His *kapa* robe would cover a living room floor. He wears an aloha shirt on top that could serve as a tent.

And pink flip-flops.

He sees me glancing.

"Gifts from my girls."

I nod. "Forgive my ignorance. I know you're *kahuna*, I have no idea which type or what to call you."

"Matty works pretty well."

He pays for his kids' tickets. "Daddy's going to be in that Baskin-Robbins right over there with this nice young *ha ole*. You come get me as soon as the movie's out and we'll all have some ice cream." He frowns and purses his lips as he hands them each a dollar for refreshments. "Understood?"

They giggle, tug on his aloha shirt until he bends over, kiss him, and hurry into the theater's darkness.

We sit on a bench outside the theater entrance in the mall. Hawai'ins nod at him as they pass. A few non-Hawai'ins do. Only one or two *ha ole*, whites, do.

Matty chuckles. "A man is not without honor, except in his own home and in his country." He lifts my denim shirt sleeve gently. It sticks due to my perspiration. The softness of his touch surprises me, like butterflies lifting the cloth. "We've got to get you some real clothes."

"I don't have much money."

He laughs. "Two Bears says you're good with a *pahu*."

"*Pahu?*"

"Drum."

"He said that? Really?"

He laughs. "He also says you need to overcome your fear."

"Yeah, well."

"Tonight we get you some good clothes. Take you to Kamapua'a's Falls. The real one, not the tourist trap one. You studied with WildCat yet?"

I shake my head.

"Doesn't matter. We can help you for one night."

My stomach drops a bit.

"See? That's what Two Bears was talking about. Your fear. You fear what you don't know. Embrace what you don't know. It'll go better."

"You embrace what you don't know and it could snap you in two."

He laughs. "You see this body and you think I'm strong?"

"Well, *duh!*"

"My strength is my weakness and my weakness is my strength."

"What?"

"Because I'm strong, I always used my strength to do things. I didn't take the time to learn which body would do things best. My strength was my weakness because it never occurred to me to be anything but strong."

I nod slowly. "Ah. Okay. I get it."

"What's the next part?"

"Your weakness is your strength?"

"Tell me what that means."

"It means you being gentle lets you get more done than you being strong does."

"Very good. Now, what does it mean for you?"

———

I hold on to a hog's back as it climbs up a waterfall. It grunts as it moves. Sometimes the grunts come back to me as words. "This is the way my people have done it for years."

Two green sea turtles stand like men, big and thick, at the top of the waterfall. The hog shrugs me off. His bristles burst into flame and he shifts back to Matthias. "Aumākua, what are you doing here?"

The Sea Turtles shape shifts as Matthias' bristles burn out. For a moment their shells glisten like *Dou* and I see them as *kozane* armored Samurai. They spin and their armor fades, their appearance like Sumo, and then they are turtles standing like men again. "We watch The Brave One." One points at me.

Matthias turns to me. "Quite the audience you have."

"Thanks?"

"Are you afraid?"

"Of what?"

He laughs. "Take my hand."

I grab supple iron, smooth, flowing. His hand grows warm.

"Now stare at the stars. Always stare at the stars."

I look up.

"Now. Leap!"

He moves a second faster than I do. His momentum collects me and I feel like The Hulk carries me while he jumps between mountains.

———

"Keep looking up."

We splash into something. The current is fast, from the feel moving downhill. I go through memory; are there mountain rivers in Hawaii?

"Keep looking up."

My hand is still in his. He guides me. The water is thick, heavy, difficult to walk through even though only up to my calves, and warm but not unpleasantly so, only slightly more so than the ocean at the beach where Matthias' family lives. The air is heavy with sulphur and my eyes tear.

"From the vog."

"Huh?"

"Volcanic fog."

I start coughing.

"You okay?"

Breathing is difficult.

"Heal."

My chest aches, shifts. I remember Grandpa smoked cigarettes. Grandma, too.

And Grandpa said I could do something he couldn't do.

Heal.

My lungs clear more with each breath.

"Thank you. I don't always remember to do that."

"Takes a while to get used to."

Waves crash but far away, each crash accompanied by a rumble under my feet which comes to me as a voice counting my steps "Five more steps. Four more steps. Three more steps. Two more steps."

One. Two. We step onto dry land.

"Look at me."

Matthias is a living flame. The firelight of his hair covers his body. His flames wisp into the night.

He points the way we came. "Look over there."

My mistake. It wasn't water. We walked through lava.

"Congratulations. Pele accepts you."

I faint.

We ride the turtles back to Matthias' home. There we slide off their backs and they walk to the sea. One turns before submerging into the waves. "Good for you, Brave One. That is a true FireWalk."

Matthias' children rush out of his house. "What did you bring us, Daddy?"

He holds out an arm. His children pull themselves up on it and use him like a jungle gym. "A brother. Another child. No longer *ha ole*."

His eldest smiles from atop his shoulders. "Good for you *Kekahi Kekahi*. Tomorrow you get to walk on your own."

"What?"

~

"You already did this."

"I already did this with you helping me."

"The first time you walked, did your Grandfather help you?"

"I guess. I don't know. It was a long time ago."

"You walk okay on your own now?"

I snort.

"This is no different. The first time you walk, you need help. After that, you walk on your own or not at all."

I stare at the stars.

"Remember how you felt the first time."

I keep my eyes on the stars.

"Feel that way again. Now."

I take a step.

"You've done this before."

I take a step.

"And when you get to the other side, I'll tell you a secret."

I take a step.

And a step. And a step.

And a step.

And I step out on the other side.

I'm shaking, panting with excitement. Adrenaline makes me quake like the mountain itself.

"What were you going to tell me?"

"It wasn't really me helping you across before."

"Who was it then?"

The Fire Being, a Child of Pele, separates from me. "Me. *Kekahi Kekahi*. The Brave One. Inside you. All along."

Kekahi Kekahi merges with Matthias. "The Brave One lives in all of us. All the FireWalk does is let him out."

Chapter 94

Utsi

"You need to learn to protect yourself. Shield yourself. So you don't exhaust yourself. Otherwise you'll die for no reason. Your life will be a waste."

A northern wind blows outside his door, the season his people call Deep Winter. We sit around a warming fire. His *goahti* is small, a large hut really, so it warms quickly, and homey in a sparsely decorated way. A rune drum takes pride of place on one wall. A single hole in the roof provides a draft and through it I see the Northern Lights dance.

Utsi sees me staring. "The spirits of unborn children."

"Isn't that Inuit?"

"Don't you share?"

"How do you protect yourself?"

"I don't. I let the Universe do that for me.

"You said I need to learn to protect myself."

"You do."

"I don't understand."

"I'm not a Healer. You are."

～

Utsi brews tea and hands me a cup. I sip and grimace.

"Drink a little more."

"Because?"

"Because someone your size needs to drink a little more. Pinch your nose. You won't smell the blood that way."

I gulp.

"Christ, that's awful."

"Give it a minute."

My body starts to warm. In a moment I steam.

"Better?"

"What's in it?"

～

"My gift isn't Healing. I know plants. Herbs. Earth. Soils. Waters. Oils. What goes inside and what stays outside. That's different than you."

A woman scratches on his door. Her son holds on to her, limps, a gash flows rich red blood down his side, leaving a trail as he travels.

Utsi points at it. "That's dangerous. Bears and wolves will follow that. You take care of him. I'll take care of this."

He leaves me. Always before he stayed, made suggestions. Now he's gone. I stare at the boy, his mother, back at the boy.

My heart is pounding. Breathing is difficult. I smell the start of infection in the boy's side. My spirit-body moves through time. How long does the boy have? It stops where there is rotting flesh.

My stomach churns. My eyes cloud.

Lower-Center-Relax-Breathe.

This is what all the lessons are about.

Give freely, naturally.

The Universe will not ask of you more than you can provide.

Unless it does.

But then it'll be alright.

⁓

The boy stands and scratches his side. The wound is closed.

Mine starts to seal. Pus weeps from its edge.

Utsi runs his hand over the new skin on the boy's side, turns to me, dabs his fingers on my wound.

I wince.

"Good trade?"

I nod. "Yes."

⁓

I learn herbs. Roots. Poisons. I learn what he knows. I learn what he doesn't.

A man's leg breaks.

His brothers carry him to me.

I scream as my thigh deforms, snaps, the bone erupts from the skin. Blood. I pant and clutch Utsi's arm. My femur goes back under the skin. The man's bone follows. My skin closes. So does his.

My bone snaps back into place.

His does the same.

But I feel the pain for both.

To save him.

A child sneezes, can't stop. Her heart palpitates. Utsi points. "Flu. A gift of the white man."

Does he mean me?

My lungs fill, her lungs clear.

I can't stop sneezing, can't catch my breath. My eyes water, close, my sky darkens.

The girl takes a breath, shallow, then another, then deep, then fills her lungs and takes normal breaths.

I spasm, the illness leaves.

"Will it always be like this?"

"I don't know."

This one's skin yellows, thickens, something not-her grows, flowers, uses her flesh as soil.

My skin yellows, thickens, blossoms with flowers that itch to the point I wound myself to relieve the pain.

Utsi pulls my hand away. "No. Heal."

Lower-Center-Relax-Breathe.

The flowers fade. My skin sloughs, grows white, some falls off, healthy pink beneath.

Her skin follows.

"What's happening to me?"

"You're learning."

Teeth fall out of rotting gums.

I taste blood, pus, in my mouth, spit.

Teeth fly out followed by drool.

"Learn."

Lower-Center-Relax-Breathe.

Jaw bones strengthen. Teeth regrow. My mouth heals.

An old woman smiles.

Utsi wipes perspiration from me. "It was cancer. Did you know?"

"Did you?"

~

"We're done."

"Why did I have to come up here to learn this?"

"Because up here, in the cold, no one can hear you scream."

"I thought it was in outer space nobody could hear you scream."

"Same thing."

We travel two days to a small village where bush pilots land skiplanes.

"But why you?"

He lifts my gear from his sledframe. "Because I said no."

"You said no to what?"

"I was supposed to be a Healer, like you. But I couldn't do it. I was afraid. Of the pain. I couldn't do it. You learned herbs and roots and waters and oils, sure, and you'll learn more as you study, but you'll never need them. Or need them as a cover, to hide what you really do."

"I don't understand."

"Ever read *Childhood's End*? Arthur C. Clarke?"

"You've read Arthur C. Clarke?"

"You always let appearances deceive you? I couldn't go through with it. I was weak. So now my job is to help others go all the way. Or help them understand when they can't."

"And me?"

He laughs. "Oh, you'll go far." He pats my back. "You'll go so far you'll probably never come back."

"What? You mean here?"

"Make sure you protect yourself. Stay on guard. If people find out what you can do, they'll come to you from everywhere, drain you, suck you dry, not care that their problems are killing you, and worse, will come to rely on you to fix them rather than learning how to fix themselves."

"Sounds like what my Grandfather said."

"Never met him. Hear he was a wise man."

"Is there anybody who doesn't know about my grandfather?"

He laughs, nods. "Oh, I'm sure. And one other thing."

"What?"

"Father Werner was right."

Chapter 95

WindWalker

"Ceremonies and Rituals are not the same."

Her name is spoken quietly, with reverence, the way one speaks in a church, synagogue, or other holy place.

"Where will I find her?"

"You won't. When you're ready, she will come for you."

I walk to my mailbox by the side of the road, letters in hand, stamps in place, diligent in my correspondence with those who can not hear thoughts, when clouds gather as if herded by Aeolus, Borrum, Nilch'i, and Dogoda.

I place the letters in the mailbox, feel a hand clasp mine, hear a voice like the sun warming frost, taste a cold wind caress my lips. A laugh comes with the kiss. "Dogoda is closest."

A wind gathers me, lifts me, and I walk among clouds.

"There are many Birthing Ceremonies."

"Where are you?"

"There are Birthing Ceremonies involving the totems we're born with, involving the directions of things at our birth, involving those things which come to us to help us, and involving those things which we call to us."

"Which are you?"

"You could perform the same Birthing Ceremony for two different people and, unless you were trained as a Ceremonialist, you wouldn't recognize that the same ceremony was being performed."

"WindWalker?"

The wind rests me on an island mountaintop. The ocean is a rippling blanket on all horizons. The wind is sweet. A young woman, full bodied and made of stone, reaches out for me, offers me a papaya.

"Thank you."

The papaya leaves her hand, falls into mine, my body becomes stone, her body shrivels to a crone's.

"The same Ritual, whether it is Birthing or LifePath or PeaceWalk or Visioning or Naming, must be different for each person who the Ceremony is for."

"How can the same ceremony be different for each person it is performed for?"

"Listen. As your Grandfather taught you."

"You knew my Grandfather?"

The wind chuckles. "Ceremonies are not performed, Rituals are."

Clouds shape wings on my back. I fly to plains succulent with buffalo grass.

"Who teaches me?"

"One who wants to learn."

"You are WindWalker, then?"

"Who are you?"

I hesitate, then laugh. "One who wants to learn."

The winds encircle me, join in my laughter. "Good answer."

My skin grows wet. The air is sticky. Orange scent fills me. "Where are you?"

"Where are you?"

I laugh without hesitation. "In a place I can learn."

"Good answer."

Orange trees surround me. A tall woman, her skin youthful green bark and her eyes sweet and red like cherries, walks out from behind one. "Hello, Gio."

"WindWalker?"

"You are not afraid?"

More laughter. "Of course I'm afraid. But I feel no danger."

"Good answer."

Arms like tree limbs reach out to me, embrace me, her strength is of the earth, crushing. She pulls me into her, her bark skin wraps itself around me, consumes me, and I sit with her around a glowing green fire in a wooded glen, the trees surrounding us with loosely intertwining leaves and limbs. Beyond them is the cosmos: stars and galaxies and nebulae, some I've seen and some are new to me.

"What do you wish to learn?"

"What do you wish to teach me?"

Her head falls back and she laughs. Her tree body dissolves and a walking wind stands before me. "Have to be careful. Don't want to blow the fire out."

And we begin. She divides into the Four Winds, each a voice: the South warm and sultry, the East energetic and excited, the West sagacious and tender, the North patient and searching. Each voice tells me its story about the ceremonies and rituals I must perform for others.

"Ceremonies are unique, rituals are not. Ceremonies never change and rituals must, and how they change from one person to the next is as individual as the people the rituals surround." The South wind pauses in its whispers. "Apara taught you this."

"Yes. This was taught to me in great detail by Grandmother Apara."

The West wind creates a path before me, a series of steps, a precession and invites me to follow. "Rituals have a precise, distinct, ordered progression from beginning to end. This progression is based on the training of the practitioner, the LifePath of the person the ritual is for, the LifePath of the practitioner, the place where the ritual starts, the place where it stops, the intended outcome, the desired outcome - "

"The two are not the same?"

Laughter from the Winds.

" - and very much on the Ceremony upon which the ritual is based. One step of the ritual must follow another in precise detail."

The North wind blows on the fire and it surges. Images form in its flames. "This is a major difference between ceremony and ritual: There is right and wrong in ritual, never in ceremony. Anyone who performs the same ritual for all people isn't performing a Ceremony at all, and many people perform rituals, such as birthing rituals, without knowing the Ceremonies which drive them."

The East Wind enters me, explores my core, my being, my dreams and wishes and hopes. "All ceremonies are echoes of what's inside and what's outside the ceremonialist. The ceremony itself takes place on the boundary where internal and external meet. It is in this ceremony that the ritual must take place, itself an echo of the exact moment in the World when the ceremony is active."

The Winds join. "However, if you aren't aware of the ceremony, what's outside of you or what's inside of you - or worse, if there's nothing inside you at all! - all you're doing is a ritual. Rituals are the form, Ceremonies are the function, the substance."

"What happens when someone performs a Ritual without knowing the Ceremony which derived it?"

WindWalker stands before me at my mailbox. "Apara goes to great length to find suitable candidates to take on the role of Ceremonialist. That is why you are here with me."

She leans towards me, kisses me. The Winds separate, my mailbox rattles, dust and dirt lifts into the air, trees sway.

I watch clouds disperse. "My question..."

"Be afraid."

Chapter 96

Godmother Budapest Z

"Study enough, practice enough, and you learn everybody *thinks* in the same language. The mental-body is the same design for everyone. It accumulates rules for language, culture, society, family, job, vocation, avocation, and people will tell you they *think* in English or Italian or Bantu or Urdic or whatever."

Her accent makes understanding a challenge and she whacks me on the side of the head when she thinks I'm not paying attention. My father did the same, but meaning to hurt. With Godmother Budapest Z it's a shove. But a strong one. She's a big, round woman, a female Santa Claus. Not a Mrs. Claus, Godmother Budapest Z is a female Santa Claus. With a little Phobos thrown in. And she has a salt&pepper mustache. Sometimes she catches me staring at it.

"I am beautiful, am I not?"

"Yes, ma'am."

"Liar!" Whack!

I meet her at her university office, per instructions mailed to me along with travel instructions. Her walls are a mosaic of awards, diplomas, recognitions. She stares at me as if inspecting some strange morsel on her dinner plate.

"*Magyarul beszélsz?*"

"Beg pardon?"

"Learn."

"Yes, ma'am."

Whack!

She motions me to follow. We go to a smallish lecture hall. She speaks to the class then points at me. "Classes will be in English until he learns better."

The class turns and looks at me.

I blush. I wave.

They turn back, focus on her.

She travels widely and is much in demand for her studies in half a dozen fields. "I make sure I have time outside my duties to study my duties." She laughs. She can pun in half a dozen languages. English isn't one of them.

"You understand?"

"Yes, ma'am."

"Liar!" Whack!

She wears colorful slacks and blouses, always nature colors, bright and eye-catching without being striking. She preens putting on coats or sweaters, making sure all lines are correct, all threads are in place.

"That's how they communicate to themselves. Ask a person what language they *think* in and, even if they believe it an odd question and take a moment, will answer with the language they speak most often."

One of her students introduces himself. "You have a place to stay?"

Godmother Budapest Z is suddenly there, no hint of movement, as if falling out of the sky to stand beside us. "He stays with me."

The student's eyes go wide. He pulls back from me slightly, apologizes, hurries away.

What did I say?

"Observe someone who acquired a second language late in life and you see flaws in this logic. Even fluent, conversational, and idiomatic speakers of the second language, when alone, hear their thoughts in a pidgin dialect. True multi-linguals think in sounds and impressions, only forming words when they communicate with others. Tonal language speakers need quiet to think fully, completely. Over time, organizers of tonal languages limited allowed tones so thinking became clearer. Language signers do not think in signs but in concepts and constructs."

We go to her apartment in St. Stephen's. It's not easy to get to. Unlit stone hallways sweat moisture like an animal's skin. Stairs designed for a giant's step spiral an unimaginable axis. I get dizzy. There's moisture on my upper lip. My nose is bleeding.

Godmother Budapest Z flags me a handkerchief over her shoulder. I can't imagine how she gets up and down, in and out each day.

"You alright?"

"Yes, ma'am."

"Liar!" Whack!

"I go this way for easy for you."

"There's another way?"

"Always another way."

We come to a door. My legs ache and I massage my thighs as I wait for her to open it.

Waiting, my mind wanders back to her lecture. Something's not right, not correct, not true.

She opens the door. Before seeing her apartment I see her view.

It is wrong.

Her walls are floor to ceiling bars. Not prison, not confining or re-straining. Evenly placed bars a grown man could walk through. There is a wind coming off the Pest and Buda Hills. It shuffles gently through the bars but nothing in her apartment moves.

The Danube, the cities proper, the hills. I hold onto a bar over my head and gaze out. There are no taller buildings here? I saw taller buildings when we arrived. One at least. I remember a statistical problem-solving method, hill-climbing, a tool for determining optimal systems.

What is this system optimal for?

Her furniture is comfortable but sparse. A chandelier hangs from where vertical bars join overhead.

She points to a plush blue couch. "No matter what happens, you stay there."

I notice a downy feather, a chick's feather, on the couch. "What's going to happen?"

"Hungry?"

"Yes, ma'am."

"What kind of food you like?"

"Anything, really."

She laughs. "We'll see."

She steps towards the bars marking the walls of her apartment. I rise up. "Anything I can do to help?"

She turns, her coat changes colors. Her slacks balloon. Her arms swell into wings. Nictating membranes come up over her eyes. When the membranes recede she has raptor eyes. There is a beak where her nose and mouth used to be. It opens and Godmother Budapest Z shrills me in Hawk's voice. "Stay on the couch. You're safe there."

She hops to the bars, leans through, leaps, opens her wings, and is gone.

~

"The real language of the mental-body is the shapes of the experiences its had. Every brain stores these experiences as memories and constantly references them to understand the present and plan the future."

I glance at her students. She's talking Four-Body Work to them and none notice? None bat an eye? Four-Body Work is common knowledge to them?

"The mental-body communicates to itself and others through sharing - not shared - experiences. People who practice learn by intention: unifying all four bodies to perform a single act. That's how they derive their power. It's not just *I thought of this* or *I feel this way* or *I ache*." She glares at me. "English is weak when describing such things."

She speaks specifically about English? At a Hungarian University? And where is her accent?

"You must experience as much as possible to understand what is communicated and communicate what is necessary."

The students leave.

"You remember the way to my ..."

She hesitates, watches me.

"...home? Yes, I think so."

This Santa Claus woman stares at me with raptor eyes. "Go there. I bring dinner."

She waits for me as I open the door. Dinner plates mix with styrofoam containers. On the floor beside her is a dead rat.

"It old. I asked."

I sit down. The lesson continues.

"Few people know how to quiet their mental-body. It is not taught any more. A peculiar kind of discipline now practiced by aboriginal hunters and, in some cases, world-class athletes, the physical- mental-body axis."

She dines behind my back. I hear skin rending, bones crunching.

"Hearing the mental-body is easy. Most people, when they encounter someone able to listen, become terrified of what secrets might be revealed. Remember, because they are a thief, you must steal."

I put down my fork, turn towards her. "My Grandfather taught me that."

Hawk holds the dead rat in its talons on a bed of twigs and leaves covering the floor. Its beak is red. Its eyes are on me.

"You grew up away from your Grandfather, away from people who always spoke, felt, thought, and hoped truth, you learn that people lie."

I hear her voice. Like Grandpa's. Inside me.

"Whatever they tell you, they lie to protect themselves. From shame, from discovery, to gain advantage, to hurt you. If a young child asks, 'Who is Santa Claus?' tell them the truth. No matter how old they are, no matter what you want them to believe, tell them the truth. They are old enough to ask, they are old enough to know the answer."

Hawk rips flesh from the dead rat, lifts its head, gobbles it down.

"You are old enough to ask. You are old enough to know the answer."

~

"All your lessons at the university, the ones I sat in on, you were teaching me, weren't you? You taught them one thing and me another?"

"Tell, don't ask."

Whack!

~

A fog rises from the Danube this morning. I stick my hands through the bars. They come back wet and cold. I pull myself up to the edge, look down. I'm not used to being this high in this body. My knees weaken. I waver.

A strong hand pulls me back. "You will not fall from this nest. No human hand will throw you down and step on you here."

I look at Godmother Budapest Z. The female Santa Claus preens her mustache.

"I am beautiful, am I not?"

"Yes, you are beautiful."

~

Hawk returns, a dead cat in its talons now. The door is gone. I have not left the apartment in two days.

"You didn't bring me anything to eat?"

"Sometimes children need encouragement to leave the nest."

~

"Not passing, not borrowing. More like WildCat than not. You will meet him soon."

I hear her in my heart. Hawk leaves me in the nest, shrills to me as she journeys.

"My kind have protected this land for thousands of years. Some could see us, others not. Those who could see sometimes burnt us, killed us. Put us on crosses, called us devils."

"My Grandfather's teachings. They will hunt you down and kill you."

My flight feathers appear when I'm not looking, like the hair on my chest and back, suddenly there in my teen years. I hop to the edge of the nest.

"You fear."

"Yes."

Godmother Budapest Z's raptor eyes hold me in what was once a cold-hearted gaze. Now I see only love. "Didn't I tell you, you will not fall from this nest?"

"But if I do, at least one body will die. My physical-body will die."

"You value it above all the others?"

"I...I..."

"I will catch you if you fall."

"Promise?"

"I am beautiful, am I not?"

"Yes." Our beaks touch. "Yes."

I fill my wings, circle St. Stephen's twice, and head home.

Chapter 97

Oly Andreevna

"These have been in my family for years. My grandmother gave them to me."

Oly lays out the cards - more correctly, tiles. Hexagonals with the most beautiful, intricate images on them. Men and women on thrones in royal regalia, peacocks, gryphons, unicorns, bears, sailing ships, a skeleton in rags on a throne soaked in blood, an empty altar, the moon, stars, the sun, planets, an old man kissing a young woman, a mother and child, a blind man who's dropped his cane, and each tile with a central image and parts of other images on its side - to see my future.

"These are Russian Gypsy Cards. The oldest. A kind of Tarot."

"Not one I'm familiar with."

"No."

Oly's husband, Andre, sits at a separate table by a window on the other side of their kitchen, going over sheets and sheets of computer code on 14 7/8" x 11" continuous form paper. He glances up each time a car goes by, people walking, dogs off leash. Birds startle him. He holds down the paper with his left forearm. He has no left hand, only a stump healed over so smooth I wondered what could have removed his hand so cleanly. His right hand flips paper back and forth, a red pencil in hand. Occasionally he scratches his thick black beard or even deeper black mane. Sometimes he drops the pencil and rubs his deep set, blue eyes, squeezing a pince-nez he doesn't have. A car drives past, slows, his hand drops to his side, finds nothing there, his face pales, the car continues, he goes back to his code.

The cards are in no obvious order. Some edge tile images match - a falcon becomes whole but above it a fore body of unicorn pairs with an upside down elephant. Six edges meet six other edges until a jagged pattern forms.

"How do you know when to start a new row?"

"The cards know."

A bizarre quilt takes shape.

"Where shall I start?"

I laugh. "At the beginning?"

She smiles. "Good answer."

The reading finishes as the sky darkens. Andre brings over candles, lights them by striking a match against the seat of his pants. "You learn to hold tight when you have only one hand left."

〜

"All tarot, all cards, all wands, rods, scythes, crystals, gems, candles, stars, charts, all are tools, lenses. They help focus, sometimes guide, maybe clarify when you're not sure. But they can't become the thing in itself."

She hands me her tiles. They vibrate in my hand, living things.

"Feel them?"

"Yes."

"No, you feel me in them. When you know how to use them, the first thing you do is cleanse them. Remove me from them. Otherwise you read me into anything you do. Understand?" She points to the full moon. "You need either a woman's blood -" she points to her groin " - or pure ocean water."

I frown.

"Pure ocean water is hard to find now. Not all women will give you their blood." She puts her hand on my belly. "You learned to give birth. Use your own."

"I...uh...don't bleed that way."

She takes a small knife used to trim candlewicks from the table, reaches for my hand, jabs my thumb. A red puddle forms on the table.

"You bleed now."

———

"Master musicians, it doesn't matter what instrument they pick up, they can play."

"I've noticed that."

"Here it is the same. You learn my tiles, but you can do the same thing with crystals, tea leaves, flowerpots, rain drops on a window. What you learn is to be open, to focus. Only be open with one tool, only focus through one lens, you're blind all other times."

She hands me traditional tarot. "Read me."

———

I rub my eyes.

"Tired?"

"Everything carries a message. Everything is readable. All that matters is being open."

She draws me to the kitchen window. Andre sits with a new ream of code.

"What are you working on?"

He sits back. "You tell me."

I hear a crack. A door opens. My hands flip pages, the dot-matrix impacts tingle my fingertips. Andre's childhood. St. Petersburg winters. Caroling. Soldiers. Marching. College. "*Вас выбрали ...*" Meeting Oly. Flight. Escape. Capture. Hunger. Word comes Oly is safe, waiting. Lies. Trust. Walking. Freedom.

"You..." I shake my head.

Oly puts a hand on my arm. "Slow. Read. No interpretation. Life is not great literature, but each life is great."

～

"How do you stop seeing?"

She sighs, looks at her tiles spread out over the table. "You learn only one lens. When you're not with that lens, you don't see."

"Then why did you teach me to not use a lens?"

She walks me to her window. A Dust Devil swirls down the street. She points. "It told me to."

Chapter 98

Wildcat

Wildcat takes off his shirt. His dark skin gleams as he stands over the fire. He pulls a stick of thick kindling from the wood he's gathered and forms the fire to some purpose. He draws its smoke over him as if bathing in a stream and throws a mixture only he knows how to make over the flames.

It sizzles, blue smoke rises.

"Ah."

This is the fifth year I've come to him, the first year he's let me study.

"It is difficult working with the dead. First you have to get their attention, which isn't always easy, then you have to make sure they understand."

"Okay if I take notes?"

"No, it's not okay. You can ask questions, you can ask me to repeat something." He glares at me. "But don't do it often or we're through. Ask me to clarify, okay, but to repeat means you're not paying attention. I don't have time for that." He continues bathing himself in the blue smoke. "Remember."

"Nobody's ever taken notes? Imagine what's lost."

"Imagination is best used to discover what's new."

"But what about what's forgotten?"

"What's forgotten is what's never used."

His long white hair glistens in the firelight. Short and wiry, I tower over him when he leads me to this place, barely able to match his pace. His eyes sparkle whether he looks at the fire or the stars.

"I'd rather work with the dead than the insane. With the dead you have a pretty good idea after the first time what kind of energies they'll carry. The insane? Each one is different."

"You work a lot with the insane?"

"Take your shirt off. Imagine how much energy an insane person has to exert and extend in order to create a singular, functional reality which is widely variant with the group consensus."

I cock my head at him.

"Afraid to take your shirt off?"

"No, I..."

"Didn't know I went to college?"

He is a psychiatric social worker "in the daytime." He's taught at Harvard and done advanced research at Vanderbilt and Duke.

"I..."

"Didn't Paula tell you never stop learning. Anything? Or to know anything you must know everything?"

"I'm seeing her again this Fall."

He studies me like a hawk circling a mouse in a field.

"Tell her I said *hau*. And take off your shirt."

I take off my shirt. He throws more medicine on the fire and waves the smoke over me.

"Clean yourself."

He shows me how. I mimic his movements. He corrects some of mine. My skin tingles.

"That's right. Do what your Grandfather taught you; Relax-Lower-Center-Breathe."

"You knew my Grandfather?"

"Everybody knew your Grandfather."

My skin turns blue with the smoke.

"That's right. Listen to my skin. Again."

I close my eyes.

He slaps my arm. "That's not how you do it. You know that. Tae-Sek taught you better than that."

"You know Tae-Sek?"

He sits up straighter. "Watch."

His skin roils as if it's its own being with its own life. I hear it breathe in the smoke. His skin is still dark but now it's also blue like a clear, moonless, midnight sky.

"Everybody maintains their own reality. Most people accept the reality of the consensus. It's easier, doesn't require as much maintenance, and so on. Borrow from me."

My skin twitches like a horse shaking off a fly.

"There are times when the majority consensus is obviously in error. Nazi Germany, while establishing a working majority consensus on reality, was also an erred or flawed reality. Manifest Destiny is another example of erred or flawed reality. The mass incarceration of US citizens of Japanese ancestry is an example and the recent prejudice towards Muslims is an example.

"Most people don't have training, desire, or inclination to fix the flaws or correct the errs when they are obvious in the majority consensus."

"You sound like a textbook."

"I'm remembering a textbook. What has Paula taught you?"

"To know anything I must know everything?"

"And what are we learning?"

"To remember."

"Everything. Someday you'll study StoryKeeping. It'll be important."

"*Hau.*"

"Here's the important part: Don't like the reality you're in? Change it. After all, you made it. It's yours. You've come to study my ways. To do what I do, you must ignore the majority consensus, you must be your own reality, you must ignore what others want and need you to be, be who you truly are so you'll know how to get back."

I nod. He throws more medicine on the fire.

"No matter what your culture or training or background, everybody has a slightly different take on reality. Usually these differences are so minor as to be immaterial to those moving around them. Borrow."

My skin roils. It blues. I taste the fire's medicine on my chest, back, arms, thighs.

"To us, it means constantly working and studying to develop the ability to alter not only our own but other people's realities when necessary."

The hawk circles the mouse again.

"So, if you've been following along, you know that to do what we do you have to be somewhat insane."

I raise my head. The hawk draws near.

Wildcat rolls on to his side, convulsing with laughter.

"There's a lot of Coyote in you."

"There's a lot of Gulla Bull in you."

"*Hau.*"

He throws more medicine on the fire. Blue smoke rises. My skin roils again and itches. The horse twitches off many flies.

He shakes his head, wags his finger. "You came here to learn that. Let it happen. Learn what skin is you and not you. Your skin is you on the inside, what you decide on the outside. Most people's outside is what others want them to be. Some people's outside is some of what they want to be and still mostly what others want them to be.

"You turn that around, put what you want on the outside, make your inside and your outside the same. Then you can decide what to do with what others want you to be, accept it or reject it. In either case, once you learn, you move on."

"It's my first time doing this."

"A weak excuse. Make every time you do something the first time you do it. Find something new each time, something you didn't explore the last time, something you didn't sense the last time, something you didn't feel, didn't taste, touch, hear, see." He looks at my skin, snickers, and his eyes rise to meet mine, the snicker gone. "Or did you come here to perfect your excuse making? You're already good at that, you don't need to come here to practice."

My face reddens.

He slaps me. "You feel that?"

"Yes."

"Stings?"

"Yes."

"Good. Now you know what the outside feels like. Turn that inside out."

"I don't know how!"

"Perfect place to start. What you're doing do any good?"

"No."

"Then do something else. If what you're doing isn't working do something else. Eventually you'll find what does work."

"Makes me wish I studied Finding."

He laughs. "Except that first time a Finder finds Finding. They don't wake up for a while after that." He throws more medicine on the fire. "Lower-Center-Relax-Breathe."

I do.

"That's better. Go to your center. Whatever's holding you back, it's there."

I came to learn versipellis, skinchanging, shapeshifting. WildCat is a master of this. He took me as a student. He says he took me to work with me, that I could teach him.

Five years I came, five years he refused, walked away as if I wasn't there. This year, yes.

I want to be like him.

"No, you don't."

I forgot his awareness, his sensitivity. I look up. He is me.

My voice comes from my lips from the other side of the fire. "To help you. To understand what holds you back. This is why we shift: to understand *the other*, yes, but first we must understand *the other* in ourselves. We become *other* when we no longer have to become ourselves."

I feel pulses in my mind. Memories.

"You do not believe you're enough? No…"

More movement. My heart becomes a roadmap and I travel through my life.

"Your grandfather didn't abandon you, Gio. He never abandoned you."

I want him to stop, but too late. He is me completely. All that I am, he is.

"You've never been alone. The Universe has always been with you, waiting."

He winces with my memories, pulls away from my experiences, my betrayals, each stripping of my innocence.

"Like that, Gio. Each layer, a lesson. Everything is your teacher - "

"You decide what the lesson is."

He reverses myself in him, exposing a bolus of pain blooming like a cancer. He holds it out to me. "This is yours, Gio. Do you want it?"

I shake my head.

"But it is yours. You must decide what to do with it."

I take it, a black melon of writhing horrors, faces of those I thought friends, voices of promises broken, words thrown like weapons, hands speaking hate. Tendrils swarm like a fungus over its bleeding surface, penetrating my skin.

"Don't let it, Gio. Know what is you, what is not, what is *self*, what is *other*."

My skin grows thick, hardens, becomes stone-like. The tendrils can't break the surface.

"Good, Gio. That's one way. Can you be yourself and keep out *other*?"

Lower-Center-Relax-Breathe.

"I - "

My skin softens.

"Yes?"

" - am - "

It becomes flesh.

"Yes, Gio?"

" - not - "

The tendrils pull back, into the bolus, not seeking my being any more.

" - this."

I drop the cancer into the fire. It explodes like a sun between us.

"Excellent, Gio. What did you learn?"

"To recognize not me. To recognize *other*."

"And what can you do with that learning?"

"I can be me."

"And?"

"And not me, when I choose."

He smiles, reaches over the fire, takes my shoulder in his strong hands. "Very good, Gio. Excellent."

He still smiles, but different. The fire catches his eyes at strange angles. They seem larger. He pulls his hands back.

"What did you come to learn?"

I laugh. "About myself."

"How?"

"By studying versipellis. Shapeshifting. How to be *other*. By first learning to be me."

He reaches out and takes my arm in a large, broad, short-fingered hand.

"Better hurry."

His hand finishes transforming into a bear's paw. Fur races up his thickening arm as claws dig into my flesh. His nose extends, his ears move up his head and grow smaller. His smile shifts as fangs replace teeth, its jaws extend as non-human incisors and molars erupt through the gumline. His eyes grow further apart and see more.

I laugh. I become him changing.

The bear claps its paws, laughs with me, growls. "Oh, that's good, Gio. That's good." He continues inside. No more talk. Bears now.

I feel his last thought as we trundle into the night. "It was never about you, Gio, all those years. I wasn't ready."

"Huh?"

"It was about me. I wasn't ready to teach you."

Chapter 99

Profesora Anna

"The name is not a good translation. Some people say *PowerPlace*. I prefer *SafePlace*."

Profesora Anna walks ahead of me, my right hand in her left. The path opens before her, closes behind me. Sometimes I lose her in the forest undergrowth except for the black bowler which never seems to leave her head.

"Safe Place? My Grandpa -"

"Yes."

My jeanned legs are swallowed by the dark green plant life at ground level and my hiking boots are lost in the foliage. Rainbows fly and hop and scamper as birds and frogs and lizards move around us. Curious reptiles clamber up the sides of thick tree trunks to stare wide-eyed at me, tasting my body heat when they flick out their tongues.

"I'm glad you wore colorful clothing."

"Yes."

I stumble over two scents mingling on the trail: riotous life and rotting flesh. Plants hiss as moisture rises, there's a sound like razors stropping as leaves rasp my legs.

We stop. Profesora Anna points to her ears then to the canopy over us.

"Water? Not rain. What is that?"

"A river of air."

She stops walking and draws me beside her. We face a prismatic display of light, a cat's-eye the height of a man glowing in the forest.

"All of these places are HealingPlaces. In all of these places we do HealingPlace Work."

She steps inside and pulls me through.

~

"People call it an intersection because people call them *lines*, therefore the lines intersect at a point." She looks outside her window to the streets below. The sub-tropical sun casts long shadows on the pastel-colored buildings and reminds me of adobe canyons in the American West. It is Saturday afternoon and people are walking everywhere, laughing, singing, some street musicians take over a corner and a crowd gathers, clapping and dancing to the music. "Is that what an intersection is in life? No. Here we deal with the real, not ideas to protect us from what is real."

I say nothing. She directs me to some multicolored beanbag chairs on a woven rug, the only furniture I see, and places a bowl of *Feijoada* and a small cup of thick, dark coffee smelling of honey on a low table beside me.

"Eat, then sleep. We begin tomorrow."

The heat, food, and long bus ride on uneven dirt roads take over. I close my eyes.

~

Early Sunday morning. Chickens are awake and cluck their way down the street, little parades of yellow and brown chicks hurrying nowhere with a Keystone Cops precision. Hawks circle overhead preparing aerial assaults.

Profesora Anna guides me to the intersection outside her third story corner apartment. Looking back I realize she lives in a watchtower, able to see most of the town to the fields to the river and forest beyond.

"I will help you the first time." She Lowers-Centers-Relaxes-Breathes.

A spinning rainbow caroms down the dirt street, dances around us, bumps me aside, caresses her, lifts her long black hair in an unfelt wind, tips her bowler hat, she chuckles as if being tickled.

Her stubby, brown hands reach out to it, pull back glowing lines, cords. Her hands move quickly, suredly.

She draws from it, threads from a spindle, weaves a tapestry, forms a door of light, invites me through, follows, weaves it shut, turns around, rips out stitching I didn't know existed on the other side, another door opens, motions me through, follows.

We stand in a grassy glen. Cattle graze on a little slope to our right, a forest forms a boundary on our left.

I close my eyes, searching with my ears. "Water? Sounds like children splashing."

She turns me. "There."

"I smell water."

"Look."

A river, more a stream, so many cricks and crooks in its flow the water wanders like an old man unsure of his footing. Children splash, fill pails. Some cows mosey over, stand in the water, drink.

The sun cuts a different arc through the sky. "Where are we?"

～

"There are two HealingPlaces I go to regularly for my own purposes. One of these I've travelled to since childhood, another I've discovered only recently. There is another HealingPlace which was shown to me by my teacher many years ago and, because there has never been a need, I've not gone back to since. There is a HealingPlace only children, I am told, can reach, and there are HealingPlaces which I know of but have never journeyed to."

She teaches me to weave light like threads, to make pictures in nothing then open doors to get there. To take others there. The wounded, the tired.

Sometimes the guilty.

"But only to heal them."

We stand in the center of Hecate's crossroads made manifest. Janus wears as many heads as worlds intersect, each face towards a different world, his robes moving as if splashing in the waters of each.

"I don't understand."

"The natural lines of power and energy which surround the earth have their counterparts in the universe itself. More specifically, there are times when these naturally occurring lines on the earth cross or otherwise come together with their universal counterparts. If you can get to a PowerPlace while its earthly lines are working with its universal lines you have easy and ready access to a place you can move into and out of."

"Stories of people disappearing before people's eyes."

"If you move into a PowerPlace while the lines are working together and know what you're doing, you can stay there while the lines pull apart."

"A prison?"

"A HealingPlace. A SafePlace."

"For the guilty to heal?"

"Consider how much knowledge one needs to go there and bring someone back if that's what they wanted to do."

"Why are these places HealingPlaces?"

"Because when you are in a place which is truly safe and the power of the Universe is moving about you, Healing can rapidly occur."

I hear the emphasis in her voice. This is not the healing of doctors and men. She lets me know without words "The Universe works here."

"This is what my Grandfather taught me. When he had me capture moonlight to make gifts for my Grandmother."

"To open doorways where none exist. To travel. Remember this. For healing."

Stories of wizards waving their hands in the air and making things appear and disappear. They opened and closed doorways. Nothing more. Nothing else.

"Thank you, Profesora."

She steps back. I use Han's teachings to see two lines, pick them up, ask them to intersect, weave their energies into a gateway, wave goodbye, walk through.

Chapter 100

Grandmother Parvati

"Take your time. Catch your breath."

She is as tall as I am and her skin is colored from many suns. She looks me eye to eye and brushes hair from my face with a hand roughened by field work. Even so, her nails are clean, and bright turquoise on silver bands run up her arms.

I walk over to the edge of the cliff. The drop is so deep daylight doesn't reach the ground unless the sun is directly overhead. The winds blow quietly here and clouds are close enough to touch.

There is a skin covered lodge behind her. She goes in and returns with water in a stone cup.

"Drink."

She puts a hand on my forearm as I raise the cup to my lips.

"Slow. Drink slow."

"Thank you."

"I don't get many visitors here."

"I heard your voice. Singing. A chant telling me which turns to take, which way to go, guiding me through the passages up the face."

"WordMedicine." She smiles. "You're weak. You've been climbing for two days. Bear told me."

"Bear?"

She laughs.

I encounter nothing on my climb except rock, stone, trickling water, a scattering of Old Man Cacti, some Mexican Red-Legged tarantula.

"Bear." Behind her a piece of rockwall shifts, boulders gather to form belly and chest. Stones become arms and legs. A huge rock grows a muzzle, ears, and eyes. A great brown bear stands behind her.

I step back seeing its size.

"You see Bear?"

"I see something."

"That's Bear. Like WhirlWind. Only different."

"Like WhirlWind. Only different."

"Rest now. Tomorrow we begin."

~

Darkness. High mesa darkness. Stars so close you can touch them. Planets line up east to west. Meteors, one, two, three chase each other across the sky. Mice burrow, their voices and the shifting of the earth they displace sounding as one. Far below coyotes howl, rabbits scurry, owls hunt.

A glow grows on the eastern horizon, the sun wakes from its slumbers lower in the sky than where I stand.

Grandmother Parvati sits in a lotus position, eyes closed and she sees everything.

She motions me to join her.

I clear my throat and her finger goes to her lips. She bows her head, points to her ears.

I remember Grandpa. "*Ascolta.*"

I shake my head, unsure.

She takes my hand. My ears come alive. I hear the fires of the sun.

Her finger returns to her lips. She spreads her fingers, holds her free hand over her head.

My skin crackles. I feel the night's dew rising, individual drops climbing as the rising sun warms the earth.

Her finger returns once more to her lips. She inhales, slowly, a Lower-Center-Relax-Breathe it will take me years to master.

My lungs fill, my nose twitches. I smell HeMouse and SheMouse, HeCactus and SheCactus, HeSpider and SheSpider, HeWater and SheWater, thousands of scents I never knew existed, each separate, distinct, delicious, wonderful stories of where each He and She has been, where they will go, how they will get there.

Her finger touches her lips, her mouth opens, last night's peaches, pears, and plums tasted again, each announcing itself on my tongue. Flatbread, still hot, honeyed by Grandmother's Bees, rolled in my mouth, held in my teeth. Fresh water, untouched, called forth as needed, risen through the earth by her hand.

She releases my hand. The sun shows clearly, still low on the horizon. The western sky is still dark. Meteors still write their names.

She places her hand in mine.

"Now you. Your turn."

———

"WordMedicine?"

"May I show you?"

"Please."

She sits between the fire and a rock wall.

"There is StoryKeeper and StoryTeller. They are different."

She lifts dry earth in her hand, invites a talking wind to help.

The fire flares, the dry earth sifts through her fingers, a movie plays on the wall.

A bear stands in front of a classroom of men and women dressed in business suits.

"StoryTelling is the use of traditional mythologies and related cultural metaphors to guide the people, heal the tribe, remind, teach, et cetera. If you've ever been with someone who could hold your attention, cause your imagination to fire, make your heart pound and breath come in gasps while they told a story, you've been with someone who, in traditional cultures, would be the people's StoryTeller. StoryTeller disciplines appear in modern societies as everything from stand-up comics to psychotherapists to engaging lecturers to authors."

She lifts another handful of dry, high mesa earth and lets it fall. Individual grains catch and hold the fire's light, scatter it, the movie continues.

"StoryKeepers and StoryTellers may share a few stories in common and that's where the similarity ends. StoryKeepers are the living histories of their people. StoryTellers will create new stories based on need, StoryKeepers can't with a few specific exceptions."

Bear, I realize, is a StoryTeller. His audience listens attentively, enraptured.

"StoryKeepers' role is to preserve the history, unchanged, from generation to generation while adding each generation's story to the history of the people."

The movie fades. The fire dims.

"More?"

"Yes, please."

"We'll need more fire."

I add tinder. The fire crackles.

The movie continues, but the bear is gone. Grandmother Parvati teaches the class and I'm the only one in it.

"One thing required of all StoryKeepers is that they create a story that tells of their coming into the tradition. So the two occasions when StoryKeepers add to the people's history are when they add their own story to the tribe's tradition and as new historical elements are added and usually with agreement of the people."

"Usually?"

"Some people want a lie more than they want the truth."

"History is written by the victors?"

She shakes her head.

"One of Buppa's lessons."

She nods. We sit side by side at the fire on the high mesa.

"WordMedicine was my addition to my people's history when they asked me to become a StoryKeeper."

Meteors flare through the sky. One crashes into the fire, sparks fly into the night, a glowing message writes itself on the wall.

"WordMedicine."

Grandmother Parvati claps her hands. The fire goes out, the wind stops, the sky grows utterly dark. No stars shine, no planets ride their paths east to west.

I see her eyes light in the dark. Hunter's eyes.

"Want to learn?"

"Yes, please.

———~———

Grandmother Parvati and I sit cross-legged by a strong fire. A half-ring of stones separates us from the flames. A line of hand-fired bowls and bowl-shaped rocks is between us, about a foot and a half long. The sun sets far to the west and, it seems, below us. Her guardian snores across the fire from us. She touches her hands to her forehead then her fingers to the rim of each bowl and repeats the motion for each bowl. "StoryTelling."

I mimic her motions, forehead to bowls."StoryTelling?"

She stops my hands. "Give thanks."

I nod. "Yes. Sorry. Thank you." I start over.

"StoryTelling. The space between Word Medicine and StoryKeeping. You've learned the first. Someday you'll learn the last. Others have told you of the medicine you carry."

I pull up my sleeves, showing my Medicine Bands: Grandfather Wolf and Grandmother Spider, she of flashing red eyes and long thin threads and he of warm blue eyes and strong, white teeth.

She smiles and points to each in turn. "Yes. Strong Spider and Wolf Medicine, StoryTeller and Teacher. Hungry?"

I nod.

"Do as I do."

Grandmother Parvati pats a ball made of hand-ground flour, water, some sumac and parsley flat then tosses it onto a rock. She checks it, is satisfied, and starts another. "Tell me the difference between StoryTellers and StoryKeepers."

I recite without understanding. "StoryTellers create new stories based on need, StoryKeepers can't with few exceptions. StoryKeepers are the living histories of their people."

She flips the steaming flatbread over. "And?"

"The StoryKeepers role is to preserve the history, unchanged, from generation to generation while adding each generation's story to the People's history."

She lifts the fatbread and offers it to me. "Careful. Hot."

I take it. She licks her fingers, looks around her, talks over the fire to Bear. "Did you eat all the honey again?"

Bear rolls onto its back, four legs in the air, a dog looking for a belly rub, looks at her and smiles.

"Silly bear." She tosses the next flatbread onto the rock and watches it for a moment. We made several balls. She pats them flat and tosses each onto its own rock. At the last rock she leans back to the first, lifts the bread, turns it, and continues until all are steaming and done. "How does it taste?"

"Delicious."

She gives Bear a good, hard look. "Better with honey."

Bear collapses onto its side, its back to us, and farts.

Grandmother Parvati shakes her head. "You need a lesson in manners."

The bear snores.

"What you're talking about sounds like synaesthetic recall, hyperthymesia, and consciously controlled neuroplasticity. People trained in such disciplines have described feeling their brains making new connections."

She gives me a good, hard look. "You've been with Paula too much."She leans in conspiratorially, her eyes askance. "Don't tell her I said that."

"Is there a hierarchy? Word Medicine to StoryTelling to StoryKeeping?"

She shakes her head, her eyes on the fire, and chews slowly before she answers. "No. They share the same thing differently. Word Medicine is healing the individual and only for the individual. StoryTelling heals the individual and those involved with the individual. StoryKeeping heals the People, keeps them whole, together. Let's them know who they are."

"That's important."

She finishes chewing. "Ready?"

"I don't get to finish?"

"Toss them to Bear." She raises her voice to the slumbering giant. "You ate the honey, you clean up, hear me?"

Bear farts.

Grandmother Parvati turns, shakes her head in disgust, walks into the night.

I follow.

～

"Time for you to move on, meet your next teacher."

"No. Please."

"Your grandfather would tell you otherwise."

It is the first time she's mentioned Buppa to me. "You knew my grandfather?"

A gentle laugh. "We all knew your grandfather, Gio."

"Please may I stay longer? There's so much more you can teach me."

"There's so much more for you to learn, and from others."

"There's nothing more you can teach me?"

She looks at me. Bear pulls itself free of the rocks and rears up, challenging me.

I stand, close my eyes, sing a peace chant, WordMedicine she taught me.

"You're not afraid?"

"Terrified, but this is what you taught me to do."

She nods. "Perhaps there is one more thing I can give you."

"Thank you."

"I've carried The Peace Shield since I was your age. It's time for me to pass it on."

"The Peace Shield?"

"There are seven Shields. I carry The Peace Shield. Carry it and you can perform Peace in any situation. You can make Peace happen. But you have to carry it. Put it down and the peace will be momentary, fleeting."

I listen then shake my head. "Grandmother, I've told you about my life, about what I've done, what I've been through. I think you have the wrong person. There's nothing about me that's peaceful anymore."

"Exactly why you are the one to carry it."

"I don't understand."

"The true purpose of The Peace Shield is to find Peace with yourself. Do that, you can create Peace for anybody and anything else."

～

The day leaves me exhausted, weak, and I sweat in the high-altitude setting sun. The Peace Shield is like a feather on the wind and is the greatest burden I've ever carried.

I wipe my face and neck and chest and laugh.

She smiles. "Yes?"

"Just wondering if you ever give out certificates. To the people who study with you."

"Certificates of what?"

"I don't know. I know some people give out certificates saying you studied with them and therefore you're a shaman."

She laughs. "You want a certificate saying you've had an experience? It's your experience, Gio, no one else's. Someone's going to give you a certificate that you've had an experience?"

I share in her laughter. Behind her, Bear joins in.

I hand her a cup of ginger bark tea. "Time for me to move on."

She smiles into her stone cup. "Yes."

Behind her, Bear wipes a tear from its eye. I hear Bear inside me, almost like Buppa's voice. "Good cub, gentle cub. Stay warm, well, and safe."

"Thank you for letting me study with you. Both of you."

She lowers her cup. Her energies surround me, an unseen blanket of life and breath.

I cry. "You are powerful, Grandmother."

She rests my head on her breast and laughs. It is Bear's rumbling laugh I feel in her chest. "Ha. No I'm not."

"But you are. I know you are. I've seen what you can do."

"No. I'm just somebody who practices."

"But what about what you can do?"

"What I can do I can do because the spirits let me. If I'm a gifted pianist and I lose my hands, am I still a gifted pianist? Of course not. But I'm still someone who studies music. What if the spirits go away tomorrow and there's nothing I can do? Will I still be one then? All I can say is that I'll still be someone who practices."

"Then how do you know if you are one?"

"As long as people come to you and you can help them, you are one. When people stop coming you're not one."

"Then you are one. I see lots of people coming to you."

Again she laughs. "No, I'm not." She turns her head slightly, looks at me out of the corner of her eye. Her laugh lines wrinkle her face and I feel her smile. "My teachers, they're the real ones. I'm just practicing."

We laugh.

Chapter 101

Madame Chi Tze

"I want you teach class."

I pull back from the energy between us, a ball of brightly exploding colors, a star seen up close. "I don't know enough to teach class."

She laughs. "I know."

Students enter the classroom. Some are senior to me, see me in front with Madame Chi Tze, smile and nod.

The class fills. Madame Chi Tze bows to the students, bows to me, motions me to take the "teacher" position, and walks to the back of the class where the newest students stand.

I fumble. I demonstrate techniques I haven't mastered. I stop. I look at them, the older students smiling, waiting, the younger students seeking, expecting.

Lower-Center-Relax-Breathe.

"You know what fascinates me about Ji Gong?"

I teach for two hours without a break.

Everyone is working, practicing, I ask them to show me when they do something better than I, I show them when there's a way they can do something better.

Everyone is smiling, laughing, hugging.

Madame Tze comes forward. "Gio, good teacher. You let brothers and sisters rest now. Some need go home."

There are no clocks on the walls. Bright sunlight filled the classroom when I started, now I see stars out the windows.

My brothers and sisters who travel to class thank me before they leave. "Great class, Gio." "That was amazing, Gio." "You really know your stuff, Gio." "You're the man, Gio."

Madame Chi Tze claps her hands at those of us who stay with her. "Clean up, everyone."

I pick up a towel. She shakes her head, motions me to follow. "Time for tea."

I look around. My older brother and sister students smile, nod. Some congratulate me. "Good lesson, Gio. Good learning."

I'm unsure but nod and smile back. "Thanks."

The tea is steeping when I knock on her door.

"Come, Gio."

She pours some. I sip. "You teach good."

"Thank you, Ma'am."

"Some ask I let you teach again."

"Please don't, Ma'am."

"You ask class 'Do you know what fascinates me about Ji Gong'?"

What happened to her pidgin English?

"Tell me."

"I realized teaching, for me anyways, is about sharing my excitement, about what fascinates me, what makes me want to know more. That was the only way to develop mutual understanding."

She nodded. "When you step into the well of your ignorance you are at the top of your knowledge." She poured a cup half full. "Teach from the top of the cup and you teach what you don't know. You fail. Teach from the bottom of the cup and all you can see is all that tea above you, not what you're teaching. Again you fail. Teach from the top of the tea and you invite others to fill your cup. That's how you teach."

"But what if you have beginner students?"

"Then empty cup before do anything else."

"Does my cup ever fill?"

She snorts. "Hope not. Nothing more learn, be dead. People who die figure it out. Don't need study anymore, time to move on, to study in next place."

I shake my head.

Her pidgin drops again. "Ignorance begins where Knowledge ends. Never be ashamed of ignorance. It's a blessing. When you decide you know something you lose the ability to learn anything more or different about what you study."

Chapter 102

Pambenet

Five of us stand at the bus station. "How long have you studied with him?"

It is a cold, rainy November evening. I pull my jacket tighter. "Not long. About a year."

"What's he teaching you."

My wool hat is soaked. Little rivers freeze finding ways under my collar. "Patience."

My classmate cocks his head then looks away as a PeterPan bus approaches.

We wait as the few riders disembark, look at the crowd, find the familiar face, smile, get their luggage, move away.

The driver clicks a little counter as each rider emerges.

No one else gets off. He checks his counter, looks at the five of us, gets back on the bus, walks three quarters of the way to the back, turns, and comes forward again.

He stands in the doorway like a guardian. I think of angels with flashing swords allowing no entry to some sacred hall.

"Any of you looking for an Indian fella?"

My classmates frown. I raise my hand. Rain quickly runs down my sleeve, thankful for the opening. "I am."

"Mind giving me a hand? We got a problem back here."

I follow the driver. My fellow students follow me. I'm not the oldest. How come I got the lead?

Pambenet is snoring, slouched over and taking up two seats. He stinks of urine and cheap wine.

I nudge him. "Sir?"

He belches a stench of rotten cabbage. A moment later he vomits over the seat and floor.

The driver pushes through the five of us. "Excuse me. Excuse me." He goes to his seat, lifts a valise behind it, takes out a pair of rubber gloves, comes back. "Christ. Get him out of here, would you?"

The other students shuffle around. One by one they leave.

The driver looks at me. "Well?"

"Let me get him into my car. I'll be back and help you clean up."

~

The postcard picture shows a middle-aged man in traditional plains regalia. The flip side has "Come meet Legendary Strongman Pambenet" and listed a place, date, and time.

"I wonder how they found me?" I move around so much no address is good for more than a year, maybe two, and I pay for everything in cash hence leave few records.

Also the man in the picture is wearing the wrong regalia for the nation mentioned.

Five of us meet over a store in a small, New Hampshire town. "Did you get a postcard?" "Did you get a postcard?" Some got a call, a message left on their answering machine.

The door at the bottom of the stairs opens. Heavy feet come up the stairs.

A large, dark-skinned, middle-aged man looks through the room, his eyes stop on each of us for a moment then continue to the next. His loose flannel shirt and jeans sometimes flatten against powerful muscles when he moves. His western boots clack when he steps through the door onto the hardwood floor.

He drags a beanbag chair from the wall to the center of the room. "Long ago, Great Spirit - "

I reach into my pocket, take out a small cassette recorder, turn it on.

He points at it. "That's not right."

I shut it off, shove it back in my pocket. "Sorry. I meant no harm. It's only so I can go over my notes later."

"No notes. Remember. Learn."

～

"The next time we meet is the Old Ways."

The Old Ways? My Grandpa used that term. Not him, others around him. Who either laughed or honored him, his ways, his teachings. "Excuse me, Sir. The 'Old Ways'?"

"I have to go back home. My son needs my help. I'll be gone about a month, maybe longer. Someone will let you know when I'm coming back. Come meet me if you want to learn."

His answers are never obvious. Part of his teaching. He's spent a year talking about the dangers of interpretation versus discernment but never demonstrated either. Some of the others grow impatient.

～

No other cars but mine. The driver waves as he turns his bus toward the highway.

I look to the edges of the deserted parking lot. "Anybody here? Anybody need a ride?" I call the names of the other students. No answers.

I open the driver's door of my light blue Volkswagen Fastback. Pambenet is slouched over onto my seat. I move him over. "Come on. That shift's gotta hurt."

"Not really." He sits up. His clothes are clean and fresh. The sour smells are gone. He smiles.

"You were passing?"

"Pretty good, huh?"

"Why?"

"Little Bear charges money. I charge insight. Interpretation versus Discernment." He looks out the windshield to emptiness. "They saw something and interpreted one thing. You saw the same thing. What did you see?"

"My teacher."

"Not a drunk Indian?"

"I saw what appeared to be a drunk Indian. That's not who's been teaching me for the past year. Unless the drunk Indian was another lesson."

"Pretty good, cub."

"Good teacher."

He points back the way the bus came. "Drive."

Chapter 103

Don Alejandro

We drive up a mountain road behind a moving van. My pickup is old and I apologize for its lackluster performance.

He nods, smiles, gazes out the window as we climb. His poncho, shirt, pants, socks and sandals match the midday, lowland Autumn colored trees and I wonder if they'll shift to different greens and browns as we climb into rich afternoon pine forests. A long, black braid comes down from the bottom of an equally black bowler I've never seen him remove and I wonder if he sleeps with it on and if all native South and Central American teachers shop at the same store. His hat has a woven band with all the colors of his clothing, of the world, and it seems to move independently of him, some kind of Navajo sand painting come alive although that's not his people, not his tribe.

Sometimes his hands rest quietly on his lap, sometimes they conduct an orchestra only he can hear. Sometimes they swish flies away from me I can not see. Once in a while he lets out a deep, guttural *Ugh* and his hands rest. It sounds odd coming from a small, almost petite man.

I wonder if my constantly shifting up and down gears as the van ahead of us goes up and down grades irritates him.

He points out the window to the forests on either side of the narrow climb. "I greet these."

"The trees?"

"In my country, nothing like this." His English is good and sometimes he slips into pure rainforest.

I drive him from lecture to lecture, class to class, my payment for his time.

"You know Language of Trees?

"I know about FrostRunes -"

"No. Secret Language of Trees. Must be TreeBrother or TreeSister to understand."

"No, I don't."

He looks out the window. "*Ugh.*"

The van ahead of us downshifts. There's no passing zone, no indication of one. I chose this route thinking there'd be no traffic.

"We won't get to your next lecture on time."

He nods, keeps staring out the window. "*Ugh.*"

"A good truckdriver would pull over, give me a chance to pass him."

He smiles at the van. "Good truckdriver."

"No, I mean, he'd pull over if he was a good truckdriver but he doesn't, so he's not that good."

"He knows. I talk to trees."

"He does?"

He points to a grassy part of the shoulder. "Stop."

"We'll be late."

He smiles. "Stop."

He gets out, stands still for a moment by the still open door of my pickup, then walks into the trees, a place where the forest's thickness touches the grass on the far side of the shoulder, a doorway I didn't notice.

Does he have to pee? Wants some privacy?

His small, brown hand emerges, the shirtsleeve a pale hollyberry green, his poncho a deeper, alpine green.

His hand, so like a child's hand, motions me in, inviting me to play a game.

Voices.

I remember now.

Grandpa. Grandpa and his friends. My friends. Talked with Trees.

"I teach you nothing new, Little One. I help you remember."

An oak reaches a branch down, pats my head. A pine shakes and the scent of scotch fir envelops me like a woodland cloak. I breathe deep. Vines and tendrils and runners and roots climb up my legs until my blood turns to sap and I drink from the earth.

"See? You hear? Listen? The Secret Language of Trees."

~

We sit in my pickup. The engine won't start. I check the sun's position in the sky.

"Where I go *no importante* where I am *ahora*." He points to the sun, the trees, himself, the ground outside his door.

"Another of my teachers taught me something like that."

"*Capitán* Bill?" His "Bill" sounds like "Beehl."

"You know him?"

He mimics Bill's voice completely. "All that matters is you know where you are. What're you going to do when your ship sinks, tell the Coast Guard that you're on your way to Diamond Cay? They might never find you. But if you tell them exactly where you are, they'll come get you in maybe an hour, maybe two."

"How do you do that?"

He points to his ear, shakes his head, points to his heart, nods.

His voice echoes in my chest. "Do you know that whatever is supposed to happen where I'm going either will or won't happen regardless if I'm there or not?"

I nod.

"So whether or not I'm there doesn't matter at all, right now. All that matters right now is that I'm here, in this truck, with you."

My pickup starts without my touching the key.

"Right here, right now is what's important. Right here, right now, can only be where I am. So what's the most important thing in the world?"

~

We crest the mountain in the middle of the night and he points to a scenic turnout. We get out and he Lowers-Centers-Relaxes-Breathes, invites me to join him.

"Know how big is Now?"

"Huh?

His small, childish hands become huge, come under me, lift me.

"I remember this. My Grandpa did this."

"He tell me teach you."

"You knew my Grandfather?" Who didn't know my Grandfather?

He pushes me, stretches me, my body becomes loose, yielding, extendable, his hands working me as if kneading dough, and I become thinner, larger.

"Now you do."

I remember how it felt with Grandpa, how Don Alejandro's hand-shaped energies feel, let myself relax, let the gravity fields of the universe pull and shape me and when one has shared enough I thank it and find another until...

Until...

The Universe slows, slows, slows.

And stops.

I hear Don Alejandro in the silence of suns. "Immensity of Now. Remember?"

"Yes. Thank you."

"You stay. Play. Learn. I wait for you."

I return and find him in a shelter made of fallen tree limbs. Once he's outside, I shake it. "Amazingly sturdy."

He points to his head. "Remember what is teach you."

I want to correct his English but don't. Would I understand better if I did? Would he explain better if I did?

He walks to the driver's side door. "I do?"

I hand him the keys. "I didn't know you knew how to drive."

He grinds gears, doesn't clutch, races the engine, stalls out. And laughs. The jostling he gives us is great fun to him.

"Mind if I drive the rest of the way?"

"I okay."

More grinding gears, smoking clutch, racing and stalling engine, and laughter.

"Do you know how to drive a standard?"

"I watch you. Learn ritual, not ceremony."

He pulls over to the side, pops the clutch, stalls us out. We switch places.

He watches the trees. "You people know rituals." One hand waves in my direction. "You know how to drive, how to use phone. I watch. You go buy buy buy." He pulls his hand back. "But not ceremonies. No *Why* of the *How*."

"You've read Nietzche? 'He who has a *why* to live can bear almost any *how*'?

He shakes his head. "Understand *Why*, you know why *How* works."

Our last evening together, his last teaching, he performs his people's Color Healing Ceremony on a woman with arthritis. His hands grow and shape and move along her body contours, sometimes six inches above, sometimes three, sometimes a foot or more. He waves them. Sometimes it looks like he's juggling, sometimes like he's gathering something.

I hear voices from the audience. "What's he doing?" "Can you tell what he's doing?" "Anybody see what he's doing?"

I see. I can tell. But they can't. Two months traveling across America I realize he's been doing the same thing to me.

Some move their hands the way he moves his. He looks at me. I nod. "Ritual, not ceremony."

He smiles. "You talk for me."

I take the microphone from his host and translator. Don Alejandro's voice resonates in my chest. "Please don't do this. Don't be so foolish, so stupid, so arrogant. Think you can watch me do something once and know immediately what I'm doing."

Inside I hear him talk about all he is doing, explaining.

"No, *Patron*. Tell them such things and they'll think they know more. They won't realize they know less."

He looks up at me, away from the woman, and nods.

He stands back. She rises from her chair, her joints no longer swollen, her hands no longer misshapen, her back no longer bent, her legs no longer bowed.

He smiles. "Better?"

She hugs him. He lets her kiss his cheek. She's slightly taller than him, doesn't bow as she approaches, tipples his hat.

One hand raises up, holds it fast. He smiles, giggles almost like a little child, and points to his other cheek. "Here one, too."

He walks through the audience and singles out two young women, two young men, a young boy, a middle-aged man, a teenage girl, an old couple. "Stay." He turns to the audience as a whole. "Goodbye. Good night."

He says nothing more until everyone save those he singled out leave.

He takes my hand and walks me to each person. "*¿Que ves?*" "*¿Que ves?*" "*¿Que ves?*" What do you see? What do you see? What do you see?

I describe colors and energies and flows and motions and sounds.

"Good, good." We return to the first woman. "See green."

I shake my head. "I see white."

He shakes his. "*No importante. ¿Que ves?*" Not important. What do you see?

"Cancer?"

"*Sí*. You see white, I see green, not important. Important you know white is cancer and I know green is cancer. *Ponerse de acuerdo en lo que es, no en lo que vemos.*" Agree on what it is, not what it is we see."

I clap my hands and laugh. "Now is more important than where we're going."

He nods, smiles. "First color, now sound." We start again with the first person he selected.

He Lowers-Centers-Relaxes-Breathes and motions me to follow. Energies and entities surround the people.

"Know who you talk to when you do this."

The people he's chosen. All their illnesses.

"You smoke. Drink coffee. Alcohol. Drugs." He recites litany; TV, radio, music, movies, ... He points to his chest. "All to change what is here."

I understand. "Rituals, not ceremonies. We can heal them but if they don't change their *Why* then they'll never change their *How*."

He puts his hat on my head. "*Buen trabajo, Gio. Lo hiciste bien. Es hora de que me vaya a casa.*" Good work, Gio. You did good. Time for me to go home.

Chapter 104

Calum

"You've learned all you can learn *am Beurlad*." Pahdeval rises as I enter his kitchen.

Da Fischer sits at the table and nods. "*Feumaidh tu Gàidhlig ionnsachadh gus barrachd a thuigsinn.*"

Their words surround me, their meanings enter me; to learn more of their ways, I must learn their language.

Da Fischer pulls a chair out for me. "There is one who can teach you *bhlas*."

Pahdeval nods. "Calum Crùbach."

Da Fischer takes a *bodhran* from his kit and tips it, his hands moving from its center to a side and back, as if tuning. "*Falbh an Alba Nuadh.*"

"Nova Scotia's a pretty big place."

Pahdeval puts his fiddle under his chin. "You go. He'll find you."

Da Fischer knocks the sides of his *bodhran*, establishing a rhythm. Pahdeval draws his bow across the strings. Wind giants grow at the intersections of the sounds, their voices like clouds colliding. "Come. You are too close to the floor."

I enroll in Gaelic summer school. I study *Gàidhlig* in the morning, stepdancing and piano in the afternoon, explore in the evening. I learn my Gaelic name. Mine has two meanings. One is my name, the other is "Here it is!" I laugh. Each teacher gives me a name and rarely do they have a single meaning. In some places I am "Walks Mountain," and it can mean either "I walk through the mountains" or "I carry a mountain in my travels" depending on when it's said.

William is renamed Ulliam and is on leave from the Gulf War. I enjoy his stories but his patriotism strains after a while.

Mary becomes Mhairi and runs a call center in North Sydney, not too far away. They service many international companies and spend a week learning neutral English, neutral French, neutral Spanish, neutral whatever country they'll be servicing. "No matter where you call from, you think we're native speakers but can't figure out what part of the country we're from." She demonstrates Leeds English and says the same thing in Chicago English. Amazing.

Jack is a talented fiddler and helps another student buy her first Scots fiddle, a *Clayton*. He refuses a *Gàidhlig* name. "You know how to win on *Gàidhlig* Wheel of Fortune? Ask for an H." He pronounces it *haitch*.

Malcolm speaks fluent *Gàidhlig*. He's a science and phys-ed teacher from the Annapolis Valley and studies *pìob mhòr*, the grand highland pipes. His humor is dry and infectious. He tells stories straight-faced then bursts out laughing when people catch on to the joke. He is courteous, gracious, considerate, helpful, and openly stares at women's chests when talking with them.

He and Jack always find reasons to give the female students a big hug. Everyone laughs. One particularly buxom student hugs them right back. "Cheap thrills, boys?"

I study to the point I dream in *Gàidhlig*. Calum never appears.

It is a week until the end of the semester. I prepare for bed and wonder if I'll meet my new teacher. I shake my head at my reflection in my mirror. "Guess I'm not ready for him."

There's still a week to go.

I rest my head, turn out the light.

Sometime in the night I wake to the sounds of *pìob mhòr*, the grand pipes, and sit up.

Snoring from other dorm rooms creeps under my door.

I get up, walk to the window, pull back the drapes.

The pipes grow louder, stronger. Am I the only one who can hear them? How can someone not hear the grand highland pipes being played?

There's no lights on in the hallway, no light coming in under the door. Nobody else hears them but me.

Calum?

I leave the room half-dressed, hop down the hall putting on sneakers, pulling on clothes.

The piping's outside, nobody else has their lights on.

I run on to the quad. Lower-Center-Relax-Breathe.

A RiverCloud ripples down beside me. The cloud has Malcolm's face. He shares a joke only I can hear. My head lolls back, laughing. I cover my mouth then realize no one else can hear.

A hand forms at the edge of the cloud, reaches out. I take it and am gone.

Chapter 105

StoryKeeping

I ride a Lamers bus in northern Wisconsin heading into Michigan's Upper Peninsula. A beautiful woman wearing full jingle dance regalia walks down the aisle towards me, the blacks, blues, reds, and yellows of her tassels and beadwork shimmer like feathers in the sun. Each step is a cascade of sounds, Marley's Ghost would fall silent before her. She sits beside me.

I smile as she takes her seat.

Her lips don't move. Her face becomes a hawk's. The bells and jingles on her shirt and dress ask me a question. "Are you ready?"

"Beg pardon?"

Her face returns. Her eyes defocus and her nostrils flare. She inhales a deep draught of me, two days without a shower, without soap and water, without brushing my teeth, hurrying to somewhere, knowing I must be there but not knowing where I must be.

Grandmother Parvati told me, "When you're truly lost, take a step in any direction. It won't matter and you'll get closer to your goal."

Good advice when you've also learned "My goal is my journey, my path is my prize."

Her hand lights on my thigh, her fingers crawl further.

Her eyes remind me of the Huron's deep waters and dangerous seas. Her chest swells with each breath.

"Tell me a story, I'll see to your needs."

She blinks.

I sit by a fire under a starlit sky in a field ringed with great pine, elm, and oak, a northern forest. The fire blazes like the sun. It is difficult to look at. Warriors from several Great Lake Peoples are with me, waiting.

A hawk glides through the night, gathers its wings preparing to land, and becomes the jingle dancer from the bus.

"Tell me a story."

I blink, understanding. I am offered a great honor, to become a StoryKeeper of the People.

My empty stomach clenches and I sweat. "I'm not read -"

She brushes a hawk feather across my lips.

I nod. My feelings, my fear, my anxiety: none are relevant under a cold, starlit sky, sitting before a fire with warriors waiting.

I begin.

~

There was once a little boy who left his village and returned knowing how to journey the way shaman do. He returned to his people wearing tassels on his wrists and everybody who saw these tassels knew they were magic but nobody said anything to him about them.

Each day, the young boy helped tend the village herds and fields, each evening he ate with the old and not-so-old, the young and not-so-young in the village. He laughed at their jokes and made some of his own, cried at their grief and learned all of his own.

One evening, a little girl came to the boy. "Boy, what are those tassels you wear on your arms?"

She did this at the village fire. Everyone grew quiet to hear what the now older boy would answer.

He smiled at the little girl. "What do you see, little one?"

"I see snakes," she said. "Big, beautiful snakes. Snakes to ride on and carry me away."

The boy nodded. "Thank you, little girl. Thank you for telling me what these tassels on my arms are. Now I know they are snakes. Thank you very much."

The little girl smiled and laughed and the older boy did, too, as the little girl went off to play.

A few nights later one of the oldest men in the village came up to the boy as he sat by the fire. "What are those tassels on your arms, boy?"

"What do you see, Grandfather?

The old man thought for a moment. "They are the waves of the great waters." He paused, seemed to think again, then stared deeply at the boy's tassels, smiled and went on. "Yes, they are the waves of the great waters. And look! There! There are the great canoes my grandfather's grandfather crossed those great waters in, the same canoes which bade him safe passage to this place." The old man looked into the boy's eyes. "That's what I see."

"Thank you, Grandfather," said the even older boy. "Thank you so much for sharing with me what you see in these tassels on my arms. I did not know what they were and now I do. Thank you for telling me what you see."

The old man and the now-older boy hugged each other and the old man walked away, smiling as he remembered the great biadarkas which brought his people to this place where they lived.

And so it came, over time, that each person in the village told the boy what magic they saw in his tassels and he thanked them for the stories they told.

All, that is, except three old women. Each time they saw the boy they laughed. Finally one of the women asked, "What are those cords wrapped around your wrists?"

The boy shook his head. "I don't know, Grandmother. I always let people tell me what they are, that way I learn. What do you think they are?"

The old women huddled amongst themselves in whispers for a moment then laughed. "We thought they were strings to bind your sandals, but see you wear none. Probably just strings you found, are they not?"

The now grown boy saddened and counted this lesson as perhaps the greatest of all. He lifted his tassels and stared at them before he answered. "Why, yes, Grandmothers. If that is what you see, that's what they are."

The three old women cackled to themselves and walked away.

One day a great trouble came to the village. It came quickly and swiftly and no one was warned. Many in the village had already died when the little girl who had first spoken to the boy ran up to him and cried out, "Boy! Boy! You must do something quickly. Hurry! Our village is dying."

The old boy shook his head sadly, no. "But there's nothing I can do."

"Can you save us?"

Again the boy shook his head. "No. Each person has to save themself."

"How?" cried the little girl.

The old boy unwrapped the tassels from his wrists so they flowed like snakes upon the ground. "Tell me what you see, little one?"

"Snakes!" she screamed. "Beautiful, wonderful snakes!"

And so there were. Two huge glorious snakes coiling on the ground. They lifted their great heads up to face the little girl and slithery said, "Come, little daughter, get on our backs and ride us to safety."

And so she did and so she is safe. The terror engulfing the village reached her not.

Then came the old man. "Boy! Boy! How can I save myself?"

The old boy swayed his tassels before the old man's eyes. "What do you see, Grandfather?"

The old man calmed and smiled. "I see the waves of the great waters, and on them the canoes that first carried us to safety here."

And thus it was so. Suddenly the old boy and the old man were up to their waists in the sea with a great biadarka floating beside them.

The old boy helped the old man and all in his family into their canoe. Suddenly a great wave came and the old man, his family, and their canoe sailed away. The old man turned and waved and then the very old boy was back in his village. The old man, all his people, the great biadarka that carried them, and the waters they sailed were gone.

Each person who came to the boy now came again. As each came the boy reminded them of the magic they saw in his tassels. Each person took their magic and went away to safety. There were great eagles and stars and waterfalls and buffalo, walking trees and talking waters, all flowing from the ancient boy's tassels to the people in the village.

All except the three old women. They came to him crying and screaming, "Tell us what magic you have for us, boy, that we might be safe as are the others."

The old boy remembered these three old women but there was nothing he could do.

"Surely there is some magic in those strands for us," they demanded.

The old boy shook his head and cried. "No, the only magic in my tassels is that which others put there. All the magic I gave others they already had. I merely reminded them of the magic within them. You saw nothing in my tassels, so there's nothing I can give you. There is no magic in you for me to remind you."

The boy grabbed his tassels and tied them around his hands. Suddenly his hands and tassels became great feathered wings which carried him away from the danger to where he was safe.

———~———

One by one the warriors rise, approach me, leave their arrows and bows, warclubs and axes, at my feet. Each walks out of sight, into the night beyond the light of the fire.

Hawk Mother alone remains.

She walks to me, her hand goes to my chest, pushes me, knocks me over, straddles me, reaches for me.

She smiles. "Good story."

Chapter 106

Bolaji

He welcomes me into his home. The Comoros Islands are not easy to get to, Chissioua Ouénéfou, a mostly uninhabited island, even less so. His abode is more hut than home, made of driftwood held firm with ocean grasses.

He sees me staring at them. "They mark the change to C4 plants."

I shake my head.

"Somewhere between six and ten million years ago plant life abruptly changed everywhere on the planet."

I note he considers *deep time* a place, a where, not a when. His knowledge of deep time to modern plant biology doesn't surprise me.

He laughs, high and musical, which suits his tall, lean body, a hint of his Kenyan heritage, the coloring of his skin reminds me of a 16' oboe church organ pipe, and I'm sure his voice would carry through church halls, organ recitals, into the ocean, into the rocks, into the air. Like all native Africans I meet, he speaks several languages and I'm grateful English is one as Shimasiwa is difficult to master, with different vowel sounds and voiceless, implosive, and prenasal consonants.

"Stay long enough, you'll learn."

"It is my hope."

"Brother Andrew speaks well of you."

I smile. They all know each other, it seems, and I'm not new to any of them.

He points to a cot. "Put your things there."

"Thank you."

"We eat, we rest, we start tomorrow. Sleep well and deeply tonight."

I nod. He laughs, high and rich and it fills his home.

~

He is gone. I step outside. The sun skims the surface of the ocean, and it smells different to me. The waves scrape different salts from the rocks underneath, the sun warms at different angles, the tides come from different shores.

I listen to the water coming and going, feel the heat and light of the sun, let it surround me, practice Chan's waves, hear my Grandfather's voice, *Ascolta. Chiedi.* Listen. Ask.

Voices come across the water. Singing. Fishermen ply the waves, two to each small boat, casting nets. One man fishes alone and his net seems tangled.

I cup my hands around my mouth. "Need some help?"

He looks up, shakes his head. I don't have enough Shimasiwa to be understood. I mimic him throwing the net and pulling it in, throwing the net and pulling it in. He nods.

I wade out to him, my feet move carefully over the coral bottom.

He waves his hands. Shouts. Other men in other boats look up, see me. Shout, wave.

I stare around me. Danger? A shark? I take a step. The ocean swallows me.

A shelf in the water, unseen because of the glinting sun.

I still can't swim. Are there fish? May I borrow?

A dark shape comes over me. A hand reaches through the ocean's surface, envelopes my wrist, lifts.

The single man, his nets abandoned, pulls me into his boat, holds my head in his hands, stares deep into my eyes. "Okay?"

I nod. "Thank you."

He points to me, to the shore.

I shake my head, point to his nets.

We spend the day fishing. My skin darkens. He teaches me some words. I want to ask how he says "Big, dumb, white guy" but can't even think how to ask.

Lunch is a fish he guts and skins on the boat. Two sunbirds, their green and gold bodies shining in the sun as they groom, perch on the forward boat railing and watch. He says something to them, they hop forward. He puts two strips of fish on the railing, the birds snatch their prize and are gone.

He says something, I have no idea what, and laughs.

I do, too.

The end of day finds us at a small dock. He hands me two good size fish, hugs me.

I don't know where I am. He points to a path through the brush. It leads me to Bolaji's camp.

"Have a good day?"

"I brought dinner."

～

He's gone again.

I go outside, practice waves.

There are no fishermen.

Children laugh in the brush behind me.

Young, dark-skinned children natter amongst themselves. Many carry baskets woven of the same grass bracing Bolaji's hut. They gather seeds, fruits, nuts.

I follow. Two children look up at some fruit well above my head. I wave them aside, climb slowly, reach the fruit, toss them down.

We walk further. Another tree. Another climb.

More walking, more trees.

Insects buzz, birds chirp. An iridescent blue and green butterfly flits in front of me, lands on my nose. I go cross-eyed staring at it, unmoving while it slowly moves its wings together, a church steeple on its back, and opens them again until they glisten along its sides like aircraft wings.

I wonder if it's resting.

Its tongue zips out, samples my sweat, retreats, my guest takes off.

I'm thirsty. One child smacks a large green, melon-like fruit against a rock, holds it together and hands it to me.

I don't know how to hold it and my hands are soaked as its juices run free.

The children laugh.

We continue. The sun lowers. One more tree.

I look up at the fruit hanging well up in the sky and roll my eyes.

The children laugh. One jumps up the tree's trunk, scurries up like a squirrel wanting to hide a nut, goes higher and faster than I could do, pulls the entire fruit-laden branch until it snaps free, drops it to us.

It seems he's on the ground before the branch is.

I drop down, roll with laughter.

The children join me, give me a basket of fruit, point to a path, and I'm back at Bolaji's hut.

He greets me. "Good day?"

"I brought dinner."

He sits on the floor beside my cot. I wake to his smile. "Never hesitate to show kindness."

I rise slowly, stretch, nod.

"You've been busy."

I shrug.

"A friend's daughter is a concert oboist."

He knows about plant life's transition of C4 pathways, why shouldn't he know someone whose daughter is a concert oboist?

"No one else in the family ever demonstrated any penchant for music. One day he asked her what caused her to pursue music with such determination."

He stands up in one smooth motion, offers me his hand. I take it. "She said that when she was a child - she thought maybe three or four years old - the family went on a trip and met a friend of her father's in a restaurant. She remembers that she was fidgeting because her mother kept telling her to sit still while her father and his friend talked."

He holds a bowl of cooked fish and fruit and offers it to me. I dip my fingers in and lick them. Delicious.

"This friend asked the waitress for an extra straw. He took out a pocketknife and made a few cuts in it, then put it to his lips and started playing music with it like it was a flute."

I hold the bowl and offer him some. He gathers fingers full and munches as he talks. "Real music. Tunes you could recognize."

"Show me?"

He pulls a half hollowed stick from the hut wall. I hadn't noticed it before. He raises it to his lips, sounds one note. Lowers it.

I cock my head, shake it.

He laughs.

"Listen." He raised it again, sounds the same note, begins to sing between the notes, rhythmically beats his chest. Outside I hear children laugh, I feel them dance. Fish leap into nets. Fishermen join Bolaji's song.

"This friend then gave the little girl the straw and said, 'Here you go. Play.' She said she didn't remember who the friend was but did remember that his ability to take a common soda straw and turn it into a musical instrument was magic to her. True magic and she never forgot it."

"Wow."

"It's also what caused her to pursue music the way she did, because she wanted to give others that kind of magic."

He holds the hollowed stick out to me. "It's called a *n'dehou*. One of many flutes in Africa."

I blow a note, laugh.

"That friend was me. Her story taught me that we can never know how much the slightest act of kindness - or cruelty - will affect another's life."

I pat my chest, blow a note, don't know the words, laugh.

"Act with kindness even though you don't know the outcome. Never doubt that something you said or didn't say, did or didn't do, et cetera, changed the universe in some incredible way. The Universe's concept of the Butterfly Effect is 'You said hello to someone walking down the street whom you didn't know therefore a lifeless planet is starting to form oceans.'"

He knows The Butterfly Effect. He probably helped formalize it.

"You helped a man fish even though you didn't have to and it almost cost you your life. You offered children help when you didn't have to and realized they didn't need any help at all."

I blow notes, beat my chest, and sing "I had fun both times."

He opens the door to his hut. There is no ocean, no children, no sounds except the silence of deepest space. I see galaxies and nebulae outside his door.

He steps out, turns back to me, offers me his hand. "Come. Let us make oceans."

Chapter 107

'Bukunmi

She looks up from the books on her desk, smiles, and waves me in. "'Bukunmi?"

Her voice is wind playing with water and her accent echoes broad leaves tasting the sun. "Hello, Gio. They told me to expect you."

I glance at the books still open on her desk.

"Law. Nigerian law."

I shrug. "I don't know law."

"There are four legal traditions in my country. You must know all four to practice here."

"Sounds challenging."

She laughs and the sound tickles me. "Everything is challenging if you need it to be. But everything has its place. Know where something is placed, you know how to find it, how to use it."

I nod.

"But be sure to put things back where you find them. It's where they like to be."

"Huh? I feel those words but I don't understand them."

"Not yet. Soon. Something for the next place."

"I'm sorry, 'Bukunmi. Ms. Ma'am. I really don't understand."

She laughs again. "'Bukunmi is fine. And what a wonderful place to start."

I hear many voices singing in her words. Green pigeons land on the trees outside her office window and peer in.

She sees me staring and continues to face me. "They are curious about you."

"What a wonderful place to start?"

She laughs. The pigeons open their beaks and join her. I hear them all as a song, the many voices of a choir.

She pushes back from her desk and stands. She is tall. Taller than me, and truly statuesque, with long black hair done western-style so it hangs below her shoulders. Deep, dark eyes fix on me and laugh lines pull up long lashes. Wide nostrils flare as she takes a deep breath, looks down at her books, waves a long-fingered, graceful hand over them and they all close at once.

"Back to your places, all of you."

The books fly to different places on the bookshelves lining the walls on either side of her desk.

"You're not disturbed by what you see?"

"Not yet."

She laughs and I hear a lion's roar. "Good answer."

~

We drive east out of Ikoyi on the Lekki-Epe Expressway onto smaller and smaller roads, her BMW exchanged for a LandCruiser for something from a MadMax movie, until we're alone on a road deep in a forest. I can't see the sky and assume it is night.

Eyes, not distant, glow at me from behind and in the trees. 'Bukunmi pulls off the road, stops, faces me and opens her mouth wide.

Her eyes glow at me. Her teeth are more cat-like than not. "I'm hungry. Are you?"

"What's on the menu?"

She laughs again. It is a lion's roar. It echoes off the trees and shakes our car cum tank. "Good answer. You like oranges?"

"Oranges grow in Nigeria?"

"What was today's first lesson?"

"Know where something is?"

She lifts her hand up and to her right and it disappears at the wrist. "Know where something is and you find it there." Her hand reappears holding an orange and she offers it to me.

"Thank you. Would you like some?"

She smiles with feline teeth and I notice she's growing whiskers. Deep in the woods around us I hear growls, things walking, feel eyes staring.

Her other hand goes up to her left, disappears at the wrist, and reappears holding a kitchen knife. "Thank you." She takes the orange back and cuts it cleanly in two.

Close behind me I feel the breath of something large.

'Bukunmi chews the orange slowly and without looking at me. "You are brave."

"Have you ever noticed bravery and stupidity are often two sides of the same coin?"

She laughs again and turns the rearview mirror to face me. "Look."

My eyes are cat's eyes, my teeth have feline prominence. I'm growing whiskers. "Was that really an orange you gave me?"

More laughter. Something large jumps onto the hood of our vehicle, circles, lays down and falls asleep. "You study maths? Science?"

I nod.

She raises the knife to her right. Her hand disappears, reappears minus the knife, gathers the orange peel in her left, raises it to her left, it disappears, reappears missing the peel. "Explain this to me."

"The closest I can come up with is something in Quantum or Hyper reality. Something in other dimensions. You know where it is so it seems you're pulling something out of thin air."

"In order to touch, we must be willing to be touched. In order to see, we must be willing to be seen. We cannot act without interacting."

I nod.

"Are you willing to be touched, Gio? Are you willing to be seen? Are you willing to interact?"

"Are you willing to help me learn? To teach me?"

Her laughter is a roar. The creature on the hood raises its head, licks its lips, lowers its head and snores again. She takes my hand, raises it above us. "To know where something is, you must be willing to be known where you are."

My hand disappears. Something bumps into it, cradles itself in my palm. It moves as if alive.

The creature on the hood rolls onto its back. Its eyes open and focus on me. It purrs.

'Bukunmi lets go of my hand, guides my other one. It disappears.

The creature's purring grows louder. A giant hand rests above it. I scratch the thing my hands touch which I cannot see. The giant hand's fingers scratch the belly of the creature on the hood.

It purrs. Its paws reach up and touch a giant finger. I feel little claws gently dig into my unseen fingers. The creature draws the giant finger close, licks it, lets it go, rolls onto its feet, looks at me, jumps off and is away.

I pull my hands back.

"Remember to put things back were you find them, Gio. It's where they like to be."

I turn my hands over in front of my eyes unsure if they're where I think they are. "Yes, 'Bukunmi."

"Also so others can find them when there's a need."

"Yes, 'Bukunmi."

Chapter 108

Ouliadês

An elderly, white haired gentleman, his skin darkened from years under Cypriot suns, opens the door. He smiles a full smile of strong, white teeth and shakes my hand. His grip is strong, not crushing. Confident. He steps back, nods, and motions me in. "Welcome, *Kouros*."

I go through my memory for the translation. "Cool guy?"

He laughs and slaps my back. "Speak from Parminides time."

I shake my head.

"Something to learn."

Cyprus is not big. Limassol to his home in the center of the Troodos Mountains takes a few hours, much of that walking the final few miles from where hitchhiking leaves me to his door.

I look for a place to drop my pack. He reaches and slips it off my back.

"I'm -"

"Gio. Yes. I remember. Welcome, *Kouros*. We've been expecting you."

Sounds of plates and pots, a well being pumped, come from a room separated by a curtain.

I look at the sound.

"We're making us some lunch."

His English is quite good. Better than I remember from childhood.

"We've travelled some since then."

I take a handkerchief from my back pocket and wipe the sweat from my face, not used to the Mediterranean heat.

"Would you like to wash before we eat?"

"Yes, please."

He leads me out back to another water pump and fills a basin with water cold from the heart on the mountains. I look at the view and gaze at snow-capped Mount Olympus. It's about to cast its shadow on us.

He comes out of his home and hands me a towel and pumicey soap. A voice comes from the other side of the water pump. "Gods live there."

Ouliadês stands by the water pump. I frown and turn back to take the towel and soap. Ouliadês smiles at me and holds out towel and soap. The two Ouliadês speak in unison. "To learn. Isn't it that for which you came?"

〜

Ouliadês is a *Daskele*, an *Iatromantis*, a teacher and what some call a "medicine man" although the term is more correctly translates as "prophet-healer." He s also a master of bipersonalization. He does not call it that. "It is learning to Shadow."

"My grandfather told me about Shadows."

"Your grandfather was a wise man. We miss him."

Ouliadês uses the plural personal pronoun. "Because we are many out of one."

"You can teach me?"

"You can learn?"

"I want to learn."

"Then we begin."

"Tell us about Shadows."

We sit outside his home, facing east, warmed by the rising sun and sip steaming, dark coffee from small white cups, its fragrance so bitter its fumes make me sneeze.

He reaches into the air up and to his right and his hand comes back holding a lemon. His other hand reaches to a different place up and to his left and comes back with a paring knife.

"You know 'Bukunmi?"

He chuckles. "We know each other."

"Does everybody know everybody?"

"Don't you?"

"How would I know?"

"You would know." He cuts off a slice of rind and holds it out to me. "To sweeten the taste."

It does, and I share what my grandfather taught me. There is a bright place...

He shakes his head and sips his coffee. "That's not what he called it. Remember more. Remember better. Say it again."

I go back, wonder if there's a way to travel through time.

"That's for another to teach you. For now, remember."

I close my eyes, go back differently, remember another of Grandpa's lessons. Recreate the experience by reexperiencing every element of the experience. "A place of such brilliance..."

"Yes. Home."

He says it like my grandfather said it. I remember. "Home."

"Yes. You've been there before. Many times. The doors are there."

I stare at him. Know something I'd never known before.

Or knew without knowing. "In my father's house there are many mansions."

He smiles. "Go on. Can you tell us more."

I smile back. A chuckle permeates my words. "Many mansions means many entrances, perhaps many doors."

"Tell us more."

"You sound like my Grandfather."

"He was a wise man. We miss him greatly." He takes another sip. "Tell us more."

Another Ouliadês comes out of their home with a small silver pot and a plate of sugar cubes. He refills our cups, offers me sugar.

"I prefer the lemon, thanks."

He smiles. They speak together, Ouliadês' voice comes from two places. "Good. Go on."

I slap my forehead, something so obvious, something all my teachers are teaching me, now understood. "Many mansions. Many ways to enter. What you believe doesn't matter, only that you do."

The Ouliadês sitting with me claps his hands, stands. The pot-holding Ouliadês hands him the pot. The former leaves, the latter takes his place beside me. "Now you understand."

"A place of such brilliance."

"Home. You've been there before. Go there now."

"How?"

"*Hêsykia.*"

He offers me his hand and I move while standing still.

"*Hêsykia.*"

My eyes widen more. "Yes. I remember. Journey by standing still."

He wags his head a bit. "Close. Be still to journey."

"Yes. Of course. Lower-Center-Relax-Breathe done to its ultimate."

His head wags again. "Close. Add *mêtis.*"

"*Mêtis*? Intelligent trickery? That can't be correct."

He laughs. "It isn't. Speak from Parminides time."

I shake my head a shrug.

"Awareness? Yes, awareness is close enough for now."

"Lower-Center-Relax-Breathe..." I search for understanding. "In all my levels of awareness?"

He claps his hands, laughs, and he is gone.

Then, "Over here."

Another Ouliadês stands some ten feet from me. A different Ouliadês. More real.

More substantial?

I reach out and he offers me his hand. He points and I follow his finger.

I see myself sitting beside him outside his home and raise a small white cup to my mouth.

"How?"

"Tell me about shadows."

"In a place of such brilliance there is the one, the original, all others are its shadows projected into the world."

"And you are now in a place of such brilliance."

I drop to my knees. The understanding weakens me.

He raises me. "Be that which casts its own shadow."

I shake as the knowledge finds a home inside me.

We are back outside his home and he grips me, his hands grab and hold as if recognizing my corporality. "This sac of flesh is only a projection of what you really are into this reality. Become that which projects its shadow. Project who you really are wherever you need." He points at warblers nesting in some scrub. "The Wild does this naturally. Others have forgotten."

It takes effort. I am back in the place of such brilliance and look back to my shadow. "Thank you."

He smiles. "One more, not for today, and we're done."

"Yes?"

"Is it better to be the light that allows shadows to exist, that lights the way for others, or to live in someone else's shadow, to be in someone else's darkness?"

Chapter 109

Hawk and Mouse

Talons dig into my shoulders and my eyes tear with pain.

"What do you see?"

Hawk is my teacher today. Will I learn his lesson?

"What do you see?"

His wings don't flap, don't beat. We soar so high houses seem like dots on the ground far away. He banks. My body lifts horizontal to the ground as he begins a power dive.

"What do you see?"

The air is so thin, we are so high, I look down on mountaintops, look up and see the dark reaches of space, stars twinkle and shine, the sun is lower on the horizon than we are.

"What do you see?"

We are fully in his power dive now. His eyes are fixed on something so far away, so very far away.

"What do you see?"

"I see mountaintops. I see the sun. The darkness of space. Clouds. The ground far below and closer every minute."

Hawk pulls up, his talons release me, I fall for I don't know how many days, the earth spinning beneath me, the sun and moon chase each other through the sky.

"You see much and not enough."

I tumble through a forest of tall, green, leafless trees. They have no bark, no limbs, no branches.

A snuffling approaches. A rustling comes closer. The giant leafless trees part. A huge black orb crashes down on me. Bristles as big as tree limbs push against me, prodding me. Below the black orb a dark cave appears, white stalagmites and stalactites border a moving pink pathway. Legs gray as an elephant's but with claws so sharp they flense me as they come down on either side of me. Hurricanes suck me up to the huge black orb and stop.

I fall, bleeding.

"Gio?"

"Who are you?"

The great creature grows less and less and less. The barkless, limbless trees shrink until they are only as tall as I. "Mouse."

My wounds heal. I stand.

"What do you see?"

I look around.

Mouse lifts me on his back before I answer. We rush through the trees, stop, rush through the trees, stop, rush through the trees, stop.

"What do you see?"

I take too long to answer.

Mouse's nose twitches. His whiskers tremble. We rush through the trees, stop, he bites down on a worm unable to get back into the earth.

He stands. I tumble from his back. His forepaws hold the worm as he dines.

"What do you see?"

"I see much and not enough."

Mouse turns to face me. Its hindpaws become talons, its forelegs and paws stretch out to become wings, its head become Hawk's, its snout and whiskers become Hawk's beak.

But the rest is still Mouse.

"What do you see?"

"I do not see what there is to be seen. I see what's important to me, not what's important. I confuse my moment with the Universe's eternity and forget my eternity is, to the Universe, a moment. I look only in front of me when I should look all around me. I look all around me when I should focus on what's in front of me."

The Old One shifts again, now Mouse's legs and paws and head and snout and whiskers and the rest of the body is Hawk's.

"What do you see?"

"I see that I am seen."

"Yes."

Chapter 110

FlowerSong

I stand in my garden, unsure of what I'm hearing. The wind gently rustles the leaves. Not that. It snakes through the grass, swishing bees from flower to flower. Not that.

Then I see a vine, a thing, I've never seen before and am terrified.

It stands like a man, taller, and is woven from vines, a walking thing, watching me. It extends green growth arms and shows me white flower petal hands. Its head bobs in the wind, its white flower face, the eyes two black pistils, its eyelids and brows the stamen and filaments of the flower, two broad pink-centered petals form a walrus mustache over a mouth made of stems and leaves. It does not approach, knowing I am alarmed.

The wind overwhelms me. I am suffocating in the tastes of hyacinth and lavender.

It moves into the green, pulling back, and is gone.

I shake, breathe slowly, ashamed of my fear.

It returns the next day, more obvious than before, distinct from the trees and bushes surrounding it. Its head and face bob, nod at me, with the wind. Its hands reach out again. I stare, more willing to be curious than afraid. Why was I afraid?

And again. I think of my work with Raccoon, Skunk, Fox, Bear, Deer, Turkey, Opossum, Wolf, Coyote, all the Old Ones who come to me. I am patient with their Shadows, letting them become familiar with me until I can greet them, learn their names.

I know. I realize. I understand. This being is to me what I am to Raccoon's, Skunk's, Fox's shadows. It exists where Man exists, it comes to me as Man's Shadow.

It speaks with the wind, like Rose but different, its voice, a melody of clouds and sunshine and rain.

And wind. Like a loud whisper, its words brush me, move my hair slightly, a gentle breeze of meaning. Its breath, the scent of hyacinth and lavender.

"Hello."

"Who are you?" I've not experienced anything like it before. "You're not The GreenMan, not Jack O' the Green, not Herne. I feel none of them about you."

Its mouth moves as the wind caresses its mustache flower petals. "I am your ally, your friend."

Behind it, the sky pours through the trees. The wind parts high branches. A bolt of sunlight strikes the trunk of a tree, singling it out from the many, spotlighting its growth.

The being rises up, towering over me, inhaling the light of the sun. "Ahhhhh."

"What shall I call you?"

The whisper of Life. "FlowerSong."

"Are you my teacher?"

A sound of seasons changing. "We have much to learn."

Chapter 111

Subway at Avenue L

I open my front door and step onto a subway platform. The sign on the wall reads "Avenue L" and is blurry. I'm not fully there yet, still rushing through time and space to where I need to be.

But why?

A subway train screeches and scratches along the tracks, the sighing and hissing of its airbrakes slowing its approach until it rolls to a stop and its doors open.

I don't recognize its markings. I sniff the air. No smell of ocean. No graffiti. No trash. No smell of Boston. Or New York, San Francisco, Montreal, Toronto, London, Beijing, Rio, Moscow, Sydney, …

People of all colors exit. All wear heavy clothing, boots, and underneath they wear cultural clothing.

A cosmopolitan city? Where is it winterish now?

I move with the crowd getting on the cars, search my pockets for a ticket, find none. An intra-urban train?

A black woman with a child on her lap smiles at me. I smile back. An Asian man beside her takes off his hat, waves it at the child, creates a breeze to cool the child's face.

The car is crowded. An elderly couple stand, holding the railings. I offer them my seat. The woman takes it, thanks me.

Friendly people? Courteous? I'm running out of options.

I close my eyes. Lower-Center-Relax-Breathe. Why am I here?

My eyes open. The crowded subway car is more crowded still. Everyone's Guides stand, sit, crawl, float, fly, hover, coil, swim around them.

The car goes into a tunnel. Its lights go out.

Doors open at the far end of the car. Long, heavy coats sway with the rhythm of the car on hangers there. An old style street lantern glows in a cloudy, almost night sky behind them, and a cold blast of air, the scent of a forever winter, comes to me.

My Grandfather Spirit sits at my feet, stands, his hackles rise. My Grandmother Spirit spins a web encompassing the car, wraps me in silk, an egg sac, tucks me off to the web's edge, takes her place in the center, her legs sensing everything that happens.

A tall, thin man, roughly my age, dressed in jeans, work boots, a white t-shirt, and orange parka vest pushes the coats out of his way, exits the doors. They clash shut behind him and he doesn't notice.

The lights come on. He holds a broad-brimmed, black-banded purple felt hat in front of him, one hand holding the brim, his fingers flicking a long brown-tipped white feather in the brim, his other hand behind the hat, and held close to him.

I know this man. His admission - a truth - set me free.

Jack.

Grandmother trills her web. Grandfather stands between Jack and me.

The lights go out again.

The eyes of all the Spirit Guides, Guardians, Totems, watch me.

Except Jack's. His hide behind him, peer over his shoulders, peak out from under his arms, watch warily from between his legs, fearful of me.

Known from long ago, from what seems another life: Shame. And Guilt.

I climb from the egg sac to the center of Grandmother's web, feeling the eyes of the Spirit Guides, the Guardians, the Totems, on me, see them as stars in a black night sky.

"I do not know what is to come. Go, protect your children until it is safe."

The lights return, the clacking of the car's wheels on the rails provide a rhythm to my thoughts.

The car is empty. Only Jack and I remain.

He glances around and centers his eyes on me. "What happened to everybody?"

I nod at the hat held close to his stomach and slightly covering his other hand. "Do you plan on using that gun?"

He frowns at me, cocks his head. His eyes light with recognition, his head lifts, and he sneers. "You." His hat slides down to his side. A revolver remains, aimed at my chest. "You said you were my friend. Do you know what you did to me?"

"I don't remember ending our friendship, only ending a life I could not lead."

Jack laughs. "You didn't walk out on me?"

"I walked out on someone whose deceit wounded more people than he could imagine. I based my life on a lie. Because I so strongly believed that lie, others based their lives on my belief. I could not continue in their wounding."

His nostrils flare and yells into the empty subway car. "What about me? Didn't you think I was wounded?"

"You were not mine to heal."

He lifts the gun. "Bullshit. I saw the things you could do."

"Then why did you work so hard for so long to take them away from me?"

He fires at me. Shame and Guilt emerge to stand beside him and glare at me with mocking smiles.

Grandmother encases me in her web. The bullet passes through me, leaves no mark, does no harm, clatters to the floor behind me. She releases me but faces Jack, her chelicerae click *snickt snickt snickt* as she snaps them together and apart.

Shame and Guilt cower behind him.

"But you could continue. It was either continue or face up to what you'd done. To so many. And all stemming from what you thought was a loving lie."

"My life is ruined because of you."

"Your life is ruined because of you, Jack. I was gone. Long gone. Been gone a long time. Whatever happened from that moment in my apartment until now, it's all you."

He fires again. Once again Grandmother enwraps me, protects me, releases me.

"You couldn't know I'd be here. I didn't know I'd be here. What are you doing here?"

He throws the gun down. "Hate me. Can't you fucking Jesus Christ hate me? Can't you at least give me that much?"

"Not my style. Not what I've been taught. Not what I've learned. Not what I do."

"Oh, yeah? Then what do you do?"

The Old Question. An Ancient Question.

Am I prepared to answer it now?

The old energies soar.

"Let me show you."

〜

The subway car is again filled. People, spirits, energies, come and go and the chatter is pleasantly deafening.

"May I ask you a question?"

"You just did."

Jack smiles broadly. "How did the bullets not kill you?"

"I'm not really here. Neither are you. But we both needed this lesson and the Universe is not wasteful."

"What do I do from here?"

"Pay it forward."

The subway car slows, stops. The door beside me opens to the front door of my house. "Ah. This is my stop. Goodbye, Jack. Have a good life. Live it gladly, live it full."

Practice

Chapter 112

Robyn

She sits across from me in German class and is the most beautiful thing I've ever encountered.

I've looked back on our galaxy from galaxies not yet discovered, sat on the rings of Saturn and watched comets sail around the sun, waded through nebulae so color-rich human hearts ache at the sight of them, tasted wines no human tongue will ever know, listened to whalesongs and mountains sing in voices no human could hear, and nothing matches the woman conjugating *haben* four rows from me.

I want to share so much with her and can't even Lower-Center-Relax-Breathe in her presence.

Grandpa and Grandma made love with a touch, with a smile, with a wink, with a nudge, with the gentlest of kisses, with understanding hugs, with an embrace, and I realize, no, she makes Lower-Center-Relax-Breathe the easiest thing in the world.

My English paper is due and my typewriter is broken. "Does anybody have a typewriter I can borrow for the afternoon?"

Long blonde hair swirls as she turns green eyes on me. "Sure, you can borrow mine."

I take her to a college play, *Pippin*, and dinner as a thank you. We drive to the coast and get caught in the blizzard of '78. Turning around, we go off the road into a ditch.

"You okay?"

"Yeah."

"Sorry about that."

"What are we going to do?"

I consider. "Can you drive a standard?"

"Sure."

"Good. You drive, I'll push."

It is a small car. We are down an incline. She'll never know.

"You ready?"

"Any time."

"Little gas, little clutch. Now."

I *lift*. It is not my talent, not what I do, but I can do most things when there's a need.

But she has the car in reverse.

"You okay?"

"I'm fine. Let's give it another go. One-Two-Three." I lift.

The car skids up out of the ditch onto the road.

"You're stronger than you look."

"Wheaties."

~

"You're the first man I've dated who actually listens to me when I talk."

"I can sing while you talk. Seems impolite."

She laughs.

I make her laugh.

We walk across campus. Every ten, fifteen feet someone says hello. I work part time at the medical center. Makes it easier to do what I do.

"You know lots of people."

"I'm a friendly kind of guy."

"You know lots of women."

"I'm not that kind of friendly."

"How come you know so many women?"

"Because I listen."

~

She studies to be an equestrian. I go with her to the barns.

Heavy construction equipment is building an indoor arena close by. Too close for the horses to be comfortable with the pounding of the earth, the rumble of big diesels, the explosions of air hammers and whine of power tools.

They are nervous, jittery.

Carl, the barn manager, meets us between the stalls. "I wouldn't take anybody out today, Robyn. Too much activity. They won't be able to focus."

I walk over to one stall, one horse, Black Knight, particularly unhappy with the activity.

Carl walks over quickly. "Don't go in there. He's not a friendly horse. He'll buck you off and kick you on your way down."

I face Carl. He slows, blinks.

I open the stall door, walk in, Lower-Center-Relax-Breathe.

Black Knight snorts, backs away from me, quiets, comes up, sniffs me, nuzzles me.

I raise Grandmother Parvati's PeaceShield. All the other horses quiet as Peace moves out from me.

Carl shakes his head. "What happened?"

Robyn stares.

~

We walk on the beach. Ocean greets me. I stop, turn to the water, perform *waves*.

"How do you do that? It looks like you're dancing with the waves."

I don't hear.

"Gio?"

The power of the ocean.

"Gio?"

Moving through my arms, into my body, down my legs, back out to the sea.

"Gio?" She pulls my arm down.

Waves crash against rocks, seawater climbs up sand towards her, begins to form, to shape, an Old One, upset, she interrupted our game. I should have waited until I was alone.

I turn her to face me, turn us both so I protect her from the water, my back to the waves, her in my arms.

She looks over my shoulder. "What the..."

I ask Ocean's forgiveness. Let it know. "We will continue later."

Waves foam, recede from our feet. "Laaaterrr."

"Did you hear that?"

"Hear what?"

~

She wakes as I return, slowly, not to wake her, a mist taking human shape becoming flesh as her eyes clear from sleep.

She rises as do I.

"Everything okay?"

She stares at me. Reaches out and touches me.

"Robyn?"

"I thought..."

"What?"

"I...nothing. Strange dreams."

"You okay?"

She rests her head back down but keeps one hand on me.

"Strange dreams."

~

I make cheese omelets, fluffy and light. She walks into the kitchen, her bathrobe revealing curves I will spend my life exploring.

"Coffee's done."

"You know I don't drink coffee."

I hand her a mug. "That's why I made you hot chocolate."

"What's that smell?"

I open the oven door. "Homemade cinnamon rolls."

"When did you have time to make those?"

"I made the dough last night, let it rise, finished them early this morning, set the oven to bake."

"I want to ask you a question."

"Okay."

"I don't want you to lie to me."

"I never have."

"What you do. I want to learn it."

"Physics?"

"Don't make fun of me."

She sits at the table and looks up at me. The window frames her in morning light.

"What do you think I do?"

"Do you think I'm blind or stupid? I watch you."

"Yes, you do. What do you see?"

"I see you at peace. Rest. And when I'm with you I feel it, too. And you know where the police are. Speed traps. And all the animals in the barn quiet when you're there. And..."

I nod. I sit, take her hands in mine.

With her, I am complete.

"You don't know what you're asking, Princess."

"I know I love you. I know I'm afraid sometimes."

"You can forget me. Meet someone else. After a while it'll be like I didn't exist."

She sneers. "Yeah, right." She looks out the window. "Could you forget me?"

"Forget you, no. Wait to meet you again?"

I do a foolish thing. I show her this universe dying, a new one form-ing, suns created, worlds coming into existence, life forming. "Fifteen billion years is not too long to wait to fall in love again."

"I don't want to wait. Will you teach me?"

I sing Judy Collins' *Since You Asked:*

> *What I'll give you since you've asked,*
> *is all my time together.*
> *Take the rugged sunny days,*
> *the warm and rocky weather.*
> *She finishes. "…this is what I ask you for, nothing more."*

Chapter 113

The Child

Robyn and I stand in the grocery store checkout line. Robyn empties the front of our cart, I handle the heavy items in the rear, and place milk, a jug of laundry detergent, a bag of oranges and so on, on the belt and watch it travel forward to where Robyn and the cashier natter.

A woman wheels her cart in line behind me.

My senses flare.

Not a defense.

A Calling.

The woman arranges things in her cart. "Rusty? Russell?"

I turn.

She's looking into her child's face. "Russell? Russell?"

Her face pales. She looks up. Her eyes meet mine. "My child's not breathing."

My energies surge.

My arm pushes groceries up on the belt. I lift the child, lay him down on it, stare at nametags. "You, Chris, go to your office and call 911, Emergency, a child is choking." "You, Bob, get on the intercom and call any doctors or nurses to come forward." I check. "Tell them there's an emergency at register 7."

Bob and Chris stare at me, at the child, back at me. "Go! Now!"

Russell turns blue. His eyes close.

I turn him over.

My physical body maps onto his. I feel for obstructions. Where where where?

A strange shape, halfway down his throat.

"Did Russell have a pacifier? Something he was sucking on?"

The woman knocks things aside in her cart. "Oh my god. Oh my god. Oh my god."

Russell's muscles aren't trained as mine. I let him borrow. The pacifier begins working its way up.

The woman reaches out to me, attempts to turn me to face her.

My eyes are closed. Concentrate.

Robyn pulls the woman's hand away. "Trust him. He knows what he's doing."

Another woman comes forward. "I'm a nurse. What's going on?"

She attempts to push me back.

Another few seconds. Pass the larynx. Pass the uvula. Up. Up.

Russell coughs up the pacifier.

A siren enters the parking lot. An officer rushes in with a medkit.

The nurse pushes me out of the way, turns Russell over. "We don't need you anymore. Go away."

I fall back against the candies stacked by the register.

Robyn grabs my arm, steadies me.

The grocery store manager places our items in bags, puts the bags in our cart, offers me his hand. "Good job, young man. Good job."

I look up. He has cat's eyes.

Chapter 114

Brian

The phone rings as Robyn draws my attention to a TV newsbreak. "You know him, don't you?"

On the screen, police escort hazel-eyed, dusty brown-haired, athletically lithe and with model good looks Brian through TV crews, newspaper reports, and curious onlookers at the local airport. Brian wears dirty sweats and clutches a roll of toilet paper in between cuffed hands. An off-camera voice rises above the rest. "What's with the toilet paper?"

Brian looks around, the captor now the captive, his eyes hungry for a friendly face. "Do you have any idea what I had to do to get this?"

I pick up the phone. "Mr. Fortune?"

"Close enough."

"Huh?"

"Who's calling, please?"

"Are you watching the news?"

"You didn't answer my question."

"This is Lieutenant McGarry. We'd like you to come in for questioning."

"Seems odd you'd call me on the phone if you want me to come in for questioning. What have I done?"

"You? Nothing. A bunch of people have filed complaints about a guy you used to work with and we'd like you to come in to get a better picture of what happened."

"Have there been any complaints about me?"

"No, none. This is purely routine."

"I'll have my lawyer contact you."

"Mr. Fortune - "

I hang up the phone.

~

He is beautiful. Handsome. Tall, athletic, and lithe with a confident gymnast's build. A part-time male model, with full, wavy sandy brown hair and brilliant hazel eyes, he dresses like a page from a catalog.

"Who are your teachers?"

He enthusiastically shares names, none of them my teachers. He references trainings I'm unfamiliar with. He invites me to teach with him.

"I'm not qualified to teach."

"Sure you are. Use what you've learned to teach what you've learned. We can team-teach. You take the lead."

He watches, makes some suggestions, offers some corrections.

I feel him around me.

Like my teachers, but different.

Like, but different.

He watches me, how I do things, how things happen.

He attempts to enter, to get in. Subtle, quiet, gentle.

I smell African forests, hear elephants trumpet, lions roar. Waters flood a plain, catching me in their current, and recede as quickly. Great apes beat their chests. Bats darken the sky. Baboons rush around me, circle me, bare their fangs at something I can't see. Rhinoceros rumble past.

A quiet voice, two, whispers only I can hear. "Yootsue T'a'Anjuu."

I look at Brian and understand.

He is *other*.

"You've never studied. You claim you've studied, but you never have. You met some people and ran away before asking them to teach you."

Uncle John and Aunt Mary gather around me. Lion and Lioness roar.

"You've read and talked. You know what's possible, not how to make things possible."

Tae-Sek's muscular cat rises up under me. I remember his words. *A defense. When the time comes.*

I close doors opened for the students.

To protect, to defend.

I am safe. Not so the students. For some, too late. I mark them. So others will know: be gentle, be kind, they have been raped. Help them until they are ready. Teach them after.

I offer Brian my hand. "You are one of my best teachers. Thank you for the lesson."

I mark him last, strongest, a lighthouse he does not know he wears: Beware! Dangerous Coasts! Hostile Natives! Unsafe Waters!

〜

Two attorneys sit beside me in an office. One is my attorney, the other someone he brought who specializes in such cases.

The specialist looks around. "Good coffee and an office without interrogation equipment. Don't worry."

"I'm not worried, just confused."

Lieutenant McGarry comes in with a notepad. He sits and flips some pages.

"Do you remember..." A name.

I nod.

"How about..." Another name.

I nod.

"Okay, one more. How about..."

"Yes."

"When was the last time you had any interaction with them?"

"Years ago."

"You haven't seen them since?"

"Correct."

He nods.

"When was the last time you saw Brian?"

"The last time we taught together. Also years ago. The last time I saw the others you mention."

"What did you teach?"

"Cultural anthropology, mythology, folklore."

"Did you know he continued teaching them?"

I shrug. "I'm not surprised."

"How come you stopped teaching with him?"

"He was inept, a fool, and a liar. It became obvious he would self-destruct, somehow implode, and I didn't want to be around when he did, didn't want to get caught in the blast, so to speak."

He makes notes, nods.

"So far everyone else we've interviewed says you mailed them a letter, wrote you decided your studies took you elsewhere, offered to continue working with them if they wished."

"Correct."

He pulls a folded sheet of paper out of his notebook. "Is this that letter?"

"It is one of many, all the same."

"Lots of the people we interviewed wish they'd taken you up on your offer."

I shrug. "Nobody wants to kiss the frog until it's too late."

"Huh?"

"Nothing."

The specialist clears his throat. "Where is this going, Lieutenant?"

McGarry rocks back in his chair. He looks from my attorney to the specialist to me. There is a bear and a wolf behind him, on either side. The wolf is hungry, the bear cautious, and they want the same thing.

But not me.

McGarry's wolf talks to my Grandfather Spirit. His bear poses questions to my Grandmother Spirit.

"They want to know if I'll be an expert witness. If I'll explain to a jury how Brian could do what he did."

McGarry rocks forward. "Do you know what Brian did?"

The specialist drops his briefcase on the floor. "This interview's over."

McGarry's wolf and bear know I'm no threat. They whisper in his ears. He considers without knowing the influence.

"Off the record. Just so I'll know if you're someone who can explain it to a jury if we need to."

The specialist writes something on his own notepad. "Off the record? Really? Then sign this."

McGarry reads, signs.

The specialist takes the notepad back, reads, nods at me.

"He raped his students. The women, anyway. Used what little he knew to convince them it was therapeutic, part of some kind of healing process."

"How do you know this?"

"I study a lot."

He nods. "Okay. Now, how would you explain this to a jury?"

———

"What Brian does is no different than what professional cardsharps do, stage mentalists do. Anybody seen *The Amazing Kreskin*? Same thing. Some people call it 'cold reading'. It has lots of names."

Prosecution walks over to the jurists. "Could you give us a demonstration, Mr. Fortune?"

I *SpiritTalk* to the energies around the first four jurists, explaining what elements of the case most intrigue them, what bore them, when their mind wanders, harmless stuff.

The judge hides his smile under a hand. "Remind me not to play poker with you, Mr. Fortune."

I smile back, remembering Randy Westphal in Atlantic City. "Not to worry, I don't play cards."

"Cross examination?"

Brian's attorney huddles with him, flips through some notes. Looks up at me.

"Mr. Fortune, by your own words, nothing done and nothing you've demonstrated provide evidence for the deep understanding necessary for the type of assault my client is accused of."

"Okay."

"There is no way to provide evidence of such an understanding, is there. My client would need to spend hours and hours over several quote-unquote therapeutic sessions to develop the understanding of an individual at a level necessary to perform the assaults he's accused of, correct?"

I look at the specialist. He nods.

"There is a way to provide such evidence, if you'd like. I'll do it with you, so you'll never have to doubt such again."

He stands up, adjusts his suit, cocks his head. "Go ahead. I'm sure we'd all love to see such a demonstration."

"For the record. You want me to do this?"

The defense attorney smiles at the jury, back at me. "Yes, please." His lips curl up. "If you can."

"One more time, so I'm sure. You want me to do this?"

The judge clears his throat. I raise my hand. He blinks his eyes, suddenly dumb. My lawyer and the specialist frown from the judge to me and back.

"Go ahead. Do your best."

I sigh and shake my head. "As you wish."

~

McGarry shakes my hand outside the courthouse. "You're scary, Mr. Fortune. You know that?"

"I don't mean to be."

The specialist walks up to us. "Unanimous decision. He's going away for a long time."

"Pity. He'll probably teach others what he does while he's away."

McGarry shakes hands all around. "I've got another case coming up. Thanks again." He walks away.

My attorney joins us. The specialist opens his DayTimer. "Gio, you ever do jury selection?"

My attorney nudges him. "I saw him first."

Chapter 115

What do you do?

Jan sits in my living room, in the blue lounger in the corner near the bookcase holding several years of my journals, and her brow furrows as she scans the titles; *Nature, Science, Journal of Consciousness Studies, Cybernetics and Human Knowing, Linguistics, Journal of Scientific Exploration*, half a dozen others, and *Shaman*. I wake early on Saturday mornings, before the house stirs. The dog comes downstairs with me, goes outside to do his business, then goes back to bed with Robyn. I have an hour, sometimes two, by myself to practice, to read, to ponder. Reading helps me understand, helps me do.

"What do you do?"

I remember Grandfather's words, his teachings.

I stand and motion Jan to join me in the center of the room, away from any furniture, away from any walls, away from the fireplace and hearth. "Let me show you."

She looks up at me, her blue eyes wide, wary. She stares at an angle, not full on, her powdered, mascaraed face slightly askew, her eyes snap to the front door and back. She prepares her escape.

She thinks we will talk. Most want to talk; Talk, exchange ideas, they'll tell me their experiences and I'll tell them mine and we'll shake hands when we're done and part as friends, and they'll think we're equals.

"Stand in front of me, about a foot back. And take off your heels."

"I'm comfortable in them."

"As you wish."

I offer my hand to help her up. She stares at my palm. Her hand rises and stops about an inch from mine, hovers. Her nose crinkles.

"They're calluses."

Her hand continues slowly, fearful calluses, work, is contagious..

"Good. Relax. Close your eyes."

I separate my spirit-body from the rest of me, move it through her and up to the ceiling.

She rocks back. Her smooth-palmed hands with her perfectly manicured nails reach out and clasp empty air, her arms flail in a wild martial arts parody, her Neiman-Marcus peasant blouse balloons as she falls, the designer holes in her designer jeans expose smoothly shaved and tanned thighs as she hits the floor.

She focuses on me. "You pushed me."

"It's the heels. Your vanity separated you from the earth."

She stays on the floor, not moving, not getting up, not offering me her hand.

"You pushed me."

I walk around her and open the front door. She crab-walks from where she fell to the lounger, her eyes leave me only long enough to grab her things, then stands. She holds her bag and pocketbook in front of her, a lifeguard keeping her rescue buoy between herself and a beach drunk. She reaches over and knocks a bunch of my journals off their shelf, then looks up at me, triumphant.

I back away from the door, leaving it open.

She leaves.

Chapter 116

A Little Piece of Gum

I listen to the waves, my eyes closed, lying on the couch at our rent-
ed beach house. One to two weeks each summer on the Rhode Island
coast, this is Robyn's family tradition since before I entered her life.
Brothers, sisters, friends, aunts, cousins, uncles.

The conversations, the laughter, the smells of good, vacation cooking, burgers on the grill, corn on the cob, strong coffee in the morning
as each wakes per some internal schedule they're not even aware of.

I rejoice in the familyness of it all.

Until an energy comes to me, asking help, a winged cat's shadow. It
climbs onto me as I lay there, cushes my chest, circles, and lies down.

"What can I do, Little One?"

It lifts its head, winks at me. It needs protection.

"Who will harm you here?"

It purrs, rubs its whiskers against my beard. "*Ascolta.*"

I listen.

Robyn and her mother, Wilma.

"Oh, come on, Robyn, just give me a piece of gum."

"No. If you want a whole stick, fine, but not a piece. You always take a stick and break off a piece and leave the rest of the stick on the table."

"For someone who wants a piece later."

"But no one ever does. Take the whole stick and put what's leftover in your pocket or wallet. Don't leave it out to get all icky and stuck to the table."

It is such a small thing, this winged cat lying on my chest. I've felt its presence many times. Always when Robyn and Wilma are together. A mutual hatred unspoken, never breaking some unrecognized mother-daughter pact.

"Oh, fine. Give me a stick."

"And you'll either chew it all or put the other half away somewhere so I won't have to clean it up?"

"Yes."

"Promise?"

"Promise."

Robyn offers her a stick of gum.

Wilma breaks off a piece and drops the rest on the table.

"Goddammit, mother! I knew you were going to do this. I knew it. I can't trust you. Nobody can trust you."

The winged cat's head deforms like an amoeba dividing. Two heads pop apart, look at me, purr for help. I sit up.

"You do understand, Wilma, you've completely given me the right to disrespect your daughter, to use her, abuse her, mistreat her, basically to act towards her as if she were nothing more than shit on my shoe."

Robyn and Wilma turn to me. All other talk stops and eyes come around.

"If you would do this when she specifically asked you not to, and such a simple thing, so simple a thing to show her you respect her wishes and honor them, and breaking that trust intentionally, as they say 'with malice a'forethought', then why should I have any regard for any of her wishes in our marriage?"

Wilma's face drains. Her eyes widen. She stops chewing her piece of gum.

"Whatever comes of our marriage, it's on your head. Not mine. Certainly not hers."

Chapter 117

Whale

The early October ocean heaves and swells. No one on this whale-watch keeps their lunch down. The air is cold and the skies gray. People struggle to walk across the deck. The captain promises us we'll see whales.

Robyn's family is onboard. The whalewatch is her birthday gift. Her father sits in the main cabin reading and rereading the same page of the newspaper. Robyn, her mother, sister, and sister's best friend are on the forward deck sitting with their backs to the gunwale. Every few waves one stands, turns to face the ocean, tosses more of their lunch, sits back down. A fellow in the rear cabin reads a paperback with a small, brown paper bag in his free hand. Every few pages he puts the book down, opens the bag, vomits into it, closes it back up, picks up his book and continues where he left off. Her brother and sister-in-law are on the rear deck so he can smoke cigarettes.

I attempt to walk from the main cabin to the forward deck through roiling seas and move like a drunk marionette, my arms swinging to keep balance, my feet coming down to find the deck's dropped another foot between my steps, take my next step as the deck rises in a swell, and fall to the deck laughing my head off.

Everyone wears heavy clothing. Those who have it wear ocean rain gear. The crew hands out wool blankets to protect us from the cold.

One of the other people on board lifts a coffee to their mouth as the boat, a deepsea trawler modified for sightseeing, lurches through a wave and splashes it on the person sitting next to them. "Think the captain will turn us around, call it a day, maybe refund our tickets?"

I rise up. Stellwagen Bank, our destination, is closer than Boston harbor. And a rapid moving front from the northeast is clearing the skies where we're heading. The captain won't turn back.

The person's partner takes off their hat, wipes coffee from their face. "I hope so."

I point to the northeast. "Skies clearing. The seas might stay rough but the sun'll come out."

Coffee face mumbles to his friend. "I didn't know we had Don Kent on board."

I stand beside Robyn, her sister, sister's friend, and mother. "Sky's clearing ahead."

Robyn's mother, Wilma, raises her head over the gunwale, scans the horizon. "How do you know?"

Robyn stays seated. "He knows."

Robyn's northern European Protestant family is uncomfortable with my Mediterranean birth. Her father is happy one of his kids isn't constantly asking for money, we always pay our own way, all the others come to him for private meetings with their hands out. But Wilma remains unsure. My customs are not her customs, my manners are not her manners. Robyn's happiness is less important than I be controlled.

There's a break in the clouds. The midmorning sun glistens off the still white-capped waters. The trawler lurches less. The sea calms enough for people to stand and most still huddle on the decks.

A mate's voice draws attention. "We're coming up on the Bank, folks. Keep your eyes open. We're picking up some big ones on sonar."

I lean against the gunwale, back to the ocean, smiling at Robyn, my six-month's bride. A swell lifts the bow, crashes it back down, another swell lifts us again. I anticipate the trawler's movements incorrectly, push up when I should sit down and am launched over the side.

Water fills my boots, saturates my coat, my jeans, my wool cap becomes a weighted diver's helmet pulling my head down. I'm underwater and sinking fast. I look up, see Robyn, her sister, her sister's friend screaming, pointing. Robyn knows I can't swim. My experience with oceans is to borrow and I can't find any fish.

I wonder. Will six months be the only joy I know of her? Will she find another? Know that I love her as my Grandfather loves me, that she is my all, my reason for living, what I cherish most in life?

The surface grows further away as my winter gear fills and pulls me down.

Something changes.

A pressure. Underneath me. Rising.

Something solid provides purchase under my boots, smooth, flowing. My lungs are bursting. Fish can breathe water but I can't find any fish to teach me.

The surface gets closer. The Rising underneath me continues. I sit. Something solid, firm, loving, kind. I break the surface.

Leviathan. Behemoth. Its song rising under me like an old Sicilian melody.

I'm here, Gio. I have you.

Friend.

Beneath me, a humpback whale breaches. Inside me, a voice rocking eternity. "Breathe, Little Brother."

I'm covered in blow as the whale clears its lungs.

The whale dives. I'm still on its back. "Borrow from me."

My lungs hold gallons of air. They become a bellows powering dives into dark places. From my bottom to my toes flukes form while I still ride the whale's back.

It seems like forever and I know it's time to breathe.

The whale brings me to the surface. I hear echoes with my heart, look around. Other whales surround us.

"Breathe, Little Brother."

I'm covered in spume as the whale breathes.

We dive again. The water courses over my skin, parts, makes way. I become a part of the whale's bow wake.

I hear the whales around us. They sing their song, their history. They tell me of their Master, Lord of the Sky, a world they gave up to roam the oceans, now can only visit, how they worked to turn legs into flukes, arms into flippers, how the deepness of the sky became the vastness of the deep.

The trawler circles.

We surface, a lifesaver is thrown. I take hold. The whale descends.

Remember us, Little Brother. Gio.

Remember us.

Chapter 118

Moondance

Robyn and I walk a sleigh path through the woods. Our breaths spiral together, dancing into the frigid moonlit night. Snow crackles with each step, WinterMan's whispering voice in the dark. Speakers along the trail play Christmas show tunes and standards: Johnny Mathis, Harry Belafonte, Nat King Cole, Perry Como, Frank Sinatra, Andy Williams.

The moon climbs above the trees and our shadows grow long in the snow.

We hug. A passionate embrace.

I want her to know she's special.

The music quickens slightly. A slight jazz beat.

Van Morrison's *Moondance*.

I remember making a lampshade of moonlight for Grandma.

I collapse the moonlight until it spotlights us, take Robyn in my arms, and dance, carrying her up into the night.

We jive above the trees. She lifts her head from my chest and sees where we are. I feel her tremble inside.

I sing alongside Van Morrison.

> *Well, it's a marvelous night for a moondance,*
> *With the stars up above in your eyes,*
> *A fantabulous night to make romance,*
> *'Neath the cover of October skies.*

She forgets her fear and laughs. "It's December."

I continue, carry her in a soft winter's wind. And all the night's magic seems to whisper and hush, And all the soft moonlight seems to shine in your blush.

Over the trees, under the stars, in the shadow of the Moon, she rests her head back on my chest. "Why do you love me?"

I let us fall gently down, snowflakes finding rest beside their siblings. "Why aren't you afraid of me?"

She laughs and pulls me back to our cabin.

Chapter 119

Aunt Ruth

She sits at Wilma's kitchen table, a smiling, red-lipsticked, eyeglassed Buddha, talking with Wilma, Robyn, and Robyn's sister-in-law while watching me play Canfield, a game she taught me one long ago Rhode Island summer.

She knows I'm good with cards and doesn't question my moves.

Today I place cards randomly. I act as if considering, evaluating, then make a move without rhyme or reason.

Aunt Ruth frowns.

I place a card where it doesn't go.

She shakes her head, says nothing.

I place a ten on a three, same suit.

She cocks her head, her eyes narrow.

I turn over a card, place it sideways over the talon, nod.

"What the hell are you doing?"

I laugh. "Gotcha!"

She puts a hand to her chest, laughs, gasps. "Oh, I have to pee."

Aunt Ruth is our favorite aunt, perhaps our only aunt. Always loving, always giving, always kind. Quick to defend, quick to reprimand, quick to share.

She hates her daughter-in-law, thinks little of her children.

She comes back, sits down. "Give me the cards."

"You going to use all the cards this time? You're not going to leave a few out to get all sticky on the table, are you?"

Ruth looks at me, can't hold it in, guffaws, waddles to the bathroom again.

I wake, sit up in bed.

Ruth's energy is there, a bright column of earth warmth, wider at the center than the ends, Ruth in starlight.

"Ruth?"

The earth warmth, the starlight, sings. "I want to be with Uncle Dick again."

Yes, I understand. She's tired. Part of her knows it's time. Her husband, Dick, gone many years, calls her to join him.

"We used to ride bikes on The Cape."

"I remember you talking about it."

Her body forms inside the starlight. "I want to be a girl again."

"And so you shall. You shall be his Queen once more. Soon."

Her body dissolves into the fires of the sun. "Queen? Dick always called me his Queen. How did you know?"

"It's in the cards."

The column fades. I lay back, rest.

"Ruth's heading back to New York today. I need to see her before she goes."

Robyn looks at me.

I nod. "Yes."

At Wilma's table I move through cousins and brothers and sisters and sisters-in-law and kneel by Ruth in her chair, put my arms around her, lean in and give her a kiss. "Know you are loved, O' Queen."

I pull back. She stares at me.

"You know you are loved, don't you?"

A tear leaves her eye. She nods. "Goodbye."

Robyn gives her a kiss. "Bye, Aunt Ruth."

Wilma chews a piece of gum. "Boy, that sounds final, you two."

Chapter 120

WhirlWind

A middle-aged woman and her partner stand in front of some thirty people gathered in a classroom above *The Shining Room*, a New Age shop. "I call the energies of the cosmos and talk with them."

A man, her partner, stands to the side, giving her room to move about, twirl, pace, exaggerate moves like a theatrical actor or a dancer. The woman wears a laurel leaf crown, a flowing white robe cinched at the waist by a white rope with little silver bells attached to it, and soft white slipper-like shoes. White hair flows down her shoulders and back. "Each of us has energies we are unaware of. I see them and share their messages with you." The man is dressed casually, gray chinos, Nikes, oxford shirt. He smiles and nods as she speaks.

Robyn and I sit in the back of the room. She reads a brochure she picked up as we walked in. "You said she's a SpiritTalker?"

"She doesn't use that term but words are fluid and her claims mark her as such, and I remember Grandpa teaching everything, everything, everything is your teacher, you decide what the lesson is."

"You could teach this class."

"I wasn't asked to."

The woman flares her robe, spins, crouches as if avoiding something, looks up, spreads her fingers by her eyes, startled by something no one else can see.

"What's she looking at?"

"I have no idea."

The woman stands tall, spreads her arms, closes her eyes. "The energies of the universe take many forms. Each has a special message. The message to me could be completely different than the message to you but it comes from the same energy."

"Is she making sense?"

"It seems familiar. Could be she trained differently than me. Had different teachers, I'm sure."

"Why are we here again?"

"A chance to learn something new? Something different? From someone who studies differently than I study? You think I'd miss out on that?"

"I think you don't know who you are or what you can do."

"Shh."

"I will now demonstrate." The woman closes her eyes, raises her head towards the ceiling. "Oh, the spirits, the spirits, I feel the spirits, ah, here they are among us now."

I frown and nudge Robyn. "Do you feel anything?"

Robyn shakes her head. "No, should I?"

People raise their hands. They ask questions. "Can we be better people?" "Is it too late to save the environment?" "What can we do about world hunger?" Genuine questions. Sincere questions.

The woman answers, her voice wispy, dreamlike. "Here is what the energies of the cosmos say..."

Robyn leans into me. "You picking up any of this?"

"No. There are many spirits here but she's not listening to any of them. Not as far as I can tell, anyway."

Someone sitting a row in front of us *shhses* us.

"What would your grandfather do in a situation like this?"

I nod, remember. Another lesson from Grandpa and my teachers. "Honor everyone's experience. We learn from honoring and questioning. Show honor. When they return honor, ask questions. Respectful, always."

The lecture concludes. Robyn and I approach the SpiritTalker and her partner. "Thank you for sharing your gift. I found it fascinating. It's not how I learned to do it, and I learned a lot from you. Thank you."

The woman takes my hand, looks me in the eyes. "You learned a different way to spirit talk? Could you share it?"

I look around the room. Lots of people mill around, talking. Several gather at the refreshment table. Late Fall kept the windows shut and the number of people had warmed the room.

"I...uh..."

"Please, show us."

I look at Robyn. She shrugs.

Relax-Lower-Center-Breathe.

WhirlWind, you are always with me. May I share you now?

A wind circles the room, picks up momentum with each pass. Pictures on the walls rattle. Paper cups fall off the refreshment table. Hair lifts.

The wind increases. Papers lift from chairs, from the table where the speaker sells her wares, brochures scatter. Folding chairs fall over. People shout to be heard over the wind. Downstairs in the store things crash on the floor, displays tip over, voices shout. "Close the windows!" "But the windows aren't open!"

Robyn reaches out to me. We are the center. WhirlWind keeps us safely in Its Eye. I look up.

The woman and her partner hold each other tightly, their faces taught, their eyes squint to protect them from the wind. Other people in the room clutch each other, some huddle on the floor.

All stare at us.

At me.

I look at the woman. "I guess I studied differently than you."

Robyn hurries us out. "You don't understand what you do. To others."

Chapter 121

Blue Sky

"This is the address she gave you?" Robyn looks at the overflowing dumpster in the parking lot, the overflowing drain in its center, the "For Sale" sign in a boarded up window on the first floor store front.

I check my notes. "Yes."

"She doesn't have a sign up."

"I'll take that as a good thing."

"I thought you said there are no good and bad, only things and the values we assign them."

I listen. Voices upstairs. "Yes. I'd say something like that."

We open a door with an unlit stairway behind it and an even darker hall behind the stairs. There's a dim light at the second floor landing.

"Up we go."

Robyn looks around. "You sure?"

"I have to know."

She shrugs, follows.

The door at the top of the stairs has a crude drawing of a dream-catcher on it. Robyn reads what's underneath. "Blue Sky. Spiritual Healings. Seneca Color Ceremony."

"I didn't know they had a color ceremony."

Robyn snorts. "Wanna bet they don't?"

I knock on the door.

A petite, dark-skinned, black-haired woman opens it.

Two rottweilers charge me.

Robyn falls back. "What the fuck?"

The woman restrains the dogs. "Sorry, sorry. I didn't know you'd be a man."

"His voice didn't give it away when he called?"

The woman pulls the dogs back into her apartment. "He said he wanted to do a healing. I didn't know he meant for himself." There are two middle-aged white women inside sitting side by side on a braided rug in the middle of the floor.

"I can leave."

Robyn shakes her head, no. The petite woman puts the dogs in a room, closes the door, comes back and offers her hand. "I'm Blue Sky. I'm Mayan but I was raised by the Lakotah and trained by the Seneca."

"You said on the phone you'd studied with Grandmother Paula."

"I know her, yes."

Grandmother Paula marks all her students. I don't smell Grandmother Paula's teaching mark on Blue Sky, but there is another mark, a warning.

"Must have been a while ago."

"No, only this past summer." The dogs howl from the other room. "Come join us in the circle." She points to the heavier of the two women on the rug. "This is Julie."

The other woman smiles, waves, her eyes wide on me. "I'm Honor."

The dogs scratch at the door. "Sorry, they don't like men."

"They were abused?"

"No, they're very protective."

"Because?"

Julie stares at me. "This is a women's healing circle. We were abused by men. They don't like men."

"I'm sorry for your hardship. There was no indication this was a women's healing circle."

Blue Sky reaches under a chipped coffee table and pulls out a dime-store drum. "Let's begin."

Robyn rolls her eyes at me. I shrug.

The dogs bang against the door. Blue Sky puts down her drum. "Let me put them outside."

"Were you abused by a man?"

She turns at the door. "My husband."

"When was the last time you saw him?

"He left for work a few hours ago."

"He still lives here?"

"Where else would he go?"

She opens the door and the dogs burst through, come at me. My Grandfather Spirit rises up, Wolf bares his fangs, growls, shows The Challenge as spit flows from his flews.

The dogs fall back, behind Blue Sky. "It must be your beard."

"My beard?"

"My husband has a beard."

Robyn shakes her head. "The one you're still living with, the one who left for work this morning and will be back tonight, the one who abuses you?"

"He only beats me when he's drunk." She takes the dogs down the stairs.

Honor touches my arm. "She's a very powerful shaman."

Robyn looks at Honor's hand on my arm and back at Honor. "Is she."

"She's helped me greatly."

"You still living with your husband, too?"

"Yes, but he's not abusive to me, only our children."

Blue Sky returns. "Let's start." She sits, lights some sage, lifts her drum and plays some beats; pat pat pat stop pat pat pat stop. "The spirits are with us now."

Robyn looks around the room. "They are?"

Blue Sky reaches under the table, takes out some notes. "Let's do our healing." She reaches in again and lifts out a cootie-catcher with one red corner, one yellow corner, one green corner, and one blue corner. "Pick a color."

Robyn falls over laughing.

"Grandmother Paula taught you this?"

"I improvised based on what she said."

Julie clears her throat. "Green."

Blue Sky flicks the cootie-catcher in her fingers. "G R E E N Green. Pick a number."

"How long did you study with Grandmother Paula?"

"I met her in a store in Maine. She was talking with the owner."

"Running Water?"

"You know her?"

"A little."

"I listened to what they said."

"That was your study?"

"She told me to be careful. She told me she knew I would do this."

"I'm sure she did. To both."

Honor stands up. "You should leave now."

Robyn stands up as well, bends over, grabs me under the arm, pulls me up. "Yes, we should."

Blue Sky closes the door behind us. Inside her drum goes pat pat pat stop pat pat pat stop.

Robyn turns to me in the parking lot. "Stop looking for others like you. There aren't any. In so many ways not even you could count them all. Understand?"

And I understand why the Universe called her to me, called us to be together. Her Spirit Guide is not one of mine, and is wiser than I.

Chapter 122

Armand

He is tall, lithe, athletic, and walks like a Castilian Flamenco dancer, erect and proud. His thick black mane is echoed by the golden-haired lion sitting on his left. A beautiful, elegant lioness lies on our living room rug grooming a male cub batting her whiskers. He shakes my hand in a strong but gentle, confident grip and bumps into the blue lounger, his eyes on his right palm.

"When will I find love?"

I smile at the lioness and cub she nuzzles. "I don't understand. You have a wife and son."

"You can tell that by looking at me?"

"By the spirits surrounding you."

He sits as if on a throne: poised, regal, and with a smile that belongs on magazine covers. He crosses his legs at the ankles revealing stockings matching his shoes, leading the eye up striped gray Madison slacks and a fitted shirt opened at the neck revealing a light gold chain.

"I am the last of my line. Even in the latter twentieth century some betrothals were made fresh from the womb."

I nod.

"There's nothing you want to ask? No questions, no concerns? No judgments to make on my wife's and son's behalf?"

"I only ask what I need to know to do what I must. My only concerns are that people be aware of what they've asked of me. Judgments are not my place. Everyone judges themselves accordingly."

"Can you help?"

"Do you want to find another to love or do you want to love those already in your life?

"You can make me love my wife?"

"You already love your wife."

"How do you know?"

"Because you are here asking for my help. If you hated her you would seek someone else. If you didn't care, you wouldn't have sought me out."

"Perhaps I feel an obligation to my family's wishes. Perhaps to my own family. My wife and son."

"Do you feel guilt? Or longing?"

"I see others. Not my wife."

"And always return wanting her to forgive you but unable to tell her why. And she always loves you unquestioningly."

"She knows. Or suspects. I can feel her wanting to ask but waiting."

"She is patient."

"You are kind."

"She respects you and knows you'll tell her everything when you're ready."

"She does?"

"What you feel with your wife is guilt, not longing. When you're with others, you wish they were your wife. That is longing. We long for what is in front of us but are afraid to ask for, to embrace. We fear when we do, it will be denied."

The lioness continues to groom her cub. It continues to bat her whiskers. The lion's mane falls from its head, its body withers, weakens, falls to the ground, collapses into dust.

"What do I want from her she's not already given?"

"She's given it; you haven't accepted it."

"What has she given?"

"She respects you, not her family's commitment to yours or some obligation to future heraldry. She, like you, wants your royal ways to end with the two of you. She, unlike you, doesn't fear doing so will end your marriage forever."

A wind stirs the dust.

The lion rises, its mane full. It stands, roars. The lioness and cub look up at it. It walks over to them, licks them both. The lioness and cub rise. The three of them bow to me, walk out my door.

"I ask again, can you help?"

"Haven't I already?"

Chapter 123

SacredSpace Work

Robyn brings Gail and her young son, Donny, to me. Gail's face is red. Her heart beats as if to escape her chest. Her short, brown hair, usually coiffed close like a fuzzy helmet, is uncombed with prominent cowlicks up straight like spikes growing from her skull. Confusion swarms her like a cloud of gnats. "Watch him, please."

I turn off the radio, a speech by President Reagan about HIV AIDS, god's judgment on non-White America.

Robyn and I are the neighborhood "safe" house. Parents tell their children, "If anything happens, go to Gio and Robyn. Tell them what's going on. Do what they say." Ollie visits daily. His father knocks on my door when he comes home from work. He knows Ollie is here and Ollie is safe.

Ollie likes Robyn. "Your wife's pretty."

"Thank you, Ollie. I think so, too."

Later I tell Robyn. "You're such a heart breaker."

She laughs.

Gail's eyes ask me to respond.

"Yes, of course. Let me know if there's anything else we can do."

Her eyes meet mine. She searches.

I remember Grandpa's teaching: Do not go where you're not invited.

"I should be back in a few hours. I'll call if I'll be later."

She leaves. Her gnats split, divide, one cloud goes with her, another surrounds Donny, more than enough for both.

Donny sits in the blue lounger. "You hungry, Donny?"

He looks at my journals, shakes his head, no.

"Want to watch some TV?"

"What are these books about?"

"Things I study. Different sciences. Do you like science?"

"Are you still in school?"

I laugh. "I'll always be in school. What school are you in?"

"How come my mom left me here?"

"Don't know. You hungry?"

Gail's husband, Donny's father, is long out of their lives. She never mentions him, Donny doesn't know him.

"No." He runs a finger along the rows of journals, tick-tick-ticking along the spines. "What's wrong with my mom?"

Gail is in pain and doesn't share it. Her pain causes Donny pain and he doesn't know how to share it.

"I don't know."

"Is my mom alright?"

Ease his pain and do not go where I'm not invited.

"Yes."

"How do you know?"

"She's in your car driving down Main Street."

He looks out the window. "You can't see that from here. You're just making that up so I'll feel better."

"If you see your mom driving down Main Street, will you believe it?"

He stands up, puts his hands on the windowsill, looks up and down the street. "How can I see that?"

"Sit down, close your eyes."

I show him Gail driving down Main St. She drives fast, honks her horn when lights change color and nobody moves, switches lanes, pulls into the hospital's parking lot. I don't stop seeing in time. I remember Grandpa not stopping me from being with Mrs. Gianelli's cat.

He jumps up, eyes open, color drained. "Mom's going to the hospital."

His spirit wants to go, to flee, to be with her, and already his schooling has taught him such things are impossible. He falls back into the blue lounger, his body tense, tears fill his eyes.

"Donny, did you ever ride piggyback when you were a little kid?"

He sniffs. "Sure."

"Do you trust me?"

"Trust you to do what?"

"Ever seen magic?"

"Sure. Why?"

"Want to see some magic?"

He sniffs and leans forward. "What kind of magic?"

"Oh, I call it the best kind. It's up to you. And the moment you tell me to stop, we will. You'll be right back here in that chair."

He looks around. "We're going somewhere?"

"To make sure your mom's okay."

My bodies separate, swarm around him, I pull from WhirlWind, drive the gnats away. I lift him in a sphere of his own energy, releasing it, freeing it to do what he needs, my back lengthens, my hair turns snowy white as does my skin. My arms become legs and wings sprout from my back.

Donny's face lights up, his eyes wide, caught in the magic of the moment. "I know what you are."

I whinny. "What am I?"

"You're Pegasus, the flying horse. I read about you in one of Mom's books."

Thank goodness Gail is an avid reader. "Get on my back. We're going to make sure your mom's okay."

He floats up and onto me, his energy freed. I spread my wings and fly through the walls of our home, into the sky, over our town, following our main street as if following a map.

He points to the hospital's parking lot. "That's Mom's car."

"Hang on." I spiral down, move through a hospital wall, fold my wings. "Stay on, Donny. If you get off the magic goes away."

"Okay."

I walk the hallways, sniffing Gail's scent, my eyes wide, my head lolling left and right. People we pass look around, sensing something but not knowing what they sense. "Did you hear that? Sounded like horse hooves on the floor." "Do you smell that? Some kind of animal smell. Did somebody bring a dog up here?" "Could have sworn I saw a kid floating down the hallway. Got to stop sniffing my own anesthesia."

Gail sits beside a bed holding a woman's hand.

"That's Aunt Autumn. What happened to her?"

Gail's Guardians seek to comfort her. She is not trained, has no knowledge of them.

An eagle the size of a citadel stands on her right, a jackal as big as a house on her left. They move between me and Gail as I approach. I step back. They look from me to the woman on the bed.

"Donny, what can you tell me about your aunt?"

"She's having a baby. Mom said any day now."

A Girl spirit hovers over Autumn, her Guardians, Guides, and Totems protecting them both.

Donny waves. "Hi. Are you Aunt Autumn's baby?"

The Girl spirit nods.

"Was Autumn having problems with the baby?"

"I don't think so."

Eagle fluffs his feathers. Jackal shakes his coat.

I stand before them, protecting Donny with my wings. "Sister Eagle, Brother Jackal, I ask safe passage for me and mine."

They separate. A circle of light forms between them.

"Donny, I'm going to do some magic with your mom. Would you like to help?"

His eyes are on Gail. She still holds Autumn's unresponsive hand. "Yes."

"We have to go somewhere. I'm not sure what's there yet. Is that okay?"

"I'll go to help Mom."

"You're a good son." I step between Gail's Guardians and through the circle of light, each step transforming me from winged myth to mortal man. Donny slides from my back and takes my hand.

"Where are we going?"

"To your mom's SacredSpace."

The other side of the circle of light holds a room not deep but forever wide. On the wall across from where we enter is a single shelf spanning eternity. Bright lights shine from behind us to the shelf, showing a glass door hinged at the top with a single lock opposite our entry. China dolls line the shelf. All the people Gail's known in her life. People she encountered and forgot, people she sometimes remembers. The population of the Gailiverse in one neat row.

Except for a clattering in one part of the row, on the future side but not far in the future. It starts just after *Now* and goes on to infinity.

Donny points to different dolls. "Hey, that's Grandma and Grandpa. Look, that's Charlie. There's the guy at the bank. That's Davy behind the deli counter. There's Uncle Henry." He steps ahead of me, points and laughs. "That's me, Mr. Gio! That's me!"

I smile, amused by his discovery.

Dolls of those dead before his birth he recognizes from pictures. Dolls of those Gail is yet to meet line her future path but none have faces, are genderless in dress and shape. And only Gail understands their order on this shelf.

He scratches his head, seeming so mature for an instant. "Where's Aunt Autumn?"

"She's not here."

Donny focuses on the clattering. It grows louder. Something bangs against the glass once, then again. The entire shelf shakes, stops, shakes. Donny moves towards it. I join him. He lights up. "Hey!"

Autumn's doll. It knocks over other dolls making room for itself on the shelf. Some dolls fall over, roll away, right themselves in future positions. Others roll into the past and gather dust. Some shatter.

A giantish Gail strides to the shelf. She reaches down her shirt for a key held on a necklace and unlocks the glass door, using a metal arm at its side to hold the door up.

I listen. Autumn's life-support mechanisms ping regular and strong when she gains a place on the shelf, grow irregular and weak when the other dolls push her back.

Gail reaches for the Autumn doll and pulls her hand away before making contact.

"Why is Autumn upsetting the people in your life, Gail?"

She watches the doll. "Because she loves me."

"How come a sister loving a sister upsets people?"

"She's not my sister, she's my wife."

"And if you make obvious room for her in your life, who will not approve?"

She points at dolls. Those shattered, those falling into the past.

"Are they important to you?"

She points at Donny. "He is."

~

"Donny, what's your favorite place in the whole world?"

"My home? You mean like that?"

"Let's go there."

I step back from Gail's SacredSpace. My back lengthens, my skin grows white, my hair becomes a frost-colored mane. Donny climbs upon my back. I spread my wings and gallop through the sky to his home.

"That's neat how you can do that."

"Thank you, Donny. I work at it."

"Can you teach me?"

Donny is twice the age when Grandpa introduced me.

And if The Knowledge favors him, it is never too late. "Let's find out. Can we help your mom first?"

We enter Gail's house. I've never been inside. A glass-doored curio cabinet sits in a living room corner. China dolls fill its shelves. I walk over for a better look. Donny hurries to ward me off. "These are Mom's special dolls, Mr. Gio. You can look but don't touch."

I nod and back away.

"What's your favorite place in your home, Donny?"

"My room. That's where all my toys are." He takes my hand and leads me upstairs to his room. Cowboys ride horses on his dresser, starships fly on slender threads from his ceiling, his bedspread is stars and galaxies, planets and moons, Sesame Street puppets line his windowsill. Little yellow dump trucks and bulldozers seek construction jobs on his red and gold carpet.

Everything is in proportion.

Except a monstrous toy chest against a wall, farthest from the door to his room, equidistant from window and door, and a large expanse of rug in front where no other toys dwell.

I wander towards it.

Donny comes over and takes my hand. "Want to see my comic books, Mr. Gio?"

"What are your favorite toys, Donny? I don't want to play with them, just curious."

His eyes dart to the toy chest. "My Legos. Why?"

His favorite toys. Nowhere to be seen in his room. Cowboys don't carry them, starships don't transport them, Miss Piggy and Kermit don't hold them, construction vehicles don't build with them.

"How come Legos are your favorite?"

"I build things with them."

~

"I have some friends who are great builders."

Donny eyes his toy chest. He wanders to it.

"And they have their own Legos, too."

A sigh of relief. "They do?"

"Oh, yes. In fact, I think they make them."

His brow furrows. "They do?"

"Would you like to meet them?"

"They won't play with my Legos?" Gail's negative doll energy, an inheritance.

"I don't know. You can ask them. Or you can offer to let them. But they mostly make their own."

He taps the top of his toy chest and tests the lock. "Okay."

"We need to go out back, into the woods a bit."

We stop equidistant from an elm tree and a small earth mound.

"Your friends are here?"

"Yes."

Buzzing fills the air. "Hello, Bee."

"Hehlloh, Gioh."

A clicking comes by our feet. "Hello, Ant."

Klick klick klick "Hello" klick klick klick "Gio" klick klick klick.

"This is my friend, Donny. He needs help building something. Would you help him build it?"

Donny tugs on my arm. "What do I have to build?"

"A place to hold all your mom's dolls."

"With what?"

"Legos."

"You said they weren't going to play with my Legos."

"I said I didn't know if they would. But why don't you ask them if they want to play with your Legos?"

Bee and Ant stand in front of Donny.

"Whe dohn't neehd youhr Lehgohs, Dohnnyh."

Klick klick klick "We" klick klick klick "just need to know" klick klick klick "what they are" Klick klick klick.

"Show them, Donny. Show them what a Lego looks like."

He picks up a twig, brushes some pine needles away.

"Noht thaht wahy, Dohnnyh. Ihn youhr heahrt."

Ant's antennae stroke Donny's palms. Klick klick klick "You've" klick klick klick "played with them" klick klick klick "a lot." Klick klick klick "Show us how you" klick klick klick "play with them." Klick klick klick "That will show us" klick klick klick "how to build them." Klick klick klick.

I hold my hands in front of him, palm up. Wooden Legos appear.

"Those are wood. Legos are plastic."

"They were wood long ago when I was a kid. But I don't think my Legos will work. Show Bee and Ant yours."

Donny holds his hand out. He scrunches his face. It reddens. He squinches his eyes. He exhales sharply. A red Lego appears.

"Hey!"

Bee looks at it, taps it over with his front legs. "Whe cahn dho thihs."

"How did I do that?"

Klick klick klick. "Because" klick klick klick "what we love" klick klick klick "has a home" klick klick klick "inside us." Klick klick klick.

"We only need to bring it out."

"My SacredSpace?"

"Yes." "Yehs." Klick klick klick. "Yes." Klick klick klick.

Bee flies from flower to flower, rhododendron to dandelion to bluebells to trillium, pollen to honey to wax. Its mandibles and tongue shaping Lego bricks faster than we can follow. Smacky sounds like whispers, joy in what it does.

Each brick drops to Ant. Ant carries them to Donny. It hustles hustles hustles, joy in what it does.

Klick klick klick. "Help me build" a place to hold your" klick klick klick "mom's dolls," klick klick klick "Donny." Klick klick klick.

A wall forms, then sides, a case, a clear plate becomes a door. It grows and fills the forest, spans the universe.

"But they're all the same color."

"Youh gihve thehm cohlorh, Dohnnyh."

Klick klick klick. "Help us" klick klick klick "give them color," klick klick klick "Donny." Klick klick klick.

Donny reaches out to the nearest brick. *Poof!* It turns red.

"Whoa."

"Neat, huh? Change the color of another."

He reaches for another. *Poof!* It turns blue.

Poof! Green.

Poof! White.

Poof! Poof! Poof! Poof! Poof!

Bee and Ant stand back.

"Goohd wohrk, Dohnnyh."

Klick klick klick. "You're the" klick klick klick "man," klick klick klick "Donny." Klick klick klick.

"It's time for Bee and Ant to go, Donny."

Donny turns, flushed. "No."

"Whe muhst, Dohnnyh."

Klick klick klick. "We are" klick klick klick "here for you" klick klick klick "always, klick klick klick "Donny" Klick klick klick.

"All you have to do is keep them in your heart, Donny."

We're back in Donny's house. The shelf he built comes in through a rear wall and out though the front.

Gail is there.

⌒

Gail drops to her knees and holds Donny close. "Where have you been? I was worried." She stares up at me.

"We went for a walk in the woods, Gail. Gave us something to do."

Gail holds Donny at arm's length. "I have a big question to ask you. You know Aunt Autumn's husband, Frank? Remember him?"

"I don't like him, mom."

She strokes the back of his head. "He hurt Autumn, Donny. He hurt her bad. He almost hurt the baby inside her."

Donny folds his arms across his chest. He stands straight and tall. "He's mean, mom. She needs to stay away from him."

"I think so, too, Donny. I'm wondering if she can come here to live. With us."

Donny claps his hands. "Of course, mom. That's why we built you a new shelf. To hold all your dolls."

Gail's eyes go from Donny to her glass case.

"My dolls?"

Donny's face shifts quickly, shifts back. He opens his mouth to speak and I hear "klick klick klick."

"What we love has a home inside us, Mom."

"What?"

Another shift and back. "Thehreh's ahlwahys roohm fohr ohthehrs ihn ouhr hearht."

Gail studies his face. She looks up at me, her brow furrowed, searching.

"He's an amazing boy, Gail."

She nods, confused, unsure.

"She's going to have her baby soon. It'll live here, too."

"I'll have a little sister!"

"How do you know it's a girl?"

Months later, the divorce well underway, Autumn finds work two states away.

Gail knocks on our door. "I thought Donny might be here. I haven't seen him all morning."

"I have an idea where he is."

He stands between the elm and the earthen mound. He turns at my approach. "Bee and Ant say they can come with me, if I want."

"I think that'd be a good thing, Donny. Don't you?"

He writes me often. He asks questions only he can answer.

Chapter 124

The Frog

I drive back from the Y, late Fall, late morning, and come around a curve as a frog hops into the road.

I swerve, drive on, complete the curve, pull over, stop.

The frog continues its journey into the road.

Others will not care if this one completes its journey or not. Some might see its movements against the wet tar of the road.

Two cars come around the curve in my rearview mirror.

I get out of my car, trot back up the road, find the frog dead, crushed and flattened, three-quarters of the way across.

I grieve. I should have acted sooner. I know what is important and what is not.

I cry, ask Frog's forgiveness for not taking care of its shadow.

Sunlight comes over the hillock blinding the curve, shines on the grasses opposite me, steaming where the frog might have been.

A mist rises.

Shapes.

Coming forward.

Old Ones.

The First Ones.

The Ancients.

The True Ones of which all else is Shadow and Myth, a harmony of human and animal energies so I can understand.

A'blig'moodj, The Frog Prince, the one of whom one of my teachers is a shadow, walks forward, holds its hand up to me.

Behind him, beside him, Wolf, Bear, Stag, Eagle, Lion, Hawk, Moose, Whale, Dolphin, Salmon, Oak, Ash, Thorn, and more lost further back in the mist.

A Council of All Beings.

A Council of All First Ones.

A'blig'moodj's mist forms around me. It takes my hand. I hear it inside me. "Do not grieve, Gio. This one was old and could not survive another winter. It is good he comes Home now."

I fall to the pavement, shaking, terrified. To be in the presence of such energies. My bodies can not stand.

A'blig'moodj lifts me, holds me, stands me beside him. "You are known to us, and we thank you."

It returns to The Ancients.

I crawl to my car, unable to drive, barely able to breathe.

To be known by The Ancients.

And live.

Chapter 125

Crow

I lean against my Jeep Cherokee under a T-shaped light in the *Interface Educational Center*'s parking lot. I teach in an hour. Native wisdom. Robyn gets out of her car and comes over, reaches out to me.

"How come you didn't tell me this last night when you got home?"

I shrug.

"What did he say to you, exactly?"

"It wasn't so much what he said as what he did. He and three others in AIM jackets and hats stood in the back while I talked. When I was done, Marvin came forward and started going through my notes telling me what I could and couldn't teach."

A crow caws, flies to the light overhead, perches on one arm of the T.

"What right does he have to tell you what you can and can't teach?"

"None, but that's not what he wanted to do. It was an intimidation maneuver. That and the phone calls."

"I told you to tell the police about those."

I shake my head. "Why bother. They'll stop. Their own stupidity will catch up with them."

"But it's not right."

"Oh, Princess, please don't tell me you think in terms of wrong and right. The Universe is. What we do, the decisions we make, determine wrong or right."

"So what have you decided to do about him?"

"Nothing."

Two more crows join the first.

I take her hand, kiss it.

"Nothing? You're going to let him bully you?"

"He can't bully me without my permission. You know that, right?"

"Sometimes your philosophy sucks, you know that, right?"

"I don't know if he's upset because his tribe's wisdom keepers selected me over their own or because of the name they gave me. Maybe he's worried people will confuse us."

"He's a jerk and don't be stupid. You think people would confuse you for him or vice versa?"

The cawing becomes a cacophony. I look up. Some twenty crows gather across the T directly overhead. More gather on the light some ten spaces down.

Robyn followed my gaze. "Kind of looks like he's summoning the legions, doesn't it?"

"He didn't confront me in the way of his own people. He confronted me the way a white man, a *wasicu*, would do it. He claims I have no right to teach their ways yet doesn't know them himself."

"Surprise!"

The parking lot becomes a crow convention. They cover the lights, the ground, gather on my Jeep, Robyn's Toyota.

She looks around. "I feel like I'm in Hitchcock's *The Birds*. Where do they all come from?"

The crows gather, grow, collect, become one.

"The other side. Crows have the ability to see the other side."

Crow flaps its wings.

"Didn't you tell me you carry Crow Medicine?"

It stands over seven feet tall, grooms itself, one eye watching me.

"So they tell me."

"Who?"

Crow turns its other eye to me. "He fears your power. He fears what you can do. He feels shame that he took on the ways of his people only after he found no lasting success in white society, didn't know white society remembers only one's last, not one's best. He is more *wasicu* than you and it sickens him. He is a weak wolf who believes the pack will accept him if he attacks you."

Feathers grow down my arms. I shake my head. "Them."

Robyn looks into my eyes. "Who them?"

"He learns of regalia through books, not through elders, claims his people's ways without knowing his people. Soon his pack will attack him. You do not challenge him, he challenges himself."

I sprout tail feathers.

"Your eyes. What's happening to your eyes?"

I see Robyn as Crow sees Robyn, as Crow sees all people.

"He takes on his people's ways now to make money, not to honor his people. Learn the lesson he teaches and move on. Teach what the Grandmothers and Grandfathers taught you to teach."

"Everything, everything, everything is my teacher. I decide what is the lesson."

Crow nods, smiles. "Do you understand? Being a teacher means being constantly willing to be taught."

I caw.

"Gio?"

"Go, teach. Do not worry about him. He is someone else's matter."

I shake the feathers from my sides, my tail feathers recede, where a beak shaped my face my nose and mouth return.

The crows separate, a whirlwind of black rising into the sky, a cloud of destiny flying away.

"You okay?"

"Yes. You?"

The crows are gone. Bluejays, robins, and nuthatches land, hop around, search for scraps.

"You're freaky, you know that?"

Chapter 126

Karen

A short, heavy woman, Karen, comes to us. "Why haven't I lost weight?"

"You want to lose weight because...?"

She ignores our question. "I took a class with Dinella. She did a weight loss ceremony with me. Everybody in the class took part. Dinella told us the words to say, the herbs to burn, what things to think and pray." Tears flow down her face. "How come I'm not losing any weight?"

Robyn reaches out to her and I draw her hand back. "Who's Dinella?"

"She's a shawoman who taught at *Interface*."

"A sha*woman*?"

"She's a very powerful shawoman. She's very well known."

"Tell us about her."

Karen tells us about the workshop she attended. I follow her memories, find a crow perched outside the window peering in, ask its indulgence. It agrees and I see through crow eyes, hear through crow ears.

A squat woman paces in front of a full class. She checks herself each time she passes her reflection: in a picture covered in glass, a shiny coffee urn, a hot water urn, a mirror. Sometimes she taps her finger to her tongue and adjusts makeup, hiding jowls. Sometimes she stands in front of men in the first and second row, leans over to ask a question, her open-necked peasant shirt revealing much, her gold necklaces jingling as they fall out and forward, her gold bracelets jingling as she hurries to close the gap, brushing her long, dirty blond hair back, finally pulling it into a treated animal hide beret.

She paces, talks hurriedly, not waiting for answers. "...and it's not only for men that's why I call myself a sha*woman*..."

Crow laughs.

"...and the police stopped this woman and pulled her over and I pulled up right behind them and got out of my car and stood there and told them 'I am observing you. I see what you're doing'." She paces, jabs the air, paces.

"Thank you, Brother Crow."

Karen's face is riven, half the face she has, half the face she desires.

"Is it possible Dinella made a mistake?"

"But she's a shawoman!"

"I'm sure she is, and that doesn't answer my question."

"Can you help me lose weight?"

"How much weight do you want to lose?

"Twenty pounds."

"How long ago was this other class?"

"Two weeks ago."

Robyn shakes her head. "You expected to lose twenty pounds in two weeks?"

"No. I expected to lose it by the end of the class. Dinella told everyone there was great magic in the ceremony she performed."

Robyn rolls her eyes at me. "I'm sure she did."

"But it didn't work."

Robyn looks down, shakes her head. "And thank god it didn't! What ever made you think it was going to work?"

"Dinella said it would."

Robyn sits back, throws her hands wide. "Oh, well, then."

"Do you know any ceremonies for losing weight?"

I nod. "Yes, several. We need to select one which will work for you then translate the ceremony into a ritual you can perform on your own."

"Can't you just wave your hands or something?"

"Yes. But then you'd never learn."

$$\sim$$

Robyn watches Karen drive away. "Do you think she learned?"

"I doubt it. What I taught her was to be careful in her diet, eat sensibly, and exercise."

"You worked with her thirty days and she lost weight."

"But I didn't wave my hands. She didn't want the responsibility for her weight loss. That was the real challenge. Working with me, she made me responsible for her weight loss. Now she's by herself again, the weight will come back."

"Eat carefully, sensible diet, and exercise?"

"Something Grandmother Apara taught me: know when the best ritual is common sense."

Chapter 127

Blind

"*Vois pas moi.*"

Yve is petite, Haitian, delicate. Her French is a patois, mine barely exists, and we talk in a pidgin with the help of an interpreter, two of some thirty people who've come to study Journeying with Robyn and me, and she returns from her first journey blind.

I walk up to people, make sure they're alright, and her interpreter walks up to me, pulls me aside, whispers in my ear, I follow.

Yve sits quietly, alone, her hands outstretched, neither screaming nor shrieking.

I take her hands in mine. She smiles. I follow her back into her journey. The class's first after days of study, preparation. None journey completely, I journey with them, letting them piggyback, Daskele's practice of several selves giving each of them a ride.

She is happy and safe, I left her for a moment knowing she could find her way back.

She did, but not her eyes.

From Grandmother Paula: there are no challenges, only opportunities.

"Class, Yve is having a wonderful experience. As part of our learning, we're going to share it." I ask through the interpreter, "Okay with you, Yve?"

"*Oui.*"

I look back at the class. "Shall we?"

"Yes!" "Oui!" "D'accord!" "Certainly!" "Go for it!" "Allez!"

"Excellent. I will sit here with Yve." I draw Yve to me, we sit on the floor. "Gather round us, form a circle two layers deep." I remind them of an earlier exercise, a demonstration of how villages come together. "Remember Turtle? We'll use what Turtle taught us to bring Yve's eyes back."

I borrow from Spider, let everyone ride upon my back like a mother spider carrying her hatchlings, and follow Yve's web of energy back, back, back until we come to a Haiti that never existed except for Yve, a reality shaped from memory and desire.

"What a beautiful place." The air is Caribbean clean, the wind warm as it rustles palms and breadfruit, and carries a hint of ocean as waves break on a pristine beach not far away.

Her eyes float in the air approximately the height they'd be if her body was present.

"I can understand you not wanting to leave."

"But I do. I cannot stay. I have children who need me back home."

I look around. There are no children here. "Where is home?"

"Saint John's, where I live."

Ah. New Brunswick is now her home but only in her head, not in her heart, so she made a place of memory and desire to escape to. Seeing it for real, her eyes sought to escape.

"How about if we make it so you can come here any time you want, a place so real you can bring your children here and share it with them?"

"That would be very nice."

I invite the class to gather Turtle to them, to share the safety of its shell, and inside I ask Spider to spin a web for Yve, one she is safe to climb, one which allows her to carry her children, a place so beautiful and easy to get to, therefore easy to leave.

Drum once again signals The Return. Yve's eyes hear it this time.

"Come, I will help you find Yve." I lift them into a shirt pocket and carry them home, all the others once again on my back, understanding the beauty Yve feared to leave.

Back in the class Yve opens her eyes.

"Hello, Yve. Can you see me?"

"*Oui!*"

"*Et Robyn?*"

"Yes!"

"*Et classe?*"

"*Oui! Tout personnes!*"

"*Bien!*"

Chapter 128

Swimming in the Sea of Japan

The group sits relaxed in our living room. I make chili and nacho chips. Everyone feasts. Now we laugh.

They ask questions, simple and harmless.

Then one, David, points to Drum on our wall above our fireplace. "Can you teach us?"

"What do you want to learn?"

"I've read about journeying. The books say it's easy to do. I took a class once."

Robyn rolls her eyes.

"I probably studied differently than the people writing those books."

"So you won't teach us?"

"Do you want to learn how to do it or just have the experience of doing it?"

"There's a difference?"

Robyn shakes her head.

"Let's start with the experience of it." I explain a little of what will happen. "Everybody sure they want to do this?"

Nods, yeses, sures, roll around the room.

"Very well." I take Drum, explain The Call and The Return, demonstrate briefly with Drum's permission.

"Everybody sure they want to do this?"

Nods, yeses, sures.

"I'll ask one more time. It's okay to say you'd rather not. Robyn made some chocolate cake for dessert. You can go in the kitchen and have some. She'll start the coffee. Your call, no questions asked."

Nods, yeses, sures.

Drum begins. I flatten, spread, allow them to piggyback, carry them one by one to where they need to be, let them off, leave enough of myself to watch, ensure their safety, then off to the next, Santa Claus without the sleigh and stopping at differently shaped chimneys.

They relax. They play.

David basks in the Sea of Japan, a place of comfort years ago.

Until something bumps him in the water.

He pays no mind, continues to feel the sunshine on his stomach, chest, and face, the water holding him along his back, arms, and legs.

Something bumps him in the water.

He sees a harbor in the distance and backstrokes towards it.

Something bumps him in the water.

He rolls over, swims.

Another bump, underneath, rasping his skin.

He swims faster.

A bump on either side. A fin breaks the surface in front of him, barring his way.

I remember Grandpa and Tutor Turtle.

But also his teaching. Do not rescue. Guide. Teach.

David panics in the water, his strokes are wild. More fins surface, surround.

A moment later he and the others are back relaxing in our living room.

"You saved me."

"I did?"

"I was swimming in the Sea of Japan, like when I was in the Navy. It was wonderful back then."

"Sounds nice."

"Except I forgot about the sharks."

"Oh?"

"And then I saw one shark, larger than the rest, with a beard and glasses."

"Oh?"

"That was you, wasn't it?"

"Was it?"

"It came up beside me, let me take its fin, and swam me back here." And a statement, not a question this time. "That was you, wasn't it."

Chapter 129

Four-Body Discernment

I sit on my back porch in the cool of an Autumn evening. The sun sets, Winter approaches, but not yet. I look where FlowerSong appears, wondering. Jays, finches, chickadees, grackles, sparrows, and red-wing blackbirds flutter back and forth among our many feeders, gifts to The Old Ones, filling their beaks with their last meals of the day. A deep breath brings forest smells. I listen to the trees, The Standing Ones, wish each other Good Morrow as they pull their leaves in for the night. A barred owl perches in a nearby pine. Raven lands between the feeders. The other birds take no notice.

"Hello, Brother Raven."

He caws.

"I'm sorry, Brother Raven. I'm still learning your language. May I borrow from you?"

He prances, forming a circle, waiting.

He caws again. I hear "Good Morrow, Gio."

"Good Morrow, Raven."

"I bring you news from an old teacher. A warning."

"Yes?"

"Return to Center. Stay whole."

~

Robyn comes to me. "A woman's here to see you. Were you expecting anyone?"

Raven caws, flies into a tree. Observes, watches, patient.

"Shall I show her in?

A woman, fifty to fifty-five, heavy and strong, walks in. *Ascolta!*

I hear her body, her joints, her bones, creak with each step. She wears a wide-brimmed gardening hat with its cord tight under her chin and large dark sunglasses which she removes and puts in a huge purse heavy with things she no longer needs yet won't give up.

I point to a chair. "Please make yourself comfortable."

She falls into the chair, nothing graceful about her. A baggy, light blue men's long sleeve shirt is buttoned high to the neck, men's cream-colored slacks have elastic straps poorly hand sewn so the pant cuffs grip slightly above her ankles. Her feet bulge from blue flats matching her shirt.

I make note; she has a sense of color, of style, yet goes no further with it?

What I can see of her face has soft skin. She carries a scent from a memory, a scent of heat and heavy rains, tar or something close. Sulphurous.

I feel Grandmother Apara in me, I remember her words. Where are the bodies located? Where are the lines of separation?

My bodies start twisting, aligning themselves with hers, to understand her needs.

She looks at me closely. "I knew your grandfather."

She has no scent of my Grandfather. I recognize his work when near it.

"You knew my Grandfather?"

She smirks. "I've known lots of people like you. None of them can help me."

"Then why come to me?"

Grandmother Apara's teaching. What are the bodies telling you?

Her bodies are misaligned. She is not at their center.

She doesn't want to heal. She wants someone to heal her.

She wants someone to fail.

So she can claim they're a fake, a failure in life.

Because that's how she sees herself.

I remember Grandfather's "If I am a thief, you must steal."

~

She tells me about her family, her children once near, now grown with lives of their own. Her husband, never faithful but always a good provider, now seeing to her needs less and less, The things he once stole - stole? - for her now going to others.

Small things. To her, signs of affection. When he thought no one was looking. Secret deals. She finishes with "You understand. You're Sicilian, aren't you?

"Is that how you learned of me?"

Confusion. She hasn't thought of herself as Italian in years. Less so now. Welcome to America. Land of Opportunity.

Now opportunity lost.

Raven caws from the tree. The limb He rests on shakes with his voice. "Center, Gio. Find your Center to find hers."

"They mentioned you at *The Shining Room*." I remember. WhirlWind and I played there. Now they whisper my name.

To know her, to understand her, my bodies must go in different ways while remembering my Center. Her bodies twist. She forces them to hold together in new ways, strange ways, ways not natural.

What are her bodies telling me?

"You've run out of ways to control your fate."

"What?"

"Controlling your fate has allowed you to go where you want, not where you should be."

The smell of her becomes familiar. Her eyes become lizard eyes, her tongue a lizard tongue.

"Well, I'm here now."

Chester. Jean Reveaux and Chester.

This is where The Universe wants her for me. The Universe is efficient. Time and Space are tools it uses so we can understand what it's saying. She is a lesson.

Chester's eyes and tongue are gone. Her face remains.

"New Orleans, long ago. The laundromat. You and your husband were washing clothes."

She nods. "You came in with your grandfather.

It is a common mistake. My Sicilian blood. I tan darkly, deeply. I laugh. A different kind of passing.

"Did you use the solution Mèt Reveaux gave you?

"Who?"

"The little man in the laundry. He gave you a bottle of liquid. Told you to rub it in."

"It didn't work."

Her physical body grows on me like a skin. It remembers being healed. Many times. "No, it did. Your son, the chemist, he also developed a cure."

She straightens her shirt, clutches her pocketbook to her.

"How do you know about my son?"

"The problem is not your physical body. It's been cured. The problem is your emotional body. It doesn't want to be cured."

"What are you talking about?"

"I can't cure you. Nothing I do would work. You can cure yourself, but you won't."

"You don't know what you're talking about."

~

"Your dis-ease is a Sacred Illness, what used to be considered a gift from god, something that allows the penitent to go about, showing off their suffering, saying 'See? God has done this to me yet I still call him Lord! He gave me this to call others to penance!'"

Her eyes have vertical irises. She grows fangs. A snake's tongue whips out. She hisses, "You're a fool."

Discernment. A snake is tied to her physical body. A snake that can't shed its skin. Can't grow, hence can't renew.

"Probably so, and if true, there's no harm in letting me talk. I'll be one more you can say failed you, another checkmark on your resume of healers who can't heal."

She spits venom. "Shut up."

"You use your illness to control people, to draw them to you, keep them clustered around, force them to put you in their centers. 'Ma, I'm going on a date, not sure when I'll be back.' 'Oh, my legs, my legs! Bring me my pillows before you go.' 'That's okay, ma. I'll stay in and take care of you.' 'The guys at the office invited me to go fishing with them this weekend, Rose. I'll be back Sunday night in time for dinner.' 'Oh, my back, my back. I think it's spread. Make sure I have enough medicine before you go.' 'No, that's okay, Rose. I'll stick around in case it gets worse.'"

She stands, dusts off her pants as if dusting off my words.

"But now your house is deserted. Your Sacred Illness has betrayed you, turned on you, attacked you, your body swollen with your lies and fears."

She opens her pocketbook, arranges things within, searching.

"There's nothing I can do. You have to heal yourself. And you won't because doing so means realizing you've created your life and it's not the life you wanted, only the one you got."

She pulls out her purse.

"That is what's destroying you."

My bodies relax, return to their own alignment, to my Center.

She looks at me, wanting to see if my eyes are on her or her opened purse.

"I'm not paying for this."

Chester's face replaces Snake's. His tongue flicks out, licking cheeks, chin, forehead, eyes.

Wounds, scales, flaking, red, blistering skin forms where it didn't exist before.

My eyes remain on hers.

"You've already paid. Thank you for your time."

Robyn comes in. Rose hustles past her, pushing her out of the way. "I know my way out."

Chapter 130

The Paraclete

I walk into the hospital room. Robyn's mother, Wilma, looks up at me from her hospital bed and smiles.

"What are you doing here, Gio? Is Robyn with you?"

"She's at the nurse's station, reading your chart."

"That's Robyn. I'm in good hands. You can tell her that."

"Yes, I know."

I stare up. The Paraclete floats over Wilma's bed, a standing wave like a squared slice of cake made of ocean, a carpet made of blue, green, and gold strands woven so fine you can't pull them apart yet with coloring so distinct you can easily see each when held in your hand, its top and edges a thick, whitish sea foam like a meringue.

She follows my gaze. "What are you looking at?"

It undulates and ripples even though it appears as an unmoving wave. It makes no sound, only waits. It covers Wilma with the sweet scent of caring, compassion, and hope.

"Do all hospital rooms have such high ceilings?"

The Paraclete waits. To comfort. To transport. To help Wilma finish her journey.

I look back at Wilma, use Grandmother's eyes, see where she is diseased, how far it's spread.

A disease of the heart. It weakens her body, tells her mind it's time, asks her spirit to prepare, draws surety from her emotions.

She is ready. Also waiting. Except she doesn't know.

I gaze back at The Paraclete. "How long have you been waiting?"

Wilma glances around. "Who are you talking to?"

She hears. It will not be long.

The Paraclete comes closer. Its voices come on Infinity's winds. "Long." and "Not long." is one word that isn't a word at all.

I pet Wilma's arm. "Let me go find Robyn."

I stop her in the hall. "What did the nurses say?"

"She's fine. A little dehydrated when she came in, that's all."

I shake my head. "She won't make it through the night."

"You're sure?"

The Paraclete whispers. It has no sense of time. Clocks don't exist in its land.

"I'm sure. Not long. Tomorrow morning at best."

"I wish you didn't tell me."

"Would you be happier that way?"

We stand on either side of Wilma's bed.

"Gio, would you rub my back?"

Robyn glances at me, catches my eye. She knows now. Wilma never asks me to do such things. Thirty-eight years together and her family knows nothing of my life. I'm a good provider, keep Robyn safe, never abuse her. That's enough.

"I never knew how soft your touch was, Gio. I always thought your hands were rough."

A nurse comes in, tells us it's time to leave.

I hold Wilma's hand, kiss her forehead.

"You never kiss me."

My kiss opens her slightly to the energies gathering around her, to The Paraclete coming closer, closer.

"I only kiss you when you need it. I'll stay the night with you if you'd like."

Her eyes flick up over my head, to where The Paraclete waits.

"No, I'll be fine." She smiles a goodbye.

We hurry back to the hospital early in the morning, an emergency call, Wilma is in the ICU, prepare for the worst.

The Paraclete no longer floats over her bed, most of it's gone, only a small portion remains, waiting for Wilma to breathe her last. All that remains is the bottom edge of the carpet and a bit of the wave floating above and a bit beyond Wilma's head.

Her body is on life support but most of her is no longer in it.

The Paraclete transports her, comforts her.

"Is there anything I can do to help?"

What remains of the wave forms a mouth with Wilma's voice. "Will you be alright? Will Adam? Jeannie? Will you take care of yourselves? Will you take care of each other?"

I wait for the nurse to leave and lean over Wilma.

"It's alright, Wilma. We'll be okay. You can go now, if you want. We'll take care of each other. We'll keep each other safe. It's okay. You don't have to worry about us anymore. And look! See? Bob's waiting for you."

The Paraclete opens its blanket, unleashes its wave.

Bob, her husband, gone over twenty-five years, stands on the wave, sits on the carpet, offers her his hand, a joyous look on his face, the love of his life comes to join him, welcomes her, lets her know it's okay, her work is done.

The Paraclete gathers her in its waves, holds her next to Bob, slowly moves away.

Chapter 131

The Spirit Guide

Giselle, a tall, flaxen-haired woman with lustrous green eyes passes a framed certificate around the class. The certificate is from a Connecticut-based institute and indicates she's successfully completed a course on shamanism.

She, it declares, is a shaman.

I know of such institutes and that one can get a certificate in such things. I remember Grandmother Parvati's teaching: you are only one as long as people come to you and you're able to help them. I remember Grandpa's teaching: don't share what you can do. They will hunt you down and kill you if they learn what you can do.

But I know not everyone studies as I study, not everyone learns as I learn.

And Grandmother Paula considers experience the only real education. "Remember, everything, everything, everything is your teacher. Especially seek out those who've studied in ways you haven't." She smiles coyly. "They are often the greatest teachers of all."

"Yes, Grandmother."

"And remember, you decide what the lesson is."

"Yes, Grandmother."

Giselle carries a certificate from an institute stating she knows what she's doing.

I learn each time I do.

Definitely different from how I study, how I learn.

I sit in the back. Giselle allows each of us to share our name, a little about our work and family, nothing more.

My turn arrives. "Hi, I'm Gio. Love my wife and pets. Spend my time studying. Not much else to say."

Giselle stares at me for a moment. She turns her eyes to the next person. "Tell us about yourself."

All share, some more, some less. Giselle stands in front and lifts her arms, palms up, as if her motion will raise us from our seats. "Divide into pairs. Find someone you're comfortable with."

Lynn, one of the women who does administrative work at this training center, smiles at me. "Want to buddy up, Gio?"

"Sure."

The teacher explains an exercise to us. We are to learn about each other's Spirit Guides. "Choose which one of you will be the seeker and which the shaman. The seeker will tell the shaman what animal they like most and the shaman will tell the seeker how they're most like that animal."

I raise my hand. "Excuse me, are you talking about SpiritCalling?"

"I don't know that term. Have you studied shamanism?"

"Not that I know of, no. At least not by that name."

"Then how about you do the exercise. It'll be a learning experience for you."

"I'm always up for learning. May I do how I've learned to do it?"

Giselle waves her hand as she walks to other student pairs. "Whatever."

Lynn and I sit on the floor in the back of the room facing each other. I *go wide*, greet the energies surrounding her. One, Fawn, nuzzles her ear.

Lynn flicks back her hair. "I want to talk about mantis."

I shake my head. "Fawn."

"Beg pardon?"

"Your Spirit Guide is Fawn. We can talk about Mantis if you want, but your Spirit Guide is Fawn."

"I thought I was supposed to tell you what animal I wanted as a Spirit Guide."

"Doesn't matter what you want, only what you have."

Giselle wanders through the class, stops and towers over us. "That's not how it's done."

"Sorry. Give me a minute. Let's find out something." I face Lynn. "This morning when you left your house. You live about -" I look - "thirty-five miles from here, just this side of Fitchburg, in a wooded area."

"How do you know where I live?"

"You stepped out your door and a fawn stood by your car."

"How do you know that?"

"You heard Fawn talk. In your heart."

"How do you know this?"

Giselle puts her hand on my shoulder. Grips me. Grandmother bites her. Giselle pulls her hand away, stares at the swelling red marks, the poison flowing from the wound.

"Fawn told you not to drive your car in today. To call a friend and drive in with them."

"Who told you this?"

"Your car broke down on Route 2. Fortunately Todd was running late today and about a mile behind you. He saw you pulled over. Should've listened to Fawn. She's your protector as well as your Guide. Todd likes you, you know."

Lynn stands up, backs away.

"And it seems, according to Fawn, you like him."

I clap my hands, laugh. "You think he's gay? What makes you think he's gay?"

Lynn runs out of the classroom.

Giselle nudges me with her boot. "What gave you the right to do that? You don't even know what you're talking about."

"You gave me the right when I asked if I could do what I learned and you answered, 'Whatever.' You said to learn. I never claimed to know what I'm doing. I said I'm a student. I have learned a great deal today."

The class is dividing. Some mosey in my direction. "He knows what he's doing." Others hasten away. "He's a stalker. How else would he know that kind of stuff?"

Chapter 132

Rock and Mantis

Another class, another certified person who studied and learned differently than I. Mel, a middle-aged male, graying at the temples. "I stay slim and young by practicing yoga."

I'm impressed. "What form?"

"You know. Yoga."

I nod.

He smiles wanly and looks away. "Before class, you all received a letter asking you to go outside your house and find something - a rock, a stick, a leaf, something - that has meaning to you and bring it with you tonight. If you didn't get the letter or forgot, go outside now and find something in the parking lot and bring it back."

Two people hurry out.

I watch Mel meditate. I'm impressed at the way he hums. "What are you doing?"

"It's Tuval Throat Singing."

"Ah. I thought it sounded more like this." I create the drone low in my chest, add a layer in my throat, my natural voice, and a harmonic in my nose, vibrate my sinus passages.

"How do you do that?"

I shrug. "Practice?"

The two others return. One carries an oak leaf, the other a map. "It's all I could come up with. I use it a lot, though."

Mel asks us to introduce ourselves.

He holds up his hand when I introduce myself. "You're Gio?"

"A Gio. Can't offer more than that."

"You took a class here last year, didn't you?"

"I study a lot."

"Yes."

The class continues introductions. Mel keeps his eyes on me.

"Divide into pairs. One person will be the seeker, the other the shaman. The seeker will share the object they brought and tell the shaman its significance in their lives, what it means to them. The shaman will offer suggestions for working with the object."

"Excuse me. You want the seeker to explain the object's significance?"

"Exactly."

My partner produces a rock.

"May I hold it?"

My partner hands it to me.

"You picked this rock up in your garden. You chose it because a praying mantis perched on it. As you neared, it spread its forelegs and wings but didn't fly off, as if wanting your attention. It kept its eyes on you. You sat and talked with it. It stepped off this rock and onto you, walking up until it was on your shoulder, facing the direction you faced. It raised one foreleg and pointed in a direction. You took it. It guided you through the woods behind your house. It took you to your daughter's doll, one she'd lost."

My partner looks at me, shakes his head slowly. "Yes. How did you know?"

Mel comes between us. "You need to leave, Gio. This is not what this class is about."

I stand, offer the stone to my partner. "It's not your fault, what happened to your daughter. It happened. She's well where she is. Tell your wife. Tell your son."

Mel's hand clamps my arm.

I stare at it, at him. I show him my partner's daughter, where she is, that she's happy, she plays with grandparents, my partner's brother and uncle, waiting.

I take Mel's hand from my arm. He cannot resist. I hold it out to my partner. "Take his hand. He has something to show you."

My partner takes Mel's hand. He smiles then weeps, waves to his family on the other side of life, and smiles again. He lets go of Mel's hand.

Mel falls to the floor, convulses, curls himself into a fetal position, a child back in the womb, and wails realizing what he has seen.

Chapter 133

Bear Medicine

Sy comes up to me and smiles an anxious smile. Her laugh lines haven't laughed in a while. "That was a wonderful presentation."

"Thank you. I do what I can."

"Can you tell me what's wrong with me?"

"Wrong? Nothing. If you're asking what stresses there are in your body, you suffer from arthritis."

"You can tell I have arthritis, but you say there's nothing wrong with me?"

"There's nothing in your body causing the arthritis."

"Then how come I have all this pain?"

"How come you're wearing a bear pendant?"

"I went to a healer and she told me I needed Bear Medicine."

My brow furrows. "That's interesting. You already have a lot of Bear Medicine."

"I do?"

"Your ancestry is northern European and Celtic, correct?"

"You can tell that by looking at me?

"Bear is extremely territorial in those cultures."

"What's that got to do with my arthritis and wearing a bear pendant?"

"The territory of our bodies is defined by our joints. Bear protects and guards its territory. In your case, Bear locks or freezes or otherwise defines limits to your joints to protect you, its territory."

"What can I do?"

"Take off the pendant."

"I never take off this pendant."

"Then you'll continue to suffer from arthritis."

She stares at me. Her eyes narrow. "Okay. I'll give it a try. You coming back this way?"

"In about a month."

"Talking anywhere?"

"Here, if they'll have me."

"I'll see you then."

~

"My arthritis is gone. If Bear is part of my heritage, how come the pendant didn't help me?"

"Because the person who gave it to you saw a ritual, didn't know the ceremony, the meaning behind the ritual, didn't know the Bear Ceremonies involved in invoking Bear to do a healing."

"She studied."

"I'm sure she did."

"But not like you?"

"Not like me."

"So you're better than her?"

"Not better, only different."

Chapter 134

HealingPlace Work

Robyn looks out our dining room window across a late Spring, still frost-covered lawn. "Did you call for a limo?"

"No."

"There's one parked outside. And between the car and the driver, this could only be for you."

Parked in front of our home is a luxury car from the 1930's, an old style, two-tone white on ruby limousine with the chauffeur's compartment completely separated from the passengers' compartment. The chauffeur is dressed in a blazing white suit with cap and stands well over six feet with strapping arms and chest, a thick, dark braid runs down the middle of a back broad enough to rent advertising space, his face blurs, keeps shifting, as if waiting to settle to something it wants seen.

It waits by the passenger door which opens when I look out.

"Guess you're going somewhere."

"Guess so."

We drive through the night and stop by a house backed by woods in Petosky, Michigan. The chauffeur opens my door, I step out, and it and the car fade.

An elderly woman, still beautiful and beautifully aged, worn housecoat covered with a sweater and both cinched at the waist, opens the front door and stands silhouetted by light from the hallway at her back. "Can I help you?" She looks around for some vehicle. "How did you get here?"

"A friend drove me."

She looks around again, up into the trees towards the coming dawn, and pulls her sweater tighter at the neck. "Better come in. It's cold out here."

I enter, inhale deeply. Strong coffee but no breakfast.

And ill. Sickness. I look up, my old friend, The Gatherer, The Paraclete, the creature of foam flecked waves without an ocean, floats at the ceiling. It points to a door at the end of the hallway.

"May I?"

"Roy's in there. My husband. You a minister? A priest? He's dying. There's nothing anybody can do about it."

I knock.

A phlegm-muffled cough answers. "Come in."

The woman moves through another door. I see a kitchen beyond. "Go ahead in. You drink coffee? I'll bring you a cup."

"Real cream, if you have it."

She nods, closes the door behind her.

I enter Roy's room.

A man, once robust and strong, now shrunken and weak, lays in a bed. The nightstand beside him is covered with medicine bottles.

I sit on the edge of his bed. The Master Musician, the Tiny Dancer, spins between us. It wears bright red clothing with a white fringe and a wide blue belt, carries a drum I've not seen in many years, beats a distinctive 1,2-3 1,2-3 rhythm and sings a *joik*. It splits and its twin joins to sing counterpoint. The round comes back and it splits again, three Master Musicians in traditional dress.

The man lifts a towel to block a cough, finishes, stares up at me. "Something I can do for you?" He smiles. "Whatever it is, it better be quick." I follow his hand, scarred and mutilated. Only three fingers remain.

I look. Snow. Mountains. Fields of winter. Rifles? Hunters? Hunters and hunted.

I listen. Mortar fire. Planes fly overhead. Props, not jets, nothing modern. Rifle shots. The sounds of skis moving quickly over snow. Men yelling, some screaming. Blood on the snow. Far off diesel rumblings.

I inhale. Exhausts. Planes and land vehicles. Human sweat. Fear.

Then one monstrous explosion, a too-near nova in the sky. Even seeing through time I blink and cover my eyes.

"10th Mountain Division. You were in the Elite Alpines."

"One of the original 400. Except we weren't in the Alps, we were way up north, running supplies and such through Finland into Russia. But how do you know that? You the son -" he squints to get a good look at me - "or grandson of one of my brothers? Come to pay your respects?"

My gaze lowers to him. I touch the covers. "May I?"

"I got nothing to hide. You a doctor? My daughter send you?"

I shrug. "Not your daughter. Something like a doctor." I pull the covers back.

His body is brittle. The sheet is sticky wet on his left side. A wound that's never healed. I point.

He smiles. "Had that since our last battle. Didn't know Jerry used the area for weapons testing. Hadn't used it in months. But they did that day. No idea what they had. Everything blew up." He gently touched the wound with his three-fingered hand. "This is my trophy. Woke up with it. Won't close up. Been stitched three times and stapled twice, had so many grafts my left ass cheek's down an inch from my right. Always opens up. Nobody can tell me why." He pauses, squints at me again. "Can you tell me why?"

"It is that for which I came."

〰

The car and chauffeur appear as I exit Roy's home. We head into Petosky center along the curve of Little Traverse Bay. The moon sets over Wisconsin. A shine rises from the bay. My chauffeur pulls over, aims the headlights at it.

Ice. Broken but still there. Not a glacier, but still noticeable bergs floating like ice cubes in some god's cocktail.

Something moves among them, catches like cat's eyes in the car's headlights. Something swimming, larger than should be in these waters. The chauffeur hands me a huge bass, its mouth still working, and points towards the water.

The shine is closer.

The chauffeur and car fade as a woman breaks the water's surface just beyond the shoreline. Her voice carries tones of ancient things and people and I step into the water.

Which is bracing cold, shocking cold, and soaks my boots. I shake my head, the woman's voice penetrating me, enrapturing me.

I am near paralyzed. I want to join her in the water.

Except I have a freshly caught bass in my hands. Holding it is awkward. Its flopping fouls my path to her.

I toss it into the water.

The woman stops voicing, stops singing, dives, surfaces with the bass between her teeth. She tears through its side and chews, her eyes on me, watching. My mind clears. I step back from the water.

The sun rises and shows what's below the surface.

"Vedenemo. Mother of Waters."

She nods, holds the fish to me.

I shake my head, make sure I'm clear of the water.

She laughs. She speaks inside me to keep me safe from her voice. "You learn well."

"The Hedningarna are good teachers."

"And Ailo, too."

"And Ailo, too."

"Save my brother."

"Your brother?"

"Tuoni opened a path to Tuonela, to Lintukoto."

I remember. Tuoni. Three fingers on each hand. Roy.

Her image swirls, shifts. A frozen battleground takes her place, floats on the ice laden water. "A strange god fought Tuoni." The same scene seen through Roy's eyes now shared by an ancient god. What hellish weapon had the Germans tested that day? "Tuoni threw his hat upon those who summoned the strange one. Cast them and their god into eternal darkness." That's why the explosion collapsed like a nova under gravitational release. What energies had Tuoni collected, directed, and to where? "But Vasara also struck. A warrior there summoned him unknowing. The resulting storm fused Tuoni and the warrior's flesh. They shared a wound." Roy, caught in the blast then Tuoni's wrath and used to deliver the god's judgement. "Now that warrior dies. He takes part of Tuoni with him and so Tuoni will die, as well."

Swirl. Shift. Vedenemo returns, half submerged. Undeniable beauty above the surface, horror and terror beneath.

"Save my brother."

"How?"

"Mysteries reveal themselves when they will."

"How much time?"

She dives under the water. Her true voice parts the lake, clouds my mind. "Until the ice leaves the bay." She speaks again into my mind and the waters seal themselves behind her. "Until the ice leaves the bay. Go now. Otso will take you."

She is gone, the rising sun flickers off the tip of her tail as she goes deep.

I'm caught in a flood of headlights and turn. The chauffeur and limo are returned, and now his face is clear.

"May I say your name?"

The chauffeur bows.

"Otso."

He growls. It's the first time I've heard him speak. "Brother, Uncle, or Cousin will do."

———

"I can't save your life but I can close your wound, give you peace, make sure you arrive safely to the next place."

Roy looks up at me. "Next place?"

"You're dying, Roy. I can't change that."

"What kind of doctor are you?"

Mysteries reveal themselves when they will. "Sorry I've never asked before, Roy. What's your last name?"

"Palen. What's yours?"

"Fortuna. Chance in English. Does it make a difference?"

He coughs. "Mine's Palen in English, Paalanen in Finnish."

I nod, understanding. "Your people are Finnish?"

"It's why I chose the Russian resupply assignment. Wanted to know how my grandfolk were getting along. Never met them, barely spoke the language, thought it might be my last chance. Wore a charm my father gave me when I left home. Said it protected our people. Was going to use it to prove who I was when I met my people."

"Do you still have it?"

He reaches under his pajama top. A braided leather thong holds an ancient stone. The stone's face holds an image of a battle axe.

I lean forward but don't touch. "Vasara. Ukko's hammer."

Mysteries reveal themselves when they will.

"Always wondered what it was. Never met my folk and never found out."

"We need to go to where you received that wound."

Roy laughs and coughs and laughs. "I need help to get to the can and you want me to go to Finland?"

We stand under a dark, midnight sky on a frozen, snow-covered field, the only aberration on its smooth surface a flattened stone surfacing like Tursas from beneath ice-laden waves. Woods are in the distance. Someone flashes a light. White-clad men ski towards us, past us, towards the far-away woods.

Roy looks around, his eyes clear, no longer rheumy, no longer weak. "I know this place." He looks down. His body is young, strong. "How come I'm naked?"

He runs healthy hands over his body until a whole hand touches a wound growing on his left side. The hand withers, changes like a tree losing leaves, drops flesh until only three fingers remain.

"What kind of doctor are you?"

He gazes at the constellations overhead. Stars move, come together, a great bear forms, descends, stands behind us, twice our height, its breath hot with a soft honey scent.

Cannons fire around us. Machine guns burst and men fall.

Roy drops to the ground, uses his hands to scoop out a foxhole in the snow. "Get down, you fool!" Clothes wrap themselves around Roy, his Alpine gear shapes itself to him, an ice axe hangs from his belt. He uses it to quickly dig.

I turn to the great bear standing behind us. "Cousin, will you help?"

Otso brings the heavens down and a transparent dome forms around us.

"We are safe here. For a while."

"This is Finland. The last offensive. How did we get here?"

"May I have your pendant?"

"What are you doing?"

"Did you ever find out what weapon the Nazis tested that day?"

"No. Something hot. Lots of our boys and the Russians got bad burns. I got this wound and lost some fingers. Small price, really. Never found the Jerries, though. Nobody knows what happened to them."

I turn to the Great Bear. "Cousin, to heal Tuoni, an exchange."

Otso bares his fangs, snarls, raises a paw over me.

"A favor for a favor."

The HoneyEater listens, lowers his paw, considers.

As much as a bear can smile, Otso smiles.

~

We stand beside the flattened rock. The battle rages around us. Men scream. Shells explode. Rifles and machine guns respond. Bright lights turn midnight into day.

Something spins over us, a hollow in the sky. A giant walks among the dead, touches them. We watch their spirits rise, drop their weapons, their gear, and follow the hollow to we know not where.

The Germans drive a platform truck and a troop carrier into the field. The crunching of snow under its tires clear above the yelling, the voices, the explosions, the gun blasts.

I place Roy's pendant on the rock. The Nazis leave the platform truck, set a timer, race getting into the carrier, its engine guns and it pulls away.

They didn't know what they had, its inventors safe hundreds of miles distant, waiting for reports that will never come.

"Your axe, Roy. Strike the pendant when I say. Strike it with all your strength."

Roy lifts his axe and his body swells, broadens, grows as Otso's dome opens and exposes us to the hell about to take place.

The timer ticks its last second.

"Now, Roy! Now!"

Ukko swings Roy's hammer. Lightning falls from the sky, the heavens thunder. Tuoni turns. Otso blocks his path. The bomb fails. The Germans race their carrier to the edge of the wood, raise a mast, radio the results to headquarters.

And Roy and Tuoni are whole. The Old One retains his hat. No darkness swallows friend or foe. Tuoni continues gathering the dead and the path to Tuonela, to Lintukoto, closes as the last souls are sent on their way.

Roy lies in his bed, his wound gone, his hand whole.

"I'm still dying, aren't I?"

"Sorry, not what I came to do."

Seafoam waves on no ocean gather over Roy's bed. I ask it for one more day.

It recedes.

"You have one more day with your wife, your children. You mentioned a daughter. You'll be strong and whole for that one more day. No pain. But then you'll be gone. Waiting."

Otso is again my chauffeur. I see it and the limo outside Roy's bedroom window.

"Waiting?"

"A final gift. Part of an exchange. A favor granted."

"What kind of doctor are you?"

"Not a doctor. Something like."

Chapter 135

Joe

He sits opposite me in the hotel lounge at the end of a long, summer conference day. I speak his thoughts before he says them. His fingers grip the cushiony armrests of his chair, his face tightens, his eyes lock on me as if he's a marksman sighting a distant target.

"That's amazing. What else can you tell me about me?"

I laugh. "It's just stage tricks. Kreskin-type stuff. A keen observer would know the same. Probably more."

"No, come on. Some of the stuff you said. How could you know it?"

"I study people. Part of my job."

"As an anthropologist?"

"Yeah, sure."

"So come on, what else can you tell me about me?"

The frame of the question, the way he asks. His scent changes, his face flushes, his smile broadens.

He wants to know he is grand, one in a million, a real champ, someone great to be around.

But I am tired and know the question he really asks: am I worthy? A small squirrel hides behind his pant leg, holding on, eyes wide, not knowing if it should run or not.

"You don't want to know."

He wants to comfort the squirrel. "Yes, I do."

"No, you don't"

"Why won't you tell me?"

"Do you really want to know?"

"Yes."

"Are you sure you want to know?"

"I just told you, yes."

"One more time, you want to know what else I can tell you about you? You may not like it."

"Yes!"

He blinks, sits back, his eyes dart right and left seeking escape: he realizes he's asked too much.

His eyes widen as the squirrel becomes him. It thumps its feet, cleans his nose, smooths its fur.

I remember Robyn's teaching: Sometimes you just have to let the fool be slapped. "Your ambitions, your goals, your desires are pedestrian, the same as everyone's. Your conceit made you think them grand. What psych researchers call 'The Spotlight Effect'."

"I -"

"Your greatest secret is your belief you are unworthy of your wife. She's a minister, correct?"

"Cor - "

"And you feel like a bumbling child beside her."

"I - "

"But that's not what you really want to know if I know. Your true greatest secret comes from that, is shared by that. What cripples you at night when you're alone - and you're always alone, even though you constantly surround yourself by others - is your feeling of inadequacy, your overwhelming sense of being an imposter, of constantly fearing somebody will rise and destroy the little empire you've created. That's what you haven't shared with anybody."

He sits, watches, his nostrils flared, the squirrel wants to run, can't hide from the predator's advance.

People move around us in the hotel lobby. Some wave, some call out hi's and hello's.

"Let me take that fear away from you in a way you will not like." Grandpa's lessons surround me, instruct me. "But first, do you want me to?"

Joe swallows. "Yes."

"You're sure? Your face goes from flushed to ashen practically in time to your heartbeats. Are you sure you're comfortable with this? You want me to continue?"

"Yes."

"One more time so we're both sure. You want me to say what I'm going to say next?"

His face changes, hardens. The squirrel's features cover with rock. He believes he is strong, believes he knows the game, believes he's better at whatever it is he thinks we play. "Sure. Go ahead. Give me your best shot."

"As you wish." I sigh, sorry because he doesn't know what he's about to hear, believes the statement will be about him and it isn't.

It's about those around him, those he thinks he knows.

"Your associates already despise you for your cowardice, your un-willingness to lead, your perpetual vacillations. They do not view you the captain of the ship, only a tattered sail striven by a weak wind, the fabled wannabe revolutionary who sees a crowd running down a street and proudly proclaims 'There go my people. I must follow them so I can lead them.'"

The rock shatters, crumbles, the squirrel's face bleeds. "I - "

"Sorry, Joe. You thought I was going to say something about you. Again, as you wish, but only because you needed the other before you could recognize this: you're convinced everybody lies to you. You're convinced you can't trust anybody. Do you know why?"

His eyes remain wide. He shakes his head, his eyes not leaving mine, the squirrel feeling the hawk's talons close on it, not releasing it.

"Because you can't tell the truth. Because you're a thief, therefore everyone must steal."

"I - "

Chapter 136

Stop the Ocean

I sit with Robyn in our living room. The late afternoon sun streams in through the windows.

"Turn on the TV, Babe?"

She glances at the wall clock. "Is there something on worth watching this time of day?"

A newscast, emergency. A tidal wave in the Pacific, a thousand miles out at sea and rushing towards land.

"Stop the Ocean."

The voice shakes me off my feet and I collapse on to our couch.

"What?"

"Stop the Ocean."

I look around me wondering which spirit is telling me this. None, only the voice, stronger than before.

"Stop the Ocean."

I am not ready for this. I am alone in this.

"Stop the Ocean."

I have no choice. I always have choice.

But so strong, so compelling. The choice is not about my ability to stop the ocean, it is about trust.

"Stop the Ocean."

This is what Chan taught me. Long ago.

"Stop the Ocean."

Lower-Center-Relax-Breathe.

My body spreads out over the waters, rests on some imaginary longitude the tidal wave has yet to cross, goes deep, deep, deep into the sea, my feet feel the bottom, the ocean floor, I expand, contract, become water, become ocean, my breath leaves me as it bubbles to the surface.

The tidal wave washes over me, leaves me as yet another wave in the sea, my body thanks it for its energy, for sharing, and I give it into the earth, into the deep, where it will power our planet's furnace.

Robyn reaches out to me. "You okay?"

Another news flash. The tidal wave is gone. No one understands why. Oceanographers and related scientists are mystified. How can this be?

I nod, my attention returning to our living room, my body returning from the sea. "Yes. Why?"

"You gasped. Like you were underwater or something."

"I was."

Chapter 137

SuperPowers

He says he comes to me to learn. I shake my head. "Why are you here?"

He hesitates. "I want superpowers."

I remember watching *Tutor Turtle* with Grandpa.

But this man isn't Tutor Turtle. He is frightened, fears he is alone, or will be. He's never made a meaningful decision, instead letting friends, lovers, bosses, parents make decisions for him.

I look around him, discern his spirits: a child screaming for attention and afraid of being hit, a frog hiding under a leaf, a butterfly refusing to leave its cocoon, a dragon giving away its horde so it will be loved.

I shake my head, have him sit. "Does anyone you know have superpowers?"

He sits tall, wants to be strong. "I want superpowers."

Tutor Turtle made manifest. "What do you gain if you have superpowers?"

"I want superpowers."

Am I Mr. Wizard? "What do you lose if you have superpowers?"

"I want superpowers."

"What do you gain if you don't have superpowers?"

"I want superpowers."

"What do you lose if you don't have superpowers?"

"I want superpowers."

"Will you be a better you if you have superpowers?"

"I want superpowers."

"Will you help people if you have superpowers?"

"I want superpowers."

"Will you be a better person if you have superpowers?"

"I want superpowers."

"What will happen to you if you have superpowers?"

"I want superpowers."

"How will you use superpowers?"

"I want superpowers."

"Maybe later. Not now."

Bear and Snake come to me. "Teach him."

"Teach him what? He's a coward who won't take responsibility for what he learns."

Dragon and Whale come to me. "Teach him."

"He is a waste of my time."

Crane and Swallow come to me. "Teach him."

"I can't stand the son-of-a-bitch!"

Mountain Lion and Badger come to me. "Yes. What else can he teach you?"

~

"You wanted superpowers."

"I didn't know I'd have to use them."

"You wanted superpowers."

"You should have told me."

"You wanted superpowers."

"You shouldn't have believed me."

"You wanted superpowers."

"What gives you the right to give people superpowers?"

"You wanted superpowers."

"I didn't know you'd take me seriously."

"You wanted superpowers."

"Take them back. I don't want them anymore."

"You wanted superpowers."

"I don't want the responsibility of them."

"You wanted superpowers."

"Go away. Leave me alone."

"You wanted superpowers."

One by one his spirits leave him, slowly, over time, replaced by others. The screaming child becomes a young man who speaks when necessary and knows how to take a punch and still stand, the frog becomes the great frog Tiddalek whose laughter gave water to the world, the butterfly breaks open its cocoon and its wings are dotted with stars, the dragon shares his horde when there is a need and is otherwise content to let it grow.

"I didn't know superpowers could be like this."

"What do you know now?"

"I know I must use them. To help others. When there is a need."

He goes in peace. With no more superpowers than when he came.

But now he doesn't fear.

An amazing superpower, that, when one has been a slave to fear all their life.

My spirits, those in all my directions, those on my Shield, those I've known since childhood and meet on my way, circle me. "What did he teach you?"

"He wanted superpowers to stop being hurt by others. He thought having superpowers would stop people abandoning him. He didn't understand. He didn't realize the way to stop people abandoning him is to be someone no one wants to abandon."

"That's what he learned. What did you learn?"

"Patience."

Chapter 138

Arminius

I come downstairs in the morning, turn into our living room, and see a tall, lithe, middle-aged man sitting in the blue lounger as if he owns it. He reaches out to pet a tigress lying at his feet, crossed at the ankles, his shoes blending into his stockings and creating a deliberate visual break before hiding under tailored, blue pinstripe slacks. The tigress grooms two male cubs playing with her whiskers.

"You look like a fashion artist's drawing of male chic."

The tigress growls. The man rubs its head. One of the cubs swats at the man's hand and snags the ballooning sleeves of his gray shirt. He frees the cub's paws, nods at me, and looks away.

I get coffee in the kitchen. Robyn asks if I want breakfast. "No time. Arminius will be here soon."

The doorbell rings. Arminius stands there without the tigress or her cubs. He takes my hand and probes, but Utsi and Tae-Sek's lessons serve me and there is no entry.

"Still wary of me, Gio?"

I chuckle. "I trust you."

His head falls back and he laughs too loudly. "Yes, from when we studied with Winnake."

"Yes. There is no distrust, only trust in the negative."

His laugh quiets. "After all these years?"

"Have you changed?"

He shakes his head and his laugh turns melancholy, turns inward. "No, probably not."

I bid him enter. The Arminius on the blue lounger looks up. The two merge as this Arminius sits down. "I am dying."

"Yes, you are."

"I've come to you for help."

"Sorry to disappoint."

"Because I was your nemesis?"

"Only according to yourself. No one else thought so, no one else said so."

"I got in your way, made it difficult for you."

"You are a good teacher."

"I sought to be better than you when we studied side-by-side."

"I seek to be better than I was yesterday."

"I've used what I learned to become rich."

"You've used what you've learned to die."

"You love the woman? Help me or I will take her from you."

"Have you forgotten so much?"

He looks up at the sound of Owl's call, Robyn's Guardian. Talons reach down through the ceiling, grab the tigress and her cubs, lift away. "Enough."

"I did not make it so."

He collapses into the lounger. "Enough, enough. I have made too many enemies to make another now."

"I was never your enemy."

"Were you ever my friend?"

"I was never your enemy."

He lets it go. "I worry about my wife and sons."

"The tigress and her cubs."

"Yes. I don't want my mistakes to fall on them."

"You come to me because...?"

"Because you are the greatest of us in this generation."

"That I doubt."

"Don't. You are known wider than your Grandfather ever was."

"What do you want me to do?"

"Protect them."

"From your mistakes?"

"They are innocent."

"Did they know? Did they understand? Robyn studies, grows, learns. She chose. Your wife and sons do not?"

He shakes his head. "When I realized what I'd done, I protected them from *The Knowledge*."

"Dangerous, that."

"Will you help me?"

"I'll help them."

He stands, offers me his hand. The tigress and cubs rise, circle him, moan. His heart speaks to me. "Will you help me now?"

I surround him with swirling winds. His body granulates, goes to dust, is caught in the winds, settles in the fireplace. It blazes, then settles, and he is gone.

I stir the ashes. "Good bye, my friend."

Chapter 139

Fire

Honoré stands before me wearing heavy, fire-resistant gear. A hose runs close under his right arm from a pack on his back to a mask covering his face from forehead to neck, some clear plastic showing his sagging, sweat-covered features clearly. A helmet more fitting to combat than his teaching position secures the mask in place. The air around him is hot, dry, and crackles pop loud and grow silent around him. He ducks as something explodes in front of him but behind me, flying over my head towards him. He carries an axe in two hands, a short-handled shovel rides over his left shoulder on a strap.

He realizes I stand before him, lowers the butt-end of his axe to the ground and leans on the head. His eyes light and he smiles weakly.

"What's going on?"

"We're building breaks but the fire keeps getting around them." He waves with his free hand. "My team's back there. We're sitting in a ring of fire. I can't find a way out."

I shake my head. "You're afraid to find a way out."

"Help me."

"Of course. Lower-Center-Relax-Breathe."

I hear the fire growing closer. Honoré removes his helmet and mask. His face tightens. "That's not what I meant."

"I won't do it for you. You can do this. This is what you practiced for."

He lifts his axe and throws it down. "Not now, dammit."

I nod. "It would be much easier if we only had to act when we wanted to, not when we need to."

A column of fire comes over the hill behind him, driven by the wind, instantaneously charcoaling trees in its breath.

He falls to his knees. "I can't do this."

"I didn't teach you to fail."

"Tell me what to do."

"No, you tell me what to do. Go back to my house, to my living room, to my blue lounger. What's the first thing you learned?"

He Lowers-Centers-Relaxes-Breathes.

"Good. Now what?"

"I have to control it."

"Do you like being controlled?"

He stands, turns his back to me, spreads his arms. "Fire! I need your help!"

The column behind him stops moving with the wind. In its center, a being forms, thin, wispy, moving with the flames. The creature's head causes flashovers in the tree canopy. Its winds suck up forest floor leaves and twigs, nettles and fleeing insects.

"What kind of help do you need? What did I learn from Tick?"

"Brother Fire. Safe passage for me and mine."

Arms of flying ash lift from the creature's sides, convection columns become its legs. Hands reach to the sides of the flames. A hollow forms under a canopy of fire. Its legs spread, bracing the canopy's sides.

A wind of abominable heat brings words to us. "Gather your brothers and sisters, lead them through me here. Then leave this place."

Honoré reclines in my blue lounger. "I never want to go through that again."

"You won't have to. You've learned what to do now. The next time will be different."

"There'll be a next time?"

"There'll be a next time."

"Do you know when?"

"The Universe does everything with a purpose. It made me more and more comfortable with Ocean, working with me from being a drowning toddler to sharing in its power. And when I was asked to work with a tidal wave, I did. All my thoughts, my fears, my anxiety, my hesitation? Meaningless. Either you trust or you don't, and once you decide to trust? - and make no mistake, trusting is a decision - Then no thinking, no fear, no wondering if I could, no hesitation, only doing. The Universe is preparing you for doing."

Honoré tilts his head back and whispers. "Doing."

"But only once you decide to trust."

Chapter 140

The Hona

Our dog shakes when guns fire, when fireworks boom, when thunder rumbles. Trains and planes don't bother him. Trucks making deliveries only elicit barks. Robyn and I joke we don't appreciate him. In any given day he protects us from UPS, the mail being delivered, kids playing in the street.

But loud, explosive, sudden noises and he trembles and wants our protection.

Robyn asks if there's something I can do.

"What do you suggest?"

"Can you make them stop?"

For a moment, I forget. To comfort my dog and allay Robyn's frustration, and because sometimes I tire, I forget.

We walk the dog as dusk creeps over the land and I stop, turn my head, close my eyes, listen.

The dog stops by my side, wags his tail, he knows what I do.

Robyn looks around. "What is it?"

"I'm stopping someone from using fireworks."

I am violating the principles Buppa taught me.

I am denying what all my teachers showed me.

I am allowing part of myself to die because I'm tired and sometimes doing a right thing for one's self requires doing more work than doing a wrong thing to someone else, sometimes doing a short-term wrong thing is more expedient than doing a long-term right thing.

There are no sudden explosions in the night, no booms to bother our child. We sleep and I am haunted by dreams.

(one line space)

We wake and I take our dog for his morning walk. Outside, on our front lawn, the dog sniffs the grass as if something has marked it and it's no longer his.

There is a strange smell.

I remember it from my dreams.

There is a rabbit haunch left near our door, beside it a clean gut pile, around both, strange footprints. Something large walking on two legs but not human, not a man. The gut pile is shaped as if from a hunter. The heart, liver, and kidneys are missing. But the stomach remains.

Nothing in The Wild did this.

Robyn comes when I call. The rabbit haunch attempts to rise, fails, falls down again, lays still.

She doesn't notice.

Rabbit and Owl, her Spirit Guides and the latter her Guardian, all her heroes. Our lawn has many rabbits. They proliferate in our neighborhood and because we use nothing artificial, wildlife prefer our lawns over others.

Rabbits abound. They are attracted to her and she attracts them, learns to talk to them. They like her, trust her, and respond.

A tear leaves her eye, finds a path down her cheek. She wipes it away. "What does it mean?"

Do I tell her?

I forgot once. Do I compound my error and forget again?

No, this is for her.

"It is an offering. It is yours."

Her eyes go wide. She steps back. I feel her denial form another tear, also wiped away.

She knows. I understand. My forgetting is for her and a lesson to us both because The Universe is not wasteful. "What do you mean?"

"There must be balance, always. I caused someone to not follow their path without asking if they wished to alter their path."

She shakes her head.

"I caused someone to deny who they are. I gave them a new life, that required a life."

She frowns at me, shakes her head. "So you killed a rabbit?

"My act allowed another to kill a rabbit."

"Who?"

The Hona appears behind her. Owl is her Guide, her Protector, her Keeper. The Hona is the oldest of them, the One, the First. It appears to me as something caught between Owl and Man, both into one, and can behave as both and as neither as need allows.

"The Hona, the Hunter in the Night. The act was mine, the price was yours."

Robyn flushes, ashamed but not yet relenting. "What price did you pay?"

"Seeing you today as I explained this to you."

She stares at me but can't meet my gaze and lowers her eyes. "I'll clean it up."

I continue walking our dog.

Chapter 141

Unlocking

A great beating of wings draws me to a front window. A black-winged tufted titmouse struggles landing on a wire in no wind. It bites the wire and I fear it will electrocute itself.

Our doorbell rings. A small, dark, tightly-muscled man in light summer clothing stands there, his body so tense he shakes as if restraining himself from releasing the fury of some personal god.

I open the door. "Welcome, friend."

His eyes take in everything in a heartbeat before he utters a word.

"You have no enemies here, friend."

He nods without smiling and comes in. I offer him the blue lounger. He shakes his head, no, not uttering a word although the tension in his body makes it sing like a bow traversing a violin string.

"Would you prefer the couch?"

He shakes his head, no.

"Do you prefer to stand?"

His eyes fall onto a straight back chair in a corner where we keep the stringed and woodwind instruments and nod towards it.

"Be my guest."

He sits and says not a word.

Within minutes he sleeps.

Robyn returns from shopping, sees him sleeping in the chair. "We have a guest."

"Yes."

"Someone else falls prey to the power of Home."

"Evidently."

"Any idea who he is?"

"He didn't say a word. Home must have called him. Seems obvious he needed a place to rest."

～

His eyes open and take everything in. Robyn comes downstairs in sweats, fresh from a shower, drying her hair with a towel. "Hello. Are you hungry? Would you like something to eat?"

"What have you done to me?"

"We've welcomed you into our home and let you rest. Is that what you mean?"

"What day is it?"

"The twenty-third. You slept twenty-three hours."

His body, so restful in sleep, vibrates again, a too-taught string. His muscles cord in his arms, on his chest, ready to explode. "I have to go."

～

The black-winged titmouse stands on this winter's first snow in our front yard, pecking at the crusting snow as if picking at a scab. "Our friend is back."

I feel his vibration before he knocks on the door, as he comes onto our grounds, as he climbs our steps, and open the door. "Hello again."

He stares at me. His nostrils flare, his hands clench.

I remember Grandmother Parvati's PeaceShield, close my eyes, allow the Peace resting within me to envelop me, flow from me, to ask to be welcomed in him.

He falls forward into my arms, asleep.

Robyn points to our couch and I lay him there. She covers him with a blanket emblazoned by her Guardian. "How can someone survive all tensed up like that?"

"Look within. People see what is obvious to them. I doubt others see him as we do. We see what is obvious to us. The trick is to be willing to accept the not-obvious."

~

He wakes, sees me sitting on the floor across the room from him, stoking the fireplace. His body tenses. "Where am I?"

"Safe."

He sniffs the air.

Robyn calls from the kitchen. "Breakfast is ready."

He stares at me. "Pancakes and sausages?"

I nod, stand, motion him forward.

"I...I can't."

"It snowed last night. Did you know that?"

"What?"

"A cooling, calming, silent snow, whispering down from the skies. WinterMan walking on slippered feet, following the herds south."

He looks out the window, stares at the snow. Tears fill his eyes.

"You are surrounded by vibrations. Patterns of force. Not of your own making. Did you know that?"

He walks to the door, his eyes on mine, darting back and forth when Robyn gathers plates in the kitchen.

She opens a drawer, rustles through the silverware.

He opens the door and is gone.

~

Robyn scatters seeds for this year's hatchlings. Soon raccoons will come seeking fat-rich peanuts to fill their breasts to nurse their young.

FlowerSong walks to the edge of the wood. The wind carries the scent of her greeting.

A black-winged titmouse flutters, lands, rests on FlowerSong's neck, pecks at a petal. A car door slams. I walk around our home, towards the street.

He stands there. "There is someone back here who wants to meet you. I'll go inside, leave the two of you to talk with each other. Okay?"

I go in through our back porch. He walks around our home, stands beside FlowerSong, his body supple, fluid, dynamic.

Robyn puts down her violin. "I've never seen him so relaxed."

I watch. He kneels before FlowerSong, lifts one of her flowers, inhales. FlowerSong's whiskers shower pollen, crowning his head.

"What's he doing?"

"Breathing."

He stays until dusk. FlowerSong flows back into the wood. He drops, saddens, cries.

I come to the porch, clear my throat. "May I help?"

"Please."

~

I lead him by the hand into the deep wood.

"Where are we going?"

"To rest."

I guide him to a glen hidden to all but knowing eyes. Clouds blanket our movements. "Is it dangerous here?"

"Do you feel in danger?"

We stand in a center cleared by the sun. Bright light shows through a blue sky over us. Clouds thicken around us. Branches poke through and wave in a light wind. The scent of rain.

Warm spring rain in cool air. A drop falls on the back of his hand. He looks at it, looks up, no clouds overhead. Another drop, his other hand.

"Have you ever seen a flower unfold, drink in the rain?"

He shakes his head.

"The other day, in our backyard, what were you doing?"

"I'm a gardener. I'd never seen a vine like that. What was it?"

"A gardener who's never seen a flower unfold in the rain?"

"I want to garden. I'm learning to garden."

"Because The Wild never talks back, never accuses, never tells you you're wrong, never tells you you're a mistake, never - "

A drop like a river trickles down a branch hovering over his head. He tilts his face up, closes his eyes, smiles, inhales. "That smell. It's the same as that vine in your backyard. Please tell me, what kind of vine is it?"

"A freeing one."

FlowerSong comes up through the soil, its vines entwine him, support him, its petals surround him like arms, he rests his head back into FlowerSong's green shoulder, turns to face his lover's embrace.

FlowerSong's voice comes in the splashes of rain. "Give to me. Grow from me."

A womb forms between FlowerSong's petals. The man climbs in. A babe is born.

I hear yelling. Like my parents but not their voice.

A child. A beating.

A boy. Punished for a mistake.

An adolescent. Mocked in front of family and friends.

A teen. Humiliated by his parents for becoming a man.

A man. Cast out, abandoned, because he feels what his parents cannot.

At each point, his body opens, unfolds, the tension binding him released into FlowerSong's network of vines, runners, shoots, going into the earth, into the waters in the soil, flowing to the streams, to the rivers, to the oceans, gathered by the sun, lifted to the stars.

Rain falls on him, steams, each wisp of steam an unfolding of the babe, the child, the boy, the adolescent, the teen, the man within, his body snapping and cracking like a tree's bark exploding with growth.

His body melts into FlowerSong. They join, merge.

"I know this vine."

"Yes, you do."

His arms become shoots, his hands leaves, his feet disappear and his legs drive into the earth.

The wind mingles their pollen, the rain splashes onto the earth, a seed forms, drops between them, they wither, die, the seed germinates.

He unfolds, a budding plant in the rain, bursting from the seed, from the soil, growing tall in the column of the sun.

FlowerSong separates, kisses him with pollen-laced dew, flows into the forest.

I offer him my hand. He smiles, takes it. There is a green warmth in him, something he hadn't allowed to enter before.

"I know why flowers unfold in the rain now."

I nod. The clouds disperse. The trees surrounding the glen shake off the last of the warm Spring rain.

"Do you - "

He shakes his head. "I know my way."

I nod, shake his hand.

"Thank you."

"Thank you."

Chapter 142

Daniel

Daniel sits across from me. It is his day, his weekend. He travels far so we can work together. Not far enough but he doesn't know that yet.

I look up and to the right, away from him. My eyes focus and I smile. "Oh, Robyn's talking with one of our neighbors. Our dogs are playing in the park."

Daniel watches me. His eyes flick to where I'm looking. There's nothing there. "What are you looking at?"

I point where I'm looking. "Robyn and Debbie, Connor and Boxer. They're in the park. Connor and Boxer are playing. Robyn and Debbie are sitting at the picnic table under the roof shelter."

I teach Daniel the Solitaire Meditation, a lesson shared by several teachers. Ask the cards which ones want to be played when. I win twelve games in a row with no hesitation in my moves.

Daniel shakes his head.

Robyn is out longer than she planned. I shuffle the cards slowly, close my eyes. "What's the First Lesson?"

"The first thing I remember -"

"That's not what I asked. What did I ask?"

"About the first lesson?'

"Are you asking me or telling me?"

"You asked about the first lesson."

"Close and not correct. I asked, 'What's the First Lesson?'"

"Okay, what's the first lesson?"

"You tell me."

"I don't remember."

"Good answer, and correct. You don't."

I Lower-Center-Relax-Breathe and see to the west. "Oh. Robyn's at the grain store. Evidently we need seed."

Daniel's brow furrows.

I Lower-Center-Relax-Breathe, deal the cards, win more games.

"Are you watching me?"

"Yes. Of course I am."

"What am I doing?"

"You're winning at cards."

I shake my head. "That happens second. What happens first?"

"You shuffle them?"

I give him the cards. He doesn't ask, he doesn't listen. His mental-body overrules the others, forces them to obey. He loses game after game.

I take the cards back and win and win and win.

"It's not about winning, it's about knowing what the cards are before you touch them, as you touch them, before you turn them over. Lower-Center-Relax-Breathe. Start again."

His face tightens. His nostrils flare. He doesn't ask the cards who they are.

I get up.

"Come on. Robyn will be home in a minute. Let's help bring things in."

We stand in the driveway. Robyn pulls in a moment later. I lift two seed sacks, one on each shoulder, and walk out to the shed. Grandpa was correct. Many years working on farms made me tall and strong.

Daniel throws the sack he carries down. "How did you know? How did you know she'd pull in the driveway when she did?"

I stare at it and he picks it back up. "How did you not?"

Chapter 143

Four-Body Work

"Do you really want to get well or do you just want to get better?"

Raye opens her mouth and I hold up a finger. She reaches for a black bag on the floor beside her, a purse matching her skirt and shoes.

"Consider before you answer."

She sags into my blue lounger in my living room. It kicks back into its recliner position and I smile.

She struggles to come forward.

"Press down on the footrest with your feet."

The seat goes back to lounge position. Raye blows some bangs out of her eyes.

"I just want to get better."

"Very good. Now we can begin."

Lower-Center-Relax-Breathe.

It happens automatically now, no effort.

I smile.

This level requires no effort, meaning I am this level all the time now. Or close to.

More levels await.

"Are you starting?"

I smile at Raye. "Yes. Sorry, I was listening."

She scans the room. "To what?"

"Myself."

"How solipsistic of you."

I laugh and she smiles.

"You're not what I expected. I don't know if that's a good thing or a bad thing yet."

I shrug. "It's a thing. We'll find out soon if it's a good thing or a bad thing. For you."

I use my Four-Bodies to gauge, isolate, and align her Four-Bodies. I remember Grandmother Apara's and Ouliadês' words: Work with your Centered-Self. Be sure it's in the center of your Four-Bodies before you begin. Otherwise you can get lost in their bodies and might not get out.

I asked Ouliadês to describe what he experiences when he does Four-Body Work. He responded demonstrating directionally, showing me where and how each body travels to do what.

"That sounds like linear programming, a branch of mathematics. You're translating from one coordinate system to another."

He laughs and pats my shoulder. "If that helps you do it, do it. If it gets in the way, do something else."

Yes. I remember. Always find the way. Work to learn, to do more. No one knows everything, and we learn all we can so when we go Home we'll have wonderful stories to tell.

My bodies slide into Raye's like a new pair of clothes. I adjust them to me.

She twitches, glances down at her arms, her legs, touches her face, pats her burgundy sleeves against herself, smooths her black skirt, makes sure her pearl necklace is still in place. "What are you doing?"

My head moves diagonally back and forth, a cow lowing in a field. "Triangulating."

"What? Are you - "

"Shh. Not healing. Association, diagnostics, analysis."

She sits back.

I have sensations in my Four-Bodies as they share from hers.

Physical-Body: "There is a pain in your left lung, near the bottom. It only occurs when you breathe deep. Your right leg cramps at the calf when you lie down. Nothing seems to help it. Eventually your foot falls asleep. Your hearing is failing. You've been tasting some kind of metal for the past few days."

Emotional-Body: "You're having an affair with a man you met online. You prefer to spend time with him over your husband because you feel your husband only wants to love the you he wants you to be while this other fellow is willing to love the you you want to be. You haven't told your husband this. Your son just moved up north and you miss him."

Mental-Body: "You're confused about your job situation, whether to go out on your own or to stay where you are or to take an offer at another agency which has just been offered to you."

Spiritual-Body: "You feel drawn to a place in Russia where you had great spiritual awakenings many years ago but are unsure if you could go through similar awakenings now."

I continue cycling through her Four-Bodies, deeper and deeper, each cycle removing another layer of the onion, seeking the one challenge that's demonstrating itself as each body's difficulty.

Nothing more to see, I leave her Four-Bodies as when I started, return my bodies to me, aligning them back to my Center, letting them radiate out to fill their individual and collective spaces.

'How did you do that?"

"You can feel free to disagree with me about anything I said."

She stares at me then looks down at her skirt. She picks a white speck from it, flicks it away, and clears her throat. "I...No. I don't disagree. Ten years in therapy and four doctor visits in the past year...did somebody give you my charts?"

I shake my head, no.

"Well, do you have any suggestions for me?"

"Several."

"What are they?"

"You found some peace during a visit to Russia. In the Caucasus Mountains? You visited a monastery. Remember the very tall, very thin monk? Scraggly goatee beard, glasses?

She clutches her pearls to her throat, her fingers work like a crab closing her collar. "Brother Jorje?"

"Yes."

"How do you know Brother Jorje? How do you know I know Brother Jorje?"

I explain Four-Body Work. "Our bodies remember everything we've ever done, everything that's ever been done to us. Plus you carry his scent. Faint but it's there."

"You're frightening me."

"That's one response. Is it the most useful one?"

"It's the one I'm having."

I laugh. "Good answer. Shall I continue?"

"How do you know Jorje?"

"I studied with *Brother* Jorje," I correct her. He worked long and hard, and it warms me to use his honorific.

She shakes her head. Her hand stays by her throat but relaxes. She protects but doesn't defend. "Is there like a club you all belong to or something? Is that how you know each other?"

"No club that I know of. Besides, I'm not sure I'd want to be a member - "

" - of a club that would have me as a member. Yeah, I know that Groucho routine, too." Her hand drops to the chair's armrest. "I don't get you. You seem normal. You're pretty disarming. I want to be afraid of you but I can't."

"Shall I continue?"

She shrugs. "Yeah, go ahead."

"This is a simple exercise. It's the same as Brother Jorje taught you. It won't take up more than five minutes of your day, but it has to be done first thing in the morning."

I demonstrate an exercise from *geomantiya tela*, body geomancy, basically *fēngshuǐ* for the body. Every culture has an equivalent. She is sensitive to the Russias so I use techniques from there. I would use *Réntǐ fēngshuǐ* if she had sensitivities to southeastern China. When working with anyone, use methods from where they call home. This from Grandpa's friend, John.

"That's it?"

"That's it. Every morning, first thing, before anything else. Move into that position as I showed you and hold it for five minutes."

"What if I have to pee?"

"Before anything else. Get out of bed, do that exercise."

"What'll it do?"

"Wonders."

"Ha ha ha, what'll it do?"

"Nothing unless you do it."

"Not going to tell me?"

⁓

Raye sits in the blue lounger. "I feel so much better! I can breathe, my legs don't bother me. I can hear good..."

"Excellent. Glad things are going as you want them to."

"I don't feel a need to go to Russia anymore."

"Okay."

"And I'm almost ready to confront my husband about my affair."

"These are good things?"

"Yes. What's next?"

"Nothing. Just keep on doing the exercise. Same as before, every day. Keep it up and there'll be more changes."

⁓

Raye sits in the blue lounger. She lifts one of my journals and fans herself. Her breaths come short and quick.

"I went to see my doctor about a month ago, after our last session."

I nod.

"I showed him the exercise you gave me."

I nod.

"He told how it really worked. He said it didn't make any difference when I did it."

I nod.

"And it didn't need to be done the way you showed me." She reaches into her bag and pulls out something with a dial, metal contacts and an electric cord. "He said this would do the same thing. I should use it whenever."

She holds it out to me. I keep my eyes on hers and repeat, "Whenever."

"Whenever."

"And?"

She sits back, adjusts herself, crosses her legs at the ankles, returns the device to her bag and places it beside the lounger.

She doesn't return my stare, looks down and aside. "And what do you think?"

"I don't know. You tell me."

"Yeah, right." She rocks her head and singsongs each phrase like a child taunting another on a playground, still not meeting my gaze. "I KNOW BroTHER JORje. I knOW RUSsia. I KNOW Ge-O-Graph-ee TELLa."

I correct her. "*Geomantiya tela.*"

Her face snaps forward and she jabs a finger in my direction. "See!"

"And?"

She singsongs again. "AND The pains' ReTURNed, MY OTHer leg's BEgun TO STIFfen, AND I Can't Get MYself goING IN THE MORNing."

She pauses to catch her breath.

"And I can't focus on anything for more than ten minutes at a time. I'm lucky I could get myself here."

Lower-Center-Relax-Breathe. My bodies work, adjust, align.

"You've stopped doing the exercise."

"Well, I didn't think I had to. My doctor told me what he was having me do was enough."

"Are you feeling better?"

"No."

"Did you feel better when you did the exercise?"

"Yes."

"Then decide how you want to feel. Until then there's nothing I can do for you."

I stand up.

"Wait a second. Isn't there something you can give me? Something we can do here, now?"

"Decide how you want to feel. Until then it's all up to you."

〜

"I'm doing my exercise again."

"Tell me more."

"The pains are going away. More and more each day."

"Good. If that's what you want, good."

"Tell me what's happening. To me."

"Would it make a difference?"

"I'm curious."

"Brother Jorje's exercise exercises more than your mind, heart, and lungs. It exercises what are called The Four-Bodies. It moves your Centered-Self towards your Center."

"Did you wear lovebeads in the '60's?"

"If you can remember the '60's you weren't really there."

"What's next?"

"Do you remember our first meeting? I asked if you wanted to get better or get well."

"I remember."

"Good. You got better. Keep on doing the exercise and you'll stay better."

She sat still, her hands holding the blue lounger's armrests, and scraped her upper lip over her teeth, nibbling it. "But I won't get well."

"But you won't get well."

"I'm doing my exercise every day. Nothing gets in the way. Not weather, family, work, nothing. I feel great."

"*Your* exercise."

"Huh?"

"You never claimed ownership before. Good.

"Yeah, well. I've been feeling there's something more."

"There is."

"What is it? I'm asking. Aren't I supposed to ask? Okay, I'm asking. What is it?"

"There's something you have to decide."

"You mean about how much better I want to get? I've decided I want to get well, O' Great Swami. Not just better, but well."

"You're sure that's your decision?

"Of course I'm sure. Didn't I just say I'm sure. Goddamn, are you ever satisfied? Do you always play these mind games?"

"Who are you upset with, Raye?"

She threw her hands up. "Myself, goddamnit."

"Good. You couldn't admit that when we started. You couldn't admit that a month ago."

She cries. Her sobs are the echoes of all the denials she directed at herself, all the time she'd spent ignoring herself and her own needs.

"Good work, Raye. Good work."

Her sobs grow less. She dries her eyes, wipes her face. She falls silent. Her color changes, her face warms, her bodies lock into their Centered place.

Chapter 144

Psychopomp

Tom stands at the border between the worlds. His physical body loses strength moment by moment, multiple cancers helping him over a bridge he is unwilling to cross. Across the border are friends, people who've passed before him, a stillborn sister now a grown woman in a body only eternity could give her.

And a man in black, taller than Tom and thin with a featureless face and a head shaped like an anvil stands between Tom and the border.

Each time he wishes to cross, each time his body should breathe its last, the anvil-headed man turns him back.

"Take my hand, Tom. I can help you across."

He hesitates and Anvil Man steps between us. He drives his head into the earth between the worlds and Tom falls as if caught in an earthquake.

I lift Tom to his feet. Anvil Man pays no attention to me, always moving with Tom, only interfering when Tom approaches the border, prepares to cross.

"He won't let me."

"Who is he?"

Tom rushes the border. Anvil Man bars his path. Tom falls. Anvil Man stands over him, his movements harsh, severe, strict. He wags his finger in hard, exact movements. I hear a voice like iron. "No. You don't belong here."

"Tom, where is this place? Where are we?"

"Purgatory? Hell? I don't know. But over there is Heaven."

"How come this man is stopping you from going to heaven?"

Tom doesn't answer.

I stand before Anvil Man. "How come you won't let Tom cross over?"

Anvil Man says nothing. He points at Tom, points into the distance, slams his anvil head into the earth, points at Tom, points into the distance, slams his anvil head into the earth.

"I can't see what you're pointing at. Will you help me?"

Anvil man spreads his arms. A river flows from him back into the past, lifts up Tom, he struggles, can't swim, can't break the current, can't stand against the tide.

I jump into the water. It is not deep. It is filled with rocks. The rocks cause swift currents, whirlpools, eddies, foaming water.

But no calms.

The water opens around me. I walk on the riverbed. Beside me Tom fights and almost drowns, fights and almost drowns.

I reach for him, help him stand beside me.

The river freezes, becomes a glacier, locks him in place, forbids him to move.

I reach down, lift up a stone. It becomes a snow globe. Inside Tom flies a helicopter gunship, calls out orders, machine guns fire, rockets flare.

"You were in a war, Tom?"

"I was a Colonel in The 'Nam, flew gunships."

"Tell me more."

He can't speak. Anvil Man crashes his head into the ground creating rivers upon rivers upon rivers.

I look into the globe. Villages destroyed. Running children.

"Tom?"

"I followed orders."

I lift another stone. It becomes a snow globe. Tom is in a hotel room, not with his wife.

Anvil Man's head crashes again, rocks shatter, stone splinters go flying.

"Tom?"

He looks away.

Another stone. Same hotel room. With a man.

Anvil Man strikes the earth.

Tom knocks the stone from my hand. "Don't judge me."

"I'm not. But you are."

Anvil Man grows smaller.

"Do you believe in sin, Tom?"

"Don't you? Isn't that what the Bible tells us? Everything I did was a sin. I can't escape that."

"So you'll stay barely alive because you need the cancers to punish you for your sins?"

He points to Anvil Man. "That's what he wants."

"No, that's what you want."

Anvil Man grows smaller still. His anvil edges smooth slightly.

"You believe you need to be punished. Anvil Man is you."

Anvil Man's iron head turns to flesh, his face forms. It is Tom's.

"I need God to forgive me."

"Forgive yourself, Tom. Forgive yourself and your god will forgive you."

"How?"

"Embrace your sins. Embrace your past. Until you do, you won't fully die, only part of you. Part of you will always remain. It'll become a ghost. You'll always be tied to the earth, to those places you couldn't forgive yourself. Nobody else can do it for you. I can't. Only you."

"How?"

Anvil Man holds his arms out.

"Embrace your past. Realize the only one here wanting to punish you is you."

Tom weeps. His tears warm the river, break the ice, free him.

The water stills with his sobs.

Anvil Man takes his hand. They merge. Their bodies become one. Small bubbling worlds form around him, laughing, nuzzling him like sheep.

"What are they?"

"They are your cancers. Now that you're ready, they'll help you cross."

Tom smiles. His body relaxes, breathes it last.

He disappears into the mist.

Chapter 145

Jack and Diane

A red Toyota Celica pulls into our driveway.

I gaze out our kitchen window, wave. "Jack and Diane - "

Robyn chuckles, cuts me off. "Here's a little ditty..."

I laugh. She knows I'm a John Mellencamp fan.

They sit in our living room. Jack clears his throat. "We took a class a year ago." He takes Diane's hand in his. "Diane wasn't able to get to the Lower World. We've heard about you, but we don't want a repeat of what happened then."

"What happened then?"

Diane pushes herself back into the sofa, away from me. "I went to the Upper World instead."

"Good for you."

Jack and Diane stare at me. Jack shakes his head, Diane remains withdrawn in the cushions of the couch. "That's it? 'Good for you.'?"

"Yes. You went to a place you recognize as the upper world. Congratulations. Good for you."

Jack sits back on the couch. "I don't get it. The other - "

"The other what?"

Diane's eyes water. Her words come timorously on little mouse feet. "The other teacher yelled at me when I talked about it. She told me I didn't know what I was doing and that I wasn't helping the class get along or move on at all."

Jack leans forward and slightly in front of Diane, protecting, preparing. "What would you have done if Diane couldn't get to the Lower World?"

"I don't know, really. I probably would have asked if she wanted to tell the rest of us about it. What is your concept of lower world and upper world?"

Jack repeats as if by rote. "Shaman learn to journey to the lower and Upper World. The Lower World is…" He notices my frown and stops. "Is that incorrect?"

"I wouldn't know. I'm not a shaman."

His brow lifts and he sits back. "But people say - "

"I have no control over what people say."

We all quiet. Robyn shrugs. "Seems to me you really needed to go to the upper world."

Diane smiles weakly.

Robyn turns to me. "Wouldn't you have known if she did go somewhere she wasn't supposed to?"

"I don't stop people from going wherever they have to go on their journey to do what they need to do. Would I have known where she was going? Yes. Would it have made a difference to me? No." I take Diane's hand. "It was your journey, not mine. So long as you were happy and comfortable, go for it. Were you happy and comfortable going wherever you did?"

Diane nods vigorously. "The teacher yelling at me in front of the class and screaming I wasn't doing it right terrified me, though."

"I'm sorry you had the experience you did with that teacher, glad you visited a place you enjoyed."

Jack shook his head and took Diane's hand from me. "That's it? That's all you would have said?"

"What more would you have liked me to say?"

Diane's face takes on a beaten look. "So you can help us?"

"I'm still unsure what kind of help you'd like."

They look into each other's eyes. "We'd like to learn how to journey."

"To learn how to journey as I understand the term can take a lifetime. Regardless, it's an ongoing study."

They collapse into each other, into the couch. Diane's eyes water again. Jack takes her hand. "But the other teacher said you could learn to do it in a weekend, an afternoon, even."

"They must be amazing teachers. I'll have to study with them."

Robyn snickers. "Or they have amazing students."

I purse my lips at her. "Or perhaps we mean different things when we say *journey*. But that's not what you really want."

They hold each other's hands. Jack blinks. "It's not?"

"I think you want a healing but nothing you've done yet has helped."

Diane frowns at me. "How do you know that?"

"Healing is different. Do you want to heal because of the lump in Diane's breast?"

Jack glares at me. "How do you know about her breasts?"

What do I say? "If I am Diane, the lump is here." My fingers press my shirt.

Diane lifts her blouse slightly. "I felt you touch me. How did you do that?"

Robyn diverts their attention. "You should see what he can do with a deck of cards."

They "Huh?" simultaneously.

"You don't need me to take care of the lump, you can do it on your own, Jack."

Jack leans forward. "How?"

"Let Diane know you'll love her if she loses her breast."

Diane cries openly. "I'm going to get a mastectomy."

"I didn't say you were."

Jack looks down at Diane's chest. "What are you talking about?"

Delicacy has no place here. "You delight in Diane's body. It brings you great joy. Pleasure."

Diane blushes deeply. Jack's nostrils flare. His eyes narrow.

"She knows this. I'm not sure if you two have ever openly talked about this, and she knows this."

His eyes fleck to her profile and back.

"Ah, you've never talked openly about it. No worries, except she fears you'll leave her as she grows older, as her physical body changes. Her mental body tells it not to worry, no, you won't."

Jack shakes his head. "Physical body? Mental body?"

"These two bodies decide to test it by placing a distraction where both mental and physical body know it will be found."

Jack rears up. "A distraction?"

"Let Diane know you'll love her and be with her if she loses her breast."

"She's going to lose a breast?"

Diane winces, clutches her chest.

Jack steps forward. "What are you doing to her?"

"Nothing. What are *you* doing to her?"

He takes her arm. "Come on, we're getting out of here. This guy's a fake just like all the rest were."

Diane pulls her arm free.

A mist forms. She is replaced by a cocoon, the butterfly within ready to break free. He is replaced by a wasp, its ovipositor, once able to penetrate the cocoon's once pliable but now quite solid silk, bends and snaps in two.

The mist clears.

Jack takes her arm more forcefully. "You're not listening to this, are you?"

"How come you can't say something so simple as you'll stay with me no matter what happens?"

"Diane!"

She sits. Tension leaves her. She relaxes into the couch cushions.

Jack throws his hands up. "Argh!"

Diane closes her eyes.

Jack walks to the door. "I'm not paying for this." He leaves.

A butterfly, fresh from the cocoon, spreads its wings in the sunlight streaming in through our front windows, and dries them on our couch.

Diane opens her eyes as Jack races the Celica's engine and exits our driveway, races down the street. She stands, goes to window, watches him go away from our home, from her life. She snorts, shrugs, returns to the couch, looks at her fading cocoon, back at us, and leans back into the cushions. "Well."

Robyn reaches for her hand. "How you doing with all this?"

"I'd rather not have a mastectomy - "

"You won't need one."

"What?"

"You have beautiful breasts and always will. For quite some time, anyway."

Diane looks at Robyn. "I...ahh..."

Robyn laughs. "Don't worry about it."

"How do you know?"

Robyn shakes her head. "He can tell you your mother's maiden shoe size, too, if you'd like."

"What?"

I stand up. "The lump was benign. A cyst, maybe? It'll be gone in a week now that you're no longer concerned about losing Jack."

Diane stands as well. "Guess I always knew." She looks around.

Robyn heads for the stairs. "Shall I make up the guest room?"

"Can I use your phone, call my folks? Tell them I'm moving back home for a while?"

～

Diane knocks on our door. Robyn greets her, welcomes her in. "What can we do for you?"

"I want to learn journeying. Your kind of journeying. A journeying that works, that gets things done."

I motion her to the same couch she sat on before. "I have a better idea. Ever wanted to visit the high plains of the southwest? I know a woman there who'll be glad to know you. Won't cost you a thing except time and a willingness to learn."

Diane looks at me, tilts her head, wary.

Behind me, Robyn nods her head vigorously.

Diane glances at Robyn. Robyn nods even more vigorously.

"Okay."

Chapter 146

Mimi

Jenny sits on cushions on the floor, sobbing. "This horrible black bird came and killed Mimi. This horrible, horrible bird came and ate Mimi's head off." Others in the workshop sit around her, comforting her.

I sit next to her. She reaches out to me, buries her head in my shoulder, sobs louder.

"Tell me more."

"For the past few months, ever since I heard about this workshop, a seagull named Mimi has come to me and been my teacher when I journey. Mimi's taught me so much."

"It's terrible when we lose a teacher like that."

She nods.

"Did Mimi tell you to come to this class?"

"Oh, yes. He said I would meet my new teacher here. He's been telling me for the past two weeks that it was time for him to go, that there was nothing more he could teach me. But I didn't want him to go. I begged him to stay. He's been such a good guide and teacher to me. He's been such a good friend. I told him I didn't want him to go. Now that horrible crow killed him."

"You had an excruciatingly painful experience, the loss of your teacher, your guide, and friend."

She nods and sobs.

"Now, tell me exactly what happened."

"This horrible bird came -"

"Yes, I know that's what you think happened. Tell me what happened. You know, like on *Dragnet*, 'The facts, ma'am. Just the facts.'"

"Mimi said he needed to take me to a new place to meet my new teacher. We flew like we always do but this time we went to a place I'd never seen before. It was like a sidewalk on a beach. There was a green railing and we stopped on the sidewalk side. On the other side was a steep grade covered with boulders and rocks. It looked dangerous and I was glad for the railing. On the other side of the grade was a beautiful beach. The water, I knew, was warm and inviting, with great big breakers and dolphins playing out in the water."

"That sounds nice."

"Mimi was on the sidewalk looking up at me. 'I have to go,' he said. 'This is as far as I can take you.' I told him not to go, that I didn't want to learn any more if he had to go. He said it wasn't like that. I said I wasn't going to let him go. Then he looked up. I heard something in the air and looked where he was looking. This huge crow came flying from out over the ocean. He flew directly onto the sidewalk and landed right beside Mimi. Mimi just stood there and this crow snapped off his head. Mimi fell, bleeding, and the crow pecked at him for a second. It seemed like he wanted to make sure he was dead."

"Or maybe to let you know Mimi had completed his time with you and, if he stayed, you couldn't move on, learn more, grow, hence it was better than he died to you?"

She looks at me. "How did you know that?"

"Just a guess."

"The crow pecked at Mimi's body and said, 'Mimi's dead. Now I'm your teacher.'"

"What happened then?"

"He taught me how to fly all over again. But this time I was able to fly out over the rocks and ocean. He took me to places I'd never been before." She smiled with the memory. "When you called the return, Mimi told me that I had a new teacher now, and it would be okay to journey with him."

"I thought Mimi was dead?"

"I thought so, too. When the crow brought me back we passed over Mimi, still on the sidewalk but now all right. He shouted up those things to me."

"I know it hurt to lose your old friend. Let me ask you some questions, though. What really happened - and correct me if I'm wrong - was that Mimi as a Seagull had been telling you that his time was over and you wouldn't let go. Is that right?"

She nods.

"And Mimi told you you'd meet a new teacher here."

She held my hand. "Yes."

"Only I'm not your new teacher. Crow is. Is it possible that you wouldn't let go of Mimi so the only way Mimi could go away was to have Crow come and kill him, specifically by devouring his head, by showing his knowledge is greater than Mimi's? Is it possible that those things had to happen so you'd let Mimi go?"

She cries again. "Yes."

"And what you think happened was that this horrible bird came and killed your friend, Mimi."

"Yes."

"And what you're feeling, the emotions and the pain and the loss, that's what's happening to you, isn't it?"

She nods again.

"So you see, there's a big difference between what really happened, what you think happened, and what happened to you, isn't there?"

"Yes."

"Good, good. Don't ignore your feelings, honor your belief in what goes on around you, and always always always remember that in the

Universe, there only *is*. There is never good or bad. This will help you to recognize the differences among what happened, what you think happened, and what happened to you."

Chapter 147

Martin Can't Heal People

An energy, a longing.

The Master Musician, the Tiny Dancer, summons me east, along the coast, to a small town, to a health center.

But I don't feel the surging. I'm not called here to heal.

I walk inside, read the names on the board. A receptionist, a short man, blond hair, Don "Miami Vice" Johnson beard scruffling his chin, cheeks, and below his nose, smiles at me from a desk central to a wall, opposite from where people sit, where children play with stuffed toys and multi-colored building blocks. "Can I help you?"

I watch the children. "Do you disinfect those toys before different children play with them? They often carry disease."

The short, blond man's smile fades. "We take all the necessary precautions. Can I help you?"

Mothers and fathers, guardians and grandparents, look at the toys children play with. Some pull the toys away and offer gum, mints, juiceboxes in their place.

"Just waiting. Is that alright?"

He nods and goes back to his mobile.

I go back to the board. My eyes catch on a name. Martin? Who can't play Bach? He's a doctor now?

There's a "Meet Our People" pamphlet on a coffee table.

Yes, Martin.

Older, of course. Heavier. Balding. Mustached. Glasses riding low on his nose, readers. A tablet in his hand, stethoscope around his neck, looking up into the camera, a smile, a look of interest, a look of paternal, patient concern.

I remember high school, a night listening to music at Hugh Maiger's house. Inside The Moody Blues *Threshold of a Dream* album is a picture of the band standing in what appears to be a park against a foggy background: Justin Hayward, John Lodge, Ray Thomas, Graeme Edge, Mike Pinder. Ray Thomas stands center facing the camera, arms crossed over his chest, left side slightly forward, thick hair and mustache, thin.

Martin points to Thomas. "Doesn't that guy look cool?"

I chuckle. Because that's what you want to look like, Martin?

The memory steps aside, waits.

What is calling me here now?

Martin comes through the clinic doors to the waiting area and checks the tablet he holds. "Mrs. Thompson?"

A woman rises and walks towards the doors he holds open. Waiting, he smiles vacantly at the others who are also waiting. His eyes fall on me.

They stop perusing the waiting others. He smiles and frowns simultaneously, patient, paternal concern colliding with a dimly remembered past, but he says nothing, follows her in, the doors close and he is gone.

The doors close and he is gone.

Memory flows again. Martin's brother flunked out of RPI. Martin tells me his brother doesn't get along with the professors. He continues at a state school and after many years earns a PhD.

Martin applies to Tufts Medical but doesn't have the grades. He attends Albany Medical and applies to Tufts until they take him in, gets his degree, goes into practice.

And all failures, all dismissals, all negations, are someone else's fault.

The memory steps aside a second time.

What am I doing here?

I sniff the air carrying the patients' woes to learn of their diseases. None will be healed, only made comfortable.

I frown.

To those who don't know, isn't that enough?

Martin practices medicine by the book, never varies, always asks others their thoughts, notes who suggests what, then acts.

But only if it's in the book. Only if it's as the majority rules, if it follows the known and safe path, the path laid down by others.

He never explores a path of his own

You cannot learn if all you practice is your excuses.

Martin comes through the doors with the woman, walks to the receptionist's desk with her, smiles, shakes her hand, hands the receptionist a script.

He checks his tablet and eyes come back to me. A smile, a frown. "Mr. Davis?"

An elderly man rises. Martin holds the clinic doors open for him. They walk in.

I stand and watch for a moment, letting the lesson find its place in me.

Martin stuck to a path I could not see and is happy there for reasons I could not divine.

All the jobs I've held, all the masks I've worn, and how many times I've longed for the simple life Martin must have lived, which to him was the most complicated life of all.

Martin's never listened to the wind, talked with the rain, midwifed stars, helped form oceans...and never learned to play Bach.

Martin can't heal people. He may take away their pain, stop their discomfort, and sometimes, yes, stop an illness.

But sometimes isn't that enough?

And we cannot miss what we don't know exists.

Who is to say one man's light is better than another man's darkness?

Martin is one of my greatest teachers.

Chapter 148

The Student

Robyn watches a bright orange Yugo pull into the restaurant parking lot. She waves, turns to me. "That's her, that's Ann."

I wave. A mid-20s woman, all teeth, freckles, and glasses, navy beret, brown hair down to her waist, big jangly earrings, minimal makeup except for eyeliner highlighting her gray eyes, muslin cheesemaker's blouse, rainbow printed peasant dress, jangly bracelets matching her earrings, thick gray wool socks, and Birkenstock sandals gets out of the car, closes the door on her dress, can't open the door, throws her hands up in the air.

Robyn shakes her head.

"Shall we go help her?"

"Can we turn this into a test? If she can figure this out, she can study with us, if not, no?"

Ann tears off a piece of her dress, frees herself from the door.

"Not the solution I hoped for."

Robyn nods. "It was a small piece."

The maître d' escorts her to our booth.

She smiles as she sits opposite us. "I called you last year and asked to study. You told me to come back in a year. Well, I'm back."

"Let's order lunch. Or early dinner. Or whatever suits you. You'll be our guest."

She asks lots of questions. We don't have lots of answers.

"I'm still not clear what made you choose us."

She sits back, spins her teacup on its saucer. Her eyes narrow. "My husband. He...has a challenge."

"Okay."

"We paid two other people lots of money to work with him."

"How did that go?"

"They had lots of money and my husband is still challenged." She spins her cup rapidly, her long-nailed fingers clacking against the porcelain. "Is there something you can do to help him?"

"That's not the question you're really asking."

Her eyes open wide, her hands lie flat on her booth seat, push her back and away from us. "I...No, there's no other question. I just want to know if you can help my husband."

Robyn says nothing, sighs. I shake my head, look down at the food on the table. "That's not the question you're really asking."

I close my eyes, look for her husband, find him.

"Your husband's injury occurred several years ago." Robyn turns her back to me so I can explain.

I point. "He has pains here, here, and here." Robyn turns back to the woman. "One physician you talked with suggested corrective surgeries, another suggested deep massage therapy. The two people you gave money to. One claimed to be a Reiki Master, the other a Native Healer."

Robyn shakes her head. "They asked for money? Before they did anything? Actual money?"

"The original injury was due to a riding accident when he was ten.. eleven...twelve? Yes, that's it, twelve. He fell from a horse onto his right hip. The shock traveled up his spine into his shoulders. Now he has backaches." My eyes are closed and I squint. "Looks like hairline fractures, too, and pinched nerves."

I open my eyes.

Robyn taps the table, her eyes on our guest. "Close your mouth, Ann."

"How do you know that?"

"You came to us with a question you haven't asked yet. I gave you your answer."

Her hands come up on the table. She plays with her napkin.

"Everything you said. It's true. When you started talking, I had a sense of movement through me and around the table, like something came out of you and entered me, then went off to my husband."

"Okay."

"I came here wanting to know if you folks are for real."

"That's the real question you wanted to ask."

"Would you take me on as a student?"

"How about you take some time and decide if you really want to study with us. It's not easy and takes lots of time."

"I understand. I want to study Women's Medicine and Psychopomp." I nod.

"That shouldn't take too long, right? Maybe a few days or a weekend or two at best? And you can heal my husband? We can make that part of the agreement?"

Robyn stares at her.

I shake my head. "I'm still learning both myself. And I've been working on both for years now."

"I'm a good student, though."

I wave for the check. "Sorry, I couldn't give you the necessary time. I don't think I'd be a good teacher for you."

She stands quickly, not quite free of the booth. Her eyes narrow. She sneers. "You two are fakers. You don't really know what you're doing."

"Yes, correct. Exactly so."

"You don't want me to expose you. That's what I did with those other two. Told everybody they were fakes."

"Good for you."

Her nostrils flare. "Bastards."

"And it didn't cost you a thing except a drive, some time, and sitting with us through lunch."

"Assholes." She gathers her things and walks out.

We watch her walk around her car in the parking lot. She gets in on the passenger side, fumbles over the shift, opens the drivers' door. A small piece of cloth flutters to the slush covered ground. She slams the door, revs the engine, drives away.

I give Robyn a hug. "As Pambenet says, sometimes the best thing a teacher can teach you is that they're not supposed to be your teacher."

I agree. "Yes, and she's an excellent teacher."

Chapter 149

BirthingWork

They sit on my couch opposite me. Mirth crosses slender legs at the ankle, her feet over to her left with sensible, low-heeled, comfortable tan shoes and smooths her tartan skirt with her free hand. Her other hand rests on top of both of Paul's with a gentle, reassuring touch. Her white blouse ruffles as she breathes and she blinks at me rapidly.

"Would you like something to drink, Mirth?"

She turns to Paul who sits straight-backed in chinos matching Mirth's shoes and a creme-colored, oxford shirt. "Would you like something to drink, Paul?"

He shakes his head, his eyes always on me.

I nod. "You are terrified that someday soon you're going to beat your wife. You are terrified that when this day comes you won't simply beat her, you will kill her."

Paul pulls back.

I take a slow breath, go wide with the exhalation.

"You've never touched her in anger. So far you've never touched anyone so dear to you in anger. But the anger -"

Another breath, this time through my mouth so Grandfather Spirit's long tongue can rake itself across Paul's face and taste whatever messages his sweat shares.

" - not anger, rage. The rage comes more often now and nothing anyone has been able to do has been able to stop it. Now you can't stop it. Now you are terrified to be here because you don't know if I can stop it."

Grandfather Spirit's tongue rolls back into my mouth.

"Don't worry. I can't. I can only do something to help you stop it."

Grandfather Spirit's nose becomes mine. My nostrils flare. A familiar scent, friend, coming from Mirth. "Your grandmother came to my lecture once. She's High Irish, knows Bridgit's ways, knows the *na gig*. You do not. She knows what troubles Paul. She sent you."

Mirth stops blinking. Her hand tightens on Paul's and she turns to him. "Is that proof?"

Paul's face tightens. His eyes narrow.

"Decide; do you want to get well or not?"

Mirth turns to me. "Are you asking him or me?"

"I'm asking you both. The two of you have to decide. Nobody gets well alone."

Paul remains silent. Mirth takes his hands in both of hers. "Could we have a moment alone?"

They hold hands as partners when I return. She breathes easier. Grandfather Spirit smells Paul's fear, warns me Paul will challenge. "Do you think I don't love my wife?"

"Doesn't matter what I think, only what you believe. Do you believe you love your wife?"

"I believe I do, yes. It's these uncontrollable moods that come over me."

Mirth takes his hands in hers. "I'm not afraid Paul will hurt me." A moment's hesitation. "Or the children." Another beat. "Or anyone else."

Paul pulls his hands free of her, sits back from her. "I am terrified of this anger and rage. She's not."

Mirth's chin quivers.

"But the verbal abuse is growing?"

She lowers her head, stares into her empty hands.

He breathes deeply. "Yes."

"He wants to leave me. Us. The children and me. So we'll be safe."

"Come back in two days. I need to do some work before I can help you."

Paul and Mirth cock their heads towards each other and frown simultaneously. He blinks. "What kind of work?"

The work WindWalker talked about, the work The Grandmothers of The Three Women's Nations taught me, the work Grandmother Parvati insist I learn, I master The Male Birthing Ceremony. "I need to figure out a ritual that'll work for you."

Mirth shakes her head slightly. "A what?"

———

They return and again sit on my couch. Their clothing patterns are reversed; his pants are tartan with a white jersey top, she wears a tan blouse and white slacks. I smile at Paul's pants choice. "You've decided to move forward."

He lifts his head, frowns slightly. "How do you know?"

"Order in chaos. You want a way out of your nightmare." I point to blankets and a pillow on the living room floor.

"We're going to do a Birthing Ceremony. I'm going to teach you how to give birth."

Mirth frowns. "I have three children."

"Not you, Paul. Paul's going to give birth to the emotions he can't accept he has, the anger. Anger denied becomes rage, a child acting out more and more to get its parents' attention. Paul knows why he has them, he's not willing to admit the reason to himself, to face that issue, hence what's made him angry grows into a rage."

Mirth clasps Paul's hands. "But why at me?"

"We will find out. He's going to watch his emotions live, grow, and die. Once that's done, he'll be free of them, except for the grief of their loss, and he'll be able to go on from there. Hopefully any new angers will be dealt with before they become rage."

Paul looks out one of the windows. "How am I going to do that?"

"I'm going to midwife you, help you give life to what's already growing inside of you."

He and Mirth stare at each other then back at me. Mirth holds his hands tighter. "Should I leave?"

"You have a role to play, too, and only if you're willing."

"What's that?"

"You're going to be the elder through all this, the wisewoman of sorts, the one who'll help Paul through the birth. We're going to move Paul out of his maleness to a universe of opposites. If you choose to come along, you'll be move out of your femaleness, as well."

Paul looks at the blankets and pillow. "What do you expect us to do, exactly?"

"Exactly? I expect you, Paul, to get on floor, on the blankets. Mirth, I expect you to support him through this."

"We don't have to...ah..."

I laugh. "God, I hope not. But there's one more thing, Mirth, and a lot depends on how much you love Paul. Remember I said nobody gets well alone?"

She nods.

"We know Paul will give birth to some emotional issues he's not dealt with. He's going to externalize them, which means you'll see them, learn what they are, what they're all about."

Paul holds up his hand. "Wait a second now."

She pulls back from him. "Do you know what this is about?"

"Part of him does, yes, but most of him doesn't, and the part that knows is buried deep and festering. If it were a boil, it would rupture, but it's not. So again I ask, how much do you love your husband."

She takes his hands in hers. "I can do this."

Paul lies on the blankets. Mirth rests on her knees beside him. I chant a song of moving.

Paul takes a deep breath, opens his eyes to a white sky with some high, blue, cirrus clouds and a black sun. "Where are we? What happened?"

Mirth leans forward, her eyes also open. She catches herself before she falls over and looks around. "How did we get here?" She leans back, puts a hand down to her side to steady herself, looks at the grass under her hand.

"We came here to do the work we need to do. This is a land of opposites."

Paul's eyes go wide on Mirth's face. "Mirth, what happened to you?"

Mirth focuses on Paul's face. "Your face." Her eyes lower. "My God! You're pregnant."

I kneel on Paul's other side. "As I said, a land of opposites."

"Are we outside?"

"A land of opposites."

"I'm a woman?"

"Here, yes." I catch Mirth's eyes on me. "And yes, you're a man."

"How?"

"Not important, really. What's important is you still recognize each other. Do you?"

They stare at each other, their eyes exploring. They touch hands, their hands move to each others' faces, continue to explore.

"Yes."

"Yes."

"Good. Ready?"

Paul takes Mirth's hands in his. "There's more?"

"Mirth, Paul will experience emotions from the female perspective, things he has no knowledge of. He'll need you to guide him through that."

Paul's face contorts. His eyes bulge. "Oh, Christ, that hurts."

Mirth takes his hand. "What's wrong? What is it?"

"Feels like..." He searches for the word. "Movement."

Mirth sighs. "Good. That's what it's supposed to feel like."

I look at the colors swarming around his body, multicolored bees preparing a harvest. I watch the emotions preparing to leave his body. "You'll give birth soon."

He groans and pulls his knees to his chest. Mirth takes his legs and moves them down, spreads them. "No, don't do that."

Paul starts gasping. "The pain."

Mirth wipes his sweating brow. "You're doing fine. You're my good man."

His breaths come in gulps.

Mirth puts a hand on his chest. "Remember what we learned in birthing class? Like this." She reminds him how to breathe.

He mimics her.

"Better?"

"Better. Yes." He looks at me. "How much longer, doc?"

I laugh. "As long as it takes. And you're doing great. Better than lots of men who've been through this."

"You've been through this?"

"Several times."

"Does it hurt like this each time?"

Mirth laughs. "Gets easier each time."

"The first takes the longest. You learn to isolate what needs to be born, makes it easier."

The clock ticks. Four hours, thirty-five minutes.

The crown appears. "Oh, Christ, I put you through this three times?"

Mirth laughs softly, dries his face. "Push, Paul. Now."

A dark cloud, laced with lightning, rises from between Paul's legs.

Mirth grips Paul's hands, places one of her hands over his eyes. "What's that?"

He pulls his hands but is too weak to free them. "Move your hand. I can't see."

"It's okay, Mirth. That's his rage, anger directed against himself."

The cloud grows, changes shape, takes a human form. It floats between Mirth and Paul, lowers to the blankets, rests there, grows within a few minutes from suckling babe to troubled adult.

"Talk to your child, Paul."

"What do I say?"

"I'd start by asking why there's so much rage."

Paul sat up. Rage mimics his movements, its cloud face staring into his.

"Hello." He looks at me. "Son?"

I nod.

"Hello, son."

"Hello, father. Thank you for giving me form."

Paul and Mirth pull back. She shifts to get around it, be on the same side of it as Paul. "You didn't tell me it would talk to us."

It flashes lightning at her.

"Ask it why it's so angry."

It flashes lightning at me, then returns its gaze to Paul. "You've carried me for a long time, father."

"How long?"

"Fifteen years."

Mirth stares at Paul. "We've been married fifteen years."

Paul looks down, away, sighs. "Yes. And our families were against it."

"Yes, but - "

"And you lied about why we should get married."

"We talked about all this."

"Yes, we did, and it still hurts."

"Have you been unhappy with me?"

Paul's gaze goes from Mirth to Rage. "Unhappy? No. And I love you. But sometimes I've wondered."

"Wondered what?"

He snorts. "We've done well, sure. But everything we've done, every place we've gone...always the right people, the right things, the right places. And it's all because of you."

"I thought you wanted those things."

"I wasn't like that when we courted. You courted me because I was all those things your family wasn't."

I clear my throat. "This is where you confess, Mirth."

"Confess what?"

"Why did you really marry Paul?"

"Because I love him, of course."

"And?"

Rage turns to her, raises its hands.

Paul reaches out to it. "Don't ever raise your hands to your mother." He shakes his head and blinks. "Christ, I can't believe I'm saying these things. Did you drug us?"

"Nope."

Mirth draws back, Paul's words striking her more than Rage could. "So I could fix him. So I could show my mother how it's done."

Rage's face turns into Paul's face in torment. "I want to know how my life might have been."

"And that desire to know your different life has grown stronger and stronger, especially in the past year. Your uncontrollable emotional outbursts have been Rage kicking in your womb."

Rage continues to age, bends with old age, shrivels as years pass in seconds. "Now you know. Now you know." It withers, dies, fades, the storm passes into the land of opposites, a place where rage released becomes joy captured in infinity.

Paul and Mirth stare where Rage sat and cry.

"Is the rage still there, Paul?"

"No. At least I don't feel it anymore."

"Are you curious about how your life might have been?"

He frowns. "Well, sure. I guess. Kind of. Who wouldn't be? Doesn't everybody?"

"In your case, it might be good to go see what it was like. Otherwise, you might be giving birth again in another fifteen, twenty years."

"You can do that, too?"

"I can show you what your life would have been, if you want."

"How?"

Paul returns without Mirth. "Mirth wants to know if I'm going to leave her."

"That's for you to decide."

"What do I do this time?"

I light a sage stick, pick up a big, richly-plumed turkey feather. "You relax."

I wash him in the sage smoke.

"Close your eyes. I'm going to help you do something basic. It's called Relax-Lower-Center-Breathe. You're going to feel something moving you from the outside in. That'll be me. All you need to do is that Relax-Lower-Center-Breathe part. We'll do the rest."

"We?"

"Drum is going to help us."

"Who's Drum?"

I point to Drum, hanging over our fireplace. "That's Drum."

He shrugs. "After our last visit, yeah, sure. What else can happen?"

I turn down the lights.

Drum sings Journeying Drum.

Sage's smoke ascends.

My spirit body moves out, embraces his, helps it move up, out, away.

We journey to his other life.

There is no Mirth.

It is an equally ideal life: a wife, a boy, a dog. A house in the suburbs. A boat docked at an ocean pier.

We stay and watch for hours.

Ella, the woman he marries on this LifePath has always been honest and true. But in this life Paul remembers Mirth's cute little lies and insecurities and how they'd endeared her to him when they were together. But then one summer he'd met El and this led to that. And he was happy here. Until he remembers his two years dating Mirth and he wonders, wonders strongly in this life, what his Mirth-filled life would have been.

And we return.

"Could I be alone for a while."

I leave him, go outside, into the woods, let the energies of his two conflicted lives leave me, drain heavenward, wish them peace.

I hear sighs, then sobs, then deep, gut-cleansing wailing inside my house.

I remember Grandpa's teachings. No one can look into the face of God and live.

Chapter 150

LifePath Work

"Edward, isn't it?"

A tall man, middle-aged handsome, well-groomed, health-club aerobic thin, sits in the blue lounger, dressed for this warm summer day in a pink IZOD and blue, lightweight slacks, no socks and white deck shoes. His skin shows a healthy tan. He has clear eyes that see much. Crow's feet show he laughs much but is cautious with his laughter. He has a small diamond stud in his left ear.

"Raye recommended you. You helped her a while back."

"Yes."

"What did you do for her?"

I repeat Grandpa's teaching. "I will tell you your story and as much of my story as you care to hear, but I will never tell you anyone else's story nor will I tell anyone else your story."

He shakes his head and looks down. He shuffles. "She said she could tell something's bothering me but didn't know what it is. You teach her to do that?"

"Some people get a taste and it stays with them."

He nods. "What do I do?"

"Do you understand what we're going to do?"

"No, not really. Does it matter?"

"Specifics, no. I need to be sure you want to go through with this. Once you become aware, you can't become unaware. Once you know, you can't unknow."

"Yeah, Raye told me that part."

"It might be better if you went to a psychiatrist. Or a therapist, maybe."

"And take years and years and still not be done. Raye said you work in hours or days what it takes others..."

He waves it away.

Again I remember Grandpa's teaching: ask three times. "Are you sure?"

"Yes."

"Are you sure?"

I feel his energy dropping. He stares at me, wondering. "Yes."

One more time, and slower. "Are you sure?"

He faces me and his eyes dart down and left. He considers. He takes a deep breath and his eyes meet mine. "Yes, I'm sure."

I hand him a red and auburn blanket with phases of the moon and stars on it. "Wrap yourself in this."

He takes it from me and frowns. "It's the middle of summer."

"You can shrug it off if you don't need it."

He stands, wraps it around his shoulders, sits again, crosses his left leg over his right. His right foot taps the air like a metronome.

"When do we begin?"

"We already have."

Edward and I walk back.

Back.

Back.

~

"Where is this place?"

I sense. "We are twenty-three? Twenty-four? Not quite twenty-five years ago. In your past."

We walk through a wood on a well-graded dirt road. Snow clings to the trees, not melting.

"Do you know this place?"

Edward pulls the blanket tighter around his shoulders. "No clue."

I breathe deeply. "It smells like north."

"North has a smell?"

"North of Ottawa maybe, but somewhere right along the Quebec border."

Edward stops and points with his chin. "There's a cabin there."

"There's only one road in and one road out but it seems to me there's another road and it's not taken."

"What are you, Robert Frost? There aren't any other roads around the place."

"Something happened there that changed your life. There was a road you wanted to follow and refused."

Edward looks around. He blinks. He sees. He remembers.

"No, nothing happened here. I want to go back now."

"As you wish."

〜〜〜

"I want to do that again."

"Same conditions as before."

Three times yes, three times back. Back. Back.

We are at the cabin in the woods.

"Yes. It was twenty-five years ago. Thereabouts. Just about Christmas time. I didn't remember before. I didn't want to remember. I put it out of...out of my life."

A fire glows through the cabin windows.

"I'm here with a friend. A close friend."

We're at the windows. There is a heat coming through them, not entirely from the fire. From the people, from the voices within. Their words crack and snap like logs caught in flames.

"You going to look in?"

"This is not my story."

"I want you to look in."

Two men yell at each other. One is naked, one covers himself with a blanket.

I turn back to Edward. His face is red, tight, his nostrils flare, his eyes are wide. "Well? Aren't you going to say something?"

"This is not my story. I have nothing to say."

"That's me in there." He flaps tonight's blanket around himself like wings. The moon and stars catch the fire's light and shroud him. "I'm gay."

I shake my head. "You're not sure." His Spirit Guide, a long-necked, graceful swan, an adult shedding its childhood down, trumpets to me. I thank it for clarifying the situation.

"Sorry, my mistake. You weren't sure."

"I'm gay and that's Brian and this is a cabin just on the Quebec side of Ottawa Falls, dead of winter. He proposed to me here."

"The life you were supposed to have, not the one you chose."

"I said no because..."

The voices in the cabin yell, shriek. The swan flares its wings, stretches its neck, calls across the years as if calling across a pond.

"...I thought I had to."

The Then-Edward opens the cabin door, puts on clothes as he walks, sits in the snow to put on boots, walks around back to a jeep, pats his pockets, throws up his hands, walks into the night.

"It was a mile to town. Damn near froze to death walking. Decided my parents were more important. A good job was more important. This was thirty-five years ago, you understand. It was a different world back then."

The cabin, the woods, the snow start fading.

"I married my wife, Andrea, on the rebound. Don't get me wrong. I love her. Dearly. And our kids."

My living room shapes around us.

"And I've never done anything. Been too terrified. Always watching myself, making sure I didn't do anything, give my feelings away."

We are back. He pulls the blanket tighter.

"Will anybody learn about this?"

"Only if you tell them."

"I don't regret my life. I want you to know that."

"But?"

"But."

~

"You call this stuff LifePath. You said I chose one path when I wanted the other. Can I get back to that other path?"

"I'm not sure what you're asking."

"You got me there. Can you..." His face reddens. "Can you leave me there? So I can walk that other path?"

"You want to change the Past?"

He nods. "But only if Andrea and the kids don't get hurt."

"You'll never meet Andrea if you walk that other Path. Your children will never be born."

"What do you mean they'll never be born. I drove them to school this morning on my way here."

I shake my head. "You change the past, you change everything that happens since that change to the past. You stay with - "

"Brian."

"Thank you. Brian. You never meet Andrea. You never have children."

He looks at our fireplace, clean but cold, unused in the summer. "Can you show me what is on that Path? Just show me, not put me there?"

"What you ask is dangerous. Depending on the energies involved, depending on the energies unleashed, especially if they've been waiting to escape some kind of prison - "

He frowns at me.

" - you could return to a different place entirely."

"Is it cold in here?"

I hand him the blanket and describe piggybacking. "You'll feel something. Relax. Have you ever scubaed?"

He shakes his head. "Not in years. On a vacation once. In Hawaii."

"Remember the sense of rising to the surface? Buoyancy without moving? It'll be a little like that."

"What should I do?"

"Hold on. You'll feel like you're riding something. Moving. It's important to keep looking forward. Understand?"

He holds his hand up. There's a white line where his wedding band rested. "Wait."

"Yes?"

"We'll come back to here, now, right?"

"I will. I can't guarantee for you."

"But that'll mean we never met, you never did any of this."

I gaze to someplace other, focus my attention there. "Correct."

"You're looking down that other path, aren't you?"

"Yes."

He inhales deeply, closes his eyes, exhales. "Can you tell me what you see?"

"Yes."

"And?"

"I will share it with you if allowed."

I ask the Edward-other if I can borrow him. He is grateful for my presence and holds up one finger. "On one condition."

I agree.

The Edward-other smiles. "Then please do." I take his four-bodies and place them on this Edward. They fit like loose clothing.

"You and Brian grow well together. You are accepted to graduate school at Boston University, he at Brandeis."

This Edward snorts. "Another reason my family wouldn't approve."

"You study and grow. He takes a job as an academic counselor at MIT. You volunteer and become a staff member at...*Interface*? Then at *The Stowe Center*? Is that correct?"

He sits back. "I used to be into that stuff."

"You learn Brian has AIDS, that he's been unfaithful, but you don't leave. Instead you make plans to move to Hawaii. They are more open to alternative relationships and their needs there. Hospice care is readily available."

"I've heard that."

"You stay with him, nurse him, care for him, won't leave him the last days of his life."

This Edward gently weeps.

"Six months after he passes, you discover you have AIDS. There are new medications, better possible outcomes. You refuse. Your family won't talk to you, all your friends are there, you want to be with Brian, exploring the indigenous flowers. It became a hobby."

"He always knew their names."

"You died alone, but happy."

Edward cries openly, sobs into the blanket. "Thank you."

I gather the Edward-Other's bodies, hold them close, dear, until my work with this Edward is done.

He repeats. "Thank you." He stands, removes the blanket from his shoulders. "I don't want to go back. I love my wife and children too much. But I will tell them the truth, let things fall where they may."

"Good choice."

He looks up at me. "Huh?"

"You're deciding to move forward, not back, and taking responsibility for what's been done, for your life as it is. Good work, that. You're demonstrating that you respect others while respecting yourself. A rare quality. At least not one I encounter often."

He takes a handkerchief out of his back pocket and dries his eyes. "Thanks. I guess."

I rise and shake his hand. "Should you ever want to study, learn what I do, let me know. I'd be honored to work with you."

———

I carry Edward-Other's Four-Bodies back to Hawaii, to his cottage on the north of the big island, back in the trees aways and still able to smell and hear the waves on the ocean.

"You came back."

I remember. "I keep my agreements. I do what I promise."

"I met one like you, at *Interface*."

"Yes."

"Do you do DeathSongs?"

"Yes."

"Please?"

I begin.

One by one, his four bodies depart.

The last one turns as it takes flight.

"Thank you."

"Thank you."

Chapter 151

Eliana's GiveAway

Eliana, a farmer-strong, middle-aged woman with waist-length, thickly-braided dark brown hair, cerulean blue eyes, and wearing a paisley blouse with matching peasant skirt, sits opposite me.

Carefully, almost religiously, she places a small, well worn, red-velvet pouch tied with an equally old, faded red ribbon in my palm. Once there, it feels heavier than I would have thought and I realize there is something inside.

Once the pouch is in my hand, Eliana fixes her eyes on mine for a moment then returns her gaze to the pouch, ribbon, and whatever is hidden within. "Please open it for me, Gio."

Only an old ribbon - which looks it would split if I breathe on it - secures whatever the pouch holds, and I am unsure of her offering.

Eliana shivers and closes her eyes. "I can't. I can't let it escape."

I focus on the unmoving pouch in my palm. "Is there something alive in there?"

A deep sigh lifts her blouse slightly and she shakes her head. "No. Do you know what it is?"

My free hand's fingers feel the form hidden within, touch it softly, gently, respectfully. "Some kind of horse? With a crown, I think."

"It's a unicorn."

"Ok. You can't open it because it'll escape, and I can open it? Are you sure you want me to open it?"

Tears flow from her closed eyelids. Her head falls back, her throat hollows, and deep, quaking sobs escape from some long, hidden place as if she is a volcano rending the bowels of the earth.

"Ever heard of GiveAways?"

She shakes her head.

"In old cultures, with anyone who knows and still practices The Old Ways, a GiveAway are an exchange of things carrying great emotional energy, nowadays its often great family energy."

She keeps her eyes on the pouch. "Like passing on family heirlooms?"

"Quite so. Literally entrusting one's history to another."

"It's not an heirloom."

I nod. I know it is. A family memory.

"There's also often an oath of some kind. A promise from the givee to the giver."

"Sounds like some kind of social contract."

"Very good. Here's the important part. The giver must part with the item in order for something else to come to them, such as the givee's oath. This can't be something we give away then take back."

"I don't want it back. I want it gone."

"This has real power over you. A memory of some kind and you've managed to put it in one place, to tie it up, to bind it so it can't hurt you anymore, to put a noose around it and keep it and you safe. I'll accept your gift and I won't open it until you're sure you want whatever this represents set free."

She looks at the pouch again. "Do you know what the memory is?"

"No."

"My father repeatedly raped me when I was a child. Every time he raped me he would go out and buy me a unicorn. Through the years I've given away all the unicorns except this one."

"Because...?"

"Because he stopped raping me when I had my first period. This was the last unicorn he gave me."

The symbolism of the unicorn bound in the red pouch astounds me. Even more so because she demonstrates it non-consciously, unintentionally.

Through all the work she's done she is finally able to GiveAway, to release all that energy. She is ready to give it away, ready to move beyond.

"I need you to open it. You won't let it hurt me. I trust you not to let it hurt me."

"Let's open it together. I'll hold the pouch, you untie the ribbon and let the unicorn out. The moment you feel that the unicorn is going to hurt you again, I'll close my hand so it won't escape."

She nods and her sobs return, except now she's released all she carried, all she withheld. She bursts the dam and lets the water run free. She sobs and rocks as she unties the ribbon and pulls a beautiful, tiny carousel-style unicorn out of the pouch.

"It's beautiful."

Eliana nods.

"You released all that energy, Eliana. It no longer has power over you. You're free. And beautiful."

There are some stains on the unicorn and she uses her tears to wash them away, then places the unicorn back in its pouch, ties the ribbon back up, curls my fingers over it and cups her hands underneath mine. "Thank you."

Chapter 152

SoulWork

I read the paperwork Francis' parents, Kim and Sally, hand me. The paperwork is from the director of a psychiatric hospital that calls me in when all their techniques fail. Many of the technicians, therapists, and doctors there do not understand me and view me as a challenge, which I'm not. They reference me as "the guy in the funny yak gut headdress." I laugh. I've never owned, had, or used a yak gut headdress, funny or otherwise. The director doesn't understand me and she likes me, sometimes flirts with me. I'm flattered and she knows I'll never take her up on it, a violation of trusts.

I read through the notes a second time, put them down, and focus on Francis. Dr. Davies and her group suggest SOA - Sudden Onset Autism. A safe diagnosis because there's no known cause or cure. "You folks were on vacation when this happened? Was he ever left alone?"

Francis sits between and at the feet of his parents who sit on my couch. He doesn't smell autistic. His energies are not the energies of an autistic. His colors are not those of autism.

Kim and Sally shake their heads simultaneously, Kim's eyes always on his son. "No, never. Can you help him?"

"Did Dr. Davies explain how I work? What I do?"

Sally places a protective hand on Francis' shoulder. "She said you always get results. She said - "

Kim cuts in. "She said you're expensive. And our insurance wouldn't cover your costs. Help our son and nothing else matters."

I chuckle, wave my hand dismissively and watch Francis. He stares straight ahead and glows with protective energy. His Guardians work hard, so hard they can't relax to tell me what's going on.

Strange.

"Expensive has many meanings. Let's first figure out if I can help your son." I look through Francis' past for social interactions, developing relationships, communications which could present this way.

I shift in my lounger.

Francis shifts with me.

Sally and Kim don't notice.

I shift again, intentionally.

Francis matches my movements.

Again.

Same.

Strange.

I turn the lounger, revealing some trinkets on my bookshelf. Francis stands, walks to it and takes an old, green and yellow polka-dotted, stuffed wolf toy given to me by a child in a hospital.

Kim reaches for his son. I hold up a hand. "Has he ever spontaneously engaged in play like that before?"

Kim sits back. "Not in a long time. Do you think it means something?"

"Everything means something. We just need to understand what it means."

Francis plays with the one toy, soft and delicate, ignores all the others. He rubs the wolf against his face, coos at it, pantomimes it walking around, all types of play a younger child would engage in.

I shift my four bodies out of their intersections and alignments until I expend as much energy to maintain their positioning as Francis expends to maintain his.

It exhausts me, but Francis is aided by his Guardians. They do this to protect him.

From what?

"Would you be willing to let Francis spend the night here? You may stay with him, of course."

"Do you think you can help him?"

"I think he can help himself. I'm going to show him how."

~

I stand in the woods. It is a moonless night. I face the window of the room where Francis and Kim stay.

Owls hoot. Raccoons and opossum chitter. A skunk trumbles past.

Francis stares from the window.

"Can you tell me what happened?"

"The wolfman wants to hurt me."

I ask my Grandfather Spirit to manifest.

Francis is not disturbed.

"Not this kind of wolf?"

"No. Wolves are friends. The wolfman is not."

"Can you take me to the wolfman, Francis?"

"I'm afraid."

"How about if my Grandfather Spirit protects you?"

"He isn't strong enough."

"Who's strong enough?"

"You are."

"Are you afraid of spiders?"

He shakes his head.

"Would you like to ride my Grandmother Spirit with me? You'll need to tell her where to go."

"Are we going to find the wolfman?"

"Is that okay?"

"Will you protect me?"

Wolf stands on my left, Spider on my right. Around me, The Standing People raise their voices as wind through their leaves. I hear rustling behind me. Frog, Deer, Elk, Mountain Lion, Coyote, Eagle, Whale, Zebra, Bee, Ant, Badger, Opossum, River, Mountain, Stone, Fire, Night, Moon, The Council of All Beings.

There is a chorus. "We will."

"Okay. I'll go."

Grandmother spins her web amongst the stars and climbs with us on her back, weaving through space, weaving through time. She shoots an anchor line down to the earth, to a place not far north of where I live, an amusement park, *Santa's Village*, and climbs down from the skies.

"Here?"

A tall, dark-skinned, man, flat-faced with a long black braid down his back, dressed as Santa Claus, walks behind the amusements smoking a cigarette.

Francis slides down Grandmother's round body, hides behind her. "Him. That's him. He hurt me."

She turns, strokes him with her pedipalps. "Fe-ear-n-no-ot, Ch-h-hil-ld-d. Hh-e-e-ca-a-an-n-n-no-ot-hu-ur-rt-yo-ou-u-u."

Francis stays protected in Grandmother's grasp.

I send my energies forward seeking his.

A weasel, a ferret, a vole, all foraging in dead, Autumn leaves. "What is his name?"

The vole stops, looks up. "Marvin Many Horses."

"I feel no power in him, barely any life. Is he well?"

The ferret comes up, sniffs me, searches in my pockets. "Do you have any food?"

"Sorry, no."

Marvin tosses down his still lit cigarette. The weasel picks it up, takes a puff, coughs. "Ugh." He throws it down, turns away. "Then go away. Why should we help you?"

"There is a boy. Somehow his energies became confused with Marvin's. The boy is ill, needs help. To help him, I must help Marvin."

"You can make him well?"

"What's troubles him?"

The vole looks at Marvin walking away. He pulls a Santa Claus beard from a pocket and puts it on, tucks his braid inside his jolly red coat, pulls a big red hat fringed with white hair from inside his jacket and puts it on. "He wants to die and doesn't know how."

~

I stand outside an RV parked at the end of a dirt road. A half-constructed sweatlodge awaits finishing on its left, its firepit long cold, its lodgepoles charred.

"Hello the camp. I'm looking for Marvin Many Horses."

He opens the RV's side door and steps out wearing cowboy boots, jeans and white t-shirt under an AIM jacket. A black western hat with a red felt band, a feather pinned to the band, shades his head. He squints behind black rimmed glasses and shuffles as he walks as if chains hold his feet to the earth. His regalia is old and doesn't show honor.

"What do you want with him?"

"I want to talk with him about a little boy."

He turns his back to me. "I don't know any little boys."

"How about the one inside you? The one who remembers The Old Ways? The one you've been trying to kill for the last forty-five, fifty years? You no longer believe but he still does."

My Grandfather Spirit leaves me, stands beside me, raises his head and howls. A pack call. A summoning.

Wolf Spirit separates from Marvin, acknowledges my Grandfather Spirit's call, howls back.

Wolf. Francis' fascinating with my stuffed wolf toy. His fear of a wolfman. Not a wolfman, a wolf-man.

I hear Dharghie, feel myself sharing her canoe sailing down the Milky Way. "Which pups does the alpha attack the most?"

"The one who will someday challenge him to lead the pack."

"That is your answer." She rocks the canoe. I fall out and float like a feather down to the earth. She continues her journey through DreamSpace.

"You saw power in a child and lashed out. You once had power? No, you once wanted power. What happened?"

Grandfather Spirit talks with Marvin's Wolf Spirit.

"Your elders said you're not worthy of teaching? Didn't you realize they were testing you? Those who give up can never learn. So you saw a child who could learn and lashed out?"

"He was white."

"Are you a fool?"

"What are you going to do about it?"

"Me? Nothing." I pointed to the vole, ferret, and weasel spirits at his feet. "They? Much."

The spirits joined, grew, became a crippled Marvin clutching his tarnished regalia, shaking a toy bow and arrows in the air in front of itself, yelled at me hoping to frighten me.

"Is this what you've become? A frightened man who believes he's strong because he frightens children?"

Grandmother Spirit spins a thread down from the sky, entangles Marvin as he heads back into his RV. She pulls him up, makes him a tight, little package, hangs him high enough crippled Marvin can pierce him with toy arrows, dance around him with mock war cries.

"Is this what it means to frighten children?"

Wolf Spirit lifts a leg high, pisses on him, washes shame down his face, mixes with his own tears. "What am I supposed to do? My own people don't respect me."

"For what you did? Why should they? You were supposed to protect them, protect children. All children. What did you do instead?"

He doesn't answer.

"Did you give them reason to respect you?"

"I don't know how. I suppose you know how, *wasicu*?"

I laugh. "*Nitakola*."

"What makes you think I need a friend?"

His spirits look to me, wait.

"What must he do?"

Crippled Marvin separates into weasel, ferret, and vole. Their voices create a harmony. "SoulWork."

Marvin cries out from the confines of Grandmother's web. "No!"

"It's your soul at risk. Continue as you are and you'll be lost forever. Put the work in now, you can be saved. Your choice."

"Will you help me?"

"No, but they will."

Frog, Deer, Cougar, Dolphin, Mountain, Star, North Wind, and others walk out of the woods.

Cougar's claws cut through Grandmother's web. Marvin falls to the ground. Cougar tears his AIM jacket and tarnished regalia from him, rips his jeans and tshirt off, leaves him naked.

"Do you know the story of *Mani He*, Marvin?"

"Walks Mountain? How he came to know who he was when he opened himself and let the Spirits teach him?"

I nod.

The Standing Ones part. A path through the woods opens. Mountain lifts itself, a hill forms, the path leading up its side.

"Your call, Marvin. You wanted power. Here's your chance."

He gets up, takes a step. "The boy?"

"He's up the path waiting for you. Teach him as you are taught. Part of your SoulWork is to free his soul."

Marvin walks into the woods. The path closes behind him. The Spirits fade into the woods behind him. The Standing Ones drum, their branches beating against each other in the wind.

A wolf howls.

I hear Marvin. "Do you see? All your brothers and sisters come round you. They are your kin. Mother and Father, Sister and Brother. You are with them, a Wolf like them. Howl, Francis. Howl!"

I hear Francis laughing.

A moment later, a young cub howls.

Chapter 153

WordMedicine

Robyn and I teach.

"The nature of StoryTelling and WordMedicine in particular is that it's quite in the moment. It's the instantaneous transmission of information from one reality to another and the revelation of that information from the other reality back to the first. Often StoryTellers don't know what they're StoryTelling about, only that they are and that they trust it will have some interesting and probably different affects upon those listening."

A gentleman asks for examples of each.

I look to the class, several dozen people forming a circle around us. "Is someone willing..."

A tall, thin, fair-skinned, blonde woman stands before I finish, comes into the center.

Energies swarm, surround, focus. My Guides open a Gate and a great brown bear stands beside me. Grandmother Parvati smiles. This will be WordMedicine.

"Listen. Watch carefully. This will happen once and never again."

I motion to the floor. The woman sits opposite me.

My eyes close. "The moving of the water. The surface. The feeling of the surface. Sunlight on strong waters. Rushing. Breaking the surface. Climbing. Higher. The Eagle. Opening Wings. Your arms. Spreading wide. Feeling wind. Seeing sky. Breath. Filling lungs. Spreading breasts. Eagle. Talons. Leaping. Grasp. Climb."

She comes off the floor, her arms outstretched and spinning for balance, her legs spreading for support. She falls sideways, halfway off the ground, tucks and rolls, stopping a few feet from where she sat.

"You okay?"

She is fine. No bruises. A little shaken. Her partner comes forward and helps her back to her seat.

"That's WordMedicine."

The same man as before scratches his head. "But what happened?"

I motioned towards the woman. "Would you be willing to share your experience with us?"

She hesitates, whispers to her partner, comes forward.

"As soon as you started speaking, my -" she looks around " - experience shifted. Everything you said. You said it the moment it happened, like you were watching it happen."

"Was I leading your experience?"

An important question, the difference between those who can and those who want to.

"No, like I said, it seemed you were watching it happen, echoing it, not making it happen."

"Go on."

"It started with me remembering seeing some fish swimming in the ocean near our home, seeing them leap out of the water and back in. Then seeing an eagle circling over them, going lower, getting closer. I had this weird sense when I saw the eagle that the eagle and I were one."

"Is that completely accurate?"

She blushes. "I came here tonight because I've always believed my spirit body is an eagle's."

"Go on."

"It was as if what you were doing gave me permission to become the eagle. I didn't hesitate."

"What happened at the very end?"

"I was complete. I wasn't a woman anymore. I was the eagle. I was diving. I was going to carry a fish away."

"And you fell?"

"I got scared. I'd never felt anything like that. It terrified me. I didn't want to be the eagle anymore. I wanted to be a woman again."

"And?"

"I stopped being an eagle and fell from the sky."

I nod. "Both StoryTelling and WordMedicine have no power over what is happening. Both have only the ability to realize it."

Chapter 154

StoryTelling

The class is curious. "Were you afraid?" "Did you really feel like an eagle?" "Did you have to eat the fish?" "Was it like a dream?"

The man walks over to Robyn and me. "What's StoryTelling, then?"

The class's attention turns.

"StoryTelling works without the StoryTeller's incidental knowledge of what is happening. A StoryTeller doesn't know what they're going to say; the story comes to them from the guardians, guides, totems, et cetera, around the person the story is being told to. Acting as liaison between an individual and their spirit partners is explicitly the StoryTeller's function: to communicate via story and metaphor a message the individual's guides, totems, guardians, healers, helpers, et cetera, haven't been able to communicate directly. StoryTelling usually has more of a narrative flow, structure, and style to it. Also, StoryTelling usually only has meaning for a specific person or group."

"Can we get an example?"

"Part of my training is 'I will tell you your story, and as much of my story as you wish to hear. I will never tell you someone else's story and

I'll never tell someone else your story.' That's in the handout I gave you, yes?"

Many nod. Some shuffle through papers on their laps.

"To demonstrate StoryTelling, I need someone who'll let me share their story with you all."

Shuffling. Whispers. Nudging.

An aerobically thin, dark-haired woman with sparkling blue eyes and big hoop earrings comes forward, her round face full of smiles and starlight.

I offer my hand. "Hello, I'm Gio."

The class chuckles.

"I'm BonnieJean."

"I will ask you three times if I can share your story. Wait before you answer. Okay?"

She nods.

"May I share your story?"

"Yes."

"I don't know what I'll say. It could be total pee-pee or it could be the center of your life."

She smirks. "Sure, go ahead."

"One more time. Once I start, I won't stop. Are you sure you want other people to know about your life?"

She stares into my eyes. This one stops her. Her lips purse, her jaws work. Unfamiliar flavors slide over her tongue.

She hesitates. "Yeah. Okay."

I take her hands in mine. We sit down facing each other. I hold her hands, close my eyes, search for the energies in her life.

"I will tell you of BonnieJean and the Magical Dancing Shoes."

～

Once upon a time there was a little girl whose name was BonnieJean. BonnieJean, her mother, her father, her brothers and sisters and everyone else she knew lived in the deep, dark, dankness of night.

This wasn't because there was no sun or day where they lived, it was because they lived deep under the ground and worked in the darkness therein. And even though they lived deep underground, they knew there was a sun. At times they could even see it. But when they did the brightness of day frightened them so much they would work even harder to dig even deeper to live even further under the ground.

One day, as all the people and even BonnieJean worked harder and harder to live deeper and deeper into the ground, they heard a tapping coming down the walls of their caves. Some asked, "What is that?" and some answered, "It is a monster."

And in the darkness of their caves they saw little tinkling lights dancing down from above in the darkness.

Some said, "It is the monster's eyes," and some huddled in fear.

Some said, "It is the monster's teeth," and others agreed and joined those already huddling in fear.

But BonnieJean saw the tinkling of the lights and heard the tapping along the walls and said, "No, I don't know what it is but I think it is something else entirely," and she started to walk towards those tinkling lights and tapping sounds.

Her family reached out for her. "No, BonnieJean!"

Those who saw a monster with horrible eyes and teeth hissed, "That horrible child!"

Those huddled in fear called out, "Grab her! Don't let her go!"

But it was too late. She turned around a bend in the cave wall and came face to face with...

A tall person in a flowing robe. The person's face was so high off the ground BonnieJean couldn't tell if it was a man or a woman.

"Hello, BonnieJean," the tall person said. The tall person's mouth was so far away that it sounded to BonnieJean like it came from a place she'd never been.

In fact, she realized, the person's head was so high up it couldn't possibly still be in the cave. It was so high up that BonnieJean saw glittering, twinkling, blinking little pinpoints of light high over her own head. "What are those?"

The tall person answered without looking. "They are stars."

BonnieJean squinted to see the faraway stars. "Stars? What are stars?"

The tall person reached into its pockets and tossed tinkling little lights far down onto the ground. "These are stars."

Suddenly the whole cave was lit with the twinkling starlight the tall person tossed down.

Far back in the cave BonnieJean heard her people say, "Oh" and "Uh" and "Hah" but never heard them step forward to see what she could see.

"What do you toss stars down for?"

With that the tall person threw back their head and laughed. "So I can dance!" The tall person held its sides and laughed and laughed and laughed.

Now BonnieJean squinted to see the close up stars. "Dance? What's 'dance'?"

"Ah, BonnieJean, I thought you'd never ask." And the tall person's robe came up just enough so that BonnieJean could see beautiful black shoes, shoes not the black of the caves she lived in but shoes richly black as the star filled sky she now saw overhead, shoes which glistened and flickered and echoed the little brightly shining starlights the dancer threw down before it danced.

And with these lights of the night sky glistening and shimmering off its richly night sky black shoes, that's just what the Dancer did.

BonnieJean had never seen anything like it. She'd never heard anything of it. The sound of the Dancer's shoes as it swept up the stars and shuffled on the cave floor and hopped and skipped and stomped and stepped made the sounds of her family's hammers and axes and sickles and picks sound tired and dull. The movement of the Dancer's feet made the rhythms of the cave people's lives seem much closer to the grave than they already were.

"Can I do that?"

The Dancer's feet stopped. Its robe fell and covered its shoes. The stars on the cavern floor winked out. "I don't know, BonnieJean. You must find out if you can."

Once again, BonnieJean found herself in the darkness she'd known all her life. Only now it caused her pain and sorrow. "Don't go!"

"But I must."

"How will I find you?"

"Don't find me, BonnieJean. Find the shoes."

"How will I find them?"

Again there was the mountain of laughter. "Follow the moon, BonnieJean. Dancing shoes are on a hook on the moon. Should you get there, you can take them down and..." the Dancer's voice faded before it finished what it said, but BonnieJean finished the sentence for it, "...dance."

The people came rushing forward from far below. BonnieJean heard them. She looked towards the end of the cave where the people had once seen the sun, looked back at the dull, aching sounds of their running feet rushing towards her in the darkness, looked back towards the sun and left.

But neither she nor anyone she knew had any idea of what a "moon" was.

Her first experience of walking on top of the earth was exciting. She'd heard there were many dangerous things there so she was quite careful and took special care with each of her steps. There was a path before her and seeing that it was easier to walk on the path than not, she did just that.

But she still didn't know what a "moon" was.

Soon she heard an awful racket. It sounded like some poor animal was dying a horrible death. As she came around a large oak tree she saw this huge man wrestling some kind of hideous monster. The monster had wrapped itself around him and was trying to get down his throat. The man was grasping the monster's belly and squeezing it under his arm. His hands were holding the monster's tail and trying to pull it out of his mouth. Meanwhile the monster's young, still attached and standing straight up out of the monster's belly, were crying and screaming and making this horrible racket waiting for the monster to feed them.

BonnieJean raced forward and grabbed the monster from the man. She threw it to the ground and started stomping on it with all her might.

"What are you doing?" bellowed the huge man. "You're destroying my pipes!"

BonnieJean was by now rolling with this beast on the ground, strangling it best she could and waiting as it made its last, dying sounds.

The man grabbed his pipes from her. "These are my pipes!"

"Don't worry. They won't hurt you again."

The man checked his pipes over closely and again fitted them to his mouth.

"What are you doing?" BonnieJean asked.

"I'm going to play my pipes."

"You mean that was music?"

"The best kind."

"I'm sorry. I thought someone was dying."

"Hmmm."

"Well, I *am* sorry. May I walk with you? Perhaps you can help me."

The man once again began wrestling with his pipes. "Oh, all right then. What help do you need?"

"I need to know what a "moon" is and where I can find one."

The man laughed. "Not a problem at all. Listen." And he started playing his pipes. He blew and he blew and he blew. The monster's belly grew and its children stood up straight and tall on its back and they grew and they grew. First they fit under his arm, then they fit under both, then they were so tall they could stand beside him, then they were as big as a tree. The huge man played and played and played and now, beside his pipe-monster, he wasn't so huge at all.

And it was a music. Sort of. At least BonnieJean agreed it could be. Like the monster itself, it kind of grew on you.

The man played on. His pipes - BonnieJean now agreed they could be pipes - grew larger and bigger still. They grew bigger than the trees and bigger than the caves BonnieJean had once called home. They grew bigger and bigger until the man came off the ground playing them. They grew grander and grander until they blocked out the sun.

And there, far away in the sky, was the most beautiful thing BonnieJean had ever seen. "What's that?"

The man took his mouth off his pipes for just a second. "That's the mo...ooo...ooo...ooo..." and the air rushed out of his pipes as if he'd taken his lips away from a balloon. BonnieJean barely heard the "n" of moon before the huge man *whoosh*ed across the sky holding onto his pipes all the while.

BonnieJean watched the man go sailing away. "Thank you. Thank you for your help." She didn't know if the man heard or not, but it didn't matter because the sun was setting and the stars were coming out. "Stars," she said. "Stars like those the Dancer gave away. I must be getting close."

She walked further. It was getting to be night and cold. BonnieJean was used to dark and warm but dark and cold was something quite new to her. "I'll have to get warm."

She started hugging herself and walked further along her path. At another bend the woods opened up onto a field and in the center of the field was a fire. "I can warm myself there."

She raced to the fire and, among the bursting and cracking of the wood, she heard a gentle plinking-tinkling sound. It reminded her of the Dancer's dancing on stars and she thought perhaps whoever made the fire could help her get closer to the moon.

A beautiful woman with long blonde hair and pale, thin arms sat by the fire. In front of her and resting against her shoulder was a strangely shaped tree. Webbing ran from under the top bough of the tree to the top of the bottom bough. The woman kept pulling her fingers from the webbing but they kept getting caught all the same. BonnieJean, remembering that what she thought was a monster was actually the huge man's life, thought that perhaps this beautiful sounding thing might be a monster in disguise.

Then she saw the woman's head stick to the side of the tree and the woman started to cry.

"Don't worry," cried BonnieJean. "I'll save you!"

The woman looked up. "No, Stop!"

"But you're crying."

"Because the music I bring is so beautiful."

"But your fingers are getting caught in the webbing."

"That's not webbing. That's my hair."

BonnieJean looked and sure enough, what she thought was webbing was strands of bright blonde hair.

The woman said, "Listen," and her fingers once again got stuck and unstuck on her webbing hair. The plinking-tinkling sounds came out.

"Is that pipes?"

"Pipes?" The woman laughed. "No, it's a harp."

"Can it get you closer to the moon?"

"Watch."

Her hands started moving in circles along her harp's webbing hair. Her fingers started plucking and plinking and the harp started tuckling and tinkling and soon the air was filled with sound.

Just when BonnieJean was about to ask the harpist what the point of all that circling and plucking and tinkling was, some magic happened. The harpist's hands started reaching further and further and faster and faster as they circled to pluck the strings of the harp. They started moving so fast and circling so far a great wind started coming up around her.

"Wow, that's quite –" started BonnieJean but the harpist said, "Hushhh," and BonnieJean hushed.

The harpist's hands flew higher and further and faster and faster and BonnieJean began to see that the harpist's hands were going so far into the sky she was able to touch the moon. Her hands moved faster and further still and then, when it seemed she would be able to hold the moon, the great winds her hands created began to lift her off the ground. She played faster and harder and the air filled with the sounds of her magic webbing hair as the winds lifted her and her harp up to the moon and beyond.

BonnieJean waited until the harpist had faded from sight and the sounds of her harp could no longer be heard. "Hmmm," she said. "Maybe I should have asked if her harp could bring the moon closer to her."

But BonnieJean saw where the moon was going and followed.

That's when she came to the bridge. It was an old bridge over a rushing river and its timbers and beams looked like they'd break before they'd let BonnieJean cross.

But that's where the moon was, with all the stars around, and when BonnieJean squinted directly at it she thought she could see the peg where the Dancer's magic dancing shoes were held.

She decided to get across.

No sooner had she put one tiny, light, graceful little foot on the bridge when a huge, growling, terrifying, horrible voice called up from below by the river. The voice rumbled like mountains grinding in the night and the bridge shook with it. "You are not worthy to cross this bridge this night."

Frightened as she was, BonnieJean wanted to get to the moon and get those dancing shoes. "Is there another way across?" she asked as she looked around to learn what kind of monstrous beast could make sounds like that.

Just when she looked one way a huge, horrible, ugly, smelly-stinky disgusting old ogre came up the other way and bellowed, "You are not worthy!"

BonnieJean put her hand on her chest and shook her head as the ogre's breath engulfed her. It smelled of things long dead and things even deader longer. "But I want to get to the moon. That's where the Dancer's magic dancing shoes are."

The ogre lifted its head and laughed. Clouds gathered and lightning crashed and heavy rains came over it as if to answer its summons. BonnieJean thought the lightning didn't do justice to its horns and horribly pimpled ears. "The dancing shoes?" The ogre lifted her and peered through one ear as if he could see out the other then put her back down. "You are not worthy to hear the magic dancing shoes."

BonnieJean thought about that for a minute. She thought about the musics she heard she thought were monsters and the monsters she'd heard and thought was music, then thought about the sounds the shoes made when the Dancer danced. "But I already have heard them. I heard them when the Dancer danced in my people's cave."

"And?" the ogre stood right over her and glared with its one, open, weeping, pus-filled eye.

"And I never confused their music with monsters."

"Harrumph." The ogre turned its back on BonnieJean. She thought it could use a good brushing. Then the ogre spun back to face her and stared deeply into her eyes and cried "You are not worthy to see the magic dancing shoes" and its voice shook the bridge and almost stopping the river from flowing.

Again BonnieJean thought. She thought about the piper and the harpist and what she'd seen them do, then thought about the rich night sky black of the Dancer's shoes and how the Dancer didn't try to grab hold of the moon, only use it as a guidepost for its own journey. "But I did see the magic dancing shoes when the Dancer danced."

The ogre eyed her more suspiciously than ever. "And?"

"And I never thought they were anything other than shoes. Not monsters or anything else."

"Hmmm."

"The Dancer told me to look for them on a peg on the moon."

The ogre shook the world with its voice. "But there is no Dancer here now."

"No, there isn't." BonnieJean looked up into the ogre's rune-lined face. "But there's me. And I want to dance."

"You are not worthy to touch the magic dancing shoes."

BonnieJean was growing tired of this. The ogre was being more a nuisance than a threat. "Maybe I'm not."

The ogre nodded agreement with BonnieJean's words. "Hugnh."

"But then again, maybe I am."

The ogre groaned and rocks slid down mountains in the distance. It spoke again, but this time slowly, making each word fall heavily onto the ground at BonnieJean's feet. "You...are...not...*WORTHY*...to wear the magic dancing shoes."

"That we will never know unless I wear them at least once, first."

The ogre stared at her, its hot, tumescent breath billowing like clouds from all four of its nostrils.

Then the most horrible thing happened.

The ogre smiled. It didn't have many teeth and those it had looked as rickety and old as the bridge itself.

Then it laughed.

It laughed and laughed and laughed and with each laugh it changed. First the clouds over and around it gathered and draped themselves like cloaks around its body, then lightning and thunder came and knocked off layers of skin, then rains came and washed everything away and all the while the ogre laughed.

Until there wasn't an ogre standing there anymore and The Dancer stood in its place.

"Do you see your shoes on the moon, BonnieJean?"

"I think so. I think I see the peg."

"That's right. You do. The shoes aren't there just yet."

"What? After all I've been through and everything I've done?"

The Dancer laughed. "The shoes are full of magic, BonnieJean. But only because you put it there. Come, walk with me."

The Dancer threw down some stars and the bridge changed into a solid block of stone arching over an ocean beneath. As they walked, BonnieJean could hear the Dancer's shoes tapping and clicking and shuffling over the star-strewn bridge.

On the other side was the moon. On the moon was a peg. Both were just out of reach. And there were no shoes there.

"Reach, BonnieJean."

"But there are no shoes there."

"And Dancers and ogres don't really exist, and harpers and pipers can't get you to the moon, and you've come this far and been through so much, how much more can it hurt to reach?"

BonnieJean stretched. She felt her arms would come out of their sockets and her back would snap in two.

"That's it, BonnieJean, S...t...r...e..t...c...h"

BonnieJean did. Suddenly her feet left the ground. Suddenly the dancing shoes hung on the peg. Then they were in her grasp.

"I'm floating."

"You're dancing. Put the shoes on, BonnieJean. Now it's your turn to dance."

BonnieJean did. Her pockets filled with stars and she didn't turn back, even when that one particular dance was done.

That's why now, if you're very quiet at night and sometimes even during the day, you can hear a little twinkling and crinkling, a little shuffling and tapping and playing.

That's BonnieJean. Who found her magic dancing shoes by finding her magic within. And letting herself dance.

~

BonnieJean takes her hands from mine, wipes tears from her face. "That's quite a story. You just made that up?"

"I had lots of help. Are you upset?"

"No. Your story - "

"No, your story."

"My story explains quite a bit. There are some things I've needed to figure out."

Someone in back raises their hand. "Do you know what any of that meant?"

She looks to see who's asking. "Everything he said made sense. How he knew some of that stuff, I don't know, but everything made sense." She blushes. "I want to be a professional dancer. I'm Scottish. It's kind of in my blood."

Chapter 155

JourneyWork

Friday night. Robyn and I begin a basic journeying class. I explain the goal is to give people a taste, Robyn and I will help them, to journey on their own requires much practice.

Robyn lights some sage. "Has anyone studied journeying before?"

Irene, tall and thin, short dirty blonde hair and cat eye glasses, pulls out a piece of paper.

I read it. A certificate from a well-known shamanic training institute states she is a shaman and can journey. "Thank you. Perhaps you can help us if something unexpected happens."

She answers with a beautiful Danske accent. "It will be my pleasure to assist."

Sunday afternoon and everyone is satisfied. All have an experience to share with others, although none have journeyed on their own. From here we will learn who can go further, who will study more.

Irene lingers.

"Did you get what you came for?"

"I wanted to know how you did things because what you offer isn't how Michael trained us."

"Fair enough. We often take classes with others to learn what is different, what is the same."

I help Robyn pick up cushions and backrests.

Irene lingers, watches, joins us.

Robyn takes some cushions from Irene and walks to a closet. "Was it different?"

Irene nods without smiling. "Yes."

I hand Robyn some cushions. "Oh?"

"Yes. When Michael encountered any kind of problem he slapped the person's face."

I drop the cushions still in my arms. "He did what?"

"And if that didn't work he told them to leave the class, that they weren't paying attention or weren't doing the work."

Robyn stares at me, squats to pick up the fallen cushions. "That's... not...quite...the way..we were taught...to do it."

"So I now know. And what you call a journey is very different than what he calls a journey."

I push folded chairs up against the wall. "Is that a good thing?"

Irene smiles. "Didn't you tell us there's no good or bad, there only is?"

I chuckle. "Yep, I did. Good catch."

"What you do is much better. I felt love and community the entire time, and when people had trouble, you assisted. Where did you study?"

"Lots of teachers. Lots of different places."

She waits. Robyn nods. I pull out two chairs and offer Irene one. "JourneyWork involves ceremonies. How people journey is the ritual specific to them and the exercise being done. It is the ceremony which is significant in the Practice and not the ritual inside."

Irene pulls out her phone. "May I take notes?"

I remember Pambenet when I asked if I could record a training. "That's not right."

"Is that a yes or a no?"

"That's a 'that's not right.' You decide."

She puts her phone back in her pocket.

"Different cultures have different concepts of worlds. The most common division is lower, middle, and upper worlds, but many who teach that division teach it as a hierarchy and don't understand the concept of balance. The Celts didn't have those concepts at all."

Irene shakes her head. "Balance?"

"We are the balance point between the upper and lower worlds, but there are a multitude of worlds and when we acknowledge them, to acknowledge them, we must be at their center."

Irene closes her eyes, shakes her head. "Are you sure I can't take notes?"

"Your decision, that."

"How do you remember it all?"

"Practice."

She turns to Robyn. "Will you sit with us?"

Robyn pulls out a chair.

"And you. How do you remember it all?"

"Listen, then practice."

I lean towards Irene. "I'll go slow. It helps if you ask lots of questions. Also if you repeat to yourself everything I say."

She looks from me to Robyn. "You'll go slow."

"As slow as you need us to go."

Chapter 156

The Teacher

He hands me some hundred pages in a manila folder. I open it to the first page, read "Digging Out: Life-Changing Tools For Personal Growth From My Astonishing 5 Year Journey with a Sicilian Mystic."

"What would you like me to do with this?"

"What do you think of it?"

I read the opening paragraphs, skim through the first chapter.

He interrupts. "I didn't want to call you a Mystagogue."

"Good. I'm not."

He blinks.

"Are you upset?"

"You wrote this because...?"

"So people could learn."

"Learn."

"From me."

"Okay."

"You're upset."

"Amused."

"I hoped you'd be flattered."

"Okay."

"You're not, are you. Why not? Aren't I doing what you taught? What you learned?"

"What was I taught? What did I learn?"

"Didn't one of your teachers tell you to teach from the well of your ignorance? Something like that?"

I chuckle The pieces and parts some hold, the pieces and parts they drop. "Madame Chi Tze. 'When you step into the well of your ignorance you are at the top of your knowledge. Teach from the top of the cup and you teach what you don't know. You fail. Teach from the bottom of the cup and all you can see is all that tea above you, not what you're teaching. Again you fail. Teach from the top of the tea and you invite others to fill your cup. That's how you teach.'"

"How do you remember such things?"

"How do you not?"

"So I can teach from the top of my cup? That's okay?"

I excuse myself, make tea, return with two cups, hand him one. "Show me the top of the cup."

He points at the rim.

"Drink from there."

He tips the cup so the tea rises to his lips.

"No, you're changing the situation. Change the situation and you change where you drink from, change what you drink. You can't drink from the top, there's nothing there."

Chapter 157

The Knowledge of Sacrifice

Robyn lies in a hospital bed. Machines I could never imagine keep her soul tethered to her body.

Lower-Center-Relax-Breathe.

But I can't. I can walk through suns and become creatures leviathans fear and am paralyzed for fear of losing her.

None of my teachers answer my call.

I sit at home on the floor. Our dog rests his head on my lap. Cars drive past and he raises his head, looks to the door. "No, pup. That's not her."

My tears wet his head. He licks my face, his eyes search mine, find nothing and he rests his head again.

He lifts it again, but looks out back, not to the door. He rises up, wags his tail, barks in recognition. I look out our backroom into the woods where I've made so many friends.

FlowerSong stands at the edge of the wood. "Robyn?"

"Not here. Have you come to collect her? Take her Home?"

"Not her. You."

"Me? She's dying, not me."

"Heal her so you can go."

My heart sinks. "I can't. I don't know why. I've tried."

FlowerSong shakes lambsfoot and sunflower petals framing its face. "No. You are afraid."

My face flushes. I stand and yell at the entity who's so long been my friend. "Afraid? Of what? I stopped oceans and formed oceans. I've ridden WhirlWind to give galaxies their spin and bind universes together, to create ripples in time so others could live other lives. Of what am I afraid?"

My rage doesn't faze it. It closes Morning Glory eyes and raises thick grapevine arms unsupported by arbors. "Failure. Your own death."

My lips purse. For a moment I hate who I am, what I've learned, what I can do.

I hate myself.

I hate my fear.

I go whenever the Universe calls me.

The Universe knows I fear.

And of what.

Of losing her.

And of healing. Because I give of myself to heal others. Father Werner's words echo in me.

The Universe teaches. Will I give of myself to heal her? To heal others? I watch The Paraclete come for others, never for myself.

FlowerSong's voice rises with the wind. "Is your fear lessened if you do not act?"

I pull back. No, my fear is not lessened. I fear failure. Failing her. Learning my whole life has been a lie, my parents were correct, those I've known who refused to understand understood more than I.

Failing her.

And myself.

I don't want to die.

And she is. If I allow all that I am to save her, I must take on all that she is.

And she is dying.

I don't want to die.

But if to save her I must?

I pet our dog. My dog. I do not want to leave him, not knowing where I've gone, when I'll return, waiting for me.

FlowerSong's voice rustles the leaves. "What is life if it's not worth giving?"

And I understand.

FlowerSong dissolves back into the wood, into the brush, into the falling leaves of Autumn.

Father Werner was correct, and not.

Lower-Center-Relax-Breathe.

The old energies surge. Our dog barks, jumps on and off the couch, bows, wants to play.

My joints bend. My bones crack. My muscles tense until my bones snap like twigs in a storm.

I fall to the floor. Our dog comes by, sniffs, barks, nudges me, brings his bone over, drops it on my hand.

The phone rings. The answering machine catches it because I can't move, can barely breathe. "Mr. Fortuna? Gio? This is Doctor Mulvany. Good news! Great news! Call me as soon as you get this message."

Because there is no greater love.

I am whole.

Chapter 158

My Friend

Robyn watches TV in the backroom. I sit on our porch and watch the wildlife move through our yard. "Hello, Skunk. Hello, Woodchuck. Hello..."

An old presence, one not felt in years, shapes on the grass by the birdfeeders. Black-and-white polka dot boxers, readers balanced up his face and just after his horn, and pink.

"Phobos! Hello, my friend. I thought I would not see you again."

He takes my hand, caresses my face with rhinoceros toes, stares into my eyes.

"Where is your pointer?"

"Has it been a good life?"

"Yes. Yes."

"And your voice. Far gentler than I remember."

"You hear fine now."

"I didn't then?"

"You were fearful then."

"I'm not now?"

"Are you asking or telling?"

"Rhetorical. I believe I know the answer."

"Which is?"

I look inside, see Robyn knitting. She picks up the remote, changes the channel. "Not now."

"Good answer."

"Where have you been all these years?"

"Close. Beside you. Inside you."

"And now?"

"Time for me to move on."

I nod. "You've been a great teacher."

"Fear...our own, deep, personal fear...our unspoken fear...is often our greatest teacher. You realized yours."

"What was it?"

He laughs, adjusts his glasses. "Do I have to get my pointer?"

"There are no closet doors here."

A screen forms beside him. He has a reel of Super8 film in his hand. His other hand lifts a pointer. His voice is soft. "To always love. To embrace love. To give freely so long as I give love."

"And?"

"To understand that the giving of love is the giving of self, even unto death."

"Yes. I understand that now."

"Now the last piece."

I scowl. "Last piece?"

"Those who love never die to those who live beyond them. They live on in the beating of others' hearts." He fades. "In the caresses of the body." The screen, the reel, the pointer, are gone. "In the lessons of the spirit." Only a pink outline remains. "In the memories of the mind." I only see his spectacles floating man-height above the lawn. Birds fly through where he had been. "Time for me to go."

"Goodbye, Phobos, my friend."

Chapter 159

The Gift

Those who work with me gather.

"There is one more teaching for those who are willing."

They lean forward. "Tell us."

"A gift. This life's last. Psychopomp, helping those who fear The Paraclete to accept its embrace, to ride it on their journey from this life to their next."

Some shy away. Some remain. "Tell us."

"A great concern among my teachers is that people with little more than a few days training go out into the world not realizing their lack of knowledge and experience may be more traumatic to those involved than the experience of death itself. Brother Andrew told me 'We die alone. We come into this world through the body and into the arms of another, and there is often someone there to help us gather our first breath. But too often we die alone. The psychopomp makes the passage from this life to the next as merciful as was the passage from the last life to this.'"

More shy away. Fewer remain. "Tell us."

"Some of you know of NDEs, Near Death Experiences, the survival of death via altered states of consciousness."

Raye frowns, looks back through her studies. "The *Kamarupa*?"

I smile. "Yes. One of many names for it. The word 'psychopomp' comes from the Greek *psychopompús*, 'conductor of souls'. The Greeks believed both Hermes and Charon were psychopomps. The Chakras via the direction and gifts of the Chakras, one-eyed Oden to the Norse, the Inuit's SnowWalker, Runes are used in some cultures, Egyptians have the jackal-headed god Anubis."

"Has any of this survived in modern culture?"

I consider. "The Christian mythologue 'Death'. The fantasists' and cultural Grim Reaper imagery. The role of psychopomp survives in thanatologists."

More leave. A handful remain. Edward raises a hand and I nod. "Who taught you?"

"My grandfather, first. WildCat, my last."

"If they taught you didn't they know how to do it for themselves?"

"In both cases, they weren't doing it for themselves."

"Who then?"

"For me. A gift. In both cases, the last they taught me."

Edward clears his throat. "So not just a lesson."

"Correct."

Raye looks around at the others, back at me. "Also a test."

"An opportunity for learning."

"Learning?"

"There's so much you have to learn yourself. You know what you need to know. Now you've got to go find out what you don't know and learn that."

Only Donny, Irene, and Honoré remain.

"Teach us."

Ending

Chapter 160

Farewell, My Brother

Roger - A'bli'g'moodj - comes to me. "It's my time, Gio."

"Yes."

"Do you remember the day you met your Power Being?"

"WhirlWind. Yes."

"Tell me."

"You asked me to teach beside you."

"I asked you to learn beside me."

"Yes. Did I?"

He laughs. "I'm here now, aren't I?"

"Because?"

Tears of joy run down his face. "Because you make things so obvious. You're the only one of us who could figure out some of the old ways, bring them back, make them active in the world again. You used the tools you had to create new tools and find old ones long forgotten, lost."

"Mercea's teachings, that."

"You used Mercea's teachings to go places Mercea couldn't imagine."

"I have good teachers."

"We have a good student."

He improves, he fails, he improves, he fails.

"I would like to ride WhirlWind to my next place."

"I will ask."

He places his hand on my arm. "I would like WhirlWind to lift my bodies, nothing more."

"As you wish."

He doesn't lift his hand. "For yourself as much for me. More so, perhaps."

I stare into his eyes. Deep mysteries still dwell there, slowly reveal themselves.

"Yes, I understand."

I do what he and others taught me.

Smoke rises around us. The Breath that Goes to Heaven. "For all you gave me, for all you taught me, for the pieces of you I carry with me."

WhirlWind lifts him. The Paraclete welcomes them both.

I wave. "I love you, my Brother. Pleasant Journeys and Safe Harbors. I give you The Wind."

Chapter 161

Le meas, Mo Charaid

I feel Calum pass.

We finish our breakfast and I look out the window, step onto the porch, stare into the woods.

Robyn follows. "Everything okay?"

"Calum crossed over."

She takes my hand. "You alright?"

"I always hoped to study with him one more time."

She nods.

"Did he work with anyone else? Maybe you could meet with them..."

"I don't know. He never mentioned it. I think he taught his daughter. I'm not sure."

"You told me about the night he called you."

"Yes. He was always there and never revealed himself until that last day."

"You bought t-shirts for everybody for the final song at the *ceilidh*."

"And I needed his help to translate the English."

We laugh.

"Wish I had seen the look on Catriona's face when everybody showed up wearing their shirt."

"How did I know what he gave me as a translation?"

"She was a Scottish schoolmarm if ever there was one. A Presbyterian minister's wife, wasn't she?"

"I asked for 'Don't know the words, don't know the language, can't carry a tune, gonna wing it!' and he gave me '*Chan eil a' Gàidhlig agam, Chan eil na faclan agam, Chan urrainn dhomh fonn a thograil, Fhalbh's càc.*'"

"Don't know the words, don't know the language, can't carry a tune, fuck it!"

"*Tapadh leibh*, Malcolm."

We laugh again.

"And it wasn't until later that night, long after we all laughed ourselves into exhaustion and gone to bed, he called me. I asked if what I experienced was him, Malcolm, and he corrected me, 'Calum'."

She nods.

I quiet, look into the sky, searching for RiverCloud. "He taught me *Gàidhlig* curses. The culture, the people, the Way of Ocean and Earth. From the Outer Isles. He was one of the last of the Celtic Storytellers."

"And he took you on. Don't forget that."

"He had a tale for everything. Teaching stories, thinking stories, ..."

"Growing stories."

"Lore."

"He asked you to help him translate fairy tales into a colinear *Gàidhlig-am Beurlad* to keep the language alive."

"He did it to teach me. To get me used to the rhythms, the meanings. The *why* of the Celts and Gaels."

"Ceremony versus ritual."

"Did I ever tell you about the night he taught me the *fios agam* behind *Uisge-Beatha*?"

"Scotch? Yes."

"He taught me to sing the *waulks*, to summon the seas and quiet the earths, to see through the present to the past, into the deep past. He taught me Rime writing, how to read ice hanging from the trees. And to respect the Old Ones of the Isles for choosing to reveal themselves to me and not to others."

"And the name they used to call you."

I nod. "He's moved on. *Stad gu math, a' Chalium.*"

Two Wind Giants come down on either side of me. I go inside and get three small glasses, pour a taste of *Uisge-Beatha* in each. Three glasses of water beside them. I return to the porch. Pahdeval and Da Fischer wait.

We inhale the musk, let the peat share its story, close our eyes, lift our glasses.

"*Le meas, mo charaid.*"

Chapter 162

Such Good Children

Donny comes to me when I rest. "It's tough to get through to you."

"I block a lot now."

"How come?"

"I'm old. Tired. It's easier for me. I wonder if I'm the last."

I suggest people for him to study with.

Sometimes he laughs. "Already been there."

Sometimes he nods. "Yeah. I've heard of them. They're on my list."

Honoré knocks on my door. I open it, smile, he waves at me with a glove-covered hand. Both hands are covered. I cock my head.

"I'm learning control." He removes his gloves and shows me a small tag inside the left one. They are asbestos lined. He puts the gloves down, turns his hands over, palms up.

Miniature bonfires glow in his palms.

I nod.

"You asked for all my notes when I pass. Do you still want them?"

"Yes."

"What will you do with them?"

"Burn them."

I nod. "Yes."

Donny goes to the window as a car pulls up. "Irene's here."

"Yes."

The door opens for her. She walks in, they embrace. She moves to Honoré.

He holds up his hands. "You can hug me but I can't hug you."

Irene frowns.

"Perhaps you can teach each other control."

Honoré laughs. "The *hariegia*." He focuses. The flames go out. He and Irene hug.

They are quiet, nervous. They shift their weight from leg to leg, foot to foot, no one sits but me.

I smile. "Why are you all here?"

They answer in unison. "To wait with you."

They hesitate. Again in unison. "But that wouldn't be useful."

"Go on."

Donny starts. "If we spend whatever time you have with you…"

Honoré continues. "…then we will not be working with others…"

Irene finishes. "…and what you've taught us might be lost forever."

They're such good children.

Chapter 163

The Interview

"How do you self-identify?"

I chuckle. "Self-identify. I don't know, really. It depends on the reason someone is asking. On my own, I don't self-identify as anything, not that I'm aware of. I'm more curious how others classify me than how I classify myself. People claim to know lots about me. More than I know about me, anyway. How do you self-identify?"

He puts down his pen, laughs himself. "I've been with you too long. I don't, either."

"Good." I pause. "How do you identify me?"

No hesitation. "Teacher. Counselor. Wiseman. I'd use the "S" word but you've taught me not to." He lifts his pen, stares at it.

I nod. "Grandmother Parvati's lessons."

"You called her a powerful shaman and she laughed."

"Yes. What she said is true for me. For everybody, really. Not everybody knows it."

"What got you started?"

"My Grandfather. He is a Sicilian Mystagogue. Or was while he was here."

"You used present tense, 'He is,'."

"One of his lessons as well as from many others: Nothing is lost, only waiting."

"Waiting where?"

I point down and to my left.

He lowers his pen again, stares after my finger.

"Don't look at my finger, look to where I'm pointing."

"Another lesson."

"Many lessons, many teachers."

He reaches into his pocket, takes out his phone. "Sure I can't record this?"

I shake my head. "Pambenet wouldn't allow it."

"You took out a microcassette recorder and he pointed at it and said, 'That's not right.'"

"And because studying with him was more important than recording him, I shut it off, put it away."

"Anybody ever try to get the better of you?"

"All the time."

"Anybody ever succeed?"

"All the time."

He laughs. "Yeah, right."

"Sometimes you have to let the other person win. You learn a lot about people by how they handle success."

"Have you handled it well?"

"One, it depends how you define 'success.' Two, by my definitions of success, no, not always."

"Is there anything about your life you'd change?"

"No, not one thing. But I don't want to relive my life, either. Once was enough."

"You'd not change anything, but you'd not repeat it?"

"Correct. Every joy and sorrow I've had got me here, you and me talking. I might not have met Robyn, I might not have played with my dogs, greeted the wildlife that came to me, studied with my teachers, ..."

"All joyful moments."

"Do you know why life is joys and sorrows?"

He shakes his head.

I draw a sine wave in the air between us. "Because ups and downs are the heartbeats of life. If you have a life of all joy or all sorrow, a straight line of either, you're dead."

"Do you think you'll die?"

I smile. "Are you asking if I'll leave this place? Yes." I look into my hands. "Probably soon."

He stares at me and frowns.

"Don't worry. Not yet. Not today. Not with you right now. I have a while yet."

"You worked miracles. Magic!"

"No, most of what I did was help others release the magic in themselves."

"You've probably forgotten more than most people learn."

I shake my head. "WildCat's lesson: We forget what we don't use. I make it a point to use everything. Every day. To remember."

"You have so much more to teach."

I shake my head again. "I have so much more to learn."

He puts down his pen and pad. A tear forms in his eye, trickles down his cheek. "Please no, not yet."

I take his hand, kiss his palm, breathe knowledge into it, fold his fingers over it, make them clench tight. "There. Everything I've ever learned, all in one breath. Never let go, hold it tight. You'll know more than me when you're done."

He lifts his hand to his mouth, inhales as he slowly relaxes his grip, closes his eyes and journeys through galaxies humans don't know exist, delves into energies that hold matter together, walks with dinosaurs, swims with creatures in distant oceans, greets Pele in her lava-rich home, feels the beating heart of sacred mountains, warms himself in the center of the sun, frolics in lapping waves knowing they are the smiles of Water Giants at play, grows leaves, talks with Bee, Ant, Spider, Wasp, Coyote, Raven, Robyn, creatures too small to be seen and creatures with bodies spanning star systems, feels the breath of Frost Giants sharper than swords, studies with No-Face daemons robed in ceremonial black, sees into his own being, boards a ship that folds smaller than an atom so he can explore the universes within.

And within.

And within.

His tears come more easily. "I don't want to lose you."

I smile. I go to his center, give comfort. Nothing is lost, only waiting.

He nods, wipes his eyes, nods again.

Chapter 164

In These Hands

I spend time on our back porch watching the raccoons, the fox, the deer, all The Wild who've accepted me over the years.

Each day I look into my hands.

I pour two Scotches. RiverCloud comes and we drink. We talk about where I go next.

Donny knocks on my door. His eyes are bright. He's explored universes with them. He sees the books he's sent me over the years beside my chair: everything from children's books on bees and ants to advanced myrmecology and apiology texts, all signed by hand, honey, and antennae.

I smell peaches.

"Gio."

"Yes, Buppa?"

"He will use what you've taught him."

"Wrongly?"

"Incorrectly."

"Will he hurt people?"

"He will learn. You taught him that. Everything is his teacher."

"Will we lose him?"

"For a while."

"And?"

"And he will find his way."

"Will he be lost long?"

"You found your way."

Irene walks through the woods. She smells of European forests. "I wasn't sure if there'd be time if I took a plane."

I nod.

Honoré knocks on my door, the sound of hard knuckles on hard wood. He waves without gloves. "I had a feeling."

He comes in, greets Donny, gives Irene a kiss on the cheek, looks around. "Where's Robyn?"

"Waiting."

We sit, the four of us, laugh, chatter.

I inhale deeply. The scent of peaches.

"Is there anything more I can do for them, Buppa?"

"Teach them to sing."

Chapter 165

Farewell

The trees drop their leaves.
The birds withhold their song.
The woods grow quiet.
Clouds hold their positions in the sky.
Stars weep.
The Universe whispers. "I have lost a friend."

Appendix: Principles

What follows is a living document. Things are added. To date (45+ years), nothing's been deleted. Some comes from things my Grandfather taught me, some from life, some from my own studies, journeys, and what have you. A friend, learning much came from my Grandfather, nodded and congratulated me for keeping my Grandpa's teaching alive. "We've lost the elements of honoring the elders," she said.

Someone once asked me if I've lived up to the Principles myself.

"Hell no. That's why I write them down. So they can be a guide to me, so I'll know when I am not following them."

Like so much in my life, they are for me. If others benefit from them, wonderful (and it seems many do). But first and foremost, they are for me.

You may not like them all. You may only be comfortable with one or two.

Good start. Work to integrate them all. Find that difficult? As noted above, if they were easy for me to follow I wouldn't write them down.

I will offer you can't pick and choose. Or at least it seems most people can't. I haven't met anyone who's done so successfully, known many who have tried and failed.

One fellow studied them for a while and told me he couldn't find any contradictions in them. They seem internally consistent.

Reassuring, that.

"Does that mean you'll follow them?"

"No way. I've got a life to live."
And so it goes.

1. Do unto others as if they were you.

In other words, cut out the middle man. Treat others the way you treat yourself. People do this anyway. All we do is suggest you become aware of it.

2. Trust yourself.

Until you do this, you'll never be able to trust others and you'll put what trust you have in people who will hurt you.

3. Be Honest.

With yourself first because it makes it easier to be honest with others. Honesty will cost you and what it returns is worth it. Tell tall tales, lie with the best of them and exaggerate all you want when people know that's what you're doing. The rest of the time, be honest.

4. Respect people's boundaries and limits.

There's a difference between being selfish and being selfless. Realize what this means for you and you'll realize what it means for others.

5. Keep it Simple.

Because it's so much easier that way.

6. Take responsibility for your actions.

When you make a mistake and before anybody else knows the mistake has been made, raise your hand and say loud enough for others to hear you, "That one's mine. I did that." If the people around you are more interested in pointing their fingers at you and distancing themselves from you than helping you clean things up, you're standing around the wrong people. Let them distance themselves. They won't be around you when you succeed, and you will, because you'll have learned how to stand up tall, proud and free by recognizing, owning up to and cleaning up your own mistakes. From this you'll also learn compassion and dignity and how to help others clean up their mistakes, as well. Along with this ...

7. Mistakes are just that; You can reach again.

So learn to stretch when you have to and to recognize when what you're reaching for isn't something you'd want to hold in your hands. You'll be better for it and so will those who love you.

8. Innocence is not Naivety and vice-versa.

Think of this as a self-recognition of " ... wise as serpents and harmless as doves."

9. Your rights end where your willingness to harm and hurt begin.

If you need this one explained or you needed a moment to put this into a context you could get comfortable with, you are either intentionally ignorant (never a good plan) or hoping to excuse yourself for your. behavior towards others (also not a good plan)

10. Language is a tool, like Maslow's Hammer.

Some people think everything's a nail. Be neither. This is part 1.

11. Language is a tool, and can be Eliadeian.

Some people are or can become 2nd order thinkers. Be both. This is part 2.

12. Faith is with the heart, but the confession of faith is with the lips.

So until you can say it to at least two others, it ain't true and you and others will know it.

13. Everything is that simple.

As soon as you begin saying things are not quite that simple or that things aren't that easy, you've demonstrated you don't understand the true nature of the problem.

14. Be wary of those who only tell you of their successes.

They do not have a full view of life.

15. It is not easier to get forgiveness than permission.

Attempting to do so demonstrates a lack of concern and consideration for others.

16. Be thee not a respecter of men (or women).

Respect is earned through actions that are closely aligned with words, and both are externalizations of thoughts, beliefs and ideas, which brings us back to what you get when you squeeze an orange.

17. Do not go where you are not invited.

This, in all things, because being unwelcome can be a painful experience in more ways than one, and the corollary is that you'll always find your way to where you're wanted and loved.

18. Do not do what you are not asked to do.

Because until you are asked, you're doing it for yourself, not for them, and it may not be what they wanted in the first place.

19. People who don't ask for what they want deserve what they get.

So go ahead and ask. All a "no" means is that there must be other avenues you haven't explored yet.

20. Never, via your direct action or intentional inaction, allow

others to come to harm.

And the minute you begin debating what "harm" is, you've already allowed it to happen.

21. If someone is drowning don't ask them "How wet is the water?"

Make sure your questions are relevant to the situation you are asking about. Think before you speak, otherwise be prepared for those around you to care more about keeping themselves dry than helping you to safety.

22. You are not your brother's (or your sister's) keeper.

Show people enough respect to let them make their own mistakes. That way they'll be able to appreciate their own successes.

23. If you can't think outside the box then you'll spend your life as someone else's package.

And maybe you're comfortable with that. We're not.

24. Don't feed someone when you're hungry.

You'll be jealous of what they eat and there's no guarantee there'll be any left for you when they're done.

25. In the Game of Life, let the other person win once in a while.

You'll learn to be humble, they'll learn to be gracious. At some point in time they'll figure out what you did, then they'll learn to be humble and you'll learn to be gracious.

26. What is a Dark Mystery to you is Perfectly Obvious to someone else (and vice versa).

So when you explain something to somebody, explain the obvious. When you leave something out and they don't get it, you're the fool, not them.

27. *Everybody knows there are classes in society, any society.*
Wise people don't speak of it. The wisest people don't show it.

28. *Respect people who know the name of their waiter or waitress.*
It shows they value people.

29. *Everything is possible.*
When you decide something is impossible all you've done is demonstrate the limitations of your resources.

30. *To each of us is given a measure, to some great and to some so small as not to be noticed in the light of day.*
How can we know that the greatest measure, without the efforts of those barely noticed as foundation or support or crown, will be enough? Therefore never slight nor be jealous of those whose measure is greater or less than yours, because to each of us is given a measure. It's not the measure that makes us great, it's what we do with our measure that gives us greatness.

31. *You don't always need a reason to get something done.*
Sometimes things just have to be done, and that is reason enough.

32. *Own your history. Don't be owned by it.*
You are the only one who has the power to change the universe you live in.

33. *Sometimes you just have to let the fool be slapped.*
People know when they're not being upfront, honest, above board, … , and nine times out of ten they want to be caught because it gives shape, form, and substance to the world around them. You honor them and yourself by catching them. Regarding that one out of ten that doesn't want to be caught? Put up walls between yourself and them. They will be a danger to both themselves and to you.

34. *Never be afraid to appear a fool when asking a question.*

It's the ones who won't ask questions who are truly the fools.

35. *Be wary of people who enjoy casting large shadows.*

It is better to be the light that allows shadows to exist, that lights the way for others, than to be in someone else's darkness.

36. *Courage is not the absence of fear. Courage is what you do when you're afraid.*

Be Courageous. It will cost you relationships, no doubt, but you'll be able to sleep at night.

37. *When someone is hanging onto a cliff by their fingernails, don't ask them if they want to play catch.*

Another example of making sure your questions are relevant to the situation. People in need, people under stress and strain, when distracted, suffer. Make sure you help rather than hurt.

38. *Let your dreams create your capabilities.*

Never believe that what you are now is all you ever shall be.

39. *Some will ask, "What do you want?" Others with, "Who are you?" To answer either, you must first answer "Am I who I want to be?"*

Whether known or not, spoken or not, it is the first question that must be answered.

40. *Laws are the boundaries societies place upon the spirit.*

Be boundless. You may be in a society of one, but being alone is often the price of freedom.

41. *Never allow yourself to be blinded by those who lack*

vision.

Surround yourself with those who encourage you to see, even if they can not. It is much to be preferred than to be around those who won't allow you to see because they themselves can not.

42. *Shame is a gift given by someone who fears you.*

This can be a hard lesson to learn. The only reason for someone to make you feel ashamed is to control you, and love has no need for control.

43. *If you follow your path long enough, eventually you'll discover your dreams.*

Therefore it is up to you to make sure your dreams are something you want to discover.

44. *and in keeping with the above, Paths reveal themselves to you if you let them.*

They are not always straight and often not obvious, therefore it's up to you to follow or not as you decide.

45. *Acceptance is not Understanding.*

Keep separate the things you accept and the things you understand. A few items will be in both camps, a lot of items won't. Knowing the difference means knowing what you're willing to change versus what you're willing to let change you, and the world of difference is there.

46. *As with most things, if you're willing to go just a little bit further than you've ever gone before, an entirely new world* 47. *is opened onto you.*

Explore to the limits of your abilities and willingness. It's the only way to know how big you really are.

48. *Is it better to see the end, to hear its answer when you call*

its name, or to be there?

Answer these and you'll know what eternity means to you.

49. True Authority becomes such by acknowledging, understanding and incorporating all points of view, especially those that disagree.

Authority can not exist without growth and change, and authority that can't include or disprove disagreement is no authority at all.

50. Success is not synonymous with Achievement.

People can have successful careers and have achieved nothing in their life, while people who've achieved but one thing are successful beyond measure. Success means you've grown (no small achievement, that). Achievement means you've helped someone else grow (and to be willing just to take on that task indicates you're a success).

51. "Chaos, once defined, can be the most organized system there is." and "Don't burn your bridges before they hatch." are two orthogonal statements and their intersection is you.

Take the time to realize that these two statements are equations of existence and that they define a universe of possibilities. Recognize that if they intersect you are the intersection and that if they don't intersect you're denying yourself a universe of possibilities.

52. Always be willing to share your story and always be respectful of the stories of others.

Tell people "I will tell you as much of my story as you wish to know, but I will never share your story with others nor will I share another's story with you." Understand this and you'll understand your own and other's boundaries, where you begin and end and how your words can heal and hurt others.

53. If you can't clearly say "No" then nobody will know when

you're saying "Yes".

So be clear and concise in all your communications when a "No" or a "Yes" will do. People will appreciate it and confusions will quickly melt away.

54. Handing over control is not giving up responsibility.

Hand over control of something to someone else and they become your responsibility as well as whatever you have control of. Consider this an opportunity to teach, yourself and them.

55. Never let your limitations be someone else's limitations.

You've probably worked long and hard to get the ones you have. Don't share them. Similarly, honor the ones others have that you don't. They worked just as hard to get theirs as you did to get yours.

56. Sometimes the best lesson is recognizing that someone is not your teacher.

It can save both of you a lot of pain and sorrow.

57. Paddle Plato's Life Boat with Ockham's Razor.

Find a theoretical structure that supports all data, even conflicting data, and find a theoretical structure that supports it all without resorting to unnecessary entities. This is where The Principle of Rich Observation meets The Principle of Parsimony. Live there. Be there. Be it.

58. You must be dancing yourself if you want to dance with somebody.

You can not find what you're looking for until and unless you're willing to first be it yourself.

59. Eliminate Variables, Remove Ambiguities.

You are going to make mistakes in life (see Principles 6, 7, and 22). It's possible to minimize those mistakes by eliminating as many unknowns as possible from the situation before you act. You can further minimize mistakes by removing all ambiguous information before you act. It isn't possible to ignore ambiguous information and it's usually possible to act in a way that doesn't require making use of the ambiguous data. Be patient. Ambiguous situations tend to resolve themselves given enough time. How do they resolve? By eliminating unknowns.

60. Be An Enemy of the People, point out the naked Emperor, protect The Old Man and tell people about The Rock.

You may be the only one who knows the truth and in truth, you're the only one who can know your own truth. However, that doesn't make the truth incorrect and your sharing it can possibly save lives. Even if it costs you yours.

61. It is perfectly useless to know the answer to the wrong question.

So before you answer another's question ask yourself if the question is worth answering at all.

62. Never cure a singer of their voice.

Sometimes people's gifts can frighten or disturb us, hence their gifts go unappreciated. Take a moment to make sure your goal is to be just and that your pursuit isn't just for yourself at the expense of others.

63. Choice is better than no choice.

This isn't Free Will versus Predestination, this is right here, right now, do you want to be in control of your life or give up control? The latter leads to victimization and can't be healthy for anyone involved. The former leads to opportunity and possible sacrifice, but it'll be your choice to sacrifice if you do.

64. Don't label people (for both your sakes).

It's sometimes helpful to assign labels to people so long as you remember that people are not objects, labels are like boxes and boxes can become coffins. For both of you.

65. Work honestly, accurately, and unbiasedly.

Doing so will be your testimony. And while some may despise you, the majority will recognize that you honor them through your work and return that honor a hundred-fold.

66. A worker is worthy of their wages.

Recognize that nothing is free. That's first. Somebody is paying some where at some time any time some thing is done. Directly paying the worker for work done demonstrates you value them and their work, that you recognize them as equals in a fair-exchange, and (perhaps most importantly) that you respect yourself enough to know your own value is not in question. That last one throw you? Then go elsewhere. The only time people want something for free is when they're not sure of the value of their own efforts because the price people are willing to pay is a measure of the value they place on their request. Want something for free? Then it has little value to you. Willing to pay? Then it's important to you. It's as simple as that.

The other side of this is that the worker can ask for wages in other than coin of the realm (and barter doesn't count. Barter is mutually agreed to coin of the realm). Recognize that the only commerce besides coin of the realm is with a piece of yourself — your time, your strength, your thoughts, your word, your knowledge, your wisdom, your friendship, your oath. Be careful with these. Coin is far cheaper than heart.

67. Act with kindness even though you don't know the outcome.

Never doubt that something you said or didn't say, did or didn't do, etc., changed the universe in some incredible way. The Universe's concept of the Butterfly Effect is "You said hello to someone walking down the street whom you didn't know therefore a lifeless planet is starting to form oceans."

68. Until you've gathered all the data available and understood its significance in the situation under study, your decisions regarding the situation are inherently flawed.

Even if they're the correct decisions, the decision process is flawed and outcomes are reproducible due more to luck than knowledge because you never know if the lacking data is contributing 1 or 99% to a complete solution. Explaining observed outcomes without complete knowledge of what's causing them is a fool's goal.

69. Forgive others so that you can be released from their grasp.

Forgiveness isn't done for others, it's done for yourself, to help you let go of the emotions that bind you to someone who wronged you. This does not mean you must love them, only that you may let them go.

70. Faith, until it is tested, is just an opinion.

It doesn't matter if faith takes the form of fealty to a friend, a place, a country, a product, an idea, a life-partner or a deity, until that faith is tested it is just opinion about your relationship to a friend, a place, et cetera. Tested, you know the limits of your faith and limits are just that, neither failure nor triumph, only today's boundaries and limits, only how far you'll go today in this particular test.

71. Technology is not how we make and keep relationships. We make and keep relationships because of who we are, not what tools we use to stay in touch.

Everybody's lives are hectic. If you can't get everything done you want to do and are missing appointments/meetings/friends/what-have-you, getting more technology won't organize your day because time isn't your problem, you are. You have as much time in your day as Michelangelo, Galileo, Newton, Einstein, Gandhi, Mother Teresa, Buddha, Socrates, ...

72. An individual can only receive a certain benefit if others are willing to take on a certain burden.

Remember, the Universe works in balance. From Principles 1, 4, 6, 9, 20, ... , remember that what you take you owe. Think you don't often enough, think this doesn't apply to you often enough and you'll find yourself on the long end of burden. Not a happy place.

73. When someone shares their success with you, focus on them, not you. There's no need to compare their success to yours. This is their moment, not yours.

Imagine your toddler or a friend's toddler taking their first step. Would you tell them about your first step? This Principle is a corollary to 14. Help people celebrate their successes. Especially those they struggled for. And earned.

74. Only teach those willing to be taught.

People demonstrate a real learning desire by how they ask and what they do with what you give them. Don't teach because you believe you have something to share. You may not teach what they want to learn, they may not want to learn what you want to teach.

Real teaching is about helping people discover their own way, their own doors, their own understanding. We teach best by our actions. Be careful with yours.

THREE QUESTIONS FOR YOU

1. *Did you know most readers rely on other readers' reviews and comments to make their book buying decisions? Ongoing research begun in mid-2022 indicates reviews and comments are better decision drivers than video teasers, author interviews, author blogs, and everything else combined.*
2. *Did you know most on- and off-line bookstores - from the smallest indie to the largest megastore - rely on reader reviews and comments to decide which books to put on their shelves?*
3. *Did you enjoy* The Shaman?

Help Northern Lights as a publisher and Joseph Carrabis as an author by reviewing The Shaman *on Amazon http://nlb.pub/Shaman Goodreads http://nlb.pub/GShaman, Barnes&Noble, BookBub, NetGalley, your favorite reader Facebook and LinkedIn groups, TikTok, Instagram, anywhere and everywhere.*

Let's Kick It Up A Notch!

Send a link to your online review of a Northern Lights Publishing book to Reviews@NorthernLightsPublishing.com and we'll give you a 35% discount on your next Northern Lights Publishing ePub or Print book.

Not Enough? Let's Kick It Up Another Notch!

You can share that 35% discount with up to ten friends, family, neighbors, we won't mind, and you'll have our thanks.

Join Northern Lights Publishing's Journey
http://nlb.pub/JoinNorthernLights

Join Northern Lights Publishing's Journey
http://nlb.pub/JoinNorthernLights

Coming Soon From Northern Lights Publishing

Stay up on early reads, special offers, and gift opportunities! Join our mailing list at http://nlb.pub/nlbmailings

December 2023: Search

Two young boys and their guardian go missing in the Maine woods. No one has a clue, no one comes forward offering information, and the police are powerless to provide the boys' family with any answers. The boys' older sister learns about Gio Fortuna through a friend and asks him to help. Search chronicles one life-changing event in The Shaman's life, an event causing Gio to realize the use of his grandfather's teachings and their purpose in both his life and the lives of others.

March 2024: Tag

Two teenagers, Eric and Julia, seek tree grafts on the outskirts of their medieval village as a summer storm clouds the sky. Sullya, a witch hiding among the trees, grabs Julia. Eric swings his axe and severs Sullya's hand from her arm. Sullya seeks refuge in the deep bole of an old oak. Her hand falls onto the same oak and crawls up the trunk to join her.

Eric wants to flee but Julia, believing they are safe, torments the witch. Sullya curses them, their families, their crops, their livestock, and their eastern European village.

Crops wilt, livestock dies, and much of village falls ill. The village priest, Father Baillot, is often seems ignorant of church ways and proves ineffective against the curse.

The elders seek help elsewhere, specifically from a distant priest, Father Patreo, who knows the Old Ways as well as the New.

Patreo is out of favor with the Church because he makes no effort to hide his belief that progress comes from exploring all paths, not just those the Church decrees acceptable.

He and Verduan, one of the elders, investigate, and what they discover changes the face of Eastern Europe forever.

June 2024: The Book of the Wounded Healers

Ben Matthews and his son, Jiminy, are enjoying some bonding time together at New York City's South Street Seaport watching jugglers and other buskers on a warm late summer day, eating fried dough covered in brown sugar and cinnamon, and getting to know each other.

Suddenly the East River and beyond because a vast desert. A warm wind blows sand in people's faces. In the distance, three creatures walk towards the City.

Havoc ensues. People run, carts are overturned, mounted police work at crowd control to no avail, and Ben loses Jiminy in the chaos.

Ben grabs the leg of a mounted officer asking for help and is knocked down as the horse turns.

The three creatures walk up to him, stop, and peer down. The one in front says, "We are Healers from the Land of Barass." It points to the one on his right. "He is Cetaf, who cries for his own pain." It turns to the one on his left. "This is Jenreel, who tends to his own needs. I am Beriah. I will tell you how I feel. We are Healers from the Land of Barass."

About Northern Lights Publishing

Northern Lights Publishing/Press is an association of five professionals (one graphic artist, one marketer, one editor/book designer, one copyeditor, one editor/educator/author) and a rotating group of ten published authors and poets all of whom are passionate readers. Financial backing is provided by a small group of investors led by Susan and Joseph Carrabis through the NextStage Evolution Corporation. Everyone receives remuneration and owns an equal share of the company with the exception of Susan and Joseph Carrabis.

We're developing our publishing/marketing model so we're not accepting submissions at present.

We'll open our doors to submissions (and announce it through various social networks) once we're sure we can break even and preferably turn a profit. Until then, wish us well.

It's an exciting journey and one we'd love to share, but only after we're sure we can successfully navigate the publishing seas.

Join Northern Lights Publishing's Journey
http://nlb.pub/JoinNorthernLights

About The Author

Joseph Carrabis told stories to anyone who would listen starting in childhood, wrote his first stories in gradeschool, and started getting paid for his writing in 1978. His work history includes periods as a long-haul trucker, apprentice butcher, apprentice coffee buyer/broker, lumberjack, Cold Regions researcher, mathematician, semanticist, semioticist, physicist, educator, Chief Data Scientist, Chief Research Scientist, and Chief Research Officer. He was an original member of the NYAS/UN's Scientists Without Borders program and held patents covering mathematics, anthropology, neuroscience, and linguistics. After patenting a technology he created in his basement and creating an international company, he retired from corporate life. Now he spends his time writing fiction based on his experiences. His work appears regularly in anthologies and his own novels. You can often find him playing with his dog, Boo, and snuggling with his wife, Susan.

You can follow Joseph on BookBub, Facebook, Goodreads, Instagram, LinkedIn, Pinterest, or Twitter.

Become a member of Joseph's blog - http://nlb.pub/JoinJoseph